Sub

JM Turner was born and raised in a leafy suburb of a town that used to be in Middlesex but is now North London.

She lives with her dog Teddy in another suburb in Norfolk.

She hopes that what happens within the pages of this book have never and will never occur in either of these suburbs.

Facebook.com / authorjillturner

Twitter: @JillMTurner

BY JILL TURNER

Books for Children:

*The Seelie Princess * Rise of the Dragons * The Seelie Queen * Trouble at Christmas * Carlotta and the Wizard * Terence the Clumsy Dinosaur*

Books for Young Adults:

*Nan Nose Best * Sunshine Girl * I Love You Most*

LRL PUBLISHING
First published in Great Britain in 2022 by LRL PUBLISHING
77 Park Lane
Wymondham
NR18 9NG

Copyright © 2022 JM Turner
All rights reserved

JM Turner asserts the moral right to be identified as the author of this work.

This novel is entirely a work of fiction. The names, characters and incidents portrayed in it are the work of the author's imagination. Any resemblance to actual persons, living or dead, or events is entirely coincidental.

All rights reserved.
No part of this publication may be reproduced, stored in a retrieval system, or transmitted, in any form or by any means, electronic, mechanical, photocopying, recording or otherwise, without the prior permission in writing of the publishers.

Suburbia

Suburbia
~noun~
the suburbs or their inhabitants viewed collectively:
"the sprawl of suburbia into the surrounding countryside"
synonyms: outlying district, residential area, dormitory area/town, commuter belt, conurbation, fringes, outskirts, garden suburb…

Foreword

If you take a stroll in any town located close to a city in England's green and pleasant land, you will come across a variety of landscapes, depending upon the locality and wealth of the people living there. What you will see will vary from leafy streets with large, detached family houses, each set back from the road with driveways circling well-tended front gardens, picket fences and roses around an arbour, to concrete jungle tower blocks sporting, at their base, broken children's play equipment the children dare not use, people who lean against street corners passing small packets to other people who are willing to pay for what is in them, and desperately young girls who make their money on their backs.

Of course, most towns will also contain other types of property: small terraced houses with postage-stamp gardens that have recently sprung up having been built on green- and brown-land, despite the furore raised by nimby's losing 'their' green space, even if they never actually used it prior to construction beginning. These properties are more commonly known as starter homes. Of course, these starter homes are mostly unaffordable for people actually starting out because the deposit required to secure them is a ridiculous percentage of the asking price. This means a large proportion of them are owned by corporations which let them out, at vastly overpriced sums, to those same people who were not allowed to buy them but need a place to live and can, magically, afford the inflated rents asked. The irony, of course, that they would pay less if they were allowed to take out a 100% mortgage passes over most heads – apart from of those who rent them, of course.

One such town is Crickleby, a suburb of Deffolk located just far enough away from the ocean to have lower house prices than the equivalent in the neighbouring Borough of Mudchurch. In Crickleby, the affluent live in Avenues or Lanes rather than Roads or Streets, and the grammar school picks from the cream of the crop before accepting children they deem to be somehow lesser because of their address, even if their intelligence is far greater than those who have wealthy parents. In short, snobbery abounds in Crickleby.

But is it justified? Does having money equal better morals? Better ethics? Nicer people? Or is it that bad behaviour is somehow justified, better tolerated, when wealth is involved?

This story takes place in an atypical road, where, if it were public knowledge, the behaviour of some of its inhabitants may not be quite so well-tolerated...

The Lakelands, Crickleby

The inordinately long road known in its entirety as The Lakelands begins close to Crickleby town centre. It starts off as Lakeland Road, becomes Lakeland Avenue at its mid-point, and ends as Lakeland Lane right at the top, beside the lakes which give the road its name. The lakes separate Crickleby from its neighbouring town of Mudchurch and woe betide anybody who mistakes the two areas.

The people who live along the road come from a vast cross-section of society. Lakeland Road begins with small houses, some of which have been sub-divided into flats, each crammed one on top of the other, mostly terraced, not all with their own gardens. Some are council stock, some Housing

Association, several of them have been purchased by their tenants for a much lower price than is available on the housing market. These people either work very hard for a living (and are generally between one and three pay cheques away from homelessness) or are supported by social funds.

At number 24, which is up a bit from the edge of Crickleby Town where the houses are marginally larger and the owners seemingly better off, lives Sarah. Sarah keeps to herself and works from home. Her neighbours know she has broadband (it caused quite a stir when she had it installed although the majority of the road now benefits from super-fast fibre) and that she works 'in finance'—they presume she's a bit of a high-flyer for a tech company. Sarah is in her early twenties but looks much younger as she doesn't tend to use make-up, a fact many of her neighbours have lamented upon amongst themselves but never to her face.

Despite their nosiness, none of her neighbours is even close to understanding what it is that Sarah does for a living, nor why she goes to such trouble not to draw attention to herself when she's out and about. Sarah does, indeed, work online but she doesn't work 'in finance' – although the financial rewards she receives for what she *does* do, are quite substantial (and, possibly, equally as ethical). Inside her house, when she's working, Sarah wears a long dark wig and stage make-up and looks very, very different.

Another young girl lives at number 77, Lakeland Road. Unbeknownst to either, this girl, Madeleine, has a similar job to Sarah, but Madeleine's role is more ... hands-on. This girl has long, auburn hair which is her pride and joy. She doesn't hide it. She likes to wear make-up, likes how she looks, and why shouldn't she? She believes that nobody is going to admit that they know her, should they meet her in the street, so why should she look any different when she isn't working?

***

Whoever designed the Lakelands appears to have done so to confuse any locum mailperson. The numbering along the lengthy road has also been split into three segments: The more common part, Lakeland Road, starts at the edge of town at number 1 and ends at number 210. Separating it from the next house along is a small park which children use to kick a ball about on during the summer months, driving the local residents mad with their shouts and hollers. The houses that follow have a Lakeland Avenue address and are a far cry from the dwellings in Lakeland Road. These houses are larger, much larger and because this part of the road is now Lakeland Avenue, the numbering begins again and ends when Lakeland Avenue becomes Lakeland Lane, the area where the truly affluent live. These houses have no need of numbers. These houses have *names*.

There is an inordinate amount of un-talked about snobbery about the addresses and if the postman delivers to the right number but the wrong part of the road, he has committed a cardinal sin. Thankfully unbeknownst to the postman, a jovial man named Jim who has followed this route for many years and is well aware of the numbering situation, he made an unfortunate mistake in one of his deliveries and set in motion a chain of events that would cause quite a stir…

Chapter One
Monday

77, Lakeland Avenue

Graham Dalgleish, who lived with his long-suffering wife, Caroline, was expecting a special delivery in the mail – the sort of delivery he didn't want his wife knowing about although, as is the way with wives of long standing, she knew exactly what he was up to and turned a blind eye to it for the sake of an easy life – and, typically, the postman was late. He'd been peeking at the curtains for over two hours when he spotted him coming and opened the front door just as Jim began to walk up the pathway.

"Beautiful afternoon!" he said brightly, subtly pointing out the fact that it was past midday when the mail should have arrived by 10.30 at the latest, and holding his hand out to receive it.

"Aye, it is that," said Jim, passing over a stack of letters and the inevitable junk mail that came along with them and ignoring the dig.

"Have a great day," Graham said briskly, pushing his foot against the door in an attempt to close it behind him, despite knowing that he would need to turn back and close it properly before their husky, Chutzpah, got wind of it being open and made a bid for freedom. He separated the junk from the genuine mail, dropping what he didn't want onto the parcel shelf in the hallway and rifling through actual letters to see what was his and what belonged to his wife. The large brown envelope addressed to him he tucked down the top of his trousers and covered the rest with his jumper.

Then, "Oh," he said aloud, hooking his foot around the door before it swung entirely shut and sticking his head back into the world. "This one's for Lakeland *Road*, not here. Jim... Jim...?"

But the postman had moved on to number 83 by this time and was hidden by the hedge, pretending not to hear his call. Graham raised his eyes to heaven and closed the door properly this time. He peered down at the envelope. It was creamy white, made of expensive paper, and the person who had addressed it had beautiful handwriting. Ms M Beaufort was a lucky lady to be receiving such a fine letter, Graham thought. He put it onto the shelf and took the rest of the mail through into the kitchen-cum-diner, laying Caroline's post on top of the highly polished dining table.

"Would you like a coffee?" he asked politely, dodging out of his wife's way and shifting Chutzpah from where he was sitting in front of the sink, waiting fruitlessly for scraps. Caroline was in the midst of mixing up some sort of cake that involved sultanas, which he very much did not approve of, although the house smelled divine whilst it baked.

Caroline gave him an old-fashioned look. "I'd have thought you'd be off to the office by now but yes, a coffee would be rather wonderful, thank you."

Graham filled the kettle and put it on to boil. He shifted from one foot to another in anticipation of opening his special letter.

"Have you got piles again?" Caroline asked, observing him.

Graham flushed. "No."

"Then what's with the dancing? Did you get something exciting in the post?"

Graham's face became a beetroot. "Why would you ask that?" he said, rather too abruptly.

Caroline shrugged and went back to her cake, smiling to herself.

Coffees made, Graham retired to his basement office, locked the door behind him and opened the brown envelope in privacy. He proceeded to spend a very happy hour looking at pictures of young women who had been captured in flagrante on film by various and dubious means.

Later, perhaps because of the contents of his brown envelope, perhaps because his wife was now sweating buckets as a hot flush overcame her as he sat at the dining table watching her preparing their dinner, Graham found himself unable to stop thinking about the recipient of that gorgeous white envelope.

Ms Beaufort. The name conjured up an image of a chic, sexy, well-dressed lady who wore her hair in a chignon and smoked cigarettes from a long holder—but why, he asked himself, would such a lady live in Lakeland *Road*? Surely she would be better suited to the Avenue?

"I'm just going to take the dog out," he said, jumping up and whistling for Chutzpah, who came running, tail wagging. Graham had decided to hand deliver the letter.

***

77 Lakeland Road was a council house. One of the better-maintained ones, he had to admit, looking about him, but a council house nonetheless. The white UPVC front door was clean, as were the window sills. The window itself had slatted wooden blinds, similar to those he had in the kitchen at home, and were tilted just enough to let the sunshine into the room but not enough for outsiders to see through. One of the slats was partially broken. Graham was unable to resist.

Keeping the dog on a tight leash, he pressed his nose against the window and peered through the gap. Then he stepped back, rubbed his eyes, and went in for another look.

Inside, Ms M Beaufort, presuming the person he was now looking at actually *was* Ms Beaufort, was not what he had expected, to say the least. Inside the room, a young girl with long, auburn hair, wearing stockings and suspenders and nothing else was bent over a table, being thoroughly spanked by an elderly man who was as naked as the day he was born.

With an erection that threatened to burst his trousers, Graham watched for a few minutes more as the spanking finished, Ms Beaufort stood up and turned to face the man who, he assumed, could only be her sugar daddy. Graham's mouth dried. She was truly beautiful. She had high, firm breasts, each topped by a raspberry nipple that he longed to taste, a slim waist and the longest legs he'd ever seen. Graham swallowed as he envisaged them wrapped around his face. The suspender belt she wore framed her hairless pubic mound like a frame enhances an old master. He swallowed again as she dropped to her knees and took the wrinkled man's penis into her mouth. Despite being utterly entranced by the sight of her beautiful young face and luscious full lips sucking so wonderfully hard, causing the recipient's knees to buckle somewhat, Graham decided it was time to take the dog home before the old boy reached his happy ending, perhaps quite literally from the noises he was making and the way he was grabbing at Ms Beaufort's head.

Graham dragged the dog home, still holding onto that creamy white envelope. His mind was busily hatching a plan.

77 Lakeland Road

With a quick peck on the lips and the promise of the same again next week, Madeleine Beaufort, now wrapped in a silk, floral, floor-length dressing gown, waved a very happy old Mr Tennant off, now entirely certain that they'd been spied on. She'd caught a flash of movement at the window whilst she was sucking the old boy off, and the dog turd on the flowerbed beneath her window confirmed it. There was a Peeping Tom in the neighbourhood.

Closing her front door, she sighed and picked up her phone. "Gregor," she said without preamble when the call was answered. "I know I've asked before, but could you please get someone to come and fix the blinds. I had some perv watching me earlier and if Mr T had spotted him, I'd be a client down." She listened for a moment, then sighed heavily and said, "Thanks, but does it have to be Declan? ... Oh, he's round the corner, is he? ... Oh, no reason; just, oh, it doesn't matter ... Okay, I'll expect him soon then. Cheers Gregor."

She put down the phone and thought for a moment. If she was quick, she'd just about have time to have a quick shower to wipe the day's work away before Mr Fix-It arrived. She didn't know quite why this was important to her, she just knew that Declan made her feel more uncomfortable than any of her punters ever had. With any luck, she'd be in her tracksuit and he wouldn't want the freebee Gregor dictated his workmen were entitled to, should they so wish, although Declan had never taken up that offer before. She sighed. The truth was that he put her off-guard; he obviously didn't fancy her so she was at a loss as to how to act around him.

She ran upstairs and dived into the shower, washing quickly and thoroughly. As luck would have it, the doorbell rang just as she turned off the water. She swore under her breath and wrapped a towel around herself. "Hang on," she called, tucking the ends in so it wouldn't fall down, then she hurried down the stairs and opened the door.

"Going somewhere?" Declan asked with a friendly smile, averting his eyes from her. He was standing back from the door, his tall, lithe body clothed in clean workman's overalls, steel-toed boots on his feet. He jiggled the toolbox he held in his right hand. "Gregor says you have a blind problem. Gonna let me in then? I'll get out of your hair as soon as I can, don't worry."

Silently, Madeleine stood to one side and beckoned him inside. Declan closed the door behind him and laid the toolbox on the floor. "Are you done for the day? Going anywhere nice?" he asked, bending to remove his boots so that he didn't scuff her already well-scuffed lino. "I've been busy along the road, fixing the front door for the bloke at number 12. I've worked up quite an appetite."

Madeleine nodded, drawing the towel tighter. "Yes, I'm done for the day," she said firmly, hoping he'd take the hint. "Would you like me to make you a sandwich?"

Declan shook his head. "No need, I've brought my own—it's in the van. I'll have it later; this is my last call."

Madeleine turned to lead the way into the front room. She indicated the broken blind and Declan nodded, ignoring the paraphernalia she had stored in various boxes that lined the walls.

"I hear you had a Peeping Tom?" he said. "Some people, eh?"

"So you wouldn't have looked, given half the chance?" she found her mouth saying before she could stop herself. This guy was just too good to be true.

Declan's head rocked back and his shoulders squared. His dark brown eyes caught and held hers, the solemnity in them sobering. "I like to think I have respect for whatever goes on inside someone's home," he said quietly, "so no, I wouldn't have looked."

Madeleine's face flushed. "I didn't mean... oh, look, Declan, I'm sorry. I'm too used to being around people who aren't generally ... nice."

Declan nodded, dropping his shoulders, understanding. "It's okay. Look, do you want to nip upstairs and put some clothes on? I have to go out to the van to get a bit for the blind, so I'll go and sit in it and eat my roll while you sort yourself out. Just give me a shout when you're ready."

"Yes, if that's not too much trouble?" Madeleine sighed with relief. Somehow, being fully dressed would be easier when dealing with this man.

The two moved back into the hallway and Declan slipped his feet inside his boots and bent to lace them. "I'll shut the door behind me, don't worry. Off you go."

Hesitating for an instant, and then trusting her instincts that he would do exactly what he said he would, Madeleine turned away, but as she did so the towel she wore caught on the door handle, came untucked and dropped to the floor. Both Declan and Madeleine froze.

Finding himself faced by her admittedly rather delectable bottom, a bottom which bore the fading imprints of Mr Tennant's hands, Declan cleared his throat and said, "That must have hurt. I'm so sorry some men are unable to behave nicely."

Madeleine stood stock still, quite unable to move. Her clients enjoyed seeing handprints, or even cane marks, on her bottom, and occasionally, elsewhere. She'd got used to the excitement it raised in them and, if she thought about it at all, almost wore them as a badge of honour. *Look what you can do to me*, was the unspoken message being sent. *I like being punished for being naughty. Spank me and fuck me and do it hard because I love it.* Tears of shame sprang into her eyes.

She heard him moving behind her and then, unexpectedly, felt a pair of warm hands at her back as Declan placed the towel around her shoulders. She clung to it like a lifeline. "Thank you," she muttered, and raced up the stairs to get away from the kindness.

77 Lakeland Avenue

Caroline, who had taken advantage of the few moments of bliss while her husband was out walking the dog, was sitting at the dining table, munching on a piece of toast when he arrived back home. Chutzpah raced to his mistress, smelling food. Smiling, she tore off a crust and passed it to him surreptitiously, hoping that Graham didn't notice—he was always telling her off for sharing their food with him.

"Nice walk?" she called. When her husband didn't reply, she got to her feet and walked into the hallway, just in time to hear his footsteps careering up the top flight of stairs where he was out of sight, and a door slamming.

"Well!" she said to herself as she went back into the kitchen to find the dog up at the table, polishing off her last piece of toast without a hint of remorse or fear, "I wonder what's got his goat?"

Later, when her husband had decided to honour her with his presence, and as she took the now baked fruit cake from its tin and cut herself a slice, Caroline brought it up. "So you came in in a tearing hurry earlier, did you upset someone, somehow?"

Graham snorted, his face reddening. It had taken him *hours* to get the image of Ms Beaufort out of his head and his wife, of all people, had managed to bring her right back to front and centre. "I don't know what you're talking about," he blustered. "I needed the toilet."

Caroline carefully lifted her plate and went to sit on the seat opposite her husband, where she eyed him thoughtfully. He was hiding something from her. "Your haemorrhoids *are* back, aren't they?"

"For Christ's sake! No, my haemorrhoids are *not* back. I had them once, woman, once! And you never let me hear the end of it."

"Well something's wrong. You were up there for a good couple of hours so you can't blame me for asking, can you? Last time you had them it took hours, a dose of Epsom salts and an entire box of Anusol to help clear the backlog ... A *large* box of Anusol if you remember." Caroline tried, and dismally failed, to hide her smile.

"Ha bloody ha," Graham said bitterly. It hadn't been a laughing matter. He had horrifying memories of that particular episode which had stemmed from an evening out with the kids when he'd eaten an entire Chateaubriand steak that was meant for two people and foregone any vegetable side dishes despite the warnings Caroline, and indeed,

Jasmine and Stuart, their twins, had given him. Graham took pride in the fact that he was a man who stuck to his guns. If he wanted an entire Chateaubriand steak, he was going to have an entire Chateaubriand steak, and hang the consequences.

Admittedly, the consequences in that particular instance had not been worth it.

Caroline tapped her nails on the table, side-eyeing her husband. "Did you let Chutzpah pooh somewhere and not clear it up? Did someone tell you off?"

"I can assure you that it was nothing to do with anything related to … to *that* end of either my or the dog's anatomy," Graham said stiffly. "So change the record."

"Okay," Caroline said slowly. She popped a piece of cake into her mouth, chewed, swallowed and then said, "So what was it to do with?"

Graham thought fast. "If you must know," he said in a clipped manner, "I was checking that our passports are in date. I *was* going to take you on a trip for our anniversary. So now you know. Bye-bye surprise, huh?"

Caroline's head went back. "Graham, our anniversary was five months ago."

"I know! You made me very aware of it when I forgot, remember?"

Caroline's eyes widened. For the first time in almost a decade, Graham had not, in fact, missed their anniversary. She'd received a huge bunch of yellow roses, a bottle of her favourite perfume and the biggest bar of Galaxy money could buy.

Graham noted his wife's face and pressed what he thought was his advantage. "So does that finish the matter?

May I arrange a holiday for my wife to thank her for everything she does?"

Caroline nodded and dropped her eyes.

Her husband had just lied to her face and she was going to get to the bottom of it.

77 Lakeland Road

Madeleine, who was now fully dressed in a pair of jeans and jumper, and Declan were sitting in her back room, at the tiny dining table she used for eating, each nursing a mug of coffee, Declan having fixed the blind in record time.

"You didn't need to," Declan said, nodding at the full mug, "but I do appreciate it."

Madeleine shook her head. "I did need to. It was the least I could do, actually. And … I want to thank you."

"For what?"

"For never … you know … taking Gregor up on his offer." Madeleine looked Declan straight in the eyes and held her breath. She didn't know why his response to this would be so important to her, but it was. She was beginning to wonder if perhaps he was gay, although her gaydar was usually spot on and definitely not ringing around him. In fact, Declan struck her as being a very heterosexual male indeed. A man who knew what he liked, knew what he wanted, believed in what he stood for and was extremely comfortable in his own skin. In short, Declan was your ideal man wrapped up in a hunky package. He was gorgeous, she thought, and sadly, far too straight for him to have any interest in her.

"Look," Declan said after a moment's awkward silence. "Gregor pays me for doing these jobs – that's how it works as far as I'm concerned – something needs fixing, I fix it, I get paid. Why on earth would I expect you to feel obliged to, um, pay me extra?"

Madeleine lowered her head, her chin wobbling slightly. What on earth was wrong with her? She was normally as hard as nails, viewing every transaction as something that had to be done to either give her the money she needed to survive, or by way of a nod towards Gregor – for that was what all these extra free services were. Gregor provided the people who maintained her home – she made him look good. She wasn't used to anybody not accepting the use of her body, especially if it was for free. Perhaps she was losing her touch – he'd seen her naked, after all, and that was all it usually took – but then he'd covered her up! God, that must be it, he just didn't find her attractive.

Gently, Declan reached a hand towards Madeleine's face, cupped her chin and raised her head until it was level with his own. "You don't owe me anything. Or anyone else who comes here to do repairs. Do you understand?"

"Okay," Madeleine said, her voice small. She took a deep breath and voiced the question she'd often wanted to ask. "Does he ever ask?"

"What, if we've...?" Declan barked out a small laugh, understanding instinctively what she was asking. "No. He's crass as hell but not that crass."

Madeleine nodded and they sat in companionable silence for another minute or so until Declan cleared his throat. "Do you mind if I ask you a bit of a personal question?"

"Go ahead. If I don't want to answer, I won't, okay?"

"Of course. Okay, here goes ... your next client will see those handprints on your bum. Won't it, I dunno, put him off?"

Madeleine laughed. "They'll have gone down by then, but no, I can guarantee that it won't put him off."

"How do you know?"

"Because I have an exclusive relationship with three men. They each have set days, and they each like the same things."

"Oh!"

"You sound surprised," Madeleine said wryly. "Did you think I had an open house? Was at it all hours of the day and night? Whatever would the neighbours think?"

Declan, who had actually thought that *was* how she operated, blushed. "Sorry," he said, taking a swig of coffee. Then, having gulped it down, he added, "So these three men; they *like* seeing the marks on you? Is that it?"

Madeleine took a sip from her own mug before answering. "Yep. I have to leave a day or so between them so it doesn't get too much, but yeah, they pretty much love seeing how naughty I've been, and they all get off on knowing the next guy will see what they've done to me."

"They know each other?" Declan asked incredulously, laying his mug onto the table with a thud.

Madeleine sighed. "Yes. That's how it works. The arrangement was set up by Gregor. They went to him with what they wanted, he showed them videos of his girls, and they picked me. He came to me, told me what they'd requested and asked if I'd be prepared to cater for their ... needs. At the time, everything I was doing was a bit, well, risky, so I said yes. He introduced us all one day and left us to

… talk." She glanced at Declan, hoping he wouldn't want her to elaborate on this part. The memory of catering to all three men at once wasn't a particularly good one and she didn't want to have to explain her audition to him.

Declan nodded but didn't comment, so she continued, "They liked what they met, we all got checked out, you know, bloods taken and checked so that we all knew we were clean—no STDs or HIV, and we're all checked weekly incidentally, just in case one of us was to, you know, go elsewhere—and that gives them free reign with their imaginations. So long as I cater to their needs, they don't need to go anywhere else. It's probably the safest way to operate. I know their kinks; they get their rocks off."

"But don't you get a bit sick of it?"

"It's just a job," Madeleine said abruptly. "It pays the bills; quite well actually, so I do what I've got to do."

Declan sat back and thought about it. "Yeah, I can see how that would work and it's safer for you as you know what you're getting." He winced. "Pardon the very bad pun. How old are these guys, if it's okay to ask that?"

"Put it this way, my neighbours see my two grandfathers and an elderly uncle visiting me every week. They're on nodding terms, as it happens."

"How do they know one another? The men, I mean."

"I can't tell you that because I don't actually know," Madeleine said, shrugging. "I mean, it was obvious from the start that they all knew each other well, but I thought it safer not to ask. What I don't know, can't hurt me."

Declan drained his coffee, obviously thinking about that. He shook his head. "Can I ask an even more personal question?"

"Same answer as before," Madeleine said, wondering what on earth he'd ask next.

"Do you ever enjoy it?"

Chapter Two
Tuesday

77 Lakeland Avenue

Graham woke earlier than Caroline. He could tell by her breathing that she was still in a deep sleep, so he rolled over very carefully, pulled aside the duvet and slid from the bed.

"Argleflurglearggh."

Graham froze, certain his movements had woken her. But no, his wife had merely turned onto her back. Her mouth dropped open and a decidedly unfeminine snore began to fill the air.

Graham rolled his eyes. Aiming for the bathroom where he had conveniently left the clothes he intended to wear that day (a rather snazzy pair of light blue slacks with a white stripe up the side that his daughter had bought him for his birthday, which, she assured him, suited him and brought him into the correct century, and a t-shirt bearing the picture of a lion and the legend '*Hear me roar!*'), he eased the bedroom door closed behind him. He tiptoed into the bathroom, showered quickly, paying thorough attention to his nether regions, dried himself off, and dressed. Using his towel, he wiped the mirror off and combed his wet hair into place, glad to be one of the few lucky men who had retained a full head of hair well into his fifties. Satisfied that it was perfect, or at least as perfect as it was ever going to be, he shaved and added a splash of expensive cologne to his hands and rubbed them over his chin and neck. After a second's debate with himself, he reached down the front of his trousers and rubbed there, too, wincing slightly at the sting.

Then, happy with the result, he opened the bathroom door and found his wife standing behind it, about to turn the handle.

"What the...?" he spluttered in alarm at exactly the same time as Caroline looked him up and down and asked, in highly suspicious tones, "Are you going *jogging*?"

Neither spoke for a moment, Graham frantically trying to avoid his wife's eyes while she, equally frantically, tried to pin them down with her own.

"Well?" she said, after a few seconds of playing eyeball Olympics.

"I have a doctor's appointment," Graham prevaricated wildly, looking up at the ceiling.

"Since when? And why on earth are you going to a doctor's appointment in that get-up?" Caroline said, wondering if her husband was beginning to lose his marbles. Dementia did run on his side of the family and it started early with some people.

"Our daughter bought these for me," Graham said stiffly. "I shall tell her you don't like them."

Caroline ignored that. "Would you like me to come with you?"

"Where?"

Caroline took a deep breath. "To the surgery."

"No!"

"I was only asking! No need to bite my head off!"

"Sorry," Graham said, his tone indicating he was anything but.

"What do you need to see the doctor for? You haven't mentioned anything to me."

"Do I need your permission?"

Caroline folded her arms and began to tap an angry foot against the carpet. "Don't take that tone with me."

"Or what?" Graham said, so caught up in trying to escape that he failed to read the warning signs.

"You're lying," she said, ominously quietly. "You're no more going to the doctor's than I am. What's going on? You've got up earlier than me, and that's a first, you're all done up like a teenage dog's dinner, you smell like you've drowned yourself in cat's piss and you're lying through your teeth. Are you having an affair?"

"Don't be so bloody stupid," Graham said, pushing her out of his way and surreptitiously sniffing his hands. Cat's piss? "I'm off now. I'll see you when I see you."

He took the stairs three at a time, pulled on a pair of brand new trainers he'd never contemplated wearing before today, sniffed his hands a second time, kicked the dog out of his way, opened the front door, went through and slammed it behind him, leaving Caroline at the top of the stairs, waiting and wondering what on earth had got into him.

A few seconds later, the doorbell rang and Chutzpah began his usual barking cacophony to let her know someone was waiting to come in. Caroline took her time going down the stairs. The doorbell rang for a second time just as she neared the bottom.

"Did you forget something, dear?" she asked, opening the door to her sheepish-looking husband who was dancing on the doorstep and waggling the keys she'd collected from the parcel shelf.

"Thank you," Graham said stiffly, snatching them from her hands. Then he made a smart about-turn and marched off down the garden path, leaving her shaking her head as she watched him go.

***

"So do you think he's having an affair?"

Jamila, Caroline's closest and oldest friend, reached her arms out and drew Caroline into a warm, comforting hug having come at the run after her friend's call thirty minutes earlier. "Graham, no. Not for an instant. It sounds to me like he's having a mid-life crisis."

"He's fifty-eight. As he keeps telling everyone, he's almost pension-aged," Caroline muttered, "...and that's normally how he acts."

With her head safely over Caroline's shoulder, Jamila grinned, knowing her friend was correct. Graham was the most boring man she'd ever met, and so far as she was concerned, had been punching when he met Caroline. He should be counting his blessings.

"I know you're grinning. I felt your cheeks lift." Caroline pulled herself out of Jamila's arms and searched her face. "See!" she said, offering a wry grin of her own. Catching hold of her friend's hand, she led Jamila into the kitchen, motioned her towards a seat at the table and went to a cupboard to the right of the sink to pull out a packet of peppermint tea. She waved it at Jamila and, seeing her answering nod, scooped some into the bottom of a tea pot, filled the kettle and put it on to boil.

"Well, he's not at the doctor's," she said, turning to face her friend who was now sitting in Graham's chair at the dining table inspecting her nails. "I rang to check."

"And they told you he didn't have an appointment?" Jamila asked, eyebrows rising.

"Not exactly. I made something up about a family emergency and said he'd gone out without his phone, would they please tell him to come straight home after his appointment. The receptionist said she'd make a note of it, and then she must have checked because she told me I was mistaken and that he didn't have an appointment today. I pretended I'd got it wrong and that he must have said the dentist, not the doctor. I could almost hear her eye roll." She turned back to the kettle as it began to boil and poured the hot water into the pot, stirring the loose leaves around furiously.

Jamila frowned. "Why would he lie about something like that?"

Caroline took out a tea strainer from a drawer, upended the teapot and poured tea into two china cups without using it, a measure of how upset she was. Jamila wisely decided not to comment as Caroline passed a cup to her and shrugged. "I don't know. But there's more to this. If you'd have seen him, you'd know what I mean. He went out dressed like Harry Enfield's Kevin and he'd apparently showered in that foul after-shave he only ever wears to weddings and funerals."

Jamila snorted tea and carefully picked an errant tea leaf from her lips. "Curiouser and curiouser. So what are you going to do?"

"Well, either I'm going to have to follow him or I'm going to have to ask Stuart to have one of his mates do it."

"Stuart? Do you think he would?"

Both women considered Caroline's son, each aware of the other's thoughts without voicing them. Stuart was the bane of both his parents' lives. A handsome young man, he had sailed through life so far trading on his looks. He'd made no attempt to concentrate at school but had charmed his way through all the female primary teachers with his tousled hair, cheeky grin and wide, blue eyes. Only one year had appeared to bother him, when he was faced with a truculent and hairy male teacher, but it turned out that the teacher had a bit of a thing for young boys – not enough to be called out on it, just enough to make them squirm in their seats when he looked at them like they were prey and, of course, he fell under Stuart's spell in much the same way as the females did.

By the time he went to secondary school – not the Grammar, much to Graham's chagrin after his monetary offerings were roundly refused – Stuart had discovered weed and learned that if he sat at the back of all the classes and appeared to be listening, he could while away the hours inside his own head without being caught. Most of his school reports spoke in great detail of his apparent willingness to learn but were unable to explain his utter lack of progress in any subject. In year 11, when he achieved the status of being the only boy ever in the history of the school to obtain not a single qualification, Graham and Caroline hired private tutors and stood over him, forcing him to learn until he finally passed English and Maths and didn't have to face the ignominy of repeating the final year.

Nowadays, Stuart always had a vacuous blonde on his arm – a vacuous *wealthy* blonde – and he went through them and their money like water to the degree that Caroline no longer bothered trying to remember their names whereas Graham was able to name every single one of them.

He was the polar opposite of his twin, Jasmine, who had been a studious, plain little child who had actually enjoyed school. Having Stuart as a brother was, by turns, either a cause for vaguely amusing embarrassment (her friends adored him) or the route of the deep and abiding hatred that grew all the way through school until she was accepted into the Grammar and so at least was able to escape him there. It was embedded into her bones by the end of it. She was finally reprieved when she was accepted into college to study A levels and Stuart began a long succession of jobs that never held his attention for long. That hatred of her brother had waned to a more liveable intolerance of all the shit he so blithely exuded as they both grew into adulthood but the feeling of utter contempt for him had never completely gone away.

At college, like her name, Jasmine blossomed. She grew her blonde hair long, dyed it pink and blue, learned that the blue would go green if she didn't top it up regularly, and then chopped the entire lot off in a bid to go back to her blonde roots that all her friends – friends she never introduced to Stuart – so admired. She began to stay overnight with some of them, overnight being the euphemism she used to hide the fact that they were going out on the lash and staggering back to the house of whichever of the group of girls had the most tolerant of parents.

"He might," Caroline said, responding to Jamila's question as to whether her son would help her out. "I think it rather depends on whether he's had a joint when I ask him."

Jamila's eyes widened. This was the first time her friend had ever admitted to knowing her son used drugs.

Caroline noticed. "Come on," she said, flapping her hands in the air, "even I can't pretend anymore. He stinks of skunk whenever he comes home." She raised her cup to her lips and took a deep gulp of peppermint tea and immediately started to cough and splutter.

"Do you want me to...?" Jamila said, rising to clap Caroline between her shoulder blades.

Caroline waved her away as the coughing spate abated. She stared into her cup in horror, then looked at Jamila. "Why didn't you tell me? This is *foul*!" And then she burst into laughter that rapidly turned into tears.

***

"What do you mean, Dad's up to something funny?" Stuart, who Caroline had managed to catch before he rolled his first spliff of the day, said surprisingly coherently.

"He's not himself. He took himself off early this morning wearing Harry Enfield's reject clothing and drenched in that cat's piss aftershave he only ever wears to weddings and funerals."

Stuart barked a laugh down the phone line. "So he went out wearing the clobber Jazz bought him for Christmas? Christ, what was he thinking?"

"He put the trainers on that you bought him, too."

"Had he worn them in?"

"He'd never had them on his feet before today."

"So," Stuart said, really laughing now, "I need to get one of my mates to go into town looking for a, what did you call him, oh yeah, a Harry Enfield reject – I just Googled him by the way – please don't tell me he was wearing a cap, too? So, a Harry Enfield reject who, because he'll be limping all over the place, will probably look pissed?"

Hearing her son's mirth at the picture he'd painted of his father, Caroline began to laugh too. When they both stopped for breath, Stuart said, "Do you seriously want me to get someone to see if they can follow him? Will it put your mind at rest?"

"Yes," Caroline said.

"Well, there's no point doing it today because by now he'll be wherever he was going. Text me in the morning if he disappears again."

"Okay. Thanks, Stu."

"No worries. Listen, Mum, I seriously doubt he's doing anything stupid so try not to worry."

"Okay," Caroline said, not believing it for a second.

24 Lakeland Road

Madeleine had got up early for a change having decided to go clothes shopping. She sashayed down the road towards town in a mini-skirt and tight-fitting top, her phone glued to her hand, sunglasses on despite the fact it was slightly overcast, heels clicking as they met the pavement, part of which had been blocked for the sort of repairs that meant pedestrians were required to walk into the road whilst nobody was present to do any work.

As the repairs went on for some distance, Madeleine tutted to herself, checked for traffic and crossed the road. Just as she reached the opposite side, one of her heels went down a pothole in the road (which, ironically, actually *did* need to be repaired but wouldn't be until someone suffered a serious injury), her ankle turned and over she went, cursing at her misfortune. An arm caught her before she actually hit the ground and dragged her back to her feet.

"Thank you," Madeleine said, straightening her skirt and turning to look at her saviour, a plain-looking girl with cropped blonde hair of around the same age as herself. "I thought I was a goner there."

"You're welcome. I think your shoe's had it though," the girl said, nodding towards the pothole where a single stiletto heel had torn from the rest of the shoe which was still on Madeleine's foot. "I've complained about that pothole but they won't do anything about it."

"They never do," Madeleine agreed.

"Take a picture of it," the girl said, "and send it to the council. They may give you the money for a new pair, if you still have the receipt for those?"

Madeleine, who wasn't worried about the money particularly, duly snapped a picture of her broken shoe.

"Look, I live here," the girl said, pointing to the door of number 24. "If you're desperate to get into town, I probably have a pair you can borrow. Your feet look like they're the same size as mine – 5s? I'm Sarah, by the way, and I live there alone, so no need to worry that anyone's gonna drag you into slavery…" Laughing, Sarah, who still had a hold of Madeleine's arm, began to tow her towards the house and, half limping, Madeleine allowed herself to be towed.

"You live further up don't you?" Sarah said as they walked through the front door of number 24 and into a neat hallway where she let go of her hold on Madeleine. "I've seen you before."

Madeleine nodded. "77," she said, unwilling to admit that she'd never noticed Sarah before today and not entirely sure she'd recognise her in the future because absolutely nothing about the girl stood out. She had no make-up on, wore a pair of baggy grey joggers that had gone at the knees and a voluminous oversized sweatshirt that she had rolled up to her elbows, all of which hid whatever kind of figure she had beneath them. That and her cropped hair did her absolutely no favours.

"I know, I look a mess," Sarah said, reading Madeleine's expression accurately as she ushered her ahead of her and closed the door behind them, ignoring the old man who obviously thought wearing clothes meant for a teenager would regain his lost youth and was staring greedily at them as he lurched across the road to avoid the pavement repairs. "I'm not normally this badly dressed but I'm having a day off today and I've been doing the housework. I spotted you crossing and came out to warn you about the pothole because I didn't think you'd see it wearing those." She nodded towards the sunglasses. "I was a bit late though; sorry about that."

"That was kind of you," Madeleine said warily, removing the sunglasses and walking up the hallway, passing an open door which she glanced through. The room beyond was small but extremely tastefully decorated in creams and whites. It had a highly polished real wood floor and an enormous, plush, cream and white fur rug which rested at the foot of a comfortable-looking leather sofa which was directly set opposite an enormous, plasma screen television that was playing a morning daytime show with the sound muted. A black and white photograph of an extraordinarily beautiful woman had been blown up and framed in red. It hung in the centre of the wall to the right of the sofa, the colour of the frame instantly drawing the eye to it. Madeleine's eyebrows raised briefly in surprise and kept walking to the end of the hall, coming to a halt at the closed door ahead of her and an equally closed second door to her left. Kitchen and dining room, she presumed, turning to face Sarah.

Now that her eyes had adjusted to the dimness of the hallway, she could see the girl's bone structure and the enormous clear blue eyes that shone from her face. If she did something with herself, she'd be a show-stopper. "...And you did stop me from falling flat on my face, so there's that," she continued.

Sarah shrugged self-deprecatingly. "Here, I'll dig out some shoes for you."

Madeleine wondered what she was going to be presented with, so when Sarah went to the hidden under-stairs cupboard and slid open the door, revealing three racks of the kind of footwear Madeleine adored, her jaw dropped. The racks were colour delineated and the contents varied; black shoes of all descriptions rested at the top of two of the three racks, purple shoes were on the shelf beneath, blue beneath the purple, then red, yellow, green, white... The third rack held an inordinate amount of boots, from cute ankle boots to thigh-high leather stilettos. Madeleine had never seen so much footwear outside of a shoe shop. She looked at Sarah curiously.

"I did say I was scruffy today," Sarah said, grinning from ear to ear. "Thought you'd get a pair of stinky trainers, didn't you?"

Madeleine's mouth twisted into a sheepish grin. "Kinda," she agreed. "What... I mean, do you wear all of these beauties? They look brand new!"

Sarah's face went blank. "Oh, yeah, sometimes. You know. Look, take your pick." She stood back to allow Madeleine to take a closer look.

Curiosity piqued, Madeleine went to the cupboard, her eyes darting over the shoes avariciously—and then she spotted something else. Hidden to the right of the shoe racks, tucked away out of sight beneath the lowest of the stairs, was a large box. A box overflowing with the same sort of work equipment she had in her own home. The penny dropped.

"Oh, I see," she said, turning to Sarah and swiftly adding, "it's okay, I can't judge."

Sarah's face fell. "I always forget about that bloody box. It caused no end of trouble when meter readers used to actually do their jobs, back before the days of smart meters. So now you know why I have all the footwear. Look, just take a pair and go, okay, and *please* don't tell the neighbours; they think I work in finance."

Madeleine laughed. "Girl, please," she said. "Snap." She flapped a hand at Sarah and added, "Kinda. People with foot fetishes are nothing, believe me! Good on you for finding a niche."

"Foot fetishes?"

Madeleine looked at Sarah, weighing her up. Apart from the cheekbones and eyes, the girl was really nothing to write home about. She looked again. Okay, perhaps if she put a lick of black mascara on those blonde lashes her blue eyes could be quite stunning, and if she added blusher to her cheeks and wore lipstick… But no, the lack of make-up and voluminous clothing meant it was quite obvious Sarah didn't care for any of that. So if she wasn't catering for people with a foot fetish, what was she doing? She obviously made a good living if the shoes and that gorgeous lounge room were anything to go by, but going on looks alone, she honestly couldn't imagine her being very successful at attracting many punters – certainly not successful enough to make the kind of money she so obviously did to have a home like this.

She neither looked nor sounded like the prostitutes in town who hung around street corners, dragging punters into alleys or shop doorways for a five-minute blowjob or knee trembler, or getting into cars and being taken to the waste ground on the edge of town for a quick fuck. Apart from the fact that Madeleine considered anyone who did that to be both way beneath her and extremely stupid, Sarah didn't seem the type to take unnecessary risks. She was a bit of an enigma.

Carefully, Madeleine said, "Look, I can see by the box that you, um, do other things as well, but all those shoes must mean that most of your, um, clients, have a thing for feet."

Sarah laughed. "No. I actually just really like shoes and I buy them when I can afford them."

"Really?"

"Really." Sarah nodded for emphasis.

"So what do you do then? How do you find your, um…" Madeleine said, curiosity winning out over the unspoken requirement not to ask other working girls about their working lives.

"Clients?"

Madeleine nodded, ready to tell her about Gregor who, she was sure, would be able to find someone who would pay to lick Sarah's toes, even if it wasn't a requirement that was most asked for.

"I don't find them. They find me."

Madeleine frowned. "How?"

"Well, I don't advertise, if that's what you mean. You won't find a card in a phone box."

"What's a phone box?"

Sarah shook her head. "It doesn't matter. Let's just say that I have someone who puts clients my way."

"Oh! You have a pimp. I get it."

Sarah burst into peals of laughter which went on for some time. "What decade are you living in?" she asked, once she was able. "No, I don't have a pimp. Look, I have regular clients but I don't see *anybody* face to face. I don't shag them—I don't need to."

"I don't understand," Madeleine said. "I mean, I have regulars too, but they definitely expect actual sex."

"Ah," Sarah said. "During the pandemic, I went online."

77 Lakeland Road

Muttering to himself, Graham strode down the hill away from his house and wife as fast as his blue slacks with their white stripe up the legs would allow. The crotch hung a little too low for his liking and his thighs rubbed together most uncomfortably, meaning that after a hundred yards or so he was forced to slow down and began to walk like a bow-legged ape. He now understood why teenage boys tended to walk with a half-hitched limp. He was also fast coming to the conclusion that it may have been a wise idea to do as his son had suggested and wear his trainers around the house for a bit before he wore them out. A quick glance at the back of his ankles showed patches of red seeping through his white socks. He slowed even further, scuffing his feet against the ground, trying to shuffle his feet further in but this only made matters worse as the extra millimetre of gap at the back meant they rubbed higher up his ankles with each step and the redness blossomed further. Surreptitiously, he sniffed at his armpits. Did he really smell like cat's piss?

He was approaching a couple of well-to-do, middle-aged women who were each standing on either side of their adjoining fences, putting the world to rights and was aghast at the fragments of their conversation that was carried to him by the wind.

"…him that if he did it again, I'd have him castrated…"

"I don't suppose he'll take a blind bit of notice…"

"…never do, do they? Gracie, don't turn around, but look at what's coming towards us… I said *don't turn round*!"

Graham's face flushed as the woman who was obviously Gracie swivelled her head towards him. Two pairs of eyes took him in from head to foot and two hands rose to each respective mouth as the women tried, unsuccessfully, to hide their sniggers.

Graham pierced each of them with a gimlet eye as he drew level. "Good morning, ladies," he managed, nodding politely, trying his best to walk like an actual adult male.

Both women nodded back, patiently waiting until he passed them by before the sniggers became loud belly laughter which followed him down the road.

Graham was now beginning to allow himself to wonder whether it was a good idea to just drop in on the girl at 77 Lakeland Road but the thought of that glorious hair and cheeky bottom being spanked was just too much for him to give up and he pushed aside the notion that he wouldn't be welcome and continued his painful journey. As he passed the park, the addresses changed from number 1, Lakeland Avenue to 209, Lakeland Road and excitement began to gather in the pit of his stomach. His mouth began to water. He was almost there!

His eyes searched out the door numbers and he began the countdown. 99... 89... Ahead of him, the door to number 77 opened and the occupant stepped out. Graham's eyes drank her in. Ms Beaufort, she of the glorious auburn hair, was wearing a short, short skirt that skimmed over her bottom and ended just south of the tops of her legs. A tight-fitting top showed off her flat belly and, Graham sighed, her pert bosoms. Dark glasses covered her eyes and her hair... oh, that hair... flowed down her back, cascading to just above her buttocks. Buttocks that were now walking away from him.

Graham sped up.

Watching her every step, Graham gained on her, his mind racing for ideas of how he could just bump into her, charm her with his elegance and sweep her off her feet. Literally. He spotted the pavement repairs just as she stepped off the curb and into the road. He watched as she strutted across and saw as her shoe went down the pothole and she began to fall. He began to half-run, half hitch his way to her aid and then, damn it! A slightly effeminate-looking youth had hold of her arm and led her straight into number 24, giving him a filthy look as he shut the door behind them both.

Chapter Three
Wednesday

77 Lakeland Road

For the second time that week, Graham slid out of bed before Caroline was awake, tiptoed into the bathroom, showered, forewent the after-shave just in case, and dressed in the tight jeans and plain grey hooded sweatshirt he'd bought the previous day. A new pair of soft loafers completed the look and he was down the stairs and out of the house before even Chutzpah knew what was happening.

By 8.15 he was ringing the doorbell of number 77 and biting back the excitement that was flooding through him. When it wasn't answered immediately, he rang again, practically jumping up and down on the spot.

"Hang on," came a sleepy voice from inside the house.

Graham heard keys turning in the lock and then the door opened marginally, held in place by a chain lock, and the girl with the auburn hair was in front of him and peering at him through sleep-filled eyes caked by yesterday's make-up.

"Can I help you?" Madeleine asked, rubbing her eyes and smearing more mascara beneath them.

Graham thought she looked like an owl. A beautiful owl but an owl nonetheless. Those eyes were mesmerising. He was so caught up in them that he forgot to speak.

"Well?" Madeleine said, her tone less polite.

Graham blinked. "I have something for you," he managed. "I, um, I came to deliver it on Monday but you were—"

"On Monday?" Madeleine interrupted, wide awake now. She stared at Graham. "You're the Peeping Tom!"

"Peeping Tom? I can assure you that I am most certainly not a Peeping Tom!" Graham said, astonished that she could ever consider him to be such. Then he remembered exactly *how* he had seen her and his face turned puce. "I mean, *that* was an accident. I certainly never intended to *spy* on you. I have something for you. Look." He held out his hand which was clutching the expensive envelope and her eyes followed the movement. "It was posted through my door by accident. I live at 77 Lakeland *Avenue* you see and when I arrived I, um, I could see that you were busy through the gap in your blinds." He pointed to the window and realised that she'd had them repaired. Now his neck reddened and he began to sweat. He began to tug at the top of his sweatshirt, flapping air onto his chest.

"Christ, you're not going to pass out on me, are you?" Madeleine said, instinctively slipping the chain from the lock that held the door partially closed and reaching out towards him. She took hold of his arm, not wanting the neighbours to see him standing there panting like a lunatic. "Would you like a glass of water?"

"What? Oh, yes, please, if that's not too much trouble?"

Madeleine tugged his arm.

Hardly able to believe his luck, Graham entered her house and closed the door behind him.

***

Stuart's phone woke him and he spent a couple of bleary-eyed seconds fumbling before he finally swiped the call open and put the phone to his ear.

"Yeah," he mumbled.

Shakil, his closest friend, was on the line. "Stu, you're not going to like this, but I just watched your old man going into a house."

"Shit," said Stuart, now fully awake. "Are you sure?"

"Yeah, look, after we talked yesterday, I thought I'd stake your mum's place out early, just in case. He sneaked out, walked down the road and I followed him to number 77."

"That's where he lives," Stuart said, confused.

"No, number 77 further down the road. Anyway, some young bird opened the door, they had a bit of a conversation and then she grabbed him inside."

"A young…? What? Is he still there?"

"Yeah. I'm standing outside the house having a fag."

"Stay put," Stuart ordered. "I'll be there as fast as I can."

***

"Where's my sodding father?" Stuart barged through the door he'd been hammering on as soon as it opened, causing it to bang back against Madeleine's forehead.

"What the…? Ouch!" she complained bitterly, automatically raising a hand to rub the pain away. "Who the hell are you? Get out!"

"I know he's in here… Dad… Dad! Get out here now!" Stuart yelled, opening the first door he came to and bursting straight through it, closely followed by Madeleine who was pummelling his back and screaming blue murder. He took in the variety of tools of her trade with one glance and was extremely pleased to note that his father was not in there. He turned to face her. "Where is he?"

"Who?" Madeleine said, temporarily stopping screaming as she wondered whether this irate man was a relative of one her clients who had found out about their 'arrangement' with her.

"Stuart?" came a querulous voice from outside the room. "Is that you, Stuart? What are you doing here?"

"Me!" Stuart exploded, shoving Madeleine aside for a second time and stomping back out into the hall to find his mortified father nursing a half-drunk glass of water. "What are you doing here?"

"Having a drink of water." Graham, whose face was once again puce and sweating, indicated the glass. "What are *you* doing here?"

Stuart looked his father up and down, noting the tight jeans and the, what he considered to be an inappropriate-for-a-man-of-his-age, sweatshirt. "You silly old sod," he spat. "Who do you think you are? Britain's oldest rocker?" While Graham bristled, Stuart turned to Madeleine. "No need to ask what you see in him, the answer to that is in *there*." He rubbed his thumb against his fingers and nodded towards the lounge door then turned back to his father. "Worth it, was she?"

"Oi!" Madeleine interjected, having finally had enough of the commotion that would draw her to the attention of the entire street. "Let me stop you right there! This man, your *father*," she sent an irate glance towards Graham who was now staring at her through wide, haunted eyes, obviously wondering if she'd tell the truth and silently begging her not to, and then turned her attention back to Stuart, "...came to give me a letter that had been delivered to the wrong address. He had a funny turn on the doorstep, a bit like the one he's having now, so I offered him a glass of water."

"He's been in here for over twenty minutes! Glass of water, my eye!"

"It took a while for him to get over it—and you've just put him back to square one!" Madeleine put her hands on her hips and gave Stuart her most evil look. "Now, do you want to take him home or do I need to call the police?" She thought for a moment and added, "And how did you know he was here, anyway? Do you have a tracker on his phone?"

"Yes, how did you know where I was?" Graham said, coming smoothly to his senses and determined to take the moral high ground. "I don't have my phone with me because I only popped down to deliver the letter, as Madeleine said." He frowned. "And if you *do* have a tracker on it, you can damned well remove it!"

"Of course there isn't a tracker on your phone," Stuart said. He was beginning to feel like he'd walked onto the set of a Carry On film and it was far too early in the morning to deal with all this, especially stone-cold sober. "But what have you been doing for the last twenty minutes? And don't tell me you've been drinking water all that time, it takes ten seconds to knock one back."

"We've been having a chat. Madeleine here was telling me about her forthcoming holiday. The letter was from a pal of hers, someone she hasn't seen for some time because she went to live in … where was it you said? … oh yes, Antigua. She's been invited to visit her later this year." Graham kept his eyes firmly on his son's. He was lying through his teeth and praying Stuart wouldn't know.

"Oh." The wind went out of Stuart's sails. His shoulders slumped and he massaged the bridge of his nose, a habit that drove his father mad under normal circumstances. Graham decided to let it pass.

"So no need to worry, eh? Come on then son, let's go home. Thank you for the glass of water, Madeleine. It was very kind of you." He thrust the glass he held into Madeleine's hand and stalked down the hallway, past both of them, and out onto the pathway. "Coming?" he said over his shoulder, noting that one of his son's friends was standing and watching from a little further down the road.

Shakil saw the look and decided it was time to make a clean getaway. He threw the butt of his cigarette into the road, turned tail and began to leg it towards the town centre, leaving Graham shaking his head after him.

From the hallway, Stuart stared out at his father. "Was any of that true?" he quietly asked Madeleine, whose temper finally snapped.

"So not content with barging your way in here, hurting my head in the process, by the way, now you're calling us both liars?"

Stuart sighed. "I'm sorry. My mate saw him come in and thought he was cheating on Mum. He rang to let me know, so I ..."

"...thought you'd see for yourself. Satisfied now? No shagging going on? *As if...*" Madeleine's fury was white hot. "How dare you? Get out before I really do call the police. And don't come back! Either of you!"

Stuart retreated down the hallway and closed the door behind him.

The Walk of Shame

Graham had marched about fifty yards up the road by the time Stuart got to the pavement, hoping that his son would turn around and go back to his own home. He had no idea what he was going to say to Caroline and certainly didn't want any witnesses.

"Wait up, Dad."

Graham ignored him and sped up, pleased to note that no footsteps pounded the pavement behind him. After a couple of seconds had passed, he decided Stuart had understood he had no wish to talk things over and slowed his pace just as a car horn tooted and Stuart's blue Hyundai pulled up alongside him, its driver's window open. "Get in."

Graham took a few more steps, but the car kept pace with him. Sighing, Graham stopped and turned to face his son. "I can walk it, thank you."

"I said, get in. We need to have a bit of a chat don't you think? About what the hell we are going to tell Mum…"

Graham got in the car.

77 Lakeland Road (late Wednesday evening)

Madeleine's doorbell rang promptly on the dot of nine o'clock. Knowing it would be her Wednesday client, Bobby Jones, she went to answer it and was utterly surprised when a heavyset man in his late twenties whom she didn't recognise powered on through it and closed the door behind him. He swung the lock across, grabbed Madeleine's hair and dragged her into the front room she used to entertain her 'guests' stopping just short of the table, his face thunderous.

"Wha…? What do you want?" Madeleine squealed as ice water filled her stomach, knowing by his face and stance that this man was trouble. "Where's Bobby?"

"Have you been letting someone watch you with your clients," the man asked without preamble. Keeping a tight grip of her hair, his other hand grasped her chin and twisted her face towards him.

"What? No, of course not! Why would I—?" Madeleine's voice trailed off as it came to her that perhaps Monday's client, old Mr Tennant, had in fact noticed Graham peeking through the window and had reported it to the others – but that didn't explain the second question; how would any of them know about Graham's return earlier today? Was she being watched? Her throat tightened as adrenaline began to course through her body.

The man was watching her carefully. "Mr Tennant reported someone watching you both on Monday. Is that true? Did you let someone watch?"

"No," Madeleine said, licking her dry lips.

"Are you recording their visits?" His grip on her hair tightened, hurting Madeleine's scalp.

"Of course I'm not recording them! Why would I?"

"Blackmail, perhaps?"

"I've been seeing these men for over two years," she stuttered. "If I was going to blackmail any of them, don't you think I'd have done it by now?" Wondering if she would be able to get out of this by offering herself up to him, she opened her robe with her loose hand and bit her lower lip as the man's eyes swept over her, lingering at her breasts which were over spilling the cups of her scarlet balconette bra, revealing a hint of nipple. "I love our arrangement. We make each other happy so why on earth would I want to stop it by doing something so dumb? Search the room, if you don't believe me. I don't mind."

"I intend to do just that," the man said, dismissing her overture with a sneer. He released her, shoved her to one side and proceeded to move and check every single item in the room. He checked around the windows, above the door, around the dado rail and behind cushions and throws. He went through her toy boxes and checked every item in them. He checked the large mirror she had hanging on the wall between that room and the next to see if it was two-way and then he checked all the tiny cracks in the plaster.

While he systematically worked, Madeleine tiptoed her way towards the door, fear coursing through her body in swift thrills. Silently, she reached for the doorknob, turning it easily. She began to ease the door open, ready to run.

She was too late; he'd seen her. In one swift move, he was across the room and shoving the door closed. He backhanded her face, saying, "That was stupid."

He watched as Madeleine's face fell and a livid red mark bloomed on her cheek.

Moving to within millimetres of her, he growled, "If I find out you are lying, Madeleine, the spanking you usually get from your clients won't be the only thing you have coming. Do you understand?"

She swallowed painfully and nodded. "Of course. I promise you, I'm not lying."

The man dragged her back into the room and eyed her from top to toe. He reached for a nipple and twisted it, his lip curling. Releasing her arm, he said, "You know what comes next, don't you?"

Understanding this man now wanted sex and with her heart racing like a jackhammer, Madeleine slipped off her robe and stood in front of him wearing nothing but her bra and thong. She resisted the urge to use her hands to cover herself against the scathing looks he ran over her body.

"Them too," he said nodding towards her chest and groin. "Do what you usually do."

Madeleine removed her underwear and walked to the table.

"I said—"

Hurriedly, Madeleine bent over the table, raising her bottom into the air for him.

"Spread those legs."

Madeleine obliged.

The man rummaged in one of her boxes and came up holding a blindfold which he passed to her.

"Put it on."

Hesitantly, Madeleine slid the blindfold over her head, listening as the man rummaged around some more. Without warning, a hand slid up her inner thigh, reached between her legs and forced her labia apart so that he could thrust all four fingers inside her. Madeleine was dry. It hurt.

Madeleine thought she knew what was coming. Bobby had obviously told this man what would happen when they met and she was ready to accept this guy if he kept to the agenda and it kept Bobby and the others sweet. She hoped, like Bobby, he'd just finger her for a while, stick his dick inside her and fuck her for a few minutes, spank her bottom using his hand or perhaps a slipper, and then she'd get on her knees, suck him to the end and he'd finish by giving her a pearl necklace. It was a tried and tested formula that worked for Bobby and was over fairly quickly for her.

As the man made a fist inside her and shoved upwards, Madeleine began to scream.

"Shut up."

Madeleine tried to stop screaming but the pain he was inflicting inside her vagina was excruciating and she couldn't help crying out with each thrust. When he removed his hand, Madeleine sobbed with relief and tried to stand up—and then she felt his hand shoving her back in place, pressing against her lower back, holding her down onto the table as he rammed a dildo inside her and then removed it. Again, and again he used it on her, using more force than she'd thought anyone to be capable of. Madeleine's hip bones slammed against the table, drawing blood and she cried out, but he ignored her cries and carried on with her punishment.

"You let someone watch you with Ted, didn't you?" the man said, removing the dildo but leaning against her back, keeping her pinned. "Someone else is paying you and you're shagging him, too."

"No!" Madeleine said. "I really didn't, I promise."

The man sighed. He dug his elbow deep into her lower back and used his hands to tug her buttocks apart. Then, in one practised move, forced the dildo deep into her anus. The unexpected shock of it made Madeleine scream. She began to try to push herself up and off the table, but his elbow did not move, and now he was putting more weight on her, ensuring she was unable to escape while she flailed uselessly against him.

"This is going to hurt," the man said conversationally, "and it does need to hurt, Madeleine. I think you know that, deep down."

"But why? I haven't done anything," Madeleine cried. "Please, I'll do anything you want but please don't hurt me."

"Be quiet now, Madeleine," the man said. "You know you like pain. Tonight, you're really going to get it."

Madeleine gave in. She lay over the table while he abused her with the dildo, tears of pain coursing down her face. Eventually, he stopped.

"Did you let someone watch?" he asked quietly, keeping his weight on her.

"N... no," she stammered through her tears. "I swear I didn't let anyone watch."

With his free hand, the man slapped her bottom, hard. "Did you let someone watch?"

"Ow, no, no I didn't let anyone watch! Why don't you believe me?"

He slapped her again, with more force. "The truth, Madeleine, or I will whip you and this time I won't be playing."

"I didn't *let* anyone watch," she began, hesitant to say anything else for fear of being seriously injured.

"But someone did?"

Madeleine nodded.

"How?"

"The blind was broken. Someone looked through it as I was giving Ted a blowie."

The man's hand came down twice more. Madeleine's bottom was now covered with angry red handprints. "Why did you lie?"

"I didn't," Madeleine protested. "You asked if I *let* anyone watch and I didn't. That was the truth. I didn't know for sure that anyone had until after Ted had gone."

"Semantics, my dear. Stay put."

His weight was gone, but fear kept her in place as she listened to him rooting about for something and braced herself. A whistling sound flew through the air and a loud crack filled the room as one of Madeleine's canes bounced off her bottom. She screamed.

"Did you see who it was?"

"No!" Madeleine sobbed as the cane came down for a second time, raising a long, thin weal.

"Did you find out who it was?" The cane came down again and this time it drew blood.

Madeleine whimpered. "Yes."

The cane whistled through the air twice more before it went to the floor. In the next instant, the weight lifted from her and the man was pulling her legs apart and ramming his penis inside her, riding her with as much force as he could muster. At the last second, he pulled out, grabbed his hands into her long hair and yanked her off the table, forcing her to her knees. He twisted her head around and thrust his cock deep into her mouth, instantly sending salty cum deep into the back of her throat while she choked and spluttered ineffectually.

When he was spent, he pulled himself away and wiped himself with one of the towels she always kept handy for these occasions. He tugged the blindfold from her red-rimmed eyes and tipped her head up so that he could be sure she was looking at him.

His voice was menacing as he said, "I think we need a proper chat about the merits of truth-telling, don't you, Madeleine? And you need to tell me who was watching and whether you are shagging him…"

Chapter Four
Thursday

77 Lakeland Avenue

Stuart stared at Jasmine and dry swallowed.

"Okay, you're worrying me now. What's up?" Jasmine raised a hand to her mouth and began to nibble at the skin around her thumb nail, a habit she'd had since childhood.

"Where's Mum?"

"She's taken Chutzy for a walk. I'm surprised you didn't see her, she's not long left. Said she needed to get out of the house to clear her head, whatever that's supposed to mean and no, she didn't want me to go with her."

"Where's Dad?"

"In his office." Jasmine slung a thumb over her shoulder, indicating the door to the basement. "He said he had, and I quote, shed loads of work to catch up on, and locked himself inside just after I got up. Quite rude, really, the pair of them." She raised an eyebrow and smiled. "So what's eating you?"

Stuart sighed. "Dad."

"What's he done?"

"I think he's having some sort of mid-life crisis."

"Dad's too old to have a mid-life crisis," Jasmine said, laughing. "Come on, don't keep me in suspenders. What's he done?"

"Urgh, don't say that!" Stuart said, grimacing. He flopped himself onto a second chair. "That's what he says."

Jasmine put her head to one side and eyed her twin. "This is serious, isn't it?" She began to drum her fingers against the table, something she did when she was beginning to feel anxious.

"I honestly don't know," Stuart told her.

"Look, I take it you don't want Mum to know so get on with it!"

"It's like this…" And Stuart told her about the events of the previous day, while Jasmine's face dropped and her eyes widened.

"Let me get this right," she said eventually, as she processed what she had just been told. "Dad delivered a letter that had mistakenly been delivered here instead of to Lakeland Road, Shakil followed him and saw him go into the house, and then you went round there and went off like a rocket, accusing him and the woman who lives there of all sorts?"

"I know how it sounds," Stuart said. "But they were both lying through their teeth, I just can't prove it. Dad was being … *shifty*. And he was all done up like a dog's dinner."

"What was he wearing?"

"Jeans and a hoodie."

"Jeans and a hoodie?" Jasmine burst into laughter. "Dad?"

"And on Monday he went out in those blue trackie bottoms you bought him and a T-shirt with a lion on it saying 'Hear me Roar', plus the trainers I bought him ages ago."

"How do you know?"

"Mum told me. She thinks he's up to something, too, not just because of the clothes; he'd practically drowned himself in that god-awful aftershave he puts on for high days and holidays."

"So what happened afterwards? Did you come back here with him?"

"Yeah, we pretended we bumped into each other in town. Mum swallowed it, I think."

"Does she know about the letter?"

Stuart shook his head. "I don't think so, no."

"Are you going to tell her?"

"Not yet, no. But if he carries on acting daft, I will."

The sound of keys turning in the lock of the front door made them both stop talking and turn to face their mother and the dog, who chuffed with delight at having both of them home and bounded up the hallway to greet them, his tail whirling like a dervish.

"Both of you! This is a pleasant surprise," Caroline said, smiling as she hung the lead on its hook, slipped off her shoes and coat and hung that up, too. "To what do I owe the pleasure? And where's your father?"

"I just wanted to see you," Stuart said, rising from his seat to give his mother a hug.

"Twice in two days," she said, kissing his cheek. "That is nice. Did you put the kettle on for him, Jazz? No? I'll do it now. Where *is* your father?"

"In his office," Jasmine said, jerking her head towards the door to the basement.

Caroline rolled her eyes in annoyance. "Really? Couldn't he take five minutes to stay and have a chat? We'll see about that…" She strode to the basement door, knocked once, peremptorily, then opened it and yelled down the stairs, "Graham? Come up here and spend a little time with our children, please," in a tone that brooked no argument.

She heard him grumbling to himself and then he appeared at the bottom of the stairs wearing a pained smile and began to climb towards her. She left the door open and went back to filling up the kettle.

"Um, hi kids," Graham said as he rounded the doorway, looking directly at Jasmine but not daring to meet Stuart's eyes.

"Hi Dad," Stuart said drily. "How's things?"

"Oh, um, you know," Graham said shiftily. "Are you making coffee, darling?"

"I am. Sit yourself down. Kids, would you like a slice of fruit cake?"

"Yes please," they both said in unison, grinning at each other while Graham grimaced.

"You not having any?" Stuart asked his father as the older man took a seat at the table.

"Oh, you! You know he doesn't like my fruit cake," Caroline said. "Would you like some toast, Graham?"

"Dad can make his own toast while you do the coffee," Stuart said firmly, sending a glare towards his father.

"Of course, of course," Graham said. "Don't worry, Caroline, I'll do it."

"Who are you and what have you done with my husband," Caroline trilled shrilly, then she burst into high-pitched, false laughter which the twins echoed, equally as shrilly.

The laughter stopped as Graham stalked stiffly across the kitchen and began the rigmarole of making himself some toast.

"What have you both got planned for today?" Caroline asked, breaking the silence. "Why aren't you both at work?"

"Stuart? Working?" Jasmine snorted. "That'll be the day."

"I'll have you know I am working," Stuart said, surprising the entire family.

"Really?" Caroline said, unable to hide her amazement. She dropped the teaspoon she was holding into one of the mugs that now had coffee in them and turned to face her son. "What are you doing?"

"I've set up a new business, actually."

"You've what?" Jasmine said. "Don't you need money to set up a business? Oh! Is that why you're here today? Cadging money from the olds? What kind of business?"

"Me and Shakil are doing it together," Stuart said, "and no, I don't need any money from Mum or Dad—"

"That's just as well, because we wouldn't give you any, anyway," Graham muttered, flinching as Caroline slapped at his arm.

"Go on, son, what kind of business?" Caroline asked.

"We've opened up a private eye agency. You know, hunting down missing people, finding lost pets, finding evidence of cheating partners…" Stuart studiously kept his eyes on the table as he said the final part.

Unnoticed by the twins, both Caroline and Graham's faces reddened.

Jasmine burst into proper belly laughter. "You and Shakil? The two of you are always off your faces! How are you going to become private eyes? Neither of you could find your arses with your elbows, never mind a missing person!"

"Jasmine!" Caroline snapped.

"We could!" Stuart protested. "You don't even need to be qualified, but we've been doing a level three qualification and got licensed. We're doing it properly."

"Won't that need a DBS check?" Caroline asked. "I mean, weren't you both done for possession last year? At that rave that got raided?"

Stuart flushed. "No, Mum." He didn't mention that one of the coppers who had burst into the rave had bought an ounce of skunk from them a week prior to the event, so had waved them off without recording their names.

"Oh, that was lucky!" Caroline said, with feeling. "So … a private eye? How long is the course?"

"They'll be a pair of private dicks," Graham muttered, not quietly enough.

"Really Dad?" Stuart said mildly, swivelling his eyes from his mother to his father, pleased to note the colour rising in his father's neck. "I think we'll be quite good at it, actually. And the course was done online, 160 hours of tuition and an exam at the end of it."

"Wasn't it expensive?" Jasmine asked.

"Surprisingly, no," Stuart said. "There's loads of online courses, starting at around £30 and going up from there. There are a ton of special offers on at the moment because everyone's sick of working online after Covid, I guess. Even we could afford that, Jazz."

"You've really looked into it then?" Caroline said.

"Yeah, Shaks came up with the idea and I think it's a goer."

"What are you going to call yourselves? 'The Two Dicks'?" Graham was unable to help himself.

"No," Stuart said, eyeing him levelly. "We rather thought we'd call ourselves SAS Investigations."

"Stoned and Stupid?" Jasmine said, getting in on the act.

"Soft and Sloppy?" Graham added, snorting.

"Silent and Suspicious?" Jasmine roared with laughter, ignoring the muscle flexing in her brother's cheek.

"Enough, you two," Caroline yelled. "It's obviously short for Stuart and Shakil."

"Actually, it stands for Security and Serenity. You know, a play on words for peace of mind."

"That's rather good, actually," Graham said, condescendingly. "So when do you start the course?"

"Haven't you been listening? We've finished it," Stuart said. "We started it ages ago, the exam's tomorrow."

"Bloody hell!" said three voices in unison.

77 Lakeland Road

Madeleine rolled over onto her back before she came fully awake, and cried out as her entire body screamed with pain. The results of this beating wouldn't be going away any time soon. She wondered whether her three clients had got together to organise what had happened to her and whether they would be happy about the result. They had an unwritten rule that handprints and raised welts were fine, but no blood was to be drawn. Madeleine's bottom had looked like an offering at a carvery by the end of the previous night and she was having trouble drawing breath because her ribs hurt. The room was swimming, her eyes unable to focus properly. She stumbled to her feet, her arms dangling agonisingly by her sides, and staggered to the mirror where she blearily peered at her reflection in horror. Her cheekbone was swollen. Her left eye was partially shut and beginning to bruise. The white of her other eye was red at the site closest to her lop-sided nose. Cigarette burns and fingerprint bruises from hard pinches were scattered across her breasts and both areola had dried blood around them. Full and expanding bruises littered the entirety of the rest of her body. There was a dull ache between her legs and, she realised with fresh horror, she had absolutely no recollection of getting into bed.

The chat she had had with her unexpected visitor had not been a pleasant one.

For the first time, she began to really think about getting out of this game; but how would she do it, where would she go, who could she turn to? She was trapped in a house that three men knew about, each of whom expected to be able to use her at will. She never wanted to see any of them again. She wondered if she could turn to Gregor, the – let's not beat about the bush here – pimp who had put the group together, and then she remembered Callie, an extremely young girl who had been shipped in from somewhere by a gang of traffickers and subsequently purchased by Gregor for his clients who liked pre-pubescent girls. Madeleine had seen her once, sitting in the corner of Gregor's office, and recalled a startlingly pretty little girl who flinched whenever anyone went near her.

Callie had been found floating face down in the Thames, not two weeks later.

So no, Gregor was out. She shivered as the thought came to her that if Bobby, or Ted or even Mr P, Friday night's client who had never allowed her to know his real name and always turned up under cover of darkness, complained about her, she may end up like Callie and not just battered.

Bitter tears sprang into her eyes, stinging her eyelids. She blinked them away, trying desperately to keep it together and decided that maybe a hot shower would help ease the pain. She stumbled from the room and into her bathroom, switched the shower on with her chin and dragged herself beneath the steaming hot flow, her face tilted into the water, allowing it to wash away her tears, ignoring the stinging of her skin as the water opened her partially knitted wounds and blood flowed down her legs to be washed away into the drain. She stood there for several minutes allowing the water to attempt to work its magic before she gingerly began to try to wash and found herself unable to lift either arm properly. She forewent shampooing her hair. Taking a deep breath, she sat herself down in the base of the shower, allowing the flow to run between her legs, alarmed to see fresh blood begin to flow down into the tray. Gingerly, she probed herself and a bolt of agony flooded through her and the blood flow increased. She let the water run until the flow eased and the drain had taken the blood away and then she slithered herself out of the shower and onto the bathroom tiles where she lay for a few seconds, trying to remember what she should do next. It was only when she began to shiver that she realised she needed to dry herself and tried to reach for a towel.

Every movement was painful, every blink, every twist of her head, every move of her torso—everything hurt; from the roots of her hair, right on down to her toes. What had he done to her once she'd passed out?

She ignored the fact she was still dripping wet and crawled back into the bedroom, wiped out by the simple act of showering. By a feat of sheer will, she managed to pull a long T-shirt from a low drawer and over her head then she simply lay face down on the floor thinking she'd rest, just for a moment, just for five minutes, just for an hour … Her final thoughts before she passed out for a second time was that there was something she badly needed to do but she could not remember what it was. Her mind was protecting her from the worst of things and did not allow her to recall how she had given the man all the information he wanted about the man from number 77 Lakeland Avenue.

77 Lakeland Avenue

Graham had taken Caroline shopping and Stuart had gone home to take his private investigator exam so Jasmine was alone in the house, apart from Chutzpah who lolled happily at her feet. Her mind was feverishly playing over what Stuart had told her about her father's actions the previous day. Had he just gone to that other woman's house to deliver a letter, or was there more to it than that? She didn't want to believe that her father could be unfaithful to her mum, but what if he were? How would her mother cope if she found out?

Sighing loudly, with the weight of the world upon her shoulders, she went to the sink to fill up the kettle just as Chutzpah began to growl loudly, making her jump. Amazed, she turned to look at the dog. His hackles were raised and he stood stock still, staring down the hall towards the front door, one front paw slightly raised and his entire body shivering.

"What is it, boy?" Jasmine whispered, tiptoeing to his side.

Without taking his eyes from the door, Chutzpah growled louder, and then louder still until the sound was almost a snarl. His top lip curled, exposing teeth that looked wickedly sharp, and then the doorbell rang and the dog's snarl became primal. Jasmine stared at the dog and knew she wasn't answering it. As if reading her mind, Chutzpah edged himself in front of her, barring her way.

"It's okay, Chutzi, I'm not going anywhere near the door, don't worry," Jasmine whispered, more to comfort herself than the dog, not daring to pet him for fear that he would turn on her. She had never seen him like this. Whoever was at the door was not a good person. She looked around the kitchen, her eyes falling on the knife block. She tiptoed across the kitchen and withdrew the butcher's knife, the sharpest and largest of them all, then she crouched down, hiding below the level of the countertops, praying that whoever was at the door couldn't see her movements through the small panes of frosted glass in the front door.

She was glad she had when Chutzpah suddenly turned and prowled towards the kitchen door – the outside one that opened into the garden. Jasmine found herself staring at the keys that dangled from the lock. She'd let the dog out for a wee not long after her parents had left—had she locked it again?

The dog's snarls were now almost silent. Drool dripped in strings from his jowls, his hackles were up like porcupine needles and his entire body language told her that whoever was out there was not somebody she wanted to meet; but who the hell could it be? Burglars? She kept a tight grip on the knife handle, making sure the blade faced away from her in case Chutzpah barked and she jumped and stabbed herself by accident. She watched as the dog stealthily crept towards the back door, slavering profusely.

Now she heard the unmistakable sounds of someone trying the back door handle. Jasmine closed her eyes and prayed that she'd locked it, stifling a relieved sob when the door didn't open. Next, she heard someone trying to open the kitchen window and froze. Was she completely hidden?

Could whoever it was see her? Terror engulfed her and as it did so, she felt warmth at the crotch of her jeans as her bladder let go.

The dog was now growling at the window, not taking his eyes from the pane. He barked, once, and then went back to his slavering growl, the sounds enormous in Jasmine's terror-filled head. The movements at the window stopped and she heard a male voice swear and then the sound of retreating footsteps. Chutzpah stayed in place staring at the window for a few more seconds and then he deftly turned and prowled towards the door that led into the hallway.

Her phone! Where was her phone? Jasmine patted the back pocket of her jeans and bit back a sob. It wasn't there. Where had she left it? As if conjured up by the power of her will alone, a familiar buzzing noise began to sound in the room. It was on the dining table, now vibrating madly as somebody tried to gain her attention.

Within seconds, somebody pounded on the front door. "We know you're in there, so open up. Don't make it worse for yourself!"

The pounding continued, making the door shake in its frame and Chutzpah was off, streaking down the hall, barking a dire warning to the person on the other side even as Jasmine got to her feet and slipped and slid across the urine-soaked tiles towards her phone which stopped ringing just as she picked it up. She slid her fingers across its screen and hit the emergency call button.

***

"Somebody did try to gain entry from around the back; they've broken the lock on your side gate, so you'll need to get that fixed," said the police officer who had arrived within minutes of her call and was now scratching the sweet spot behind Chutzpah's ears, sending the dog into drools of delight. "Good job you have him, eh? Who's a good boy then? Yes, you are, you are." He realised what he was doing and drew himself upright to turn his attention back to Jasmine. "Are you okay? You can put the knife down now, you're perfectly safe."

Jasmine glanced down at her hand which was still gripping the knife with a vice-like grip. She held it out towards the officer shakily but found herself unable to release her fingers. A female officer walked into the kitchen after having swept through the house and took in the situation in one glance.

"Come on then, love," she said softly, walking over to Jasmine and carefully prising the knife from her. She passed it to the other officer and then put an arm around her shoulders. "Let's get you cleaned up, shall we? Come on, come with me, let's get you changed."

In a daze, Jasmine allowed herself to be led upstairs and into the bathroom with Chutzpah close at her heels. "Have a shower love, we'll wait downstairs for you. You've had a nasty fright."

"I've never seen Chutzi act like that," Jasmine stammered. "He was, he was *feral*."

Both women turned to look at the dog who had curled himself into a ball by the side of the bath looking about as fierce as a rabbit. His tail thumped against the floor.

"Good job he was," the officer said. "He scared them off. They left the tools they used to try to break in in the lock, so they would have entered if he hadn't gone off on one.

Now, have a quick wash and come back down when you're ready. We're going nowhere, don't worry. You're in safe hands."

"What's your name," Jasmine asked, unwilling to be left alone.

"It's Chloe, love, and you're Jasmine, right?"

Jasmine nodded again.

"Good. So Jasmine, I'm going to go downstairs while you freshen up, up here. Don't worry about the kitchen floor, I'll have that cleaned up before you know it. You're not the first to have had an accident when you were frightened and you won't be the last. And nobody needs to know, okay? Just us."

Jasmine burst into tears and the policewoman threw the rulebook out of the window and pulled her into a hug. "There, there," she crooned, rubbing the girl's back as Chutzpah raised his head and whined softly. "It's okay. There's nothing to be scared of now. We'll stay with you until your parents get back."

"Promise?" Jasmine croaked.

"Promise," Chloe told her. "Cross my heart and all that. Now," she pulled herself away from Jasmine and held her by her shoulders, gazing into her eyes, "put those clothes in the wash basket there and wash up. Your gorgeous, furry guardian angel isn't going anywhere and I'll wait outside the door for you. Do you want me to get you some fresh clothes?"

Jasmine nodded. "Please. My bedroom's the first on the left, ignore the mess."

Chloe laughed. "I have teenagers, don't worry about any mess." She removed her hands from Jasmine's shoulders and went to the door. "I'll get your clothes and wait here for when you're ready for them, okay?"

Jasmine nodded again and watched as Chloe closed the door behind her. She bit back a sob and began to undress.

***

"What's going on?" Graham yelled as he and Caroline rushed into the house, alarmed by the presence of the police car parked across their driveway and even more so to see one officer standing in the hallway and another at the top of the stairs. "Where's Jazz? What's happened?"

"Try to stay calm, sir," the male officer standing in front of them said as he flashed his badge at them both. "PC Stanhope. Attempted burglary, we think. Your daughter's upstairs, getting changed."

"Was she hurt?" Caroline said, sprinting up the stairs and calling Jasmine's name.

"She's fine," Officer Chloe told her, stepping in front of the bathroom door to stop Caroline from bursting through it. "She's just showering. She, um, she spilt some water down herself and asked me to wait outside because she was a bit het up. Nothing to worry about."

"I'm okay, Mum." Jasmine's voice drifted through the door. "I'll be out in a bit, I'm fine, don't worry."

"Where's Chutzi?"

"In here with me. I'll bring him down with me."

"In there... what the hell has happened?"

"I'll tell you in a minute!" Jasmine shouted. Now she had showered her fear had abated somewhat and she was beginning to feel a little embarrassed by all the commotion she'd raised.

Caroline looked at the officer, who shrugged and said, "Shall we go downstairs and I'll tell you what I know?"

Reluctantly, Caroline stood back, watching as Chloe laid the set of clothing she'd had in her arms down to the floor outside the bathroom door, calling to let Jasmine know what she'd done. She let the officer lead the way back down the stairs where Graham, who had moved into the kitchen, was in full flow.

"...do you mean, there were tools in the locks?"

"We've got them now, don't worry, but you will need to change the locks—and if I were you, I'd consider beefing them up a little, and also think about putting window locks on the downstairs windows. There's been a spate of burglaries in the area recently and they don't seem to be bothered by somebody being home. Thank your lucky stars you have your dog." The officer nodded in emphasis.

Graham, who had never wanted a dog in the first place, gazed blankly at Chutzpah who was now trotting into the kitchen, tail wagging, his wife and a female officer behind him. "Yes," he mumbled. "He was worth his weight in gold today, wasn't he?"

"He really was," Jasmine said, having followed her mother down the stairs and slipped past her to come to her father's side.

Graham slid an arm around her waist and squeezed slightly. "Are you okay?"

Jasmine nodded. "They knew someone was in," she said slowly, remembering what the man at the front door had shouted. "They said not to make it worse on myself. But I haven't done anything wrong. I haven't hurt anyone or anything. So did they have the wrong house?"

The male officer cocked his head, his eyes narrowing. "That puts a slightly different slant on things." He turned to Graham. "Do you have any enemies, sir?"

77 Lakeland Road

It was the insistence of the person knocking at her door that roused Madeleine from her stupor although she did not, at first, recognise the fact. She prised open her eyes and looked at the clock on the bedside table. 8.40. Was that morning, or evening? She squinted at her window and noted that it was almost dark outside, so that meant it was the evening. The doorbell rang and someone simultaneously knocked on the door. A female voice called through the letterbox.

"Maddy? Are you all right? Look, I'm not leaving until you answer."

Madeleine blinked. She recognised the voice but had never had anybody female call on her before. So who was it?

"It's me, Sarah," came the voice again. "Please open up."

"Hang on," Madeleine slurred, her tongue feeling thick and muzzy. She was still having trouble focussing and knew she needed help. She got to her knees, used her chin against the bed to help her stand and stumbled to the top of the stairs. "Hang on," she repeated, leaning her hip against the bannister and slip-sliding down the first few stairs towards the voice. "Don't go. Please don't go."

She heard the letterbox flap again and heard a gasp. "That's it, sweetie, take your time. I'll wait, don't worry."

Sweet words of encouragement followed every step Madeleine struggled with, and after what felt like an age of painful manoeuvres, she managed to make her way to the front door and scrabbled with her less useless arm to unlock it. She finally turned the key by hooking a thumb into the key ring it was attached to and twisting but was then unable to turn the handle as fierce bolts of pain shot up both her arms and embedded themselves into her shoulders.

"Stand back, sweetie. I can take it from here."

Madeleine stumbled backwards and leaned against the wall. Within seconds, the door was open and Sarah was in the hallway, putting an arm around Madeleine's back and beneath her arms, catching her as her legs gave way beneath her. Keeping a tight hold on her new friend, Sarah kicked open the closest door and was just about to take Madeleine into it when she stopped and inhaled sharply. Dried blood had sunk into the grains of the table in the centre of the room and was splattered up the walls. A bloodied cane was on the floor, alongside what looked like a bullwhip, also covered in dried blood. Blood-encrusted nipple clamps lay on a chair alongside bloodied sex toys.

It looked like carnage had taken place in there.

Sarah reversed back into the hallway and half dragged the semi-conscious girl towards the next room along, pleased to note that in this room there was a comfy-looking sofa. She lowered Madeleine into it and stared at her, taking in the swellings and bruises, the odd angles at which she held her arms.

"I need to call you an ambulance," she said gently.

"N... no 'bulance," Madeleine mumbled. "P'lice'll come'n I'll be 'rested."

"No you won't," Sarah said. "But you need help, medical help. I think you have broken bones that'll need setting, and antibiotics, too."

"No!" Madeleine was becoming agitated now. "Gregor'll kill me if I go to 'spital."

"Okay, okay," Sarah said immediately, making a mental note of the name and wondering if it was the same Gregor who ran the website she worked for. She silently thanked God for her spidey senses—she'd woken with a bad feeling that morning and hadn't been able to either shake it or figure out what was bothering her. It happened sometimes; she had a built-in antenna for trouble, and she always took note of the warning. She'd racked her brains, called everyone she cared about and still the feeling would not leave. Eventually, just as she was about to get herself ready to start work for the evening, Madeleine popped into her head and she'd found herself out of her front door and up the road before she knew it. "Maddy, I need to get you some help. Is there anyone you can think of who might be able to help you?"

"D'clan." Madeleine had no idea why the handyman's name came to mind, but it popped out regardless.

"Declan?" Sarah said. "Do you have a number for him?"

"Card. On windowsill. Not here—in kitchen," Madeleine managed. And then the strain proved too much for her and she was out cold.

Sarah lifted Madeleine's legs onto the sofa and slid a cushion beneath the girl's head, checking she was still breathing before she went into the kitchen to track down Declan's details, hoping vehemently that he wasn't one of Madeleine's clients.

***

Sarah waited in the front room of the house, ignoring the mess and listening to Madeleine's hitched breathing, checking through the blinds at the window every few seconds to see when Declan arrived. She was careful not to touch anything apart from the string to the blinds which she'd had to pull on to open slightly. After what felt like forever, a Ford Fiesta pulled up outside and a man got out, slammed the car door, locked it and raced up the pathway. He reached the front door at the same time as Sarah did.

"Don't ring the bell," she hissed, opening the door slightly and keeping the chain on, not wanting to disturb Madeleine if she could help it yet knowing that if he wanted to, he'd simply push against the door and it would give way. She pulled the door to the scene of horror closed behind her. "Who are you?" she asked.

"It's me, Declan," he said. He scrabbled in the pocket of his jeans and pulled out a card that she recognised.

Sarah unhooked the chain and ushered him in with quick beckoning movements.

"Where is she?" Declan said, reaching for the handle of the door that led to the front room.

"Back room," Sarah said swiftly. "Up the hall." She led the way, Declan close on her heels.

As she opened the door, Declan inhaled sharply and turned to face Sarah. "What the hell happened to her?"

Sarah looked him evenly in the eyes, willing him to understand.

"A punter?"

Sarah nodded.

"We'll deal with that issue later. Do you think we can get her into the car between us? She needs proper help."

"She won't go to hospital. She's scared she'll be arrested."

Declan's lips thinned. He thought for an instant and then said, "I know someone who may be able to help. Let me give them a quick ring." He turned and walked from the room, his phone already at his ear.

***

Thirty long minutes later, Madeleine's doorbell sounded. This time, Declan went to answer it and returned lugging what looked to be a heavy bag and accompanied by an older woman. Sarah stared at her as she swept past her and on into the back room. She appeared to be in her late fifties, but very well preserved. Her greying hair was neatly swept into a chignon on the back of her head and her face was immaculately made up to look like she wasn't wearing any. Her bone structure was incredible; she must have been a heartbreaker when she was younger.

"Sarah, Doc, Doc, Sarah," Declan said, by way of introduction.

Ignoring him, Doc went straight to Madeleine. She pressed long, slender fingers against the unconscious girl's neck and breathed a sigh of relief. "Well, she's still alive. Her pulse is a bit thready, but it's stable. Do we know what happened?" She turned her head to finally look at Sarah and Declan, her south London accent at odds with her looks.

Sarah and Declan shared a look which Doc, correctly, interpreted. "She's not safe here then, is she? We'll need to get her to hospital but first I need to take a good look at her. Bag please, Dec. ... What's her name?"

"Madeleine," Sarah said, as Declan hefted the bag up and then put it on the floor beside Doc who began to rummage through it and pulled out a pair of sterile gloves which she put on. "I think her arms are broken; she couldn't move them properly and they looked off kilter when I arrived. She passed out soon after she let me in. And she doesn't want to go to hospital because it'll be reported to the police."

"Any idea how long she's been like this?" Doc was now drawing liquid from a small vial into a syringe which she flicked expertly and emptied into the crook of Madeleine's arm.

Sarah looked away. "I think, probably, since last night. She was okay on Tuesday and the bruises and swelling look fresh to me."

Doc nodded. "Yes, I agree. Anyone know the fucker who did this to her?"

Sarah blinked at the unexpected language and shook her head. "I think it may be one of the three men she's got an arrangement with. She doesn't have cold callers if you know what I mean?"

"Yes," Declan agreed. "That's what she told me, too, so it could be one of them." He thought for a moment. "Although ... she did have a Peeping Tom on Monday. It's not beyond the realms of possibility that he came back again."

Doc nodded. She was now examining Madeleine's face, her fingers pressing against the girl's nose. "Straight break," she said. "Can one of you check to see if she has any ice in her freezer. Put it in a clean tea towel for me and bring it here."

Declan went to look leaving Sarah to watch as Doc carefully inserted a metal rod into Madeleine's left nostril and manually realigned her nose. She then packed the nostril with gauze, leaving a small blue thread hanging which she stuck to Madeleine's cheek with an adhesive strip. Next, she placed three white strips across the top of Madeleine's nose and then stuck another more solid-looking white strip over the top of them all.

"That'll keep it in place. The gauze needs to come out after seven days, and she's to leave the splint in place for around three weeks. Will you remember that?" Doc finally looked directly at Sarah, who nodded.

Declan came back carrying a tea towel bulging with ice cubes.

"Thanks, come and hold it against her face," Doc said. "I've fixed her nose but it looks like she's got a busted cheekbone here and I want the swelling around her eyes to go down. Bastard must have done both with one swipe. There's not much I can do for that right now because I can't tell without an x-ray if it's going to need surgery. We'll worry about that later. For now, I need to examine the rest of her body. Declan, can you step out? I'll need you to stay, Sarah, is it?"

Sarah nodded as Declan went back to the kitchen, closing the door behind him. They both heard him rummaging around and then heard the sound of the back door opening and closing behind him.

"Are you ready?" Doc asked Sarah. "I need to check everywhere. Can you cope? I don't need someone passing out on me."

"Just do it," Sarah said, gritting her teeth in annoyance. "I've seen worse."

Doc's eyebrows raised infinitesimally and briefly. "Okay then." She took a pair of scissors from her bag and began to cut open the T-shirt from bottom to top. She then took the scissors to the sleeves and finally lifted the front of the shirt from Madeleine's body.

Sarah gasped, unable to help herself. Madeleine's slight body was smothered in bruises. She found her eyes drawn to the girl's breasts. Apart from cuts and bruises that looked very much like they had come from the nipple clamps she'd seen in the front room, whoever had done this appeared to have put a cigarette or two out on them and also used their teeth. Bite marks loomed large and ugly on each breast and each of those had pierced through her skin, drawing copious amounts of blood. Some of the wounds oozed and her left nipple was hanging on by a thread.

"Christ," Doc said, turning to her bag again. She drew out a bottle of some kind of liquid and ripped open a wad of sterile pads, opened the bottle and tipped a small amount of the liquid onto the top pad. The astringent smell of antiseptic filled the room. Doc wiped it gently over Madeleine's breasts, concentrating on the burns, bites and misplaced nipple.

"This needs a stitch," she said, indicating a particularly large bite wound before digging into her bag again and getting started. "Do you know if she's had a tetanus shot lately?"

"I only met her on Tuesday. I have no idea," Sarah said.

"Oh," Doc said as she worked. "I thought she was your friend."

"She is," Sarah said. "We clicked straight away. But I don't really know her."

"That's a shame. I hoped you'd be able to look after her once she comes back from the clinic I'm going to have her transported to. *If* she comes back."

"I will," Sarah said, simply and honestly. "I'd hope someone would do the same for me."

Doc smiled briefly for the first time and began to feel around Madeleine's rib cage. "Yeah, at least two broken ribs," she said soberly. "I can't do anything for that, they have to heal themselves. She'll need to take deep breaths to stop her getting pneumonia. Can you remember that?"

Sarah nodded. "Deep breaths. No pneumonia."

Doc sat back on her heels and looked straight at Sarah. "I need to examine her private parts now and I'd prefer to be chaperoned. Are you ready for that? I have a feeling things won't be pretty."

"Do I have to look?"

"No. You can pass me things if I ask for them. Put a pair of gloves on, they're at the top of the bag."

As Sarah did so, Doc turned back to Madeleine and continued her search of the girl's injuries, muttering profanities to herself as she did so. After a few seconds she asked Sarah to get her a bowl of warm water and a couple of clean towels, if she could find any. When Sarah returned with what she'd asked for, Doc cleaned away the massive amount of dried blood between Madeleine's legs and told Sarah to change her gloves.

"Is she alright?" Sarah asked having done so, when the silence in the room became too much for her.

"He's ripped through her perineum." Seeing Sarah's blank look, Doc explained, "The skin between her vagina and anus. Waste is coming through into her vagina and that's not good news. She'll need special surgery for this; a colostomy – that's where we redirect waste so it comes out of a stoma in her tummy - until her bottom heals, if it does. I can't do that here."

"Fucking hell," Sarah said quietly.

"Indeed," said Doc.

Doc drew Madeleine's legs back together and looked up at Sarah. "I need to turn her. Can you help?"

Sarah nodded.

"You take her feet and I'll take her top half. I want you to turn them to your left."

Sarah moved to the foot of the sofa and took hold of Madeleine's feet, the soles of which also had cigarette burns on them. Biting back tears, she said, "On three. One, two, *three*."

And both women stared in horror at the lacerated meat of Madeleine's bottom.

***

Declan paced around Madeleine's small back garden, staring blindly at the roses and lavender whose cloying scent was rising into the warm air and making him feel slightly nauseous. He dug into his back pocket and pulled out a lighter and a pack of unopened cigarettes, ripped off the plastic seal and pulled one out. He put it to his lips, used the lighter and inhaled harshly, coughing as the smoke hit the back of his throat. He was finding it hard to reconcile the figure on the couch with the beautiful, bubbly girl he'd spent time with on Monday, just a couple of short days ago. His head bubbled with a rage that he knew would blow out of control with just one little push, and so he paced to contain it.

"Is everything okay over there?" A small voice came from behind the fence of an adjacent garden. "Only we heard a bit of a commotion in here yesterday when, um, she had a visitor, and we've never seen you before."

Declan swivelled to face the speaker, a small elderly man who was standing with his wife, wringing his hands, an anxious look on his face. He drew in a deep breath and stalked over to the fence.

"No," he spat, still trying to keep his temper under control and failing dismally. "Did you not think to perhaps call for help when you heard the commotion?"

"Well, the thing is, we weren't sure whether she needed help or not. We tend to hear things you see; the walls aren't as thick as she thinks they are," the elderly man stammered, reading the rage in Declan accurately.

"We know they're not her grandfathers," the woman said, her face flushing. "There's not many grandfathers nowadays who visit their grandchildren every week, nor many grandchildren who would let them spank them, are there?"

Declan closed his eyes. They obviously knew what Madeleine did to survive and hadn't reported her, or even told her they knew. They'd kept to themselves—and perhaps, after what had happened to Madeleine, that was just as well for them.

"We just wanted to know if she was alright, that's all. We don't want any trouble," the man said, taking hold of his wife's arm and turning away. "Don't worry, forget we asked."

"He looked angry, you see, when he turned up," said the old woman, shaking her husband's hand away and standing her ground, "and we didn't know him. I said to Reg, I said, that bloke's not in a good mood. I hope he doesn't hurt Madeleine more than the others do, didn't I, Reg?"

"You did, aye, Mo," said Reg, nodding as his wife continued to talk over him.

"...and then we heard him hitting her and her screaming and then she just ... stopped but the noises didn't. All sorts was going on in there. I said to Reg, I said, we should call the polis, but Reg said no, he'd know who called them. So we left it. *Is* she alright?"

Now Declan could see tears welling in the elderly woman's eyes.

"Don't say he's killed her? *Please* don't say he's killed her. I'd never forgive myself if he has—or *you*, for stopping me getting help." This last she aimed at her husband, who visibly wilted.

"She's going to be okay," Declan said, praying he was telling the truth. "She's pretty bad but there's a doctor in with her now."

"Shouldn't she be in hospital, if she's that bad?"

Declan opened his mouth to say no, but stopped himself. He really had no idea whether Madeleine was going to pull through this and privately, he'd wanted to get her into hospital as soon as he clapped eyes on her. He took a final drag on his cigarette and shrugged his shoulders as he flicked it to the ground and twisted his foot on the embers. "Honestly?" he said. "I don't know." And then he had another thought. "Now, you say you know the men who visit her—can you give me a description of the bloke who came here last night?"

"Tall, heavyset, a right thug—but here's the thing; it wasn't her usual grandad visiting."

"Oh," Declan said, his heart sinking.

"But I can help you with the one who usually arrives on Wednesdays," Mo said, surprising him. "His name's Bobby, Bobby Jones. And, well, he must have known whoever turned up last night because he didn't, if you understand what I mean. Yes, Bobby Jones. Well, strictly speaking, it's Robert but he prefers Bobby. Has since he was a lad. He was chummy with our Neil at one time, before he got a bit too big for his boots. Nasty piece of work then and still is, I see."

"Neil?"

"Our son."

"How old is Neil?"

"Fifty-eight," Mo said proudly. "We don't look old enough, do we?"

"Not at all," Declan said smoothly. "You don't happen to know where Bobby lives, do you?" He held his breath.

"No," said Reg. "Sorry."

"What about photos?"

"We...ell," Mo said, rubbing her chin. "Nothing recent, but he was at Neil's fiftieth bash, so he may be in some of them..."

77 Lakeland Avenue

After the police had left with instructions for them to be careful and to change all the locks everywhere, Graham, Caroline and Jasmine sat at the kitchen table, nursing various drinks to lessen the strain of what had happened earlier.

Caroline took a sip of her gin and tonic and turned to her husband. "*Do* you have any enemies?" she asked. She found it hard to believe that he could have, Graham was far too strait-laced to court enemies.

"As I told the police; not that I'm aware," Graham said, adding viciously, "have you?"

Caroline continued staring at him, watching the minute movements of his face, certain she would know if he was lying to her and seeing nothing to say that he was. "No, of course not," she replied. "So why were there two men trying to get into the house today?"

"Could ... could Stuart have upset someone?" Jasmine ventured. She took a sip of tea and eyed her mother's gin enviously.

"He hasn't been working long enough for that," Graham said drolly between mouthfuls of the can of Heineken he was necking at a rate of knots, "and I hardly think the dope-addled idiot could have made the effort to actually get anyone really upset."

"Graham!" Caroline snapped. "Was there any need for that?"

"It's the truth." Graham drained the can and went to the fridge for a fresh one. He put the empty can on the countertop and returned to the table holding the full one.

"It may have been before, but he's turned a new leaf. Look at what he's doing, starting a new business. Can't you be pleased for him?"

Graham shook his head and popped the tab on the can. "Caroline, do you imagine for one second that he's capable of being a private investigator? Aside from the fact that he'll have trouble staying awake, he has no background in it and I hardly think some dodgy online course is going to turn him into Sherlock Homes, do you? Be honest." He tipped the can to his mouth and swallowed.

"I think it will be the making of him," Caroline said through thin lips. She drained her glass and went for a refill.

"I've never seen him so pleased with himself," Jasmine added, watching both her parents and shaking her head. "I really think he means to make a go of it."

"Oh, he'll make a go of it, and then he'll come running to us when he's got some angry husband hot on his heels, you mark my words," Graham said. "And who's to say he hasn't already? We all know that he's not particularly choosy about his partners – anything with a pulse, that one; who's to say that today wasn't down to him?" He gulped down the rest of his can and went to the fridge again for another, passing his wife as she returned to the table.

"He doesn't live here, so why would anyone possibly come here after him?" Caroline said hotly, sitting back down holding an extremely full glass which she emptied by a third with one long swallow. She burped gently and raised a hand to her mouth. "Oops, I beg your pardon."

"Doesn't live here," Graham said scornfully, also returning to the table and popping the tab. "He's here every day, eating us out of house and home. Most of the time he kips on the sofa, and don't tell me he doesn't, I'm not stupid. I can tell because the stink of his feet lingers long after he's gone."

Jasmine snorted. "And your feet smell like roses, I suppose."

"I shower every day, I'll have you know," Graham said. "My feet do not smell!"

"No, course they don't. And neither do your farts."

Jasmine met her mother's eyes and they both sniggered.

"Oh, grow up, both of you!" Graham said, draining the third can of Heineken and slapping it down on the table top.

"Rings," Caroline said.

Graham picked the can up again and shook it in the hope it still had something inside, then he shrugged and got back up, staggering slightly.

"Another one?" Jasmine asked

"We've all had a shock," her father told her as he placed the empty can next to the previous two. He opened the fridge door and began to move things around. "Is that all the cans? I could have shworn I bought more than that."

"How many are in a pack?" Caroline asked, swigging another third of the glass down. "Don't forget you've had three already."

"Four, no six, no, four. I think," Graham said. He looked at Jasmine. "Did I shay four?"

Jasmine nodded. "Can you put the kettle on while you're up?"

"Sure," Graham agreed, sliding his sock-clad feet across the floor like he was on ice skates. He flicked the switch and the kettle began to make a disturbing noise.

"I think it might need some water in it," Jasmine said.

"Oops." Graham lifted the kettle from its stand and went to the sink where he turned on the cold tap and attempted to fill it. Water splashed everywhere except inside the utensil.

Jasmine sighed and went and took it from him. She filled the kettle and, as Graham took down a glass from the cupboard and made himself a strong gin and tonic, put a tea bag in her mug and watched as her father began to make zooming noises and slid his feet across the floor towards his wife.

"You look like you're on skates," Caroline said, echoing her daughter's earlier thoughts. "Can I have a go?"

"Sure, join me." Graham put the glass on the table and held out his hands to his wife, who took them and was pulled unceremoniously to her feet. Caroline slipped off her shoes and the two of them began to slip-slide across the tiles, looking very much like two overgrown toddlers, both laughing like drains.

Jasmine was shaking her head when Chutzpah's tail began to wag furiously and he hurtled himself down the hall as Stuart let himself into the house and began to take off his shoes. He came up the hall towards them all and stood in the doorway, ruffling the dog's ears and exchanging amused glances with his sister as their parents careered around the table. They were now chasing each other.

"Shcoose me, Shtoo," Graham slurred, as he misjudged the turn and fell headlong into his son. "Where did you come from?"

"Shtoooart," Caroline squealed, sliding her way towards them both.

"Having a drink, I see," Stuart said, holding his father up with one hand and stopping his mother's forward momentum with the other.

"They're pissed," Jasmine said succinctly.

"You don't say. What's caused this then? Are we celebrating something?"

"Only the fact that a couple of blokes tried to break into the house earlier when I was home alone."

"What! Are you alright?"

"Fine," Jasmine said. "Embarrassed. I called the police. They left not long ago and our parents decided the best way of dealing with it is like *this*." She waved a hand towards them both and rolled her eyes.

"It's not even six yet."

"I know."

Stuart nodded his head towards the hall, indicating that she should follow him. He turned and made his way back towards the front door. Jasmine dodged her parents, who were now in each other's arms and waltzing around the room, and went after him.

"I've just seen the woman Dad visited being stretchered into a paramedic's van," he whispered. "She'd been beaten up. Badly. She was being carried by a couple of blokes and had an odd-looking girl and a woman who looked like a doctor in tow—well, she was carrying a doctor's bag at any rate. I'm not entirely sure the girl wasn't dead."

Jasmine's eyes widened. "Really?"

Stuart nodded. "Do you think what happened here may have had something to do with what happened to her?"

Chapter Five
Friday

The Clinic

Sarah stared out at the street, watching the comings and goings of people as they went about their daily lives unaware of what was taking place in hers. She looked around as the door to the waiting room opened and Declan walked in saying, "I got kicked out; the nurses are doing something with her now. Oh, and I put another pillow behind her head, you don't think they'll mind, do you?"

"I doubt it." Sarah smiled at the man who was proving to be a true friend to Madeleine, despite them both having only known her for a few days. He was beginning to restore her somewhat jaded faith in the male species.

Declan pointed to the seat at the end of the bench she was curled up on and raised his eyebrows.

"Of course," Sarah said, moving her feet to the floor. "Would you like a cuppa?"

"In a bit, there's no rush." He eased himself down, exhaling loudly. "Doc's due again soon, the fluid bag's almost empty and she's going to need more pain relief." He didn't mention the catheter bag which would need emptying.

The two sat in silence for a few minutes, gathering their thoughts. Neither had slept much, despite supposedly taking turns to grab a few hours. Having seen the extent of Madeleine's injuries, neither had expected her to make it through the night. As a result, both were somewhat bleary-eyed and achy.

"I think she may survive this," Sarah said, not looking at him, her voice sounding loud in the quiet of the room.

"I hope so." Declan nodded his agreement but his face told a different story. "She survived the operation and I was dubious she'd pull through that. She's a fighter. Sarah, look, I should have told you this sooner but when you and Doc were working on Madeleine yesterday, I had an interesting chat with her neighbours."

Sarah turned to face him. "And...?" she said, when Declan showed no inclination to go on.

He pulled out his phone. "Look." He held it out towards her and Sarah took it. On the screen was a photograph of people celebrating what looked to be a birthday in a hall somewhere. Balloons with the numbers five and zero floated in the air and below them, women danced while men looked on from the side-lines. They all looked happy.

"What am I missing?" she asked, passing the phone back to him.

"May I?" Declan pointed to the seat next to her, and without waiting for a response, slid himself across. With fingers that looked too big to be able to do so, he expanded the screen and held it up to her again.

Now Sarah could see a grainy image of a few men standing at the bar. They were turned to face the dancers, each holding partially filled glasses of brown liquid. Declan pointed to the man who was second to the left. "That's Neil, the neighbour's son. It was his birthday bash. Now, see *him*?" He pointed to the man standing to Neil's left. "That's Bobby Jones."

"Okay," Sarah said slowly, not understanding why Declan thought this was important.

"Bobby Jones is Madeleine's Wednesday client."

"What? How do you know?" Now Sarah was alert. She straightened her back and studied the picture more closely, dabbing at the screen to stop it from disappearing from view.

"The neighbours have seen him coming and going and recognised him from the party eight years ago. He's been friendly with their son since they were both at school, so it's unlikely they're mistaken."

Sarah's eyes became owl-like. "So you think this might be the person who…?"

Declan shrugged. "It wasn't him who turned up that night, but he may know who did."

Sarah nodded slowly. "So what do we do?"

Declan smiled, liking her use of the word 'we'. "We find him, of course," he said. "And if it was anything to do with him … well, then we teach him a lesson."

Sarah was still squinting at the photograph. "It's not very clear, is it? And Bobby Jones isn't going to be easy to search—it's a common name."

Declan's nose wrinkled. "True, I've already Googled him and got millions of hits and a reverse image search came up with nothing concrete, probably because, as you say, the picture's grainy. But there must be a way to find him; we just don't know how yet."

"So what do you suggest?"

Declan smiled again. "I thought we might hire a P.I. I'll pay, you won't need to put your hand in your pocket—"

"I want to," Sarah interrupted vehemently. "If this arsehole is out there and capable of doing this to Maddy, he's capable of doing it to someone else. And next time, he might finish the job. I don't want that blood on my hands."

The two shared a grim smile.

"I'm glad you said that," Declan said, his voice as grim as his face. "We're meeting some bloke called Shakil Barbosa at the Orangerie in an hour. Doc's agreed to stay with Madeleine."

"The Orangerie?" Sarah said. "Christ Declan, I need to get dressed up for that."

"I've ordered a cab to take us back to yours; my car's there anyway. Madeleine's in good hands here and they've got our numbers if they need us."

The Orangerie

Declan led a Sarah he barely recognised through the gloom of the inside bar, politely requesting people to move aside so they could pass through and marvelling internally as to why Shakil Barbosa had thought meeting at the Orangerie, Crickleby's most celebrated bar-cum-café, was a good idea. People came here from far and wide, and today was no exception; the bar inside was heaving, despite the early hour, the air redolent with the mixed perfumes of various clientele and the smell of intoxicating fresh liquor.

Sarah fitted right in. She was dressed in a black, all-in-one pantsuit that plunged almost to her navel at the neckline, managing to both expose and hide high, firm breasts, and skimmed over her slender hips to drop seamlessly to the floor. On her feet were heels; serious red heels. Her short blonde crop had been artfully spiked and her eyes, outlined in black kohl, were simply enormous. Her lips were painted the same shade as her shoes, outlining a luscious mouth that Declan had not taken note of earlier. Now, he was finding it hard to take his eyes off it. She looked spectacular, and the majority of the male clientele of the Orangerie appeared to hold the same opinion. Mouths dropped as she passed by, ignoring them all.

At the rear of the bar was a set of double doors that led to the centre courtyard. Catching hold of Sarah's hand so he didn't lose her in the throng, Declan pushed his way towards them and gratefully shoved one open, ushering Sarah through to the relative peace of the outside area where parasol-bearing tables were strategically and artistically set, most of them occupied by four or more people, all either eating or, having finished their meals, drinking and holding laughing conversations. They stepped into a sun trap, both blinking furiously as the brilliance of the day hit eyes that had become briefly adjusted to the dark of the bar.

As the door swung shut behind them, blocking the majority of the sounds of people having fun inside, the pair stopped and looked around them, searching for someone sitting alone, someone who looked like he could possibly be a private investigator. From the far side of the courtyard, a young Asian-looking male rose from a table where he had been sitting alongside another, equally young and startlingly handsome male, and beckoned them towards him. Both were wearing black suits, crisp white shirts, thin black ties and wrap-around shades.

"You can't be serious," Declan muttered under his breath. "They look like they're auditioning for a role in Men in Black."

"We're here now," Sarah said, "and at least they've made the effort, so we may as well see what they have to say for themselves. We don't have to hire them, do we?"

"True." Declan took a deep breath and began to walk towards the youngsters, Sarah hot on his heels.

As they approached the table, the second of the young males removed his shades and rested them on the top of his tousled curls. He pushed his ornate metal chair back from the table and stood to meet them, his hand held out in greeting. Declan shook it and was pleasantly surprised by the strength of the grip as the youngster's piercing blue eyes probed his own. He was equally as surprised that neither he, nor Barbosa, had begun to drool at the vision of Sarah.

"Declan," he introduced himself, "and this is Sarah."

"Hello Declan, Sarah, I'm Stuart Dalgleish, Stu if you prefer. I'm pleased to meet you both," the handsome blonde guy said, releasing Declan to shake Sarah's hand. "And this is Shakil Barbosa, my colleague."

The appropriate handshakes continued and when the introductions were over with, Shakil said, "Please, take a seat." He tugged a chair away from the table and ushered Sarah towards it while Declan pulled out the fourth chair and sat. When they were all settled, and drinks had been offered and ordered via the mobile phone set into the centre of the table, a feature of the Orangerie that customers appreciated, Shakil continued, "Now, we understand you would like us to trace somebody for you?"

"Before we come to that," Declan said, "I'd like to know what experience you both have. I mean, no offence but–"

"—but we look too young to be serious? Yeah, we get that a lot," Stuart interjected smoothly. "I can assure you we come with good credentials and we're older than we look. It also means that nobody expects anything of us. People we track are seldom suspicious of a couple of young guys hanging around. They tend to think we're selling drugs, if anything."

Sarah's mouth twitched; he was probably right, if they lost the suits. While Stuart was speaking, she'd been studying him. He stood around five-ten, an average height, so he could blend into a crowd, and beneath the suit jacket, muscles rippled against the sleeves as he moved his arms. She turned to Shakil and surreptitiously studied him, too. Shakil did not appear to be as muscular as Stuart, but she thought she could detect a litheness about him that belied his outward appearance.

"Forgive me," Declan said, "but I doubt anyone would think that of two blokes playing at being Will Smith and Tommy Lee Jones."

"Bags I Will," Stuart said. "Sorry, Shaks, you're Tommy today."

"I don't think so," Shakil said, grinning and circling his face with his index finger.

Sarah snorted back laughter as Declan rolled his eyes and held his hands out, palms up, by way of apology.

A waitress approached the table carrying a tray of drinks. She handed them out, lingering as she passed a drink over to Stuart who appeared to be utterly unaware of her obvious interest in him. "Enjoy your stay," she simpered, batting her eyelashes at him.

"Thanks, we will," Stuart said, dismissing her with a wave of his hand and turning his attention to Sarah. "So, are you going to tell us who you want us to trace?"

"A guy called Robert Jones. He calls himself Bobby."

Stuart nodded. "Okay. Any other information? It's not an unusual name," he said, echoing her own words from earlier.

"We know his age and we have a photograph that was taken about eight years ago," Declan said.

"That'll help," Shakil said. "Can we see it?"

Declan took out his phone, expanded the screen and pointed Bobby out to them both.

"Can you send that to us?" Shakil asked, adding a number to Declan's phone and passing it back.

Within seconds, Shakil's phone buzzed to say he'd received it. He opened the photograph, expanded it and took a screenshot of the expanded view. "It's a bit grainy," he said, "but we can work with that, don't worry. Now, why do you want him tracked?"

"Do you need to know?" Declan said.

Stuart raised his eyebrows. "If you want us to find him, we need to know why you want him found. We don't take on clients who won't tell us or who aren't straight with us. There's no judgment here, but them's the rules."

Declan and Sarah shared a look and then Sarah reached into her pocket and withdrew her own phone. She clicked open the photograph of Madeleine's face that she'd taken just before they left the clinic, and turned the phone towards them.

"We think he may have been the person who arranged for this to be done to our friend," she said. "You may as well know that she's a sex worker, but she only caters for three men. They each visit her on specific days. Bobby's day is Wednesday but he didn't turn up, someone else did."

"Aren't the police looking for him?" Stuart asked at the same time as Shakil said, "Which hospital is she in?"

Declan and Sarah shared another look.

"She *is* in hospital, isn't she? I mean, you have reported it?" Shakil asked, frowning. "We'll need to talk to her once she's able."

Again, Declan and Sarah said nothing.

"Why not?" Stuart asked, drumming his fingers against the table. "Look, we're not doing a thing until you tell us, so start talking."

***

Stuart and Shakil stayed at the table, watching as Declan and Sarah departed. As the door closed behind them, Shakil turned to Stuart and said, "You know who Madeleine is, don't you?"

Stuart nodded. "It was her hair that gave it away. Do you think they realised?"

"No," Shakil said instantly. "They'd have said something. I think they're both too caught up in their own emotions right now."

"Yeah … should we have told them do you think?"

Shakil shook his head emphatically. "They might start looking at your dad. He was there on, what was it, Tuesday?"

"Wednesday." Stuart drained his lager and put the empty glass back on the table. "The day she was attacked."

"Well, we both know it wasn't him, don't we?" It wasn't a question.

"We do, but I'm going to have to talk to him about it anyway."

"Why?"

"Because what he told me about him being in Madeleine's house doesn't add up. There's more to it than that." Stuart twisted his mouth up at the corner. "I'm going to find out what it is."

Shakil drained his own glass and sat back, rolling it back and forth between his fingers. "What should I do?" he said eventually.

"Well, first of all, we need to go back to the office and find out if we passed our exam, then we find out who's behind it all – the guy who put Bobby on to Madeleine. And to do that, I think you'll need to talk to Sarah again."

"Why?"

"I think she knows more than she's letting on."

77 Lakeland Avenue

Graham was in his office, flicking through a particularly dirty magazine he'd ordered in especially, drinking copious amounts of water and nursing a hangover while wondering what on earth had possessed him to get so drunk yesterday. His tackle wasn't responding to what he was viewing, a sure sign that he'd overdone things—either that, or it was another sign of ageing. Perhaps he needed to visit the GP and see if he could get hold of some little blue pills. He lowered his trousers further, flipped to the centrefold which showed a picture of a naked young girl being rogered by an impossibly large cock whilst also wrapping her lips around another that was, from what little Graham could see of its girth, big enough to make her eyes water – and took himself firmly in hand.

Nothing happened. His willy had as much life in it as a wet noodle and now he needed to urinate. He couldn't be bothered to go upstairs, so decided to take a leak in the sink in the corner of the room, something he resorted to on occasion, unbeknownst to anybody else. He was mid-flow and sighing with relief when the door opened and footsteps thundered down the stairs. Graham tried, and failed, to stop the flow—

another sign of age; years before he'd been able to stop and start at will.

"Dad! What the hell?"

Still, Graham's stream continued and showed no sign of abating; now he was starting to sweat. Was this going to be how he died? A never-ending urination that depleted his body of all its fluids in front of his son?

"That's revolting! I hope you don't let anyone wash their hands in there," Stuart said, the disgust evident in his voice. "Christ, Dad, hurry it up."

"I'm trying," Graham said, eyeing his dick balefully. Normally he had to coax urine out of it and would go back and forth to the toilet several times before he felt he was fully empty but presently it appeared that he'd inadvertently swallowed the contents of Niagara Falls and now it was making a bid for freedom.

At last, the stream slowed and Graham found his muscles straining to make sure he was finally empty, something he now did out of need rather than habit.

"Yeah, you're done," Stuart said. "And if Mum catches you with this god-awful magazine, you'll really be done."

"Christ!" Shame made Graham close his eyes and he tugged at the zipper of the jeans with unwarranted force. A split second later he was rolling around on the carpet, crying tears of real pain having zipped up his own foreskin.

"Hold still," he could hear a voice saying as his son's face loomed over him. "I said, *hold still*, Dad. Let me take a look."

Graham cupped himself and tried to curl into a ball. "Shit, that hurts," he moaned.

"Well, I can't help if you won't let me see," Stuart said, slapping his father's hands away. Graham lay as still as he could whilst his son investigated his nether region.

"I think we may need to call an ambulance," Stuart said after a second or so. "You're stitched up tight in there and I think I'd circumcise you if I try to, um, extract it." Then, with a note of wonder in his voice, he added, "How the hell did you manage to get so *much* of it in there? Seriously, you need some proper help here—it's going to be embarrassing though, are you going to cope with that?"

Graham nodded. At that particular moment he couldn't have cared less if a marching band had strolled on through and gawped at his predicament. He just wanted the pain to stop. Through a haze of pain, he heard his son making the call and couldn't miss the hint of mirth in his voice as he explained his father's problem.

"It's not fucking funny," he managed to say as Stuart ended the call.

"I'm not laughing," Stuart said, fighting back the urge to let loose what would inevitably be the loudest guffaw he'd ever made. Every time he looked, and he couldn't *not* look, his own penis shrivelled a little more in empathy and the urge to laugh worsened.

"This is all your fault," Graham groaned.

"How do you figure that then? ... No, don't move, Dad, try to stay still."

"If you hadn't burst in on me, it wouldn't have happened," Graham panted, trying to resist the very real urge he had to try to escape the worst pain he'd ever experienced. He moved his knees slightly further towards his belly and immediately squealed and moved them back again.

"I'd been standing here for almost five minutes before you did it, so you can't blame it on me," Stuart said, quite reasonably, he thought.

"Fuck, fuck, fuckety fuck," Graham shouted. "If I say it's your fucking fault, it's your fucking fault, do you hear me? Where's this fucking ambulance?"

"It's coming, Dad."

"Is everything all right down there?" came a hesitant voice from the top of the stairs. "I heard shouting…"

Both Stuart and Graham's heads swivelled in that direction as Jasmine began making her way down the steps towards them. Stuart caught sight of the magazine that was lying open at his father's desk and jumped up to sit on it.

"Go away!" Graham shouted, doing his best to ensure she saw nothing of his predicament and causing himself additional pain in doing so. "Aaargh! Jasmine, please go back upstairs and tell your mother to be ready to open the front door to the ambulance."

"The ambulance?" Jasmine said, her eyes wide as she saw her father writhing on the floor. Her voice raised in disbelief, "Have you been *fighting*? Stuart, *what have you done*?"

"I haven't done anything," Stuart protested. "Dad's got his dick stuck in his zipper."

"His *what* stuck *where*?"

"You bastard!" Graham roared. "Jasmine, go and get your mother!"

Jasmine turned tail and raced back up the stairs, calling for Caroline as loudly as she could while Stuart took the chance to shove the magazine into a desk drawer. He was just closing it as Caroline appeared at the double, almost missing her footing as she took the stairs two at a time, her eyes just as wide as her daughter's had been, her mouth an o-shape of fear.

"Oh God, has he had a heart attack?" she shrieked, looking from one to the other. "I keep telling him he should take better care of himself and now look, he's going to die on me!"

"He's not going to die," Stuart said, "he's just got his dick caught in his zipper."

"He's got his *what* stuck *where*?" Caroline sounded like her daughter's double.

"Don't either of you females ever bloody listen," Graham complained loudly as the doorbell rang. "Go and let the ambulance people in, will you."

"His penis is caught in his zip," Stuart enunciated clearly.

"You've called an ambulance for that? Get out of the way, Stu." Caroline put her hands on either side of her son's torso and shifted him aside so she could get to her husband. She knelt down on the carpet and said, "Let me see ... Graham, *move your bloody hands*!"

Graham's hands went straight to his sides. When his wife used that tone of voice, she meant business.

"It's only a tiny bit," she said, peering down the top of Graham's jeans. "We'll soon have you out of there, hold still…" and with one swift jerk, she yanked the zipper down, freeing Graham's bloodied tackle from captivity.

Graham screamed.

"Hold on," came another voice from the top of the stairs. A paramedic had arrived to save the day. "We'll soon have you out of there, don't worry."

"It's done," Caroline said, going over to the sink to wash her hands.

"Nooooo!" both Stuart and Graham shouted in unison.

***

Three hours later, Graham was sitting up in a hospital bed after suffering through an emergency circumcision that had taken place under local anaesthesia, his foreskin having been considered too damaged to salvage. It had seemed like the lesser of two evils; either way, someone was going to be sticking a bloody great needle into the base of his penis, and Graham hadn't fancied having his foreskin sewn up, even if it had been salvageable, because that meant the stitches would have to come out at a later date and at least these ones were dissolvable. Now his cock was covered in gauze and throbbing like a bastard. He eyed his wife angrily.

"This is your fault," he said for the umpteenth time. "If you hadn't ripped my jeans open…"

"You'd still have needed surgery," interrupted the nurse who had come to check on him, having heard him say it several times already, although not nearly so many times as Caroline. "It was the zipper that did the damage. The paramedics would have done the same thing." She didn't add that he'd have received some anaesthetic prior to them doing so, thinking it wisest to keep that piece of information to herself. She pulled the manoeuvrable trolley that rested beside Graham's bed towards her, pulled down the thin blanket that was covering his legs, raised the gown he was wearing and lifted his penis, checking the gauze for any oozing suppurations. There were none. "It's looking good.

The surgeon will be around soon to check on you and then you can go home, I expect. Oh, and have you had a tetanus jab recently? There's nothing showing on your hospital notes."

Graham looked at Caroline.

"Why are you looking at me, I don't know," she said, as gently as her fraying temper would allow. "I don't remember you ever having one."

"In that case," said the nurse, reaching towards a large syringe that was ready and waiting. "Now; sharp scratch…" She took hold of Graham's upper arm and stabbed the needle in, injecting the fluid slowly and carefully while Graham gasped and groaned. "Have you got transport?" she asked Caroline as she worked.

"No," Caroline said, looking worried. "The paramedic brought us in. I'll have to call my son to come and fetch us."

"Why don't you go and do that?"

"That's a good idea," Caroline said, jumping to her feet and heading out without needing to be told twice.

"She has no idea how much it hurts," Graham complained bitterly.

"Is it hurting at the moment?" the nurse asked.

"Well, no, but that's because the anaesthetic hasn't worn off yet."

"Well then," the nurse said, turning on her heel and walking away, leaving Graham staring after her in amazement.

Caroline came back to the ward about thirty minutes later, smelling of ozone and smoke, and readjusting her obligatory face mask.

"Have you been having a crafty fag?" complained Graham, sniffing. "I thought you gave up."

"I have," Caroline lied. "I had to go outside to call Stuart and someone was smoking near me." She didn't add that she'd cadged one from the good-looking general registrar who had also slipped out of the hospital at the same time as she and only then because she'd accidentally bumped into him causing him to drop the pack he was holding.

"Oooh," she'd said, her eyes burning a hole into the pack. "You wouldn't let me have one of those, would you?"

He'd rightly read the need in her eyes and led her to a hidden area, out of sight of anyone in authority, where they'd both ripped off their masks, sparked up and dragged deep lugs into their lungs, neither speaking, just enjoying the wind-down moment and the illicitness of what they were doing.

"Well then, see you again," he'd said, as he stubbed his butt out on the hospital wall and re-masked. "Nice to meet you."

"You, too," Caroline called after him, only then taking out her phone to call Stuart.

"Well, you were bloody ages," Graham complained as she sat in the chair beside his bed. "You missed the doctor. I can go home."

"I had to go down three flights of stairs and find a spot where I could get a signal. You know you're not allowed to ring from inside the hospital. Anyway, Stuart's on his way to get you, he should be here in half an hour or so. In the meantime, I'm going to nip into Crickleby to get us something for tea."

"You're *leaving* me here?" Graham could not believe his ears.

"Graham, you zipped your own penis into your jeans – I won't point out that I told you they were too tight for you, didn't I? And you're sorted now. The doctor tells me you're going to be absolutely fine, so long as you follow his instructions, so I hope you were listening to him?"

"Of course I was," Graham spat. "I'm not entirely stupid, you know."

Caroline's eyes involuntarily lowered to the area of Graham's crotch. "No, dear," she said, with a long-suffering sigh. "Anyway, I'll probably be home before you are, so I'll see you in a little while. Try not to move awkwardly, won't you?"

"Well, I'm hardly going to be doing cartwheels, am I?" Graham said to his wife's disappearing back.

***

By the time Stuart arrived at the hospital, Graham's mental health had gone through several stages: incredulity that his wife had left him there; anger with himself for having been stupid enough to put himself in this position in the first place, and then more anger that he was having to wait for the son whose act of catching him peeing in the sink had been the instigator to this entire mess. *And* he wasn't in any apparent rush to come and get him. This led to anxiety that perhaps Stuart wasn't coming after all as thirty minutes passed without him making an appearance, then undiluted anger that his son *hadn't* appeared within thirty minutes, closely followed by a strange kind of sorrow for his now missing foreskin. He'd been quite fond of it – it had been a part of him, after all.

He stared at the large, round clock set high on the grubby, hospital-green wall, watching the minutes tick by and winding himself up into a slightly more generalised mix of anger and anxiety. Where the hell was the boy?

So when Stuart appeared in the doorway some forty-five minutes later, Graham was not entirely happy to see him. "What took you so long?" he snapped.

"Shall I go again?" Stuart snapped back. "You can always call yourself a taxi."

Graham shut up knowing his son was more than capable of simply leaving again, without him.

"I was working. Shall we go then?" Stuart said, once it was apparent that his father wasn't going to say anything else. "I have your meds here; the nurse gave them to me as I arrived."

"I suppose so," Graham said grudgingly.

As Stuart pulled the car up to the barriers in the hospital car park and unwound his window to slide in the ticket he'd paid for, he casually said, "Dad, you know when I found you at that young girl's place on Wednesday…?"

Graham's mouth, which had been issuing a lamentation of how much pain he was in up until that point, closed.

Stuart continued, "Why were you there? I mean, the real reason why you were there. I don't buy that guff about you needing a glass of water. I think there was more to it than that." The car park barrier rose and Stuart pulled the car smoothly out and onto the road that circled the hospital grounds where he indicated to show anyone coming that he was pulling over and came to another halt at the side of the road. He yanked the handbrake up and turned to face his father.

"How dare you!" Graham expostulated. "What are you insinuating?"

Stuart waited. The training he'd done had told him that if he asked a question and then shut up, people would fill the silence.

Graham hadn't done the training. "I told you what happened," he said sulkily. "Why are you bringing it up again now?"

"Because I have a new client."

"What? You mean someone has actually hired you and the other stoner?"

Stuart waited some more.

"What for?" Graham couldn't resist asking when it became apparent that his son wasn't going to bite.

"I *just* need to know what you were doing there," Stuart said.

"I already told you—I was delivering a misdirected letter."

"Okay, supposing I buy that part, why didn't you just pop it through the letterbox?"

"Well, she opened the door just as I was about to and it made me jump and I had a bit of a funny turn. Like she said."

"Bull."

"What do you mean, bull?" Graham blustered, digging himself a deeper hole. "That's what happened!"

"Okay," Stuart said. He checked the rear-view mirror, put the car into gear, unclicked the handbrake and pulled back onto the road. "If that's how you want to play it, so be it. You'll have to lie straighter than that when the police come knocking though—and they will because I'll have to tell them you were there."

"What are you on about? Why on earth would you need to tell the police about that?"

"Because that young girl is currently fighting for her life. She was beaten so badly that she's barely recognisable now and it happened on Wednesday, the day you were there. Your fingerprints will be all over the place."

"What!" Graham felt a moment's sorrow for Madeleine, a sorrow that was closely followed by the compelling urge to save his own skin. "But you know that I didn't have anything to do with that! So you can speak up for me, can't you."

"Nice to see your caring side showing, Dad," Stuart said, shaking his head as he negotiated a roundabout. He lapsed into silence, his lips pursed and a frown on his forehead.

Graham glanced at him and sighed. "Park somewhere. I'll tell you—but first, you've got to promise not to tell your mother."

Stuart drove on until they came to the entrance to Crickleby Park. He pulled in and drove to the far side of the car park, coming to a halt in one of the many empty spaces. He switched the engine off and turned to face his father. "Start talking."

SAS Investigations Office

"How did you get on with Sarah?" Stuart asked, as he swung himself into the seat behind his desk and slapped his notebook down on top of it.

"You look stressed," Shakil said, watching as Stuart raked a hand through his hair and then rubbed his nose with the back of his thumb. "Did the talk with your dad not go so well?"

"I got to the bottom of it," Stuart said gloomily. "Turns out that my old man went to deliver the letter to Madeleine earlier in the week and caught her at work."

Shakil waited.

Stuart sighed. "She had a broken blind and he looked through it. Madeleine was with one of her clients, some old boy who was, apparently, in the middle of giving her a good spanking which culminated in her sucking him off…"

"Blimey! He watched for quite a while then?"

"Apparently so," Stuart said, reddening. "Anyway, he decided not to put the letter through the door and went back on Wednesday, he says, so he could meet her."

"Why would he want to do that?" Shakil asked, earning himself a look from Stuart. "Oh."

"Oh, exactly." Stuart was silent for a few moments, then he blinked away his thoughts. "So? How did you go with Sarah?"

"It was a bit odd actually. At first, I wasn't sure it was her because she looks very different without make-up on. She kept me on the doorstep so I wasn't able to talk to her for very long because she was just about to leave to visit Madeleine. She's in a clinic apparently and they're doing the best they can for her, from what I can gather. Apparently, all Madeleine said before she passed out was that she didn't want someone called Gregor to know."

"So Gregor's who? Her pimp?"

Shakil shrugged. "Presumably. Sarah didn't know anything more about him but I had the funny feeling that she wasn't being entirely honest with me. Nothing I can put my finger on exactly, but still..."

Stuart took that in. "Was Declan there?"

"Not so far as I know. He didn't come to the door if he was. Anyway, I said goodbye and went away, and then I had a thought. She told us that the neighbour recognised this Bobby Jones, so I went and knocked at number seventy-nine. They're a very friendly couple, thankfully. They invited me in and gave me a cuppa and—"

Stuart circled a hand in the air. "Yada, yada—get to the point, Shaks."

"They said they'd been thinking and might know the bloke your dad saw on Monday. Apparently, they regularly go to a bowls club on a Thursday night and he *may* have just become a member—"

"So if we find out what club it is; they should have a member's list."

Shakil grinned. "It's Crickleby Bowls Association. They meet at the Sports Centre every Thursday at seven. Oh, and they said they've heard her calling him Ted."

Stuart let out a short burst of laughter. "Thank God for nosey neighbours, eh? Did they have a number for whoever runs it?"

"Yep," said Shakil. "We're meeting up with Janice Longbottom on Monday."

"Monday? No sooner?"

"She's away from home at the moment; something about a daughter's wedding. She won't be back until Monday but she knew who I was talking about because it's rare for them to have had an opening at the club – people tend to stick until they croak, as she put it, and they lost one of their members recently. Anyway, she'll let us have his details then—oh, and she did recall that his name is Edgar something or other."

"Could Ted be short for Edgar; do you think?"

Shakil shrugged. "Your guess is as good as mine, but I'd say so, yes."

"And if Sarah's right with what she said about Madeleine's three clients having concocted this pact between them, Ted will know who Bobby is."

"Yeah, we'll need to tread carefully though because I doubt he'll come out and tell us, especially considering what's happened."

Stuart pushed his chair back and began to pace the room. Shakil watched him, knowing his friend was trying to figure something out. Eventually Stuart stopped pacing. "I wonder if Ted knows? And if he doesn't, then perhaps her third client doesn't know either. In which case, he could still think he's on for a visit tonight. Shakil, we are going on our first stake-out."

77 Lakeland Road

"I still think we should have just asked Sarah if she had any keys," Shakil grumbled, as he watched Stuart fiddling with the lock of the back door of Madeleine's property.

"Nearly done it," Stuart whispered. "Keep your voice down. We don't want everyone hearing us, do we?"

There was a tiny click and then Stuart was twisting the doorknob and opening the door. The two men crept through it and Shakil closed it carefully behind himself. Both men were wearing gloves so no prints were left behind them. They found themselves standing in a very small kitchen. An old-fashioned butler sink held a bloodied towel that was currently soaking in cold water. Ahead of them was another door which, once opened, led to a narrow hallway with stairs leading upwards on the left and two closed doors on the right-hand side, one of which was set into the wall closest to the kitchen and the other closest to the front door. A strange, cloying smell lingered in the air.

Stuart opened the first door and found himself looking at the area Madeleine must use as a lounge room. To his left, a sofa, covered in dried blood, rested mostly against the far wall. It had been angled slightly to face a television which had been fixed to the wall opposite the door. Blood had coagulated in a pool on the tatty carpet beside the sofa. The room itself was set in an 'L' shape with the largest area being where they now stood. The smaller part of the room to their right ran adjacent to the kitchen and to the rear of the property where a window that took up much of the wall looked out over the garden. A tiny dining table and two chairs took up much of that space.

"Let's try the other room," Stuart whispered.

Shakil nodded and turned to lead the way.

"Well this is where it happened," he said shakily, once he'd opened the door and seen the blood-splattered room beyond. The stench of dried blood assaulted his nostrils and several flies buzzed past his head and out into the hallway which Stuart swatted away. Shakil did not enter the room and put up an arm to stop Stuart from pushing him inside.

"Dear God!" Stuart said, once Shakil had moved back into the hallway so he could see. "This guy has some temper, doesn't he?" He took out his phone and silently took several photographs of the scene of devastation, then slid it back into his back pocket. "I think we'll wait out here. Those stairs look comfortable; don't you think?"

He closed the door again and the two men took a seat halfway up the stairs and began their wait.

Chapter Six
Saturday

The Clinic

Madeleine woke, or perhaps it would be more correct to say came to, in the early hours of Saturday morning. She opened her eyes and found herself staring blurrily up at a ceiling she did not recognise. A cream-coloured pendant light hung in the centre, one which definitely did not belong to her. Starched sheets were beneath her hands and a clock ticked somewhere to her right. She didn't possess a clock and never ironed her sheets; another indicator she was not at home. She licked her lips and winced at the effort it took for her to open her mouth.

"You're awake! Oh, thank God!" A male voice came from the corner of the room, one she recognised but was unable to put a name to. A worried face that went with the voice loomed out of the darkness and hovered above her head. A cool hand swept across her brow, gently pushing her hair back and off her face. Although she recognised him, Madeleine struggled to put a name to the man who stared tenderly down at her. "How are you feeling? Do you need something for the pain?"

Madeleine knew the words, knew what he was asking, but could not make them make sense. She opened her mouth and tried to ask him to say it again but could only make vague, guttural noises. It frightened her and tears sprang into her eyes and slid slowly down her cheeks.

"Ahhh, don't cry. Your throat was hurt quite badly but you'll get your voice back, don't worry. In the meantime, try not to talk, okay? Here, have a sip of water."

A straw poked its way into the side of her mouth and Madeleine automatically sucked on it, marvelling at how good the water that trickled into her mouth felt against her gums and then her throat. She swallowed and cried out at the pain that caused her. The straw was hastily removed and she found she was unable to keep her eyes open any longer and was gone again, but this time, to sleep and nothing deeper.

"She tried to talk to me, I swear," Declan told Sarah when he went into the waiting room to wake her as dawn broke. "She had a sip of water and then went back to sleep. Her fever's broken at last."

Sarah smiled and heaved a sigh of relief as she pulled herself up to a seated position. Her back ached—the padded bench looked good and was comfy to a degree, but it wasn't meant for spending nights on. She had never been so happy to hear someone say that someone else was getting better. It had been touch and go as to whether Madeleine would pull through and Doc had said that if the fever broke, hopefully, she'd have turned a corner, so she hoped Declan was right. In the van on the way to the clinic, Doc had hooked Madeleine up to an IV drip that fed her fluids, antibiotics and pain relief and once there had helped usher the stretcher into a sealed operating room, turning only to ask them both to leave so that they could do what they needed to do. Sarah had spent the past couple of days wondering who she could tell if the girl didn't survive, not liking the thought of her being buried with no loved ones in attendance.

"I'll nip up and see her," she said, swinging her legs over the edge of the sofa.

"No, have a cuppa. Wake up properly," Declan said, resting a hand on her shoulder. "You look beat."

"I feel it," Sarah said, not adding the word 'thanks'. No woman liked being told she looked rough and she was no exception.

"I'll do it," Declan said, aware that he'd said something wrong but not entirely sure what. "Stay put."

She watched as his long frame left the room to go and purchase two polystyrene cups of hospital muck and grinned to herself. She could get used to this, she thought, and then she mentally chastised herself. He wouldn't be here if it wasn't for what had happened to Madeleine.

"Here, I cadged some toast from one of the nurses." Declan came back into the room carrying a tray bearing two mugs of tea and a plate of hot, buttered toast. "Sorry."

Sarah's mouth watered even as she frowned. "For what?" She took a huge bite out of a piece of toast and let out a happy sigh. "This is just what the doctor ordered. Thank you."

"You're welcome. Sorry for saying you looked beat. It wasn't the most tactful thing to say, was it?"

Sarah half-laughed over her second bite. "No, but it's probably true. This bench isn't doing me any favours. I could do with a full night's sleep in a proper bed." She winced as the words left her mouth knowing that she sounded like a selfish cow. She'd only been inconvenienced for two nights—that poor girl in the room along the hallway was suffering far worse than she.

"Don't," Declan said, knowing what was going on in her head. "It's not just that you've not slept properly, you've been worried about Maddy and scared that whoever did it could figure out where she is and come back for her. It's a lot for anyone."

"Yeah, but so have you," she said. "You don't look tired at all."

It was true. He didn't. Declan appeared to be one of those people who life could throw things at and would prosper.

"I'm exhausted," he admitted. "Honest, I really am. I think I've got second wind – I was so pleased that she came round, even if it was only for a few seconds."

Sarah nodded as she demolished the last slice of toast and grabbed another. "I'll go in once I've finished this," she said, dipping her head towards the hand holding it. "I'll take my tea up with me. Get your head down for a while."

"I think I'm going to ring Stuart—see if they've come up with anything."

Sarah swallowed down the last of her toast and licked her fingers. She picked up her mug and got to her feet. "Let me know if they have," she said, walking over to the door to go back to Madeleine, "and thank you again. For the toast and tea, I mean. See you in a while."

An hour later, Sarah was just about to doze off on the chair beside Madeleine's bed when the girl stirred. Sarah was up and bending over her before she knew it.

"Hi," she said softly. "Welcome back!"

Madeleine opened her eyes and saw another blurry face that she knew she recognised but couldn't put a name to.

"It's Sarah, you remember? From down the road? We met in the week and I came round to see you and found you in a bit of a state. You're safe now, being looked after."

Madeleine gave a tiny nod and tried to lift an arm to rub the blurriness from her eyes. She gave a small hiss of pain when the movement caused pain to shoot up her arm and through her shoulder.

"Don't try and move. Both your arms were broken but they're mending now and you're in plaster, so don't try and turn over, will you? It'll hurt for a while though."

"Eyes," Madeleine said. "Can't see properly."

"That'll be because you took a bit of a whack to your face. Your nose was broken and your cheekbone, too. Doc put some cream in your eyes and said that'll make your eyesight blurry for a little while and they're still quite swollen." Sarah carefully didn't add that Doc had also said that her sight may never be fully normal again.

"Hurt," Madeleine said. "Hurt all over."

Sarah nodded. "Try not to worry, love. You're mending, that's what counts. You'll be good as new before you know it."

Madeleine's eyes caught hers. "'m I ugly?" she asked.

"Not at all," Sarah lied. "Just hurt. Promise."

Madeleine appeared to accept this. She sighed and instantly drifted back to sleep leaving Sarah with tears in her eyes that wouldn't stop coming.

SAS Investigations Office

"Okay, so we know Friday guy knew about Madeleine because he didn't show up," Shakil said, tapping a pen against his teeth. "And we know she didn't keep anything in the house that could connect any of the three to her because we didn't find anything."

"Yep," Stuart said gloomily. "Looks like we'll have to wait until Monday to find anything else out."

The two men sat back, each with their own thoughts. Following the guidelines they'd learned, they'd done a thorough, systematic sweep of Madeleine's place in the early hours of the morning when it became apparent that nobody was going to be showing up and found absolutely nothing that could help them.

"I've been thinking," Shakil said, laying the pen on his desk "You know your dad saw Edgar, if that is who this Ted guy is, on Monday, right?"

"Right," said Stuart.

"Well, he went back to see Madeleine on the Wednesday, right?"

"Right," said Stuart.

"And Madeleine was attacked on Wednesday night, right?"

"Right," said Stuart.

"And some people tried to break into your dad's place on Thursday afternoon, right?"

"Right," said Stuart. "Where are you going with this, Shaks?"

"I'm not sure, let me think." Shakil picked up the pen and bounced it against his teeth some more. Stuart watched for a while and then got up to put the kettle on.

"What if ... what if the two are connected?" Shakil said, as the kettle came to the boil.

"Connected how?" Stuart said, tipping boiling water into two mugs.

"Well, you said that your dad had been perving on her on Monday, when she was with Ted, right?"

"I wouldn't say *perving* exactly," Stuart said, stirring the tea bags, "but right."

"What if, when he went to see her on Wednesday, she knew that he'd been watching her?"

"Ri...ight," Stuart said, beginning to see what Shakil was suggesting.

"So what if that's *why* she was beaten up? What if Ted spotted him too? What if Madeleine told whoever beat her up that it was your dad who'd seen them? What if they thought he was paying her to let him watch her at it? They'd go after your dad, wouldn't they?"

"Right," Stuart said flatly. "And that means whoever called at Dad's and frightened Jazz were there for him. And they probably won't stop there, will they?"

"Hmmn," said Shakil.

"We need to get them out of there for a bit, don't we?"

"I think we need to get your old man in here and tell him what we think first."

Stuart picked up his phone.

77 Lakeland Avenue

Caroline was busy at the sink, washing up the lunch things and chatting about what they were going to have for dinner that night. She was happy and Graham was enjoying just being with her and making daft meal suggestions, so when his mobile phone rang and he saw that the caller was his son, his heart sank. This had to be to do with the conversation they'd had on the way home from the hospital and Graham was thoroughly fed up with talking about it. He'd done something stupid, been caught, but nobody had been hurt, had they? Well, nobody apart from Madeleine but that was one of the risks of her job, surely. So far as Stuart was concerned, he hadn't actually done anything wrong? He didn't allow himself to think about what he'd failed to tell him.

"I'll just take this outside, love," he said, scooping up the phone before she could see the name of the caller. "Work thing. Don't want to bore you with it." He slid himself off the chair he was sitting at and hobbled to the back door. Once he was outside and certain the door was closed behind him, he swiped the call open and raised his eyes to the skies. It looked like it was going to rain which he approved of. It would be good for the garden. It hadn't rained for weeks and the roses were suffering. He'd have to get the hose out later if those clouds came to nothing.

"Hello," he said glumly into the mouthpiece.

"I was just about to give up," Stuart said breezily.

"Sorry, it took me a while to get to the phone. Sore bits, you know."

"How is your, um, your—"

"Penis? You can say the word you know. You do have one too."

Stuart sighed and a neighbour who was outside in their own garden and had heard about Graham's close encounter, tittered.

"Don't make that noise at me," Graham snapped at both of them, and then quietly added, "and it's healing, thank you for asking."

"Good," Stuart said, getting down to business. "You need to come into our office today. We need a chat."

"I knew it! For God's sake, I've already told you everything I know! What more can we possibly have to talk about?"

"Well, the fact that Madeleine may have told whoever beat her up that you'd been watching her, for one thing,"

Stuart said. "Which means that your attempted break-in may not have been burglars."

Graham digested this. Eventually, he said, "Can you come and get me? I can't drive at the moment for obvious reasons. I'll wander down the road and meet you at the Cock and Feathers in an hour. Don't make me wait."

"As if," Stuart said, ending the call.

Forty minutes later, Stuart was just about to get into his car to go and meet him when his father called him back. "Change of plan," he said brusquely. "You've to come here. I've encouraged the girls to go and buy some new clothes for our holiday next month and they practically tore my arm off trying to get to my wallet. And I include your mother in that."

Stuart snorted back a laugh. His father was notoriously tight, so getting money out of him unasked must have made his mum and sister's year—and it meant that he was probably feeling guilty about something. "Okay," he said, his mind working nineteen to the dozen, "I won't be long so get the kettle on."

When he let himself into his family home, slipping the lock down behind him, his father, clad in a pair of Stuart's old joggers that he'd left behind when he moved out and a sky blue, unbuttoned to the navel shirt that exposed matts of grey hair and loose pecs, was just adding a splash of milk to two mugs. He stirred both then turned to face his son and held one out towards him. "I made tea, is that okay with you?"

"Fine," said Stuart who would actually have preferred coffee. He took the mug, blinked at the darkness of the liquid within, and hastily placed it on a coaster on the table before his fingers burned. "Do you mind if I add a drop more milk? And how are you really?"

"I'm okay. Sore, but that's to be expected." Graham hobbled over to the table, slopping tea everywhere. Stuart jumped up and rescued the mug from his hand, setting it on another coaster where, he presumed, his father would be sitting, then went to the fridge to get the milk back out. Graham sank onto the seat, wincing. "So what's all this about, Stuart?"

"I need you to tell me again, exactly what happened before I got to you on Wednesday." He added milk into his mug and shook the carton at his father. "Have you got enough in yours?"

Graham tutted and put his hand over the top of his mug. "Mine's fine, thank you. Wednesday again? I already told you. I knocked on her door – honestly, I think I had a moment of madness – I just wanted to meet her."

"Why? No lies, Dad, just the truth please."

Graham had an instant's recall of Madeleine's pert bottom as her client spanked her and another of her delectable lips wrapped around his cock and immediately wished he hadn't thought of it as his own anatomy tried to respond in kind. He squirmed. "Do you really need me to spell it out?"

Stuart nodded, his gaze steely. "Pretend I'm not your son. Talk to me, man to man."

"I already told you what I saw." Graham kept his eyes averted from his son's face as he spoke, trying to get out of it by prevarication. It didn't work.

"Tell me again."

"Oh for God's sake! She was practically naked, he was spanking her and then she … she, um, she took his penis into her mouth."

"Did you see his face?"

"No."

"Was any of it visible to you?"

Graham squirmed, unwilling to admit that he'd barely glanced at the facial features of the bloke who was the lucky recipient of Madeleine's luscious lips. "I don't know," he admitted.

"—because you weren't looking at his face." Stuart finished the sentence for him, his lip curled in disgust.

Graham stayed silent while his son digested this. He watched as Stuart's mouth twitched several times, as though he was about to speak but couldn't form the words. Into the silence, a clap of thunder reverberated through the skies and rain began to instantly hammer against the door and windows. Graham looked up and smiled; he'd been right about the weather.

"So why did you want to meet her?" Stuart asked the question he wasn't entirely sure he wanted an answer to. Graham's smile disappeared, his face fell and was replaced by what Stuart recognised as his obstinate look and that reaction made the answer become vital. "Dad, this is important."

"We've been through all this."

"Humour me."

Graham sighed. "You're like a dog with a bone, aren't you?"

Stuart held his father's eyes with his own.

Graham squirmed on his seat. "Look son, the thing is, we've been married a long time, your mother and I. Things aren't always as ... exciting as they once were. I, um, I thought perhaps I could get some tips from her to spice things up in the bedroom at home." He raised his eyes to see if his son was buying it.

Stuart put his head to one side and shook it slightly. "Dad," he said as gently as he was able, considering that this was his father and what he was saying concerned his mother, too, "that's bollocks and you know it. You have that bloody magazine delivered to your door so I know you see all sorts. If that's all it was, you'd have used some of the ideas from that, so don't treat me like an idiot."

Graham always saw red when his children swore and now was no different, not least because it had been directed at him and was, for once, justified. He snapped and began to utter words he would come to bitterly regret. "Okay! I wanted to sleep with her! There, is that what you wanted to hear? That I wanted to have sex with her? She had the most beautiful arse I've ever seen and I wanted to be able to see it and touch it just like *he* was, and then I wanted to take her from behind and feel those glorious cheeks slapping against my thighs."

Stuart closed his eyes, his heart thudding erratically in his chest. He swallowed down his visceral reaction, which was telling him to deck his father, with an extreme effort of will. "So, Wednesday. You went back. What happened?"

"I knocked on the door and told her that her letter had come to us by mistake. I told her that I'd tried to deliver it to her on Monday and she went ballistic. She'd seen me at the window, you see, accused me – *me* – of being a Peeping Tom. I came over a bit funny and she grabbed me and took me inside."

This fitted with what Shakil had seen, so Stuart remained silent. A flash of lightning lit up the kitchen for an instant, highlighting the gloom of the room, and was followed by another clap of thunder. A strong wind had risen, directing the torrential rain directly at the window panes which rattled in their frames against the watery assault.

Still at the height of his temper, Graham carried on, "She took me into the kitchen and gave me a glass of water. I drained it within seconds, obviously, because I was *in her house*! I was in her house, Stuart! My hands were shaking because she was glorious, even with make-up smeared around her eyes, she was glorious." Now, Graham could not stop talking. The feelings Madeleine had engendered within him had bubbled up to the surface and he was reliving the moment in front of his son's eyes, and the best, and worst, of it, was that he *wanted* to tell him, *wanted* him to understand what had happened during that wonderful, wonderful meeting.

Stuart, on the other hand, was not enjoying this one little bit. He held his tongue and tried to pretend that the man sitting in front of him was not, in fact, his father.

"She was so cross with me to start with. She really told me off but that only showed her fire and, oh, it was amazing! Of course, I explained that I hadn't expected to see what I saw but that it had excited me—I told her I couldn't get her out of my mind. I asked her if she took payment for it and she wasn't cross with me for asking! She said yes, she did, so then I asked if she would let me, you know, if I paid her. And she said yes!" Graham tried to catch his son's eye, wanting him to understand that it had therefore been a fait accompli, something out of his control, but Stuart was staring at the floor and not at him.

"She told me how much she charged, I took out my wallet and gave her what she asked, and she took her robe off and stood there in front of me, naked as the day she was born and twice as gorgeous. She lifted my hands and put them on her breasts and asked me to squeeze them and oh, they were so young and firm and … and then she pushed my head towards them. Her nipples were rock hard, Stuart, and I rolled them around in my mouth like I was sucking on a mint imperial. You'd have done the same!"

Stuart was beginning to think he'd never want to have sex again.

"…and then she turned around and bent over. I could see right between those long legs and she was wet. *She was already wet for me*! She said she wanted me, that she loved me! So I had her. I had her right there and right then, I didn't even take my jeans off! And it was the best sex I've ever had! She was so wet and so tight and so into it … *and then you bloody arrived and spoiled it all*!"

Stuart's head slowly rose as his father admitted his adultery. A mixture of emotions swept over him: a well of pity for his mother; white-hot rage at his father. Another flash of lightning lit up the room, highlighting Graham's face which Stuart found himself studying dispassionately. It highlighted the bags beneath his father's eyes, the wrinkles at their edges and the deepening jowls. It elevated the feverish zeal which burned in his eyes as he recounted what he'd done on that Wednesday morning in the space of twenty minutes. If he'd just got there sooner, he may have been able to stop it. Bile rose into the back of Stuart's throat as his father got to the end of his tale and told Stuart how he'd spoiled it for him, spoiled the sex he was paying for with a girl who was Stuart's own age, and he was unable to contain himself. In one swift and sudden movement, he leaned over the table, aimed his fist at his father's nose and, like someone possessed, watched himself punch forwards, watched as the chair his father was sitting on rocked back and watched as it went over, taking his father with it.

Stuart pushed his own chair back with a clatter and rose like a behemoth to his feet. He towered over his father and broke the stunned silence, his voice low and dangerous. "Get up, you faithless, feckless, excuse of a man. Get up. You've put Mum and Jazz in danger for the sake of a shag you had to pay for. It wasn't love. It wasn't out of your control. It wasn't that she couldn't resist you and she *certainly* doesn't love you. You *paid for it.*

"You make me sick, and the worst of it is that you're going to have to tell them both what you've done because they have to go somewhere else for a few weeks until we get hold of the bloke who almost killed the girl you paid to fuck. And he *is* coming for you, you can be sure of that—all because you *perved* over a girl young enough to be your daughter while she was working with someone important, from the looks of things."

Graham stared up at his son, unable to believe what had just happened. Hadn't he *asked* for the truth of what had happened?

Stuart wasn't done. "You're a sad, sad old man. Do you think she *wanted* to go with you? That you were *special* to her? Think again. You'd wangled your way into her house under false pretences. She probably thought she had no choice—she didn't know what you'd do if she said no, did she? You were a cock with money on the end of it. That's all."

He stared down at his father, contempt written all over his face. "I'm off. I'll expect to hear from Mum telling me that she's leaving you and taking Jazz with her. In fact, tell her to call me. I'll get them somewhere safe. And…" Stuart bent low over his father who was still cowering on the floor, half in, half out of his broken chair, blood streaming from his nose, "…if I haven't heard from her by, say, six this evening, I am coming here to tell her myself." He stalked over to the door that led into the hall, stopped and turned back to add, "And if you haven't told her, I'll make your life so miserable that tap I just gave you won't be the last. Do you understand?"

Crickleby Park

Keeping his feet planted on the muddy ground, Stuart rocked himself on the largest of the children's swings, nursing his sore knuckles and ignoring the rain beating down on him as he tried to make sense of what had just happened, his thoughts and emotions going back and forth, back and forth with each push of his feet.

His feet pushed backwards as anger boiled—his father had cheated on his mother. His feet pushed forwards and he was overcome by sobering shame—he'd punched his father! Backwards again—rage at his father's delight at cheating on his mother. Forwards—overwhelming shame—he'd *punched* his *father*!

It was only when he started to shiver and realised he was drenched through to the skin that he pulled himself out of his funk and got to his feet. He had to do something decisive. Something that would help his mum. He pulled out his phone and called the one person he knew he could count on to help, even if they weren't exactly talking to him at the moment, and then he went back to the office.

24 Lakeland Road

"Go home tonight," Declan told Sarah in a tone that brooked no argument as they sat themselves down at the small table in the clinic's laughable canteen to eat the Chinese meal they'd ordered in. "You're dead on your feet and that's no good to anyone. Doc's happy with how Maddy's doing, she's out for the count until the morning, there's nothing for you to do."

"I can't leave her. What if she needs me?"

"Sarah, seriously, go and get your head around what's happened and get a proper night's sleep." Declan wound noodles around his fork and expertly raised it to his mouth.

"I've got my head around what's happened," Sarah said hotly, stung at the implication that she hadn't.

Declan swallowed his mouthful and waved a fork at her. "Sarah, a girl who is in the same line of work as you was almost killed by a punter. Don't tell me you haven't even contemplated the fact that it could have been you because I won't believe you. You're human. It's human nature to paint yourself into a scenario like that. Hell, even I've put you in that scenario!"

"Thanks," Sarah said dryly, through a mouthful of Crispy Chilli Beef.

"Oh, you know what I mean!" Declan threw his hands up in exasperation.

Sarah thought about it. "Wouldn't you rather go and get a good night's sleep yourself?"

In answer, Declan reached into his pocket and took out a set of keys which he tossed over the table towards her. "Take my car. Do you know how to get to Hammond Close?"

"If it runs off Cranham Road, then yes. Why?"

Declan scooped up more food and nodded. "That's where I live; number fifty-three. Seriously, go home, get some kip in your own bed, then would you mind nipping into mine tomorrow morning and bringing me back some clean shreddies and a couple of tops? Ignore the mess, I came at a run and can't remember if I washed up and if I didn't, the kitchen will probably stink by now."

Sarah's mouth wobbled. She wasn't used to a male being kind to her. "I can do that."

"Something else you may need to think about," Declan added, about to bring her back down to earth with a bump, "and I don't want to worry you or anything, but you haven't worked since this happened. Do you need to let anyone know why?"

"I'll ring in later, let him know what's happened." Sarah was now toying with her food, her appetite dulled by the thought of having to do so.

"Good," Declan said, not noticing. He scooped another forkful of noodles into his mouth. "Good food," he mumbled. "I'll have to remember this place."

"It is, isn't it? I've not tried it before." Sarah was barely aware of what she was saying because she was busily mulling over the thought of calling Gregor, her boss, who, she knew, would be justifiably angry with her for not having shown up for the past few days. She was also wondering about Madeleine's boss having the same name and whether the two Gregors were, in fact, one and the same. If so, had any of

Madeleine's punters also logged on to view her? Some of the people she dealt with were not exactly what you'd call savoury characters and she was often very grateful that she had the medium of a camera to hide herself behind. If the two Gregors *were* the same person, he would undoubtedly be aware of what had happened to Madeleine and, as he would know that the two of them lived in the same road, could have put two and two together and come up with the correct answer as to why Sarah hadn't logged on.

"What's up?" Declan laid his knife and fork down on his plate and gave Sarah a quizzical look. "And don't say nothing. There's obviously something wrong."

Sarah sighed and put down her own cutlery, her appetite suddenly completely gone. "It's just that Madeleine mentioned her boss when I found her. She didn't want him knowing."

"Gregor?" Declan said, then, "*Gregor!* Jesus, I am so dumb! Gregor will know who her clients are! I know Gregor, he hires me to work on the houses he runs; it's how I met Maddy. I'll call him—"

"Wait," Sarah laid a hand on Declan's arm. "Let's think about this for a minute."

Declan waited impatiently. He was itching to use his phone to get the information he wanted. He stared at Sarah's troubled features and suddenly it clicked. "Gregor's your boss too?"

"I don't know. I mean, I guess so. That's my boss's name and I can't imagine there are too many of them in this industry, can you? So if I call him, he's going to put two and two together, isn't he? And that means that if he already knows what's happened to Madeleine, then he knows who did it and he hasn't done anything about it, has he? So—"

"—so that means you're putting yourself in danger, too." Declan put his phone away, stuck his elbows on the table and rested his chin heavily on his palms. He thought for a moment. "Well, one thing's for certain; you can't go back to yours now. If you're right, he'll have someone watching both your place and hers." Keeping his chin resting on one palm he now drummed the fingers of his other against the table top, deep in thought. After a moment he slowly said, "Okay—give me your keys. I'm going instead. I doubt whoever is watching will know who I am so it should be safe enough for me to go and get you a few things. Here," he thrust a napkin towards her, "write a list of what you need and I'll go get it for you. Then I'll go for a nice long drive and shake them off if anyone tries to follow me. You're going to stay at mine tonight."

Tears welled in Sarah's eyes and trickled down her cheeks as she wrote the list, scrabbled in her bag and found her keys and then passed them and Declan's own keys over to him. She looked into his eyes and said with meaning, "Thank you."

***

Declan sat in his car outside the clinic as thunder roared and rain tipped down, bouncing off the windscreen noisily. He made a call. When it was done, he drove across town and back to Lakeland Road which he drove the full length of without slowing or stopping, keeping his eyes peeled for anyone lurking in the area or anyone sitting in their car paying undue attention to what was going on in the area of both Madeleine and Sarah's houses. He spotted two. A heavyset young man was sitting in an old BMW just along from Madeleine's house. He wore wraparound black sunglasses, despite the pouring rain, and was pretending to use his phone. Declan shook his head. He really couldn't have been more obvious had he tried. He may as well have had 'thug' tattooed on his forehead. The second was equally as obvious and just as heavyset. It looked like he had been sitting on the wall of the house two along from Sarah's as he was currently involved in an argument with the people who obviously lived there and each of them were getting absolutely soaked through.

"…can sit where I like!" Declan heard as he passed, and then the high-pitched tones of a couple arguing back carried in the wind through his window. Declan smiled grimly.

At the top of the Lakelands, he caught sight of the person he'd called; Shakil was sheltering at a bus stop. Declan pulled the car up to the stop and unwound the passenger window. "Get in."

Shakil grinned at him, braved the rain, opened the car door and slid into the seat beside Declan, shaking his head like a dog to clear the worst of the rain that had instantly flattened his hair to his head. "Anyone around?"

Declan told him what he'd seen.

Shakil's grin widened. "Give me a few minutes to get down there and I'll distract him some more while you go in. Hopefully, the row will still be going on. Do you know where to park?"

Declan nodded. He'd spotted an empty house not far from Sarah's and it had a driveway. He was going to use it, jump the gate leading to the back garden and then cross the other gardens so he could enter Sarah's house from the rear. It was a risky move. If he was seen, there was nothing to say that the police wouldn't be called and he wanted to avoid that if possible.

"Make the disturbance as big as possible," he said.

"Happily," Shakil replied, nodding thoughtfully.

Declan turned the car around and drove down the Lakelands a short distance so that nobody who had spotted Shakil getting into his car saw him getting straight out again. He pulled over into a gap between two enormous houses and watched as Shakil began the long walk down towards town and sat back to give him time to achieve what was necessary. He got out his own phone and pulled up a map of the area, just in case anyone should apprehend him to ask what he was doing sitting in his car in an affluent area of town. People in big houses were generally more suspicious of those sitting outside them than those who lived in less valuable properties. This fact was borne out when an irate tapping began against his window.

Declan looked up and into the eyes of an angry, well-kept, blonde lady of indeterminate age. She wore short shorts and a sleeveless T-shirt that were sodden and clinging to her like a second skin and was marching on the spot. He rolled down his window.

"Can I help you?" the woman said sharply, leaning into the window and dripping water all over Declan.

"No, I'm good," Declan replied, showing her his phone. "Got a bit lost I'm afraid. I was after Lakeside and came here by mistake."

"Lakeside? There isn't a Lakeside in Crickleby, so far as I'm aware."

"I'm rapidly coming to the same conclusion," Declan said, offering her a cheese-eating grin. "I'm just about to call my niece. My sister moved into the area last week and wanted me to pick her daughter up as she's stuck somewhere. I must have written the address down wrong."

The woman jerked her chin in acknowledgement. "Well, don't sit here too long or other people may not be so accommodating," she said. Then she rapped on the roof of his car, turned and began to run up the hill, away from him.

Declan's mouth twitched as he closed his window and watched her in his rear-view mirror, wondering, not for the first time, why it was that rich people thought they were so much better than everyone else. He looked ahead of him. Shakil had disappeared from view. About to start his car again, he remembered what he'd told the woman, switched the ringer off on his phone, and pretended to have a lengthy conversation with his make-believe niece, just in case she asked anyone if they'd seen him do so. Then he pretend-ended the call, turned the ringer on again, shook his head and began to drive back down the hill.

He pulled into the driveway of the unoccupied house unnoticed and watched, grinning, as Shakil added his thoughts on thugs sitting on walls that didn't belong to them alongside the owners of the said wall. Both Shakil and the male owner of the house were now squaring up to the outsider. As he watched, Shakil yelled, "What did you just say, you racist scum?" and danced a little way down the road ensuring the guy turned to follow his movements. The outsider was now facing down the hill, in the opposite direction to where Declan sat.

Declan was out of the car and jumping the rear gate in one swift move. He landed heavily on a pile of abandoned black bin bags that had been ripped apart by wildlife, spilling their stinking contents all over the passageway that led to the rear garden, and fell with a thud against the side of the house. Declan froze and waited to see if he'd been heard over the noise of the torrential rain as rivulets of water flowed towards him, the ground too hard for it to be able to soak up what was falling from the skies. Nobody sounded any alarms. Already soaked through, Declan splashed his way to the fence that separated this garden from the next and peered over the top to see if anyone was looking out of a window of the neighbouring property and saw nobody moving. He jumped over, keeping himself low to the ground, and made his way to the fence on the other side. He repeated his previous actions four more times and managed to get into Sarah's back garden unnoticed by anyone apart from a sodden black cat which yowled its displeasure from where it was hiding inside an upturned flower pot.

Declan inserted the key into Sarah's back door and turned the handle. Once he was inside, he removed his sodden boots that had muck from the bins on their soles. His socks were drenched, so he removed them too, wiggling his toes to dry between them as he stared around him in amazement. He'd only previously seen the lounge room before, where he'd waited while Sarah got herself ready to go to the Orangerie, and had been impressed by the clean white lines, the splash of red of her photograph against the walls, and the luxury of the flooring. The kitchen of Sarah's house, where he now stood, was equally as immaculate. Work surfaces gleamed, spotless mugs hung from a polished mug tree, plates slotted into purpose-built spaces in a cabinet on the wall and the sink looked like it had never been used. Not a splash mark or drip of water tarnished the simple stainless steel. In and of itself, this wasn't an expensive kitchen, but it was well cared for and obviously loved. He knew, without looking, that the insides of the cupboards would be as tidy as their exteriors (although he would have been sadly disappointed by the under-sink cupboard with was much the same as everybody else's—filled with aerosols, old dusters, ancient cleaning products, washing up bottles and various other odds and ends that always make their way into such a place).

He looked down at his toes which weren't appearing to dry as swiftly as he would have liked and the reason why became clear. He was leaving a trail of water behind him that was coming from his entire body because he was saturated from the relentless downpour. Declan cursed and stripped off his sweatshirt and, after a second's indecision, his sopping jeans. His underwear would have to stay on; he wasn't going to be caught entirely naked should somebody have seen him entering the house and come to investigate why he had done so by jumping across gardens, and if the police arrived, at least they would be able to check with Sarah that she'd given him the keys to gain access and he'd only have to suffer the ignominy of being caught with his keks off.

He looked around for a towel of some kind in a bid to dry himself off a little but none were apparent. Deciding not to sully the carpet in the hall or anywhere else he began to pull open drawers and, in a slight panic, cupboard doors, one of which housed a tumble dryer inside of which was a freshly washed and dried, fluffy towel. Heaving a sigh of relief, Declan pulled it out and rubbed himself dry. Then he pulled open the neighbouring cupboard and found a washing machine. He put the damp towel inside that and, after a second's further thought, put his jeans and sweatshirt into the tumble drier and switched it on, praying it was not going to be like his mother's which rattled and crashed about as it completed its task. Luckily, like everything else in Sarah's house, the tumble drier behaved beautifully, so a dryish Declan decided it was safe to go upstairs to get the things from Sarah's list. The list that was now tumbling around in his soaking wet jeans' pocket, no doubt ruined. He was going to have to wing it.

Half an hour later, having determined the difference between the two bedrooms by the multitude of cameras and the computer in one and nothing of the like in the other, Declan had amassed an entire suitcase full of Sarah's belongings. Faced with drawers full of colour-coded, scanty underwear, none of which looked like they were the kind of things the girls he knew wore on a daily basis (although they may have been more inclined to do so on a night out), he closed his eyes, stuck in his arms, scooped out a massive handful and chucked them into the bottom of the suitcase he'd found hiding in the landing cupboard. Tops he was more comfortable with choosing and the same went for leggings and jeans. He grabbed several of each, folded them carefully, and laid them on top of the pile of knickers, trying not to touch anything skimpy. He went into the bathroom next and found a wash bag beneath the sink. Into it, he piled shampoo, conditioner, toothbrush, toothpaste and a bottle of body wash, checking everything was screwed up tightly so nothing leaked. He grabbed the towel that was carefully hung over a heated rail and then transferred everything into the suitcase.

What had he missed? He scratched his head. Declan had never lived with a woman apart from his mother but he knew women had a need for certain feminine products on a monthly basis. He had no idea of Sarah's cycle but, just in case, he went back into the bathroom, searched the under-sink cupboard and grabbed a practically full pack of tampons. A packet of Microgynon was on the shelf beside the tampons and, after a brief argument with himself as to whether he was overstepping his remit, that went into the case alongside the tampon box.

Pretty certain that he'd got everything she could possibly need for at least a week and knowing that he wasn't going to let her come back here any earlier than that, Declan peered from the bedroom window to see whether the thug was still arguing with Shakil. Nobody was in sight. Lugging the suitcase, he went back downstairs, left the case by the front door, and went into the kitchen to see if his clothes had dried off. When he opened the door to the tumble drier, warmth hit his bare skin like a caress. He reached inside, pleased to note that his sweatshirt was bone dry and his jeans now merely damp. He pulled the sweatshirt over his head, enjoying the heat and stuck his jeans back inside to allow them to tumble for another ten minutes.

Then he sat at Sarah's dining table, rested his head on his hands, and promptly fell asleep.

77 Lakeland Avenue

Caroline and Jasmine arrived back home late in the afternoon, laden with carrier bags filled with new clothes and shoes. Graham, who had heard the car pull up and swiftly headed upstairs to avoid them, watched from the bedroom window, noting their bright eyes, rosy cheeks, good moods and messed up hair from where they'd been caught in the rain yet hadn't allowed it to bother them. He felt a stab of loss as he turned to look at the packed suitcase at the end of their double bed. Graham was taking the coward's way out—the case was going out of the window as soon as they closed the front door behind them because there was no way he could explain to his wife and child that he'd had a moment of insanity and cheated on them both—because that was what he had done—he'd taken his marriage, his family, and he'd shat all over them, he understood that now.

He glanced in the dressing table mirror. His nose was swollen and he had the beginnings of a pair of smashing black eyes and had absolutely no idea how he was going to tell his wife and child that Stuart had done this to him. He'd come up with the idea of saying that he'd tripped and smacked his head on one of the kitchen cabinets, but he knew this was simply borrowing time and he'd come to the conclusion that he would have to leave without saying a word; Stuart would make good on his promise to tell them and he didn't want to be around to suffer the consequences. His stomach churned in turmoil and a small amount of gas escaped him. It stunk. Graham opened the window and wafted his hand around in a bid to disperse the smell.

Caroline caught the movement and thought he was waving at her. She waved back. Graham grimaced and, leaving the window wide open, disappeared back inside.

Caroline frowned, the shine from the shopping trip with her daughter leaving her immediately. Something was up. Normally, her husband would have been at the front door demanding to know why they were so late home and how much of his money they'd spent. Something was definitely up, she'd known it earlier and had allowed herself to believe she was imagining things; now that niggling feeling that something was amiss was yelling at her.

Jasmine gave her mother a look. "Where's he gone?" she asked, looking up at the open bedroom window in much the same way as her mother had.

Caroline shook her head and shrugged. "Dunno. Let's go inside, shall we?" She lugged her bags to the front of the house and opened the front door, ushering Jasmine inside, greeting the dog as he bounded down the hall towards them, his tail whirling like a dervish. As Caroline shut the door behind them, a dull thud sounded outside and a loud yowl screeched.

"What was that?" Jasmine asked, alarm written all over her face.

"I don't know." Caroline put the chain lock on and opened the door to peer out at the driveway. Nobody was out there, but the holly bush she lovingly tended was shaking. "I think next door's cat may have hurt itself on the bush. I can't see it, so it's probably okay. I'll check in a bit."

She closed the door again and both women dropped their bags in the hallway, kicked off their shoes and hung up their wet coats.

"Go and put the kettle on love," Caroline said, almost pushing Jasmine along the hallway towards the kitchen. "I'm just going to find out what's going on with your father."

"Okay." Jasmine went into the kitchen without any argument, understanding that a row was probably coming, listening to her mother's footsteps as she climbed the stairs.

Caroline took a deep breath and walked into the bedroom, aware of her heart thudding in her chest. Graham was perched on her side of the bed, the side nearest the door, his head hanging. He didn't look up. It was cold in the room so Caroline went to the wide-open window and pulled it closed. With her back to her husband, she softly said, "What's going on, Graham?"

"I'm sorry. I never wanted to hurt you," Graham said, his voice strangled.

Now truly alarmed, her heart racing, Caroline turned to look at him but to her utter amazement, Graham ran from the room. He clattered down the stairs as she ran after him calling his name, grabbed the car keys from the hook she'd just hung them on and raced out of the front door, slamming it behind him. By the time she got to the bottom of the stairs and opened the door again, Graham was sliding a suitcase onto the back seat of the car, closing it and jumping into the driving seat. Without looking at her, he switched on the engine, crunched the gear into reverse and backed out into the road and was gone.

"Mum?" Jasmine said, running down the hall to her mother who was now sobbing at the open front door and holding Chutzpah back with her leg to stop him escaping.

"I think your father has just left me," Caroline said between sobs. "Jazz, he's left me. That thud must have been his suitcase; he slung it out of the window. Why's he doing this? What did I do wrong?"

Jazz could only stare in disbelief as she took her mother into her arms and held her up as her legs collapsed beneath her.

***

Stuart was sitting at the bar of the Orangerie beside a very pretty brunette named Tammy with whom he'd had one of his longer relationships the previous year when his mobile rang and his sister's name flashed up on the screen. It was eight-fifteen pm. He hadn't plucked up the courage to go back to his parent's house, despite what he'd told his father.

Tammy noticed. "He's told her then," she said, having been briefed on what was going on in Stuart's parent's lives.

"I'll take this outside," Stuart said. "Hang on, I won't be long." He flashed her a grateful smile as he turned to leave the bar, already holding the phone to his ear. "Jazz, hang on, I'm just going somewhere so I can hear you…"

When he didn't return after ten minutes, Tammy, who had been left to fend off an overweight, sweaty, drunk guy within seconds of Stuart leaving, told him to fuck off, picked up her glass of wine and Stuart's bottle of Bud and went in search of him. She found him standing in the drizzle, leaning against the front façade of the Orangerie beneath one of the overhead, soft glow lights, shaking with temper. He spotted her coming and held up a hand, warning her off.

Tammy ignored it and went over to him. "What's happened?"

"Tam, I need a moment. Look, take my keys and go and wait in the van for me." He reached into his pocket and proffered the keys towards her with a shaky hand.

Tammy, who hadn't taken too kindly to being expected to travel in a manky old van when Stuart had arrived to pick her up, managed to stop herself from rolling her eyes. She took the keys and silently did as he'd asked. It was better than being chatted up by idiots and also better than standing in the persistent drizzle that was all that remained of the earlier storm.

When Stuart loped up and climbed into the van about fifteen minutes later, shivering, she kept her mouth closed knowing he'd tell her what he wanted her to know quicker if she did so.

He turned the ignition on. "Why didn't you start it? You must be frozen," he said, turning to look at her while his fingers fiddled with the heater dial, turning it up to maximum.

"Leather trousers are warm, and so's my jacket," she said, shrugging. "I was okay."

Gazing steadily at her face, Stuart said, "Are you sure about this, Tam?"

"What? Putting your Mum and Jazz up in one of my houses for a while? Of course. You know I love them both."

"You know I'll pay you," Stuart said, putting the van into gear and pulling away from the side of the road.

Tammy waved a refusal. "No need. It's empty and I'd rather someone was in it anyway—stops squatters. You can pay the bills though."

Stuart nodded, unable to speak. "I don't deserve you being this kind," he said eventually.

"No, you don't," Tammy cheerfully agreed, "but like I said, I'm fond of your Mum and Jazz was always good to me."

"The thing is," Stuart said, "they're going to need to go there tonight. Dad's walked out on them."

"Ah."

"Is that a problem?"

"It needs a clean. It hasn't been done since the last tenants vacated."

"How bad can it be?" Stuart glanced at her.

"Like I said, I don't know."

"Don't you have an agent who checks them out?"

"Yes, but the report's not back yet. They only left yesterday, so it could be in any old state."

"Okay, let's go."

Tammy's head swivelled in Stuart's direction so fast she felt her neck crick. Her eyes wide, she said, "I wasn't volunteering! I have people to do that."

Stuart gave her a side glance. "I bet they won't be working at this time of night, will they?"

"Well, no—"

"So let's go and get on with it. I can't leave them alone in the house overnight—and, um, I already told Jazz to start packing. That's why I've got the van."

"I'm not cleaning in this get up!" Tammy folded her arms and glared at him.

"Well, we've got to go and collect the keys from yours, so you can get changed then," Stuart said, quite reasonably he thought, until he looked at Tammy's furious face.

"Stuart. You. Are. Taking. The. Piss. I'll give you the address and the keys but that's as far as it goes—I won't be coming with you," she said curtly.

"Shit, Tam, I'm sorry."

"For what? Being a presumptuous tosspot?"

Stuart grimaced. "Yeah." He kept driving, trying to think up ways to salvage the situation but came up with nothing. His shoulders slumped. The only sound in the van was the steady swish of the wiper blades against the windscreen.

About a mile further on, Tammy giggled. Stuart turned to look at her. "I can't believe you thought I was serious! Of course I'll help you. Who do you think I am?"

Stuart sighed with relief. "Oh, thank God," he said with feeling. "I'm crap at knowing what to do."

"You don't say. And you're still a presumptuous tosspot," Tammy said cheerfully, "but did you seriously think I wasn't expecting something like this? You turned up in a dirty great van, for God's sake! I certainly wasn't expecting a nice civilised drink and then perhaps a meal, although the Orangerie had me fooled for a short time, so kudos to you for that. I rather thought you'd be offering a burger, if I was offered anything at all—you do have form, you know."

"I know, I know. Thanks, Tam." Stuart gave her a rueful grin.

"De nada."

Chapter Seven
Sunday

SAS Investigations Office

When Shakil let himself into the offices late on Sunday morning he wasn't expecting to find his partner curled up on the floor behind his desk, snoring like a steam train. He hesitated for a second, then turned around, silently closed and locked the door behind him, waited for a beat and then pretend-thumped footsteps towards it, rattling his keys and whistling loudly. This time when he opened the door, Stuart was at his desk, doing his best to look wide awake.

"Morning," Shakil said, not looking at him.

"Yeah," Stuart said, rubbing his eyes. "You saw me, didn't you?"

"How did you know!" Shakil pulled a wry face.

"I didn't, you just told me. Sorry, I had to come back here for something in the early hours and couldn't face the drive home. I was absolutely knackered."

"Heavy night?"

"Yeah, but not in the way you're thinking," Stuart said, and then he explained everything that had happened since he'd last seen his partner, including how he'd moved his mother and sister into one of Tammy's 'spare' houses, and ended by asking, "So what happened to you?"

"Me? Oh, I almost had a fight with someone." Shakil grinned as Stuart gaped. "Good job I've got boxer's feet. You'd have been proud of me – I dodged every single attempt the guy made to thump me and he knackered himself out pretty quickly and went running home to mummy with his tail between his legs." As he talked, he danced around the office, ducking and diving, and it made Stuart laugh. Once he'd started, he found it very hard to stop. It was contagious and

Shakil found himself laughing too. Very soon, both men were practically rolling around the room, absolutely belly laughing.

Eventually, Stuart pulled himself together enough to ask, "So how did you come to be dancing in the street? I mean, I presume you were in the street?"

"Declan rang to ask for some help. It turns out that Sarah works for the same guy who manages Madeleine and they thought that if he knew what had happened to her, which, let's face it, is a foregone conclusion really, he may think that Sarah may be involved somehow because she hasn't worked since it happened."

"I didn't know Sarah was on the game," Stuart said, frowning. "How did I miss that?"

"She's not. Well, she's in the racket but she's a sex-cam worker. She doesn't actually physically, um, *service* anyone."

"What? Like those birds on late-night telly? Flashing their boobs and talking dirty to people who ring in?"

"Something like that, I'm not entirely sure what she does, if I'm honest. I didn't like to ask."

"Don't suppose it matters really. Anyway, go on…"

"Declan wanted to go and get some of Sarah's belongings. She's going to be staying at his until this is over and he didn't want her going home in case anyone was staking her place out. He was right to be worried; a bloke was sitting in a car outside Madeleine's, and another was outside Sarah's. That's who I had the fight with—I was a diversionary tactic while Declan snuck in and got what she needed. Actually, it was pretty easy, as it goes…" Shakil explained about the owners of the house arguing with the heavy who'd been sitting on their wall and how he'd taken over on their behalf. "They gave me a cup of tea and a slice of homemade ginger cake afterwards. Nice people. They're going to ring if they see anyone else hanging around."

"You didn't tell them anything, did you?"

Shakil gave Stuart the stink-eye. "I'm not stupid. I told them I lived nearby and if they were worried to call and I'd come and help them." He watched as Stuart rubbed his eyes. "Mate, you look like shit. Go home and get some proper sleep."

"I can't. I have to go and help Mum get straight. Jazz and I managed to get the beds made up and unpacked a bit of kitchen stuff so they could have a drink this morning."

"Want me to come and help too?"

Stuart smiled. "Is the Pope a Catholic?"

***

Caroline had been up and about for hours. She hadn't been able to sleep a wink and after tossing and turning for a few hours, gave up and went into the small kitchen to make herself a coffee. If she wasn't sleeping, she thought, she might as well be doing something productive. What actually happened was that she took one look at all the overflowing boxes, sank to the floor and sobbed all over Chutzpah who was equally as confused as she.

"Why did he do this?" she asked the dog, over and over again, as she ruffled his silky ears and dripped tears over his muzzle.

Chutzpah did his best. He licked away her tears, whined uncomfortably from time to time when he was unable to stop himself, and refused to leave her side, even accompanying her to the bathroom when the copious amounts of coffee she consumed went straight through her. After the fifth trip to the loo, Caroline's thoughts hardened. Round and round they went in her head as she prowled the kitchen, picking up objects from boxes and throwing them back in again. Had she done something wrong? She'd not picked up on anything in Graham's behaviour until very recently – that Harry Enfield outfit! – that would have told her he was unhappy. He'd been his usual mardy self. So what had happened? And why on earth had Stuart and Jazz insisted that she had to leave her home with absolutely no notice? Had Graham defaulted on the final payments of the mortgage? She dismissed that thought swiftly. She had access to all their accounts and knew all the direct debits and standing orders had, and still were, being met with money to spare. The mortgage was peanuts now that it was almost at the end of its term. So why had they had to leave home?

Her thoughts went to the attempted burglary, the one that had frightened Jazz so much. Did it have something to do with Graham? Had he upset someone? Badly upset someone? She had no idea—but she had the sneaking suspicion that her son and daughter knew far more than they were letting on; why else would Stuart have turned up with a van and the keys to an address for them to go to so swiftly? Had he intended for them all to go, before Graham had walked out on them? Had, and the shock of this next thought made her legs weak, had Graham gone back to the house? Had he organised this with their son so that he could say *she'd* left *him*? Was he intending to divorce her and keep their family home? The home where they'd brought up their children? The home she loved?

Last night, she'd been so caught up in the urgency her children had painted, and so full of sorrow, that she'd allowed herself to be moved out. Now she came to a decision—she was moving back again.

Caroline began to repack and this was how Stuart and Shakil found her when they arrived to help her get settled.

"I hope you still have that van," she said, opening the door to let them both in while Chutzpah danced around in the narrow hallway behind her, "because we're going home again."

"You can't." Stuart and Shakil spoke simultaneously as they followed her through into the kitchen.

"Unless you have a bloody good reason why, I'm overruling you. I'm not infirm yet and I can make my own decisions." Caroline turned to face them, her hands on her hips and her face set. "Your father walked out on me. If you think he's having the house, you have another think coming!"

"What?" Stuart said. "He's not having the house, whatever gave you that idea?"

"Well you seemed to know all about him leaving me; why else would you have had the van ready to get us out?" Caroline said bitterly. "Did you and your father cook this up between you? Is he there now? He's not answering his phone."

"I have no idea where my father is and actually, I don't want to know," Stuart said. "Mum, you really can't go home. It's not safe for you there."

"Not safe? Why?" Caroline glared at her son and began to tap her foot, a sign that she was going to lose any semblance of self-control very swiftly. "What the hell has he done?"

"He slept with someone else." The voice came from the hallway and all three turned to look at Jazz who was standing at the foot of the stairs, her chin wobbling. "Stu, just tell her. She has the right to know what the self-serving prick did."

"You knew?" Caroline shrieked, her head turning from one to the other of her children. "You both knew he was having an affair and you didn't *tell* me?"

"It wasn't an aff—" Stuart began.

Caroline interrupted him. "How is sleeping with someone else *not* an affair? We're married, he slept with someone else, ergo it's an affair. Next you're going to tell me it only happened once—"

"Actually, it did—"

"And I suppose that's what he told you? As if he's going to admit to shagging someone regularly. How did you find out?"

"Come and sit down, Mum. I'll tell you everything I know."

"I'm okay standing, thanks. Go on then, get on with it. Start by telling me how you knew he was … he was … having sex with someone else."

"Because our first big job," Stuart pointed between himself and Shakil, "is to find out who almost killed the girl he slept with. She was attacked that same evening." And then, editing his father's decisions very heavily, Stuart explained everything and when he'd finished, Caroline ordered everyone from the house.

***

"The sad thing is if he'd told me he wanted to spank me I'd have probably let him," Caroline tearfully told Jamila on the phone, not long after her family and Shakil had departed. "Our sex life has never been particularly exciting. I've suggested trying various things over the years but he never would. What do they call it nowadays? Vanilla sex? That was us to a T. I never imagined he'd get off on abuse."

"You don't really think he had anything to do with how this girl ended up, do you?"

Caroline stared at her phone for a few seconds and then she said in a sad, little voice, "I don't know. I don't know my husband at all, do I?"

"Caro, I think he chanced this. I don't think it was planned, well, not planned before last week at any rate. What did Stuart say? That he'd been re-delivering a letter that came to yours by mistake and saw her working through a window? He's getting old, Caro. He saw someone young who was willingly letting another old bloke spank her and it went to his head."

Caroline sniffed. "The thing I don't understand is why he didn't just post the letter through her letterbox. Why look through her window at all?"

"I don't know, love."

"And why would anyone be after him? She's a prostitute. It's not like he used her and didn't pay up."

"Perhaps her client saw him watching them."

"Yes, that's what Stuart said he thinks has happened. Apparently, she only works for three men and they all know each other, so if one was seen, they'd all know about it, wouldn't they? But why go to such lengths? I mean, men use prostitutes all the time. I understand that this bloke may not be too happy about being seen, but why get people to try to break into our house? What did they intend to do to him?"

Jamila's brain had gone in another direction. "Caroline, what if it was nothing to do with that particular client? What if ... what if it's to do with one of the others? What if one of them is well known?"

"They wouldn't want it to get out, would they?" Caroline said thoughtfully. "Jamila, can I borrow your car?"

"Not today, I've got tons to do, but you can have it tomorrow."

"Can you come and pick me up? I'll tell Jazz I have an appointment with a solicitor; she'll think I'm starting divorce proceedings. We can go back to yours and I'll go on from there."

"What are you going to do?"

"First off, I'm going to Stuart's new offices, then I'm going to go and visit the girl."

"Are you mad?"

"Quite probably."

Chapter Eight
Monday

Crickleby Bowls Association

"Janice? Janice Longbottom? Shakil Barbosa, SAS Investigations, and this is my partner, Stuart Dalgleish." Shakil held out his hand towards a grossly overweight woman who was sitting behind a desk piled high with various papers in the small Bowls Association club office. She wobbled her way up from the chair she was sitting on, leaned over the desk and enveloped it in her own, slightly damp and podgy one. "We spoke on the phone last week."

"Yes, of course," Janice said, pumping his hand, then dropping it like a stone and proffering it towards Stuart who took it gingerly and received the same treatment. Both men surreptitiously wiped their palms against their trousers after the exchange as she sank back down onto her chair which creaked alarmingly. "You're after some information about one of our bowls club members if I remember correctly? Can I offer you both some tea, we're out of coffee, unfortunately?" Her voice was surprisingly deep and somewhat soothing to listen to.

"That would be very kind of you, yes, please," Shakil said, surprising Stuart as he very seldom agreed to such offers.

"Take a seat, take a seat. I'll go and put the kettle on. I won't keep you waiting." Janice lumbered to her feet again and squeezed through a door that was at the rear of the office. It swung shut behind her. Shortly afterwards, as the two men perched themselves on a pair of hard wooden chairs that were far too low to the ground for comfort, it swung open again and her head appeared. "Milk and sugar?"

"Just milk for me, please," Stuart said. "None for Shakil. He takes it black."

Janice tried to hide her grimace of distaste.

"I know," Stuart said, grinning. "Sets your teeth on edge, doesn't it?"

Janice laughed and disappeared back into the kitchen.

"I wish you wouldn't take the piss out of how I like my tea. Strong and black; best way to drink it," Shakil reproved mildly.

"It's disgusting. Black coffee I get, but tea? Don't your teeth get coated?"

"Yep, that's what tongues are for."

Stuart pretend gagged. "I can think of better things to do with my tongue, thank you."

A smile spread across Shakil's face. "How is Tammy?"

Stuart raised an eyebrow. "Interesting segue, Mr Barbosa."

"Well, I'm pretty certain she put you through your paces after she provided your family with a free house."

Stuart grinned. "A gentleman never divulges what goes on in his bedroom."

"Oh! You managed to make it that far, did you?"

Stuart laughed. "You're incorrigible, do you know that?"

Shakil nodded and both lapsed into silence and looked around the room while they waited for Janice to return. Standing against the wall behind the desk was an oak display cabinet. It housed a variety of cups, medals and photographs of proud players receiving their trophies. Various framed photographs of people in play on perfectly manicured grass had been hung on the walls to either side of the desk, some of them signed.

Janice came back in carrying a tray bearing matching china cups on saucers, a pot of tea, a jug of milk and a small, sugar basin with a tiny spoon in it. Shakil jumped to his feet. "Allow me," he said, taking the tray from her and sliding it onto her desk without knocking any paperwork over.

Stuart marvelled. Had that been him, the floor would by now be littered.

"Thank you," Janice said as she squeezed back behind the desk and slumped back onto the seat. "Shall I be mother?"

Both men nodded and watched as she began the time-honoured ritual of straining a decent cup of tea into each of the three cups. She added a dash of milk to two of the cups, offered one to Stuart and indicated the sugar basin. "Help yourself."

"Thank you." Stuart added two tiny spoonful and wondered what to use to stir his tea.

Janice pre-empted his question. "Use that spoon. I don't take sugar." As Stuart did so and then returned the spoon to the basin making Janice wince, she said, "Now, remind me. Who was it you wanted to talk to me about?"

"One of your new members, Ted something or other."

"That's it!" Janice said, nodding. "I remember now. He's just joined us. His real name is Edgar but he prefers to be called Ted. How can I help you? I don't really know much about him. Is he in some kind of trouble?"

"Nothing like that," Stuart said smoothly. "Do you have an address for him?"

"I do, but unfortunately, due to Data Protection laws, I'm not going to be able to give it to you." Janice nodded twice, her lips pursed. "I could be sued."

"We won't tell him where we got it from," Shakil said, nodding along with her. "As Stuart said, he's not in any trouble, we're just trying to track him down for a client."

"Oh? Come into an inheritance has he? That's what you private eyes do, isn't it? Track people down so they can claim what's owed to them?"

"We do," Shakil agreed, still nodding. They had had a few enquiries of that nature and were working on them at the same time as running this case. "It's one of the main things we do, actually."

"Ah, bless him. What a stroke of luck for him, eh?" Janice said, her eyes sharp. "How did you trace him to here?"

"Pure luck actually. We were chatting with someone who said they thought the new chap here could be the person we're looking for," Shakil said.

"Who would that be?"

Stuart interjected, "Unfortunately, we can't divulge that information."

"That's a shame. That's a shame," Janice said, rocking back in her chair and nodding some more. "Indeed, that's a shame."

"Indeed," Stuart said, "so can you please let us have his address so we can let him know?"

"I wasn't born yesterday," Janice said, abruptly stopping the rocking and sitting upright in her chair, "so why don't you tell me the real reason why you want his address? What's he done?"

Stuart and Shakil exchanged a glance and then Stuart said, "We don't know that he's done anything just yet, it's why we want to talk to him, to find out."

"Find out what, exactly?"

"If he had anything to do with something ... *bad* ... that happened to our client."

"What kind of bad?"

Stuart shook his head and got to his feet. "We're sorry to have troubled you, Janice. Come on Shakil, let's leave this lady to go about her business. Thank you for the tea." He took Shakil's cup and saucer from him and began to lay it, along with his own, on the tray on the desk.

"Hang on, hang on," Janice said very quietly, looking up at him. "I meant what I said about Data Protection laws. I *can't* legally give it out to you. Tell me this though; was anybody hurt?"

Stuart continued messing around with the tea cups, clattering them and nodding almost imperceptibly.

"Yes. Very badly. Not necessarily by him, but by somebody we think he knows," he said, equally quietly, still pretending to balance the cups on the tray.

"Female?"

Again, almost imperceptibly, he nodded.

Janice inhaled sharply. When she was sure she had both men's attention, she flicked her eyes, obviously trying to indicate something behind her. Stuart left the tray alone, stood up and casually looked at the cabinet again – and spotted something he'd missed earlier. A tiny red light, just bigger than a pin prick, was almost hidden between two trophies.

"Your team must be successful," he said loudly, moving his eyes swiftly on from the light to take in the rest of the contents, "going by the amount of trophies you have. My dad's often thought of joining a team. Do you have any vacancies?"

"They are successful, yes, and no, we don't have any vacancies at the moment. Would you like me to put his name down on our list?"

"Yeah, that's a good idea. Thank you."

They watched as Janice slid open the drawer to her right and took out a large black ledger. She licked her finger and flicked through the pages, then turned it and passed it across the desk, keeping her body in the way of the camera. The pages were open and completely filled by various names and addresses. Janice tapped one with her fingernail. "Put his name and phone number here and I'll contact him once we have an opening. The list is quite long though, so it may be a while. Do you need a pen?"

Stuart bent down to the desk, taking the pen Janice passed to him. Making sure he remained in front of her so that what he was doing was not recorded, he scrawled down the information she had indicated on the palm of his left hand, then stood, dropping that hand to his side, palm facing away. As he stood again, using his right hand, he reached into his jacket pocket and passed one of their cards across the table to her.

"If you change your mind about being able to help us, you can find us on that number. It's a shame you couldn't help us any further but we understand about Data Protection laws. Thank you for your time."

"You're welcome. Sorry I couldn't be of more help to you." Janice got to her feet for a third time. "Let me show you out."

The Clinic

While her son was out visiting Janice, Caroline broke into his office. She'd spent the entire previous evening learning how to open the lock on the back door of Tammy's house without using a key, having logged in to Stuart's emails (he still had the same password he'd had since he was old enough to have his own email address, she'd have to tell him to change it one day), found the emails containing links to his Private Eye training, and searched through them until she found what she needed to know, and then she'd practised until she could do it successfully over and over again. Stuart's office had been easy pickings. It only had a yale lock opener, something else she'd have to casually mention to him at some stage.

Once inside, she searched through their filing cabinet, looking for details of where the girl, Madeleine, was currently staying. It didn't take long. They only had a few cases so far, and this was the biggest by far. She read all the notes on the case, then found a notepad and pen and jotted down all the names and addresses she came across: Sarah, Declan, Madeleine's home address (which she already knew and wasn't actually going to help her because the girl wasn't there at the moment), a bowls club and the address of a private clinic on the other side of town. Caroline smiled grimly, made sure she put everything back exactly as she'd found it and left the office. She wasn't able to lock the door again and guiltily hoped nobody would break in before the boys got back. Then she got back into Jamila's little car, programmed the postcode of the clinic into the inbuilt satnav, and drove to it.

It wasn't what she'd expected. From the outside, the building didn't look like a clinic. It looked very much like a big old house that had been allowed to go to rack and ruin. Dark blue paint peeled in strips from the front door and window sills and the windows themselves needed a good clean. Overgrown bushes sprawled over the front lawn and, dotted here and there, out-of-control rose bushes bloomed their last of the season. Caroline went up the pathway to the front door which opened when she pushed against it.

Inside, she found herself in a small foyer with a reception desk bearing a bank of computers. Sitting behind them was a young man who looked up at her and smiled. "Can I help you?"

"Yes," Caroline said, having not thought this far ahead. "I've been told my, my daughter has been brought here. Madeleine..." For an instant, her mind went blank, and then she remembered the girl's surname, "Beaufort. Madeleine Beaufort."

The young man keyed into one of the computers. "Ah, yes," he said, smiling up at her. "She's in the Lilac Room. Just up the stairs and along the corridor. First door on your left. Please sign in." He slid a book towards her and offered her a pen.

Caroline thought swiftly. She carefully wrote the name Marie Beaufort in the gap provided and inserted Madeleine's name in the space asking who she was visiting. She left the car registration space empty as she'd parked around the corner and not in the clinic's car park. She passed the book back and the young man simply closed it and gave her a pass to attach to her coat. Caroline duly did so, and then she walked through the double doors to the right of the reception and headed up the stairs.

When she got to the Lilac Room she paused and peered through the small window in the door. Inside, a hospital bed bore a young girl of around her daughter's age. She was hooked up to a multitude of drips and medicines and her eyes were closed. Caroline opened the door as quietly as she could and the girl did not stir. She tiptoed towards the bed and stared down at the mass of titian hair surrounding a face filled with bruising. She stared at her two black eyes, her splinted nose, the plaster casts around both her arms and suddenly she found herself crying, great gulping sobs that she tried desperately to hold back but was unable to stop. What man in his right mind would have done this to this poor child?

Madeleine heard her and painfully pried her eyes apart. Light hurt them and her vision was still not stable so she could only make out the blurry face of a woman she was pretty sure she didn't know. "Ooh are ooh?" she slurred.

"Oh God, I'm sorry!" Caroline said, trying desperately to stop crying. "I didn't mean to disturb you."

"S'kay," Madeleine said. "'m not going an'where. Not talked to an'one t'day. Ooh are ooh?"

"I'm Caroline," she said, deciding to tell the truth. "I'm Stuart's mum."

Madeleine frowned. "Ooh?"

"Stuart. He's one of the men who is trying to find the person who did this to you."

Madeleine tried to shake her head but the pain it engendered stopped the movement. She was pretty certain she didn't know any Stuart. "Dunno," she managed, hoping Caroline would understand.

"It's okay. Your friend Sarah hired him to help you. He needs to be found and stopped from ever doing this again to anyone else."

"Ooh know ooh did 'is?"

Caroline nodded. Her maternal instincts kicked in and she leaned across and gently lifted a strand of hair that had fallen across Madeleine's face. "Robert Jones," she said. "Is that right?"

A silent tear slid down Madeleine's cheek as she tried to shake her head. Caroline reached into her handbag, pulled out a tissue and wiped it away. "Don't cry, honey. Don't cry. We'll get the bastard, don't you worry. He won't come near you again. I promise."

"'ot 'obby." Madeleine knew she was making no sense, she could 'see it in the woman's eyes; and now her own were beginning to droop again. She was unable to stay awake for longer than a minute or two, and she wasn't sure, in her rare moments of clarity, whether it was due to the injuries she had sustained or the drugs being pumped into her.

"No problems. Would you like me to sit with you for a while? I, I told them I was your mum, I hope you don't mind."

Madeleine tried to smile. "No' go' a mum," she mumbled as she drifted away. "S'nice."

Caroline sat with her until ten o'clock that night when the nurse who had been coming in and out, checking fluid levels, changing her catheter and injecting further drugs at regular intervals came in to turn the lights down. "You have to leave now; we need to close up for the night. Go home. Get some rest and come again when you can," she said kindly, helping Caroline to her feet. "She won't be awake again now until tomorrow. We're hoping to reduce the drugs that knock her out a little over the coming days, so she's going to need all her friends and family around her then."

Caroline, feeling vaguely guilty for asking as the nurse escorted her to the door, said, "Tell me honestly, is she going to get fully better?"

"We hope so, but there's no guarantee. She was pretty banged up and the punch to her face has possibly damaged her eyesight permanently. She's not responding in the way we'd hoped but you being here may have helped a lot. She's not had many visitors, so her mum being here can only be a good thing." The nurse stopped and looked Caroline directly in the eyes. "Come back," she urged. "I know you've probably found what she does for a living hard to cope with, but come back for your daughter. She needs you."

Caroline swallowed hard. She nodded. "I will."

The Wrong Address

Stuart and Shakil sat in Shakil's car outside the address provided to them by Janice, staring up at the derelict house in dismay.

"So Ted has something to hide," Shakil said eventually, taking out his phone to call the number she'd provided them with and was greeted with a loud squawking noise and a recorded message telling him he had dialled an incorrect number. He held it out so Stuart could hear.

Stuart sighed. "Yep. Back to square one. We'll have to go to the Bowls Club after all."

"Let's hope nobody saw us knocking."

Both men surreptitiously glanced around them. Nobody appeared to be taking any notice of them at all.

"Let's go," Stuart said. "We're going to draw attention to ourselves sitting out here and we don't want that."

Shakil started the car.

Borddulac Chateau

As he paid the cab driver, Stuart stared up at the flamboyant brass lettering set into the red brick arch above the door to Tammy's enormous, detached, lakeside house and bit back a grin. He'd never had the heart to tell her that it should read 'Bord du lac'—she'd been so proud when she'd thought up the name and found someone to construct it for her.

"It makes me smile, too," she said, mistaking the grin for admiration as she waved her arm at a small piece of metal set into the wall beside the door. The door swung open.

"How did you do that?" Stuart asked, blinking in surprise as they went through it and into a hallway that was as large as his entire apartment. The door closed automatically behind them and locks could be heard clicking quietly into place.

"Apple watch. It's new. Daddy knows somebody. Brilliant, isn't it?"

Stuart, who knew only too well how careless Tammy was with her belongings, was wondering whether the movement had been observed by the cab driver who was still circling the driveway. He kept his thoughts to himself. "It is," he agreed. "I've never noticed that you don't have a door lock."

"But I do," Tammy said, pouting. "I just used it."

"Yeah, I meant one that uses … oh, never mind. So," he said, changing the subject and twirling a strand of her hair between his fingers, "what are we doing now?

Tammy curled a hand around his neck and arched an elegant eyebrow.

"Aren't we eating first? I'm not a cheap date you know."

"I know," she said dryly. "You've cost me an entire house so far."

Stuart grinned. "Touché."

"I'm not touchy! I don't mind, I keep telling you."

"No, I didn't say … oh, never mind, come here…" Stuart pulled her into his arms properly and bent his head to kiss her.

"Mmmn," she murmured as they came up for air a few moments later. "Are you really hungry?"

Less than a minute earlier, Stuart had been so hungry he could have eaten anything put in front of him. Alcohol had that effect on him and they'd spent the best part of the evening in a tiny wine bar pouring champagne down their throats. Now he was experiencing hunger of a different kind. "Not for food," he said, putting his arms around her waist and lifting her until she wrapped her legs around him.

"Take me upstairs then," Tammy whispered. "I'll find you something to eat."

Stuart didn't need asking twice.

Chapter Nine
Tuesday

SAS Investigations Office

Stuart approached the door to the office, keys in hand. He inserted one and was alarmed to find that the door moved against his fingers without him having turned it. He turned to Shakil, who had arrived in the car park at the same time as him, put his finger over his lips and then pointed to the door.

"On three," he mouthed silently, holding up his hand to show first his index finger, then his middle finger and finally his ring finger. Both he and Shakil burst into the office, fists raised, roaring an attack.

Nobody was inside. Both men came to a standstill without touching anything and looked around them. Nothing appeared to be out of place.

"What the...?" Stuart said, walking over to the desk and opening drawers. "You did lock up I take it?"

"Of course," Shakil said, offended. He went over to the window and looked out. Nobody appeared to be lurking in the vicinity and nobody was sitting in any of the cars in the car park. He turned to face Stuart. "So what's gone?"

"Nothing, so far as I can make out," Stuart said, picking up a pencil. "I think whoever came in was after information and they weren't too clever about it, look." He held up the notepad that sat on the top of the desk, laid it back down again and began to lightly scrawl over the clean white sheet at the top of the office notepad and then, "Aha," he said triumphantly, tearing the scribbled-on page from the pad and holding it aloft, "I was right. Somebody has written down a list of names and addresses in Maddy's case. Now, who could possibly want that information?"

"Do you think it could be Bobby Jones?" Shakil said, taking the paper from Stuart's hand and inspecting it.

"I don't see why it would be. He doesn't know we're after him, does he? We haven't even caught up with Ted yet."

"True. But what if Janice has told him we want to talk to him?"

Stuart thought about it and shook his head. "I don't think she would. Not after she learned that somebody was hurt and he was possibly involved and don't forget he gave her the wrong address and phone number."

"Shit, the clinic is at the top of this list," Shakil said, pulling out his phone. "I hope we're not too late—I'm going to warn them that somebody may try to get to Madeleine—she needs a guard."

"I don't think there's any point, we don't know when we were broken into, do we? Whoever it was has probably already been to the clinic. Ring them on the way, but try not to alarm them," Stuart said, taking out his car keys. "Let's go."

***

Stuart and Shakil took the stairs at the clinic two at a time, the receptionist hot on their heels and shouting for them to stop, come back and sign in. A slightly-built, ashen-faced nurse came to see what the commotion was all about and bravely barred their way into the Lilac Room.

"Stuart Dalgleish and Shakil Barbosa. Is she safe?" Stuart asked, as the receptionist danced about between them and the nurse, not entirely sure which of them he needed to try to deal with first and equally as unsure as to whether he could actually take on either and win.

The nurse ignored his question. "You need to speak with security," she said, planting her five-foot-nothing body firmly in the doorway and glaring at them fiercely. Although a strong breeze would probably have knocked her over, she had an aura of righteous indignation that meant neither of them was prepared to cross her. "Conrad, can you take them?"

"Sure," said the receptionist, backing away down the corridor and silently praying the two angry men would follow him. "Come on, come with me."

Glad the nurse was on the ball, Shakil and Stuart exchanged glances and duly did as they had been asked. Further along the corridor, they reached a door bearing a plaque with the word 'Security' engraved into it. Conrad knocked on the door and waited. When there was no response, he knocked again.

"Can't just go in, I'm afraid. Tarquin would have my guts for garters," he explained apologetically.

After the third, slightly louder knock, a voice that was filled with annoyance sounded from within. "For crying out loud, what now?"

"We'll take it from here." Shakil dismissed the receptionist with a wave and waited as Conrad first hesitated and then walked sheepishly back to the nurse who was guarding Madeleine's door and still glaring up the corridor at them. Shakil grinned at Stuart, pushed the door open and both men walked into a room that stunk of vinegar.

An enormous man in his late forties was sitting with his feet up on a desk, shovelling chips into his mouth and reading a dog-eared paperback. Without looking up, he waved them towards a bank of chairs that was set against a wall to their right and continued eating.

The two men stayed on their feet, only the redness creeping up on Stuart's neck and Shakil's fisted hands giving away the fact that both were becoming very upset. After a few moments, Stuart opened his mouth and then closed it again abruptly when Shakil tugged on his arm, shook his head slightly and opened his own. "Excuse me," he said quietly.

The security guard failed to pick up on the tone. Still with his head buried in his book and a mouthful of half-chewed chips, he said, "Hang on, I'll be with you in a—"

Shakil moved so swiftly even Stuart was alarmed. He darted around the desk, grabbed the book, threw the chips onto the floor, knocked the guard's feet off the table and grabbed his lapels in a flash. Then he leaned close and growled into his face, "Get up, you lazy bastard. Get up, grab your things and get out. You just quit."

The guard scrambled to his feet and pushed against Shakil's shoulders in a bid to shift him. He failed. "Who do you think you are? You can't fire me, you ain't my boss!"

"I didn't fire you," Shakil said, still growling, still nose to nose with the much larger man. "I told you, you quit. Unless you want to stay a bit longer in one of the private rooms?"

"Oh yeah? Who's gonna put me there then? You, you jumped up streak of piss? Don't make me—"

Stuart blinked in amazement as his partner swiftly brought both his arms up and inside the guard's, knocking one aside with ease and blocking it with his body while he grabbed the other. Keeping it in a vice-like grip, he dodged to the rear of the guard, twisting his arm upwards and back, yanking it up behind the man's shoulder blades. He kicked into the back of the guard's knees, making him buckle, and brought him crashing down to the ground with an ease that was astonishing to behold.

"Give me a hand," Shakil said, from where he lay across the guard's back, holding him in place while the man tried to buck him off, swearing profusely. "Get the cuffs out. I'm nicking this bloke."

Stuart played along. "What's the charge?"

"I'll think of something. Colourful language? Being a total prick?"

"What about failure to do his job?"

"That'll do."

"You can't nick me for any of those things," the guard protested. He'd stopped struggling and was now lying more quietly. "Why didn't you tell me you were Old Bill?"

"Shouldn't need to. You're employed to *guard* your patients. You should have been alert, especially after you received a call telling you you needed to be on the lookout."

"What, I have to jump when some twat thinks someone's after the hooker? Yeah, I got the message; didn't believe it. Whoever done her over prob'ly thought he'd finished the job. He won't be back. I seed it all before."

Shakil growled and pushed the guard's arm further up his back. He squealed. "I've got arthritis and you're gonna snap my bones! That's aggravated assault, that is!"

Shakil pressed his elbow into the small of the guard's back. "Seen it all before, have you? Pipe down and stop struggling and it won't hurt so much, you pathetic pile of cow dung. That little nurse out there has bigger balls than you."

"Mate, you have two choices," Stuart said, walking around the desk, opening drawers and having a good rummage through them as he spoke. "Either tell us who's in charge here and we'll let him know you had an emergency call and had to leave without giving notice, or we can take you to the station and book you."

"For what! I ain't done nothing wrong!"

"How about possession?" Stuart bent and waved a transparent baggie filled with a huge block of cannabis under the guard's nose. He raised the bag to his face, opened it and sniffed. "Skunk," he proclaimed, "and there's too much here for it to be for personal use; there's enough here to put a battalion into a coma."

The guard went limp.

"Let him up," Stuart said, pocketing the drugs. "He's going to behave now."

Shakil released his grip and sprang to his feet, using his elbow against the guard's lower back for leverage. The guard squealed again and then pushed himself to a seated position where he sat and glared at them both.

"What the fuck do you both want?"

"Just think how much better this could have gone if you'd only asked us that in the first place," Shakil said, shaking his head in wonder. "You wouldn't be unemployed now, would you? So, why don't you get up and sit behind your desk like a good chap, eh? Write out your resignation and we'll tell your boss what we said we would. You had an unexpected family emergency."

"I can't write now, can I? You've prob'ly broke my arm."

"Type then," Stuart said, fed up now. "One fingered if you have to." He turned the laptop that was open on the guard's desk and woke the screen up, his face falling when he saw the screensaver; a still shot of a very young naked girl being sexually abused by two men whose faces had been cropped from the photograph. The link to what was probably the full film was at the bottom of the screen. "On second thoughts," he said slowly, "you don't need to write your resignation; this speaks for itself." He pulled back his arm and, in a carbon copy of what he'd done to his father only days earlier, knocked the guard out cold.

***

When the real police had been and carted Tarquin away, and after Stuart and Shakil had given statements and passed the laptop over as evidence, they began to make their way back towards the Lilac Room where the nurse was still standing guard. She was now wearing a smile.

"Pathetic pile of cow dung?" Stuart said, bumping Shakil's shoulder as they trudged back along the corridor.

Shakil reddened. "I couldn't think of anything else. Bit naff?"

"Nah, personally I enjoyed the moment."

The two men shared a glance and then both began to chuckle.

"Is he gone for good?" the little nurse called as they approached. "Maddy's fine, by the way. Nobody's been in to see her apart from her mum, yesterday. She was here for a while and I think it did her good, Maddy, I mean."

"That's great," Shakil said, answering her smile with one of his own. "And yes, that's the last you'll see of Tarquin. Did you send us down there deliberately?"

"Yes," the nurse said unapologetically. "I recognised your names. You're both down as safe visitors. I checked who was and who wasn't after you rang to warn us someone may try to get to Maddy."

"Thank you," Stuart said. "We'll have a man stationed outside her door from now on, just in case. If you spot anyone wandering around that shouldn't be here, don't hesitate to call us."

The nurse nodded. "Are you allowed to tell me what you found in his room?"

"Probably not," Stuart said.

"Pornography? Young girls?"

Shakil frowned. "You knew?"

The nurse shook her head. "Not for certain but his behaviour hasn't been the best and we're all wary of letting him anywhere near the patients unaccompanied. There have been one or two complaints; nothing bad enough to act on, just patients saying they don't like him, that he makes them feel uncomfortable. He's ... *shifty* ... overly fond of checking in on patients under MIC, do you know what I mean?"

"MIC?"

"Sorry, I always forget people don't understand our acronyms; medically induced comas," the nurse said, flushing slightly. "When someone has received severe injuries they sometimes need to be kept asleep to start the healing process."

"Those patients—young, were they?" Shakil asked.

The nurse nodded. "Under sixteen, in the main."

"Have you told anyone?"

The nurse sighed. "Only about a dozen times. The Head of Security is one of Tarquin's buddies; he wouldn't listen. He laughed at me—laughed at anyone who said anything actually. He seems to think that patients brought here instead of the general hospital don't count for much."

"Charmer," Stuart said, understanding her meaning. "What's his name?"

"Gordon King."

"Stu," Shakil said, "why don't you go and get us all a nice cup of tea? I'm sure Nurse…?"

"Gerrity, Trudy Gerrity," the nurse supplied.

"…Trudy could do with one. She's had a nasty shock, after all."

Stuart stared at Shakil in surprise. Shakil nodded his head towards the stairwell without meeting his eyes.

"Oh, yeah, sure," Stuart said, hiding his smile. He turned to Trudy. "How do you take it?"

"We're not supposed to really," Trudy said, looking up at Shakil, "but, well, yes, that would be nice. White, please. No sugar."

Before Stuart headed for the canteen on the ground floor, he went back into the guard's office and completed a very thorough search of the room. He found what he fully expected to find in an old shoe box that had been hidden practically in plain sight in one corner of the room, resting beneath an artfully placed dust sheet. He pulled on a pair of gloves, opened the box, saw the DVDs, sighed and rang the police a second time.

Next, he headed down to speak to Conrad, the receptionist, where the pair decided that locking the front door and finding out who was there *before* they were admitted would probably be an extremely good idea. He also checked the sign-in register and noted down the name of Madeleine's mother, Marie Beaufort.

***

Jasmine rolled out of bed at midday having slept through her alarm. She frowned, wondering why her mum hadn't woken her, then staggered out of bed and went for a quick shower to wake herself up fully. Once she was dressed she went down the unfamiliar stairs and into the kitchen, certain her mother would be in there and probably sitting at the tiny table, fretting over her father.

But Caroline was not there. Instead, Jasmine found Chutzpah nosing his food bowl towards her and wagging his tail forlornly, and a note propped up against the kettle.

Jazz, I've had to pop back to Jam's, I left something there yesterday. Should be back before you get back from work. Have a good day, sweetie xx

Jasmine screwed up the note and tossed it into the bin understanding now why she'd been left to oversleep. She fed the dog, made a cuppa and, as she sat down to drink it, her phone rang and the name 'Shitbag' flashed across the screen.

"Hi Stu," she said, answering it. "What's up now?"

"Nothing, just checking that you're both okay? Where are you?"

"At the house."

"Well?"

"Well, what?"

Stuart sighed. "Are you both okay? Honestly, it's like pulling teeth with you sometimes."

Jasmine laughed. "Yes, Stuart, I'm okay and I presume Mum is too although I haven't seen her since the day before yesterday."

"What!"

"Relax, she left me a note this morning. She's gone to Jamila's to collect something she left there yesterday, so as I said, I presume she's okay."

"Oh. Well, that's good, I suppose. How did she seem to you when you saw her last?"

"Oh, happy as Larry, how do you think?" Jasmine said sarcastically. "I mean, it's not like she's just discovered our dear father has been screwing prostitutes and dropped us right in the shit, is it?"

"Yeah, okay," Stuart said heavily.

"What are you up to? Any closer to detecting who the jerks who are after us all are?"

"Yes, actually."

"Good. I want to go home. Where are you now?"

Stuart laughed. "I'm at the clinic where the girl was taken after the attack. I'm killing time, actually."

"Why?" Jasmine asked, unable to resist.

"Shaks is chatting up one of the nurses."

"Shakil? Chatting someone up? No! So what's she like, this nurse?"

"Sweet," Stuart said, "which is why I've left him to it. It's about time he got some action."

"Nice," Jasmine said, shaking her head in disgust. "You couldn't just say it was about time he met someone nice, could you?"

"Oh, come on. The last time Shaks scored was in 2018. If he doesn't use it soon, it'll shrivel up and fall off."

"And that, brother dearest, is why I don't date."

"Nothing to do with the fact that nobody'll have you?"

"Oh fuck off." Jasmine ended the call and sat glaring at her phone, smarting a little. She'd had a crush on Shakil since forever and the thought of him with someone else stung; he'd been so reliably single for so long.

Her phone rang again.

"What now!"

"Sorry, Sis. I know you fancy him so I've got to ask—why the hell haven't you let him know?"

"I do not *fancy him*," Jasmine hissed. "What on earth makes you think that?"

"The fact that you turn into a tongue-tied twit whenever he's around, that's what."

"Ohhh, go to hell, Stuart!" But Jasmine was talking into an empty line. Stuart had hung up.

77 Lakeland Avenue

Sitting in the lap of luxury in his room at The Crickleby Hilton, toying with a plate filled with foie gras and truffles, Graham was staring at his own phone, wondering if it would be a good idea to try to call his wife. He knew his marriage was falling apart but failed to understand that it was entirely his own fault. He scrolled through the various text messages he had sent to Caroline, Jasmine and even Stuart. Not one of them had had the decency to respond to him. Hadn't he suffered long enough?

He picked up a bone china cup and sipped at the tepid contents. Expensive tea wasn't all it was cracked up to be, he decided, give him a cup of PG Tips any day. He put the cup down, pushed the plate aside and went over to the window rubbing his eyes. Despite the luxury, he had barely slept since he'd been forced to leave home. The view over the lakes was as spectacular as always but Graham was itching to be back at home, sleeping in his own bed, watching Caroline as she pottered around their house, seeing Jasmine off to work (even though he wasn't keen on her choice of career; with her qualifications, she could have done anything, so why was she wasting her life working in a shop, of all places?) He even missed walking Chutzpah, probably the only member of his family who would actually be missing him.

Graham decided enough was enough; it was time to go home. He packed his bag, ensuring he took all the soaps, shampoos and other complementary items from the enormous ensuite bathroom – he was paying enough for the pleasure, after all – and headed down to the hotel reception to check out, wincing at the extortionate price for less than a week's stay and thinking it would possibly have cost him less to buy a second property. He forewent leaving a tip.

He had the doorman bring his car around for him and ignored the disdain on the man's face as he stared at the bruising around Graham's eye. He pulled up in the little Ford Fiesta, leaving the engine running for him and the driver's door open.

"Would Sir like some help with his luggage?" he asked snootily, brushing down his uniform with a white-gloved hand and planting himself back into his usual position beneath the awning.

"Not with my luggage," Graham said, equally as snootily, "but be a good man and check the oil for me."

The doorman glared at him. "I will happily escort you to your car and attend to your luggage, *Sir*, but I am afraid I am not a *mechanic*, although I can, of course, recommend one should you believe your vehicle to be unroadworthy?" He picked up Graham's bag and carried it down the steps to the car, opened the boot and packed it inside, none too carefully. "Will that be all, Sir?"

Graham pretended to think. He rubbed his chin, put his head to one side and was just about to speak when the doorman darted around him.

"Madam Johnson, so nice to see you this morning. Shall I bring around the Bentley?" he said obsequiously. He turned back to Graham. "Sir, would you be so good as to move your vehicle so that I can attend to Madam?"

Intending to say something nasty, Graham turned to look at Madam Johnson, an elderly, pug-faced woman who was dripping in diamonds and red lipstick. Faced with real money, Graham gave in. Muttering to himself, he stalked down the stairs, got into his car, put it into gear and promptly stalled it. Red-faced, he turned the key and smashed his foot down on the accelerator. The car lurched forwards and stalled again. Graham took a deep breath and tried again. This time, he was able to drive away from the hotel without further incident although it took him a solid five minutes to stop sweating. He pounded on the steering wheel out of sheer temper, ignoring the looks from other drivers when he accidentally hit the horn and made himself jump.

He pulled up on the driveway to his home and sat there for a few moments, staring up at the windows. Was she inside? Would she let him back? There was nothing for it, he'd have to go and find out. Graham tugged on the handbrake, knocked the car out of gear and switched the engine off. He got out and went to the boot, studiously avoiding looking back up at any windows in case anyone was watching him, took out his bag which smelled suspiciously like some of his purloined bathroom lotions had burst from their containers, and walked up to the front door. So far, so good. He put the key into the lock, twisted, and the door opened. Nobody came to shout at him. Chutzpah failed to appear. Caroline must be out walking him, Graham thought, heaving a sigh of relief. He was inside his own home and he wasn't leaving again for anyone.

He locked the door behind him and removed the keys so that his wife would be able to let herself in. Then he went into the kitchen, laid his bag on the floor, opened it and confirmed that his purloined lotions had emptied themselves all over his clothes. He opened the door to the inbuilt washing machine and tipped the entire contents inside. Then, after several tries, he closed the door and stared at the controls, scratching his head. Whites? Coloureds? Short rinse? Long spin? Christ, he only wanted to wash them, surely a degree in engineering wasn't required? Caroline and Jasmine operated the thing all the time. How hard could it be? He turned the knob until a little blue light came on and decided that would do. About to press the start button, he realised he needed to add detergent and began to search for the big box of powder he remembered his mother using decades previously. Instead, he found a plastic box with a lid that appeared to have been welded shut beneath the sink. It smelled as he remembered his clothing smelling after Caroline had done it for him so he fought with the lid for a good few minutes, then, having thoroughly lost his temper, took the butcher's knife from the knife block – the only knife in it, he noticed – pushed it through the box just beneath the lid and sawed around the entire top of it. Inside were a couple of squishy pod things, each with three segments holding a different colour liquid in each.

"Bloody stupid idea," he muttered to himself, opening the machine drawer he'd seen Caroline use on previous occasions. Inside were small compartments labelled one, two and three. Graham used the same butcher's knife to carefully poke a hole into one of the pod's segments and squeezed the white liquid into compartment one. He repeated the performance with the light blue liquid which went into compartment two and the final dark blue liquid he squeezed into compartment three, grimacing as the sticky liquid coated his thumb and index finger. He found and pressed the button marked 'start' and waited until he heard water chugging into the machine. "There," he said triumphantly, running his hands under the cold tap to get rid of the mess on his fingers, "that wasn't so hard, was it?"

He went to make himself a nice mug of PG Tips in the special mug that had been bought for him for Father's Day when the children were young, not noticing that it was the only mug on the tree. He frowned when he saw the cutlery drawer was empty and opened the dishwasher muttering under his breath. Why had his wife allowed every single item of cutlery to be used before she washed up? The dishwasher was empty barring a teaspoon that was hiding at the very bottom having evidently fallen out of the cutlery basket. He went to fill the kettle but that too had mysteriously disappeared. Had his wife gone mad? Was she replacing the entire contents of the kitchen? He opened the cupboard that held the saucepans – only the ancient, burned milk pan was inside. With a growing sense of anger, he filled it with water and put it on the stove to boil, then when it had, carefully tipped it into the mug before realising he had failed to add a tea bag. He opened the cupboard door that held all the drink-making things; teabags, coffee, sugar and cinnamon and swore when he found that cupboard, too, was empty. Graham emptied his mug into the sink and refilled it with cold water from the tap.

Carrying his mug, Graham went into the lounge and his jaw dropped. Only his chair and the wall-mounted television were inside. The sofa had disappeared along with the kitchen contents. Refusing to believe his own eyes, he switched the telly on and sat down in his chair to wait for his wife to come home. He was going to have a few things to say to her! On-screen, a bunch of angry women screeched and cackled about how disgusting it was that the prime minister had allegedly been caught receiving a blow job from the woman who was now his wife. "Lucky bastard," he mumbled, just before he dozed off.

The washing machine woke him as it tried to escape its confines when it came to a full, rattling spin. It sounded like an angry helicopter and obviously needed a service. Graham rolled his eyes. More expense. He closed his ears to the noise and looked up at the clock. Caroline was still not home. Where was she? Had she seen his car in the driveway and decided not to come in or had she ... for the first time Graham entertained the thought he'd been warding off ... had she left him? Properly left him? He reached for his phone and dashed off a text message:

Caro, I've come home. Where are you and where are all our things? We need to talk.

and pressed send. As soon as it disappeared from his screen he realised that he should have perhaps been a little less terse and tried again.

Caro, sweetheart. Please come home.

and then he sat back and waited for her reply. By the time night fell, he was still waiting.

Chapter Ten
Wednesday

SAS Investigations Office

Stuart answered the office phone when it rang with a sigh. He was just about to go and speak to a man who wanted his wife traced and was going to be late if this incoming call took too long. He'd spent several hours putting client files into their newly acquired filing cabinet and was already running a little late.

As he'd filed, he'd brooded about Madeleine's case and had to admit to himself that they were getting nowhere fast. They couldn't do anything more until they had spoken to Ted, which wouldn't be happening until tomorrow, although further bookings, mostly of the lost cat, dog and errant husband variety, were certainly beginning to come in thick and fast and were giving them both something else to work on.

"SAS Investig—" he began before a distorted voice cut him off.

"You don't know who you're meddling with, so for your own safety, stop the investigation into what happened to Madeleine Beaufort. Now. You won't receive a second warning."

"Is that Bobby?" Stuart said calmly, his heart rate picking up. "Robert Jones? We'd very much like to speak with you—" But he was speaking into a dead line.

"Shaks!" he yelled to his partner who was in the kitchen, making himself a cuppa. "We need to try and track a number. Have you had any luck getting your mate on board?"

Shakil came back into the office drying a mug with a tea towel. "Seeing him later on," he said. "Why, what's happened?"

"We're treading on someone's toes. I've just had a call telling us to back off trying to find out what happened to Maddy."

Shakil grinned. "That's good to know. Did you get the number?"

"Well yes, that's why I asked if you could track it."

Shakil laughed. "I'll pass it—"

"Cooee, it's me, Mum."

Shakil stopped mid-flow and both men turned towards the door as Caroline pushed through it, her face flushed. "I suppose you know by now that I've been to see the girl."

"How did you ... oh! *You're* Marie Beaufort? Did you break into the office yesterday, Mother?"

"You really need to change the locks you know," Caroline said. "I want to help you."

"What, you're going to change the locks for us?"

Caroline huffed. "No, Stuart. I want to help you catch Robert Jones, the man who beat Madeleine to a pulp. That poor child!"

Stuart blinked in surprise. "I would have thought you'd be the last person to want to help her."

"Why, because of your idiot father? Give me some credit, Stuart, what he did and what happened to that little girl are two utterly separate issues. What can I do?"

"How good are you at using a computer, Caroline?" Shakil asked.

"Not too bad. I'm on all the socials—I had to be, to try and keep a track of my children over the years when they were in the habit of shoving photos of all their stupidities all over the net."

Stuart's mouth dropped. "You didn't!"

Caroline smiled grimly. "Remember your 'friend' Shaniece? The girl who wouldn't go out with you?"

Stuart's mind flashed to a picture of a stunning blonde. "I was at school with her."

"Were you? Were you really? Remember her well, do you?"

"Well, not from school as such. But she remembered me and obviously I accepted when she sent me a friend request because she knew me—"

"And she's gorgeous, isn't she? So of course you said yes."

Stuart glared at his mother. "That's you?"

Caroline waggled her eyebrows at him, a small smile playing on her lips. "It was so much fun, turning down your advances, especially since I knew all the girls you were dating at the same time as you were trying your luck with her."

Stuart barked a laugh, unsure whether he should be laughing at his mother's ingenuity or angry with her for spying on him. He also felt slightly foolish—he'd really wanted to meet Shaniece.

Shakil roared with laughter. "Nice one, Mrs D. I think she's earned her credentials, don't you, Stu?"

"I've also been working through your Private Eye course," Caroline admitted, not meeting either of the men's eyes.

"How?"

"I downloaded it all to my laptop. You really need to use different passwords for everything, Stuart, even I know that! Did you know that your computer will generate a really strong one for you and save it? You don't even need to write it down."

Stuart gawped at his mother as Shakil began to clutch at his stomach, laughing fit to burst. "Owned. You've been owned," he managed to stammer out, wiping his streaming eyes. The two others watched, shaking their heads until he managed to get himself under control and asked, "Caroline, can you do a reverse search of a picture?"

"I can try," she said. "Who is it?"

"Robert Jones, we hope," Stuart said, gathering his thoughts and shaking his head at his mother's craftiness, "although you've probably already seen him, considering you've snooped through everything. The picture was in the file." He went to their newly acquired filing cabinet and pulled it out, then passed it to his mother. "We can't pay you, you know."

"That's okay," Caroline said, studying the grainy image. "I don't need paying. I want to help you catch this bastard. Do you know anything about him at all?"

"Not yet, we're going to see Madeleine's Monday night client tomorrow. We know where he'll be so we're hoping we can get some information from him."

"Where are you meeting him?"

"The local bowls club."

Caroline nodded, pressing her lips together, deep in thought. After a moment she looked up. "Have you had any luck tracing the third client?"

Stuart shook his head. "We staked Maddy's house out last week but he didn't show, so he's obviously been told what's happened to her."

"Who is he?"

Stuart shrugged. "We just know him as Mr P."

Caroline frowned. "I wonder why he's known as that. Don't you think it's odd?"

"Yes," Stuart said curtly. He wasn't entirely sure he wanted his mother to help them out. This was *their* business and she had a habit of taking over.

Caroline waved the photograph at them both. "I'll try to find this guy for you, but then I'm going to see Madeleine again."

"You're what?"

"Stu, don't you have somewhere to be?" Shakil reminded, tapping his watch. "I'll keep your mum company for a bit. At least until I have to go and meet Terry."

"Terry the Tech?" Caroline asked, smiling. "Such a nice boy. Now, Shakil, are you ever going to put that tea towel down and put the kettle on?"

"How do you know Terry?" Stuart asked, adding, "Actually, never mind, I'm not sure I want to know. See you later."

"Got it, Mrs D." Shakil grinned as he went back into the kitchen to do as he'd been told and Stuart darted from the office to go and meet his client.

The Clinic

"Who are you?" Sarah said, jumping up when Caroline opened the door to Madeleine's room in the early afternoon. "You can't just walk in here, you know."

Madeleine turned her head to see who Sarah was talking to and recognised the lady who had visited her before. She smiled, wincing as her cheeks lifted with the movement.

"S'Mum," she said croakily, her words only slightly mumbled.

"Oh! I'm sorry," Sarah said, making way for Caroline to enter. "Here, have a chair. I'll just go and grab you a coffee if you'd like one?"

Caroline nodded, not correcting the mistake. She smiled down at Madeleine and took the girl's hand in her own, being careful not to move the cast. "How are you feeling, sweetie?"

Madeleine nodded slightly. "Bit better," she said slowly but much more clearly, "but sore."

"You will be for a bit," Caroline said, taking in Madeleine's face. The swelling that had been so evident on her last visit had reduced and some of her bruises were now beginning to yellow. "You look better than you did."

Madeleine cleared her throat and grimaced. "Still look pretty bad though, eh?"

Caroline smiled, careful not to show her pity. "Bruises heal, bones knit back together. You'll be back on your feet before you know it."

"I'll take your word for it," Madeleine said. "I can't see properly – you're still blurry – and I'll never be a mum. The doctor who came in to see me today told me."

Caroline remained silent but gently indicated her empathy with a small squeeze of her fingers.

"Do you mind pretending to be my mum?" Madeleine asked, her eyes downcast.

"Not if that's what you need, no. Do you mind if I ask you why?"

"Don't know S'rah well enough," Madeleine said, her voice becoming hoarser with each sentence she spoke. She swallowed painfully.

Caroline frowned. Madeleine didn't know her at all yet she seemed to trust her more than she did the other girl who'd been in the room. "Is Sarah the girl who's gone to get coffee?" she asked.

"Mm." Madeleine began to cough and tears sprang into her eyes with the ferocity of the attack and the pain it caused to her ribcage.

"Would you like a drink? Would that help?" Caroline said, trying to hide her alarm. "Do you need a nurse?"

"Drink please, no nurse," Madeleine managed, watching as Caroline poured some water from the pitcher on the bedside table into a glass and took a fresh straw from its paper casing, bent it at the junction, put it into the glass and held it to her lips. She sipped and swallowed gratefully, moving the straw from her mouth with her tongue when she'd had enough. "Thank you."

"You're welcome," Caroline said, taking the glass and putting it back on the bedside table. She bent to smooth Madeleine's hair back from her face with gentle fingers. "Are you in much pain?"

"Not really. Drugs are good." Madeleine gave her a half-smile. "I hope I don't get addicted."

"I expect they'll wean you off them before they let you go," Caroline said, smiling in return. "Madeleine, do you trust Sarah?"

"Don't know. Only met her once before. Think she found me—prob'ly saved my life."

"So why aren't you sure about her?"

"Think her boss is my boss. She said it when she thought I couldn't hear her. Couldn't open my eyes or speak but I could hear her talking. Don't want him coming here. Don't tell her!" Madeleine's eyes opened wide in panic.

"Of course I won't," Caroline hurried to reassure her. "Madeleine, last time I was here I mentioned Bobby Jones. Did he do this to you?"

A guarded look came over Madeleine's face and she averted her eyes. "No," she said.

"You don't need to be scared," Caroline said gently. "There are guards at your door and people out looking for him. He'll be caught, don't worry, and you'll be safe. Madeleine, if it wasn't Bobby Jones, could he have hired someone, do you think?"

Madeleine shut down. She turned her head, closed her eyes and refused to open them again, even when Declan appeared at the door bearing an enormous bouquet of flowers and an equally large box of chocolates.

***

"She's gone," Declan said softly as the door swung shut behind Caroline. "You can open your eyes now."

Madeleine, who had actually drifted off to sleep while Declan and Caroline sat in awkward silence for almost an hour, stirred and opened her eyes. She looked around the room and offered him a half-smile. "Mum's gone?"

Declan nodded. "How are you feeling? The doc tells me you're going to be fine."

"Okay. Did you tell her about Bobby?"

"Your mum? No, that's the first time I've met her."

"She knows about him. How?"

"I wasn't aware that she did," Declan said, his eyes narrowing. "I wonder how she found out. Do you have a phone number for her? I'll give her a ring and tell her not to … not to get involved." Declan bit back what he had been about to say, that her mother would be best not to do anything stupid like trying to find Bobby.

"I haven't got her number," Madeleine said, a tear trickling down her face as she thought of the real mother who had disowned her long ago and subsequently died from a heroin overdose. "We lost touch years ago. She needs protection. If Bobby finds out she's asking questions, he'll be after her, too."

"How did she know you were here?"

"I don't know. I didn't ask her."

"Christ," said Declan.

***

Shakil, having contacted Terry the Tech to ask him to find out what he could about the number that had called to warn them off, turned his attention to Gregor, the guy who potentially provided clients to both Madeleine and Sarah. He called Sarah to ask her for the name of the website she was on, and after she was satisfied that he wasn't simply going on there to perv at the girls, she told him, adding, "…but you won't see anything until you go past the paywall. It's not cheap, Shakil."

"So I see," Shakil said, having already searched out the site and come across it. "Thanks, Sarah. Don't worry, I'm not interested in looking at anything I shouldn't and if I come across you, I'll definitely keep scrolling."

"Thanks," Sarah said dryly.

Shakil was already mentally kicking himself. "Not that I wouldn't want to, er, look, um, obviously, but…"

"I'd shut up while you still can," Sarah interjected. "I know what you meant. I was having you on."

Even though she couldn't see him, Shakil blushed, and as if she knew, Sarah laughed.

"Right, er, thanks then," he said, ending the call with relief.

He looked at the obviously high-end website. Sleek lettering beckoned him to enter and girls' faces flashed up in rotation on the screen, each of them either smiling or pouting suggestively. He clicked the button and was instantly taken to a registration page which was asking for his personal details as well as his method of payment. There was no menu and nothing else he could click on to try to dig into details of the site owner. He exited the page and thought for a while, then he rang Sarah again.

"It's me," he said when she answered. "Look, the site isn't giving anything away. Before I spend anything – and bear in mind that it will ultimately be you and Declan who pay for this, not us – when you log on to work, what do you see? I don't mean the punters, obviously, I mean, do you have any way of contacting your boss, this Gregor?"

"Bloody hell! How could I have been so stupid?" Sarah said, her anger at herself evident in her voice. "Declan said he knows Gregor. It's how he met Maddy; he does the girls' repairs. He'll be able to tell you whatever you need to know. Forget the website; give him a ring."

Shakil rolled his eyes, glad he hadn't paid anything out. "I'll ring him now."

"He's probably at the clinic," Sarah warned. "His mobile might be turned off."

***

Shakil took the stairs at the clinic two at a time. He tapped on the door of the Lilac Room, inserted his head and nodded for Declan to come out.

"Who's that?" Madeleine asked.

"A colleague," Declan said. "I was supposed to be fixing some flooring with him today and forgot."

"Don't lose work because of me," Madeleine said. "Go on, go then. I'll be fine, don't worry."

Declan nodded. He stared down at Madeleine's bruised face and then, in one quick and sudden move, bent and dropped a kiss onto her forehead, leaving as a growing smile spread across her face.

"You do work for Gregor," Shakil said without preamble as the door swung closed behind Declan. "How do you contact him?"

"I don't, generally he contacts me."

"Okay, I'm going to need his number."

Declan pulled a face. "It always shows as a private number."

"How does he pay you? Is it always cash?"

Declan shook his head. "No, never cash. I go through his books legitimately. It's always by bank transfer."

Shakil smiled triumphantly. "Then you have more information than you realise. How does it show up in your account?"

"I'm not sure."

The two men stood aside as a nurse bustled up the hallway. They waited until she'd entered another room and the door had closed behind her then continued their conversation.

"It must show up as something on your statement, can you remember what?" Shakil asked.

Declan thought for a moment, then shook his head. "I'll need to log in to find out," he said. "I haven't got it set up on my phone and my laptop's at home. Let me just cancel the job I was going to do this afternoon and we'll go back and find out."

The two men left the clinic as Declan made the call and gave Shakil his address. "I'll meet you there," he told him, opening the door to his trusty and ancient Ford Focus, "unless you want to come with me? I can drop you back here again afterwards?"

Shakil eyed the car warily.

"It looks worse than it is," Declan said, patting the car's roof before he slid into the driver's seat. "It's up to you, obviously."

Shakil went to the passenger side and pressed the handle to open the door. Nothing happened until Declan reached across and opened it from inside, his face red. "Yeah, that's a thing," he said as Shakil got in. "At least nobody can get to you from that side, eh?"

Shakil grinned wryly and put his seatbelt on.

Later, at Declan's house, the two men poured over Declan's bank statement together.

"It looks like it comes in via an umbrella company," Declan said, pointing out several transactions that coincided with dates he'd worked for Gregor. "See here?"

Shakil already had his phone out and was searching for the company online. He showed the screen to Declan. Over eleven million hits of that company name were showing. They scrolled through the first few pages and then looked at each other.

"This is useless," Shakil said. "Honestly, these guys are as slippery as eels. I think we'll have to wait until tomorrow to get anywhere."

"What's happening tomorrow?"

"We've tracked down where Ted, Monday's client, is likely to be. We're paying him a little visit." Shakil told him about the Bowls Club and Ted being a new member.

"I'm in," Declan said immediately. "You don't think he's going to tell you anything, do you? I'll wait outside and follow him home."

Chapter Eleven
Thursday

Crickleby Bowls Club

The day dawned fine and bright. The perfect day for watching old men play bowls, Stuart thought darkly as he showered and dressed in his second-best suit, the first having been put into the dry cleaners over the weekend. He made a mental note to remember to collect it later. He hadn't slept at all well; he had been woken several times by the slightest of noises and it wasn't the first time, it had been happening ever since they'd started the business up. He checked his phone for messages, replied to a couple, and then put it into his back pocket. Next, he looked through the window and checked the street for signs of anybody lurking around, and when he was satisfied nobody was lying in wait for him, double-checked the locks were in place on all the windows of his flat, grabbed his keys and left, double-locking the door behind him.

Stuart was feeling the effects of not having had a spliff for a couple of weeks and was decidedly jittery. He and Shakil had made a pact that, once things really picked up with the Agency, neither would smoke weed and they had, so far as he knew, both stuck to it. He certainly had. He recognised that the anxiety and irritability he was feeling was par for the course for quitting cold turkey in the way they had, but his paranoia level was high this morning and his eyes felt gritty from the lack of a decent night's sleep. As he walked to the car, he continually looked around him, alert to the threat of danger. So when a passing pigeon dropped a slimy, chalky deposit on the top of his head, he jumped about a foot in the air and let out a yell.

A small child, who was walking along the road hand in hand with his mother, laughed. "Birdie pooped on your head, Mister," he yelled.

"I know," Stuart said, wiping as much of the stuff off as he could and then wiping his hand against a garden wall, the best he could do unless he went back inside and washed his hair. "Naughty birdie!"

The little boy carried on up the road yelling, "Naughty birdie, naughty birdie," over and over again until his mother tugged at his hand and told him to stop.

"It's supposed to be good luck," Stuart muttered to himself as he let himself into his car and switched the engine on. His guts roiled.

It was in this grim frame of mind that he met up with Shakil around the corner from the car park of Crickleby Bowls Club and acknowledged him with a curt nod.

"He's not here yet," Shakil said. "None of them are, apart from Janice. She saw me."

"How did she see you?" Stuart snapped. "Weren't you even trying not to be seen?"

"What's bitten you?" Shakil said. He nodded to the vehicle behind his own. "That's her car. When I arrived, she was bending down to get something and I didn't see her in it. Her head popped up as I switched the engine off and it was too late to drive away."

"She'll be expecting trouble then. Let's hope she doesn't warn Ted. Why the hell doesn't she use the car park?"

The reason became evident as time passed by. Partially hidden by an overgrown hedge, the two men sat on a wall and watched as various cars, driven by various people of various ages (provided you considered anything from seventy and upwards to fall under the category of various) began to pull into the car park. It was a miracle there wasn't a serious accident as not one of them could park. They pulled in, slung their vehicles into an approximation of the marked slots, and tottered out, greeting each other with waves, grins and shouts of greeting whilst dodging incoming cars that appeared to be aiming directly for them and toting bags that looked far too heavy for them to cope with.

"Christ on a bike they have an average age of ninety," Stuart said, shaking his head in wonder as a brand new BMW side-swiped a brand new Mercedes, leaving a streak of exposed metal a foot long. The driver looked to be an ancient skeleton with wrinkled, transparent skin and he waved a skeletal hand at the driver of the Mercedes, an equally old man who appeared to have the same hairdresser as Michael Fabricant, by way of apology. "If you still know me at that age, put me out of my misery—or at least, take away my car keys."

"Can any of them *see*?" Shakil said, equally as shocked. "They should have their licences revoked, surely none of them are fit to drive? They'd never pass an eyesight test."

"Is Ted one of them, do you suppose?"

Shakil shrugged. "Honestly? I can't imagine a single one of them being able to get it up, can you?"

Stuart laughed. "No. And I seriously cannot imagine Madeleine allowing any of them to be one of her clients."

Shakil put his head to one side. "We don't actually know her though, do we? She may do."

Stuart raised his eyebrows and nodded. Shakil was right, they didn't really know Madeleine, although it felt as though they did.

After the old men had doddered their way into the club, another car arrived. This one was driven by a man who, whilst old, was not yet in the same bracket as the others. The driver pulled up by the side of the road, looked into the car park and shook his head. He got out of his dark blue Jaguar, reached into the back seat and pulled out a bag, and then went directly into the club without once looking in their direction.

"That's him," Stuart said, staring at the man as he walked away from them, more nimble than the other members. "I'd lay odds on that being Ted Tennant."

Shakil was already on the phone, relaying the make and number plate to Declan. "Let's go," he said once he was done. "Let's go and make this bloke squirm."

Janice looked up from the table she was sitting at as Shakil appeared around the corner of the club building and began to walk towards the bowling green, following the man they suspected of being Ted Tennant. She tipped her head fractionally towards the man he was following, rose and walked over to a small group of geriatrics and began to engage them all in conversation.

Ted waved for her to come back to the table but Janice's head was turning towards the group of men she was with and she either didn't see the wave or was choosing to ignore it. Ted didn't seem to mind. He kept walking, passing the empty table and heading towards another small group of cadaverous men who were laughing at something, while Shakil closed the gap between them.

"Mr Tennant?" Shakil put his hand on the man's shoulder and tugged.

The man automatically found himself turning towards Shakil, his eyes widening. "I say," he said. "Who's asking?"

"Mr Tennant, may I have a quiet word?" Shakil briefly flashed a fake badge in front of Ted's nose and just as swiftly whisked it away again.

Ted shrugged off his hand. "Not here," he said and began to walk back the way he'd come. Shakil kept pace with him. "I suppose this is about Madeleine?" Ted said quietly as they walked. "How is the girl?"

"You knew then?"

Ted nodded. "I received a message to say she'd been attacked, poor love."

"From who?"

Ted looked at him blankly. "What do you mean?"

"You said you received a message. Who did the message come from? Was it via text or telephone?"

"Text," Ted said.

"From...?" Shakil put his head to one side and stopped walking.

Ted didn't which rather put Shakil out. "Mr Tennant. Unless you want me to start shouting questions at you, may I suggest you stop walking," he said loudly.

Around the corner, Stuart grinned. He was ready to join in should Ted prove tricky to deal with.

"Mr...? Actually, you failed to provide me with your name or rank, which leads me to suspect that you are not in fact a policeman," Ted said coolly, "which, of course, means that I am not required to speak to you."

Stuart made his appearance and blocked Ted's way while Shakil caught up with them.

"Oh, another idiot thug. Why do you always travel in pairs?" Ted said, running his eyes from Stuart's feet to the top of his head. "Did you know you have bird shit on top of your head?"

"It's lucky," Stuart said. "Are you feeling lucky?"

Ted laughed. "Ah, the cliché. Come on then, Al Capone, let's talk. I have nothing to hide."

"I'd like to know where you were last Wednesday night from nine onwards," Shakil said as the three of them continued to walk. They were now in the car park, moving surprisingly swiftly considering Ted's age, each dodging around the randomly parked vehicles.

"Let me see," Ted said. He stopped walking and stood rubbing his hand against his chin and pretending to think. "Ah, yes, last Wednesday I had an early night. I was tucked up in bed by ten." He began to walk again and now all three were close to the car park exit.

"Anyone with you?" Stuart asked, positioning himself in front of Ted to stop him from walking any further and getting to his car.

A flash of annoyance distorted Ted's features. "I rather think that's none of your business," he said smartly, sidestepping.

Stuart moved with him. "Maybe not, but it could provide you with an alibi."

Ted stopped walking. "An alibi for what? Beating ten shades of shit out of the girl I've been visiting, as I'm certain you already know, for the past couple of years? Why would I?"

"Because you thought you were being watched on your last visit to her."

Ted tutted. "Still no reason to beat her up, is it? I can't control what other people do, can I?"

"No, but if you thought she'd set it up, you might think differently."

"Had she?" Now Ted's eyes narrowed.

"So was anyone with you on Wednesday?" Shakil cut in smoothly. "Can they confirm you were where you say you were?"

"What? In bed? I dare say my wife would be able to confirm it, but let me tell you now that if you approach her about this in any way, shape or form, it won't end well for you."

"Is that a threat?" Stuart asked, adrenalin pumping. "Did you just hear this guy threaten us, Shaks?"

"Sure did," Shakil said. "Big mistake. For starters, we're not tiny girls who can't fight back—and for seconds, you just told us you have something to hide."

"All I told you was to leave my wife out of this. I had nothing to do with what happened to Madeleine. I was as shocked by it as she was—"

"I sincerely doubt that, considering you instigated the attack on her. She was almost killed and she's been in a coma ever since." Stuart's voice began to rise as he spoke. "Did you know your mate Bobby broke her nose, her cheekbone, both her arms and several ribs? And that's only half of what he did to her exterior. Do you want to know about what he did to her internally?"

"I don't believe you," Tom said, but his voice faltered slightly. "He told me he'd had her punished because he believed she slept with the guy who saw us. He said he used the whip, so not to visit her for a week or two ... Bobby wouldn't go that far."

Shakil took out his phone. He'd taken several photographs of Madeleine when they first went to visit her and now he shoved them under Ted's nose. "Wouldn't go that far?" he spat as he scrolled through them, showing the extent of the damage to Madeleine's almost unrecognisable face, the two arms in plaster and the various drips she was hooked up to.

"I ... I had ... I had no idea!" Ted stuttered, his eyes widening and a look of horror spreading on his face as picture after picture appeared onscreen. "Is that really *Madeleine*? Look, I promise you, I had no idea about this. Are you sure *Bobby* is responsible for this?"

"Where can we find him?" Stuart pinned Ted with his eyes. "He needs to be stopped from ever doing anything like this again, don't you agree?"

Ted's head dipped in an abrupt nod. "I do. I can give you a telephone number but I don't know where he lives. Can you ... would you tell Madeleine I'm sorry? I wouldn't have mentioned it had I known what would happen."

"The number?" Shakil said.

"I don't have it on me. It's stored on a burner phone and that's in my office."

"Let's go," Stuart said, taking hold of Ted's arm. "We'll take your car. Shaks, you okay to follow?"

Shakil nodded.

***

After they'd retrieved Bobby's phone number from Ted's office and returned to the Bowls Club so Stuart could collect his own car, Declan took over surveillance. Whilst the two men had been talking to Ted, he'd placed a tracker with audio listening enabled beneath the Jaguar, and now he could see exactly where Ted went after Stuart and Shakil had left him at his office; a large, sprawling building in the heart of Crickleby that was owned by a company called 'Compliance Assured'.

The man's first stop was to a leafy house in the suburbs of Crickleby. Declan, in his works van, pulled up along the road from the house and watched as Ted used a key to enter. The door closed behind him. Declan noted down the address and waited. He didn't have to wait for long. Around twenty minutes later, the front door opened and Ted came out, now clad in a suit and tie, followed by an elderly, grey-haired lady who used a stick to help her along. Ted waited until she was safely down the step and on the pathway before he locked the door behind them, helped her into the car, and then got back into the driver's seat. The car passed Declan's van and Ted didn't even glance his way; he was too busy telling the lady, his wife as became abundantly clear later, about the imaginary game of bowls he hadn't played and the woman was responding with a variety of bored-sounding oohs and ahhs. Declan could hear everything the pair were saying extremely clearly. The conversation, an entire fabrication on Ted's part, was dull, to say the least.

Leaving it for a few seconds until the car had turned right at the end of the road, Declan began to follow the signal from the tracker being careful to remain out of sight. Ted was driving back into town. On the way, a squabble broke out between the pair on the merits of stopping outside the dubiously entitled *'Hair Today'* salon, the evident destination of their journey.

"Edgar, there are never any wardens around. Tell me the last time you ever saw one?" the female voice said.

"Last week actually, just after I dropped you off," Ted replied. He sounded defeated already.

"Oh, don't be so stupid. If you get a ticket, you know you can call and have the matter dropped. It's not like you haven't done it before, is it? Patrick must have them on a hotline, the amount you receive."

"June, it's not really that easy…"

But the woman wasn't listening to any arguments. "Just pull up outside. It only takes a second and I'll be out of your, ha ha, *hair*."

"Very funny, dear," Ted said, allowing his wife to win the squabble by pulling over on a set of double yellows outside the salon. He scuttled around to the passenger door and began to help her out. A traffic warden approached and Declan, who had pulled up into a designated parking space further up the road, watched with some amusement as Ted angrily waved the warden away, indicating his wife's need for assistance. The warden shrugged and wrote the ticket anyway, sticking it firmly beneath the windscreen wiper blade as Ted and June entered the salon. It really wasn't turning out to be a good day for Ted Tennant and Declan's amusement increased when Ted returned to the car and tried ineffectually to remove the ticket. In the end, he left it there and drove off, muttering to himself about his fucking wife, the fucking ticket, and the equally fucking miserable traffic warden.

Declan allowed him to pull away and watched as Ted merged the Jag into the rush hour traffic. He wasn't worried about losing him; the tracker appeared to be doing its job as admirably as the audio listening device. Now Declan heard the sound of a phone ringing and he pressed record on his own phone.

"You bloody lunatic!" Ted shouted when the call was answered. "Whipped her? You nearly fucking killed her!"

Declan smiled grimly: Ted had called Robert 'Bobby' Jones.

"Did you see the state you left her in?" Ted was saying now, not letting the other party to the call get a word in edgewise. "You fool! If this comes out, we're all done for. You should have finished her off!"

Declan's blood ran cold and thundered in his ears so he missed the next few words. When he was able to hear clearly again, Ted was saying, "... awake and obviously talking. Does Gregor know? ... What about Paddy? ... No, you're telling him, not me ... Yes, I know he's going to be upset, of course I do! Do you think I'm a fool? ... Did you tell him the same as you told me? That you'd given her a good whipping? ... More fool you then ... We need to meet, decide what we're going to do next. There are a couple of thugs after you, by the way ... Oh, you knew did you? Thanks for the heads up! ... ... I have around an hour now. I'll meet you at the GC in ten minutes, and you'd better bloody arrive by then or I'll call Paddy myself."

Declan watched the tracker as Ted drove on into the centre of Crickleby Town and parked up at the rear of the Gentleman's Club, known locally as the meat market, a place where businessmen from all over went either to arrange dubious deals or to ogle naked 'lap dancers'. He'd never felt the need to visit it before and had heard rumours about what actually went on inside; lap dancing being strictly a euphemism. He parked in the closest multi-storey and rang to let Stuart and Shakil know what was happening, where he was and what he was planning to do, then he got into the back of his van and changed from his work attire into a suit.

He arrived at the back entrance to the GC just as Ted and another man were climbing the steps to go inside. Declan's eyes widened when he saw who was accompanying Ted. He pulled out his phone and took several photographs which he emailed to SAS Investigations, and then he followed them in. As he topped the stairs, he saw both men passing through a door that was guarded by two bouncers. Inside the front door, a woman sat at a booth, idly filing her nails. She looked up.

"Which room?"

"That one," Declan nodded towards the door he'd seen Ted and the other man go through, praying that there wasn't some sort of special word he needed to use. There wasn't. The woman rang up the extortionate amount the club charged for access to that room and held out her hand for payment. Declan paid in cash, wincing internally at the cost, had his hand stamped with invisible ink, and then read the discrete, stylised black card the receptionist handed to him.

Den of Iniquity
What happens within these walls, remains within these walls.
You have been warned.

He went through the double doors that led into a large open bar where several groups of men stood around, drinking malt whisky and other spirits, heading straight to the door at the rear where he held out his hand and one of the seriously huge bouncers flashed a metal wand at it. A circle appeared briefly and disappeared as soon as the wand moved away. The bouncer moved aside and allowed Declan to pass through. Without looking around, Declan headed inside and made for the bar where he ordered himself a scotch on the rocks. Once it arrived, he allowed himself to turn and look around, letting his eyes acclimatise to the dim lighting and his ears to the loud music that boomed from invisible speakers. He scoped out the clientele, a motley crew of mostly older men who were standing around the edge of an 'L' shaped catwalk where three naked girls were performing around poles. He watched as one of the girls jumped down and went over to a man who had been waving a wad of notes at her. The man reached for her breasts and began to play with her nipples, then he pushed on her shoulders, urging her downwards. The girl relieved him of his cash, dropped to her knees in front of him, unzipped his trousers and began to perform oral sex on him, cheered on by a crowd of onlookers.

A second girl appeared from nowhere to join the party, allowing anybody holding out cash that she swiftly removed from them to touch her wherever they pleased. Smiling and writhing sinuously, she lifted a leg onto a low table for one particular man, allowing easier access for his hand and moving her pelvis against him. Within seconds, he had her bent over that same table and was taking her from behind, while yet another inserted his penis into her open mouth, accompanied by loud cheers from the rest of their crowd.

Sickened, Declan swallowed his scotch in one gulp and looked away. Ted and the other man weren't part of that crowd. His eyes skimmed darkened booths until they found his targets. The pair were engrossed in a deep, and from the looks of it, angry, conversation and were ignoring the kerfuffle by the stage. Declan took out his phone again and snapped a couple of quick shots while pretending to check his messages.

"Can I please you?" A voice speaking broken English came from Declan's right shoulder and he pocketed his phone swiftly. He turned to see a brunette standing beside him, smiling. She was young and pretty, too young and pretty to be doing this kind of work. She took the glass from his hand. "May I please fill this again for you? You like?"

Knowing she would be in trouble if he refused, Declan nodded. He peeled off a twenty and passed it to her. She nodded and passed the glass over the bar to the bartender, then returned it to him filled with ice and a lousy half-measure of scotch. There was no change. The girl had a piece of ice in her hand and, as Declan watched, she slid it suggestively down her chest and then around each of her nipples, making them stiffen. "You like?" she said, sliding the ice lower. "I make this melt then I make you melt?"

Declan stayed her hand with his own before it reached where she intended it to go. He shook his head once, pulling a face that showed regret for the benefit of anyone watching. "I'm just here to watch," he said gently. Then, because he couldn't help himself, he added, "Why are you doing this? You're far too young and pretty; isn't there anything else you can do?"

The girl's face showed an instant of fear, and Declan released his hold on her arm. Her smile was back before Declan could really register what he'd seen. "I like you," she said, rubbing her breasts against his arm and tonguing the almost melted ice cube suggestively. "You buy me champagne and come to back room with me? I make you very happy."

"No," Declan said firmly, moving away from the girl.

"Come here my darlin'," a drunken voice called. "You can make me very happy."

The girl bit her lip and turned towards the sound of the voice. Plastering a smile on her face, she sashayed across the couple of feet between them and was soon busy on her knees, sucking more than an ice cube.

Declan turned his attention back to Ted's booth. Ted was now on his feet, leaning across the table and hissing something into his partner's face. He slapped the table once, then pulled himself up to his full height and stalked away, pushing through the crowds of men in his haste to depart. Declan watched him go and sent his eyes back to the man at the booth.

The third dancer was now seated on his table, leaning back in front of him, legs splayed one to each side of him, while he used an open beer bottle as a replacement penis. Declan pulled out his phone and pretended to send a text as he recorded what was happening. Then he drained his scotch and went home. He knew where they could find Bobby now.

***

Shakil was having a somewhat better evening despite several inadvertent attempts to derail it. He'd arranged a date with Trudy, the nurse from the clinic, and was currently sitting opposite her in the garden of The Orangerie. He'd managed to book the final open table and the pair were deciding what they were going to eat and sipping iced Margaritas in the warmth of the night air. The sun was just beginning to make its final descent and the sky was streaked with pinks and purples. Citronella candles burned at each of the tables to keep wasps away and fairy lights twinkled merrily around the walls and fences of the entire garden. Shakil thought it looked magical and it matched the feeling he had burning in his belly. Trudy was just as lovely outside of the clinic as she had appeared inside it.

"I think I'm going to have the peppered steak, a side of fries and salad," Trudy finally announced to the waitress who was patiently waiting for their decisions. "I've heard good things about it."

Shakil had decided on the maple-glazed chicken breast and told her so. "...although the steak here is divine," he said, blinking at hearing himself saying the word divine. He capped it off by kissing his thumb and index finger in the way he'd seen chefs on the telly do, and winced.

"I'll take your word for it," Trudy said, biting back a smile and wondering why this lovely man was so evidently nervous.

"Any sides, sir?" the waitress asked.

Shakil coloured. "Yes, fries and a side salad for me, too, please." He turned to Trudy, "And shall we have a bottle of Prosecco?"

"Can we just have a bottle of red?" she said. "I'm not keen on fizz."

Shakil smiled properly for the first time. "Thank God," he said. "I hate the stuff too. I thought all girls liked it."

The waitress smiled and added it to their order. "I'll be back with your wine shortly," she said. "Bon appetite."

"Bon appetite to you, too," Shakil said unthinkingly.

Both Trudy and the waitress giggled.

"I'm not doing a very good job here, am I?" Shakil said wryly. "I'm not usually this…" He raised a hand and waved it in front of his face, "this inept."

"I wouldn't be here if I thought you were," Trudy said gently, taking and keeping hold of his fluttering fingers. "I don't date often, and you're the first person who has offered to take me out when I'm at work that I've said yes to. I have a rule—no dating patients or their visitors—they're usually full of heightened emotions and that makes for lousy dates. I *wanted* to come out with you."

Shakil offered her a grateful smile and squeezed her hand slightly. "I'm glad you said yes."

The evening got a lot better from that point…

Chapter Twelve
Friday

SAS Investigations Office

Stuart and Shakil were just having their morning cuppa and discussing the things they were supposed to be doing that day. Stuart's first stop was to meet a middle-aged woman who believed her new partner was not divorced at all and still living with his wife. She'd caught him telling one too many tall tales and had asked the firm to follow him. Stuart was meeting with her to find out a little bit more and to discover the best time to catch him out if, in fact, he was cheating on her.

"It's just, I've never been the other woman and I have no intention of continuing things with him if that's what he's turning me into," she'd said on the phone, sounding both cross and sad at the same time. "I really like him."

They were meeting in the park where the woman walked her dog every day as she was reluctant to come to the office in case she was spotted entering or to invite them into her house because, "the neighbours would talk and if he isn't cheating on me, it'll look like I'm cheating on him."

Shakil was supposed to be meeting up with Terry the Tech who, so far, had been unable to discover the owner of the phone who had called to threaten them. It appeared to be a burner and untraceable.

All that changed when Declan appeared in the doorway saying, "Did you get the pictures I sent you?"

Stuart shook his head.

"They'll be in your emails." Declan was now pacing the floor. "Quick, open them. I want to see your reactions."

Stuart opened his laptop and, while he waited for it to boot up, Shakil joined him on his side of the desk. Once the email was opened and the attachments on screen, both men's eyes widened.

"*This* is Bobby Jones?" Shakil said.

Declan nodded grimly and played them the recording of the phone conversation Ted had had in his car prior to the meeting at the GC.

"But this is—"

"Robert Flanaghan, our local Member of Parliament, if I'm not mistaken," Declan said, "and he's some piece of work. I hope you haven't had your breakfast yet—look at what I took later, inside the club."

"Shit just got real," Stuart said glumly after a quick glance. "No wonder we were warned off."

"Now what the hell do we do?" Shakil said.

"Why didn't the neighbours who told us about 'Bobby' realise he wasn't who they thought? Robert Flanaghan can't have been the same person who went to school with their son, can he? Men don't tend to change surnames."

"They probably recognised him because he is who he is, and got a bit confused," Shakil said, hitting the nail on the head without knowing it.

"Hmmn. So what next? Do we arrange to meet him and tell him all this is going off to the papers if he doesn't talk to us?" Declan asked. "We all have copies now, don't we? And, no offence here guys, but you really need to beef up the locks on your office door. A kid could break in."

Shakil glanced at Stuart. "He's right, and so was your mum."

Declan frowned. "Your mum?"

"My mum," Stuart acknowledged, shifting uncomfortably. "She wanted to know about Dad and broke in to try to find out. You may as well know that she's been to see Maddy, too."

A light bulb flicked on in Declan's head. "Hang on a minute," he said angrily. "Why didn't you tell me Madeleine was your sister? And what does your father have to do with any of this?"

Stuart's face was almost comical. "What? Madeleine's not my sister. Look, sit down," he told Declan. "Let me call and put my client off for an hour; it's a long story…"

***

Graham was feeling terribly perturbed. His texts to his wife had all gone unanswered and now he was beginning to feel a little hard done by. What had he done that was so bad? There were plenty of men who had long-standing affairs and he'd only had one moment of madness. Surely that was forgivable? He'd been a good husband, hadn't he? He was also beginning to feel hungry and knew that he ought to go to the supermarket, but he had nothing to cook food in, and, he thought angrily, buying food was Caroline's job. He went into the kitchen and checked every cupboard again in the hope they'd magically filled and he'd dreamed it all, but no, they were still all empty. Even if he did buy food, he had nothing to store it in – she'd taken the fridge freezer.

His mobile phone rang and he grabbed it up, snatching the cord that was charging it from the outlet. "Yes, Caro, it's me, I'm here. Please come home," he said, hearing the sound of desperation in his voice.

Jasmine's snort hit his ear. "It's me, not Mum."

"Sweetie, where are you both? Please can you try to get Mum to come home—and you, obviously."

Jasmine snorted. "You have a snowball's chance in hell of that happening, Dad. What the hell possessed you to sleep with a prostitute?"

"Is that why you called me? To tell me off? Where are you both?"

"Tell you off?" Jasmine's hand shook with anger as she pressed her phone to her ear. "Do you understand what you did? Do you have no fucking clue how badly you hurt her? I'm not ringing to *tell you off* Dad, I'm ringing to tell you to stop sending bloody stupid messages to her. In fact, I'm calling to tell you not to contact her again. She's divorcing you. Do you understand now? She's divorcing you and I'm glad—you deserve everything you have coming! You disgust me."

Graham stared at his phone as the line went dead. Caroline was divorcing him? That couldn't be true ... could it? What had Stuart told them? He dialled his son's number and it went straight to voicemail. Graham left him a lengthy rant, laying the blame entirely on his son's shoulders, and then hung up the phone triumphantly, a triumph that evaporated swiftly when he had the thought that his son may very well let his mother hear what he'd said. He rang back again and left another message apologising profusely and asking his son to call him, ending the message by saying, "I'm back at home by the way, although I can't really call it home when everything's been taken from it. Please can you ask your mother to come home again? She won't listen to me and your sister tells me I should be leaving her alone."

He paced the kitchen for several minutes, expecting Stuart's return call to be swift. When it didn't happen, he grabbed his keys and took himself off to the supermarket. He didn't intend to starve while he waited for his family to come to their senses.

He returned having purchased a new microwave, a mini fridge, and a week's worth of groceries and lugged them all into the house. He installed the new electricals and unpacked the bags of food, then realised he'd forgotten to buy milk or tea bags. He grabbed his keys a second time and went back to the supermarket.

As he pulled back onto the driveway, he spotted a man lurking in some bushes further along the road and the back of his neck prickled. He pulled up the handbrake, got out, locked the car and let himself into the house, triple locking the door behind him. He went into the kitchen and drew down the blinds, then he tiptoed around the rest of the house, drawing curtains and pulling down blinds so that nobody outside would be able to see him. When nothing happened; nobody knocked on the door and nobody came through the garden, he relaxed a little and realised he'd forgotten to buy himself a kettle. He put some water into the manky pan and put that onto the stove to boil. He put a teabag into his mug and, when the water was at boiling point, added that too.

He was just settling down in his chair in the lounge, ready to watch the afternoon film, when the doorbell rang. Graham froze with his mug halfway to his mouth. He pressed mute on the remote control and stayed in place, his heart hammering in his chest.

The doorbell rang again.

Something scrabbled at the front door and then a voice rang out. "Dad, let me in! It's me, Stuart. Why have you locked yourself in?"

Graham jumped up with relief and went to open the door. Stuart came in and shook his head as his father locked it again behind him.

"Why's it so gloomy in here?" Stuart asked, walking into the lounge once his father was sure nobody was going to gain access through the front door.

"I drew the curtains. A strange man was hanging around just up the road."

"I know, he's one of ours. He's keeping an eye on the place while Mum's away and let me know someone had come in; that's why I'm here."

"Didn't you get my messages?"

Stuart shook his head. "I've been busy."

"Your mother; where is she?" Graham turned pleading eyes towards his son.

Stuart shook his head, his lips curling downwards, hardening his heart against the yellowing bruise surrounding his father's eye. "I'm not gonna tell you, Dad, especially if you're thinking of staying here. She's already been through enough without you adding to it. And you really shouldn't stay here, you know. Whoever got to Madeleine is extremely likely to come after you, too. You should have stayed put wherever you scuttled off to."

"I didn't scuttle off," Graham said indignantly.

"You ran away without coming clean about what you did and left it to me to sort it out. I'd call that scuttling off, wouldn't you?"

Graham deflated. "I wasn't thinking clearly."

"You haven't been thinking clearly for quite some time, have you?"

"Stuart, you have never been faithful to one woman in your entire life," Graham said incredulously. "Aren't you being a tad hypocritical?"

"I'm not married to any of them, am I?"

Graham sighed. "Look, son…"

"Don't," Stuart said sharply. He paced around the room and then turned back to his father. "What the hell are you doing back here?"

"I wanted to come home," Graham said wistfully. "I miss your mother."

Stuart plonked himself to the carpet and stared at his father in disbelief. "Dad, this isn't your home anymore. Mum's divorcing you and she's keeping the house."

"Not if I have anything to do with it," Graham said, his mouth dry. Jasmine had been telling the truth. Caroline was going to end their marriage and there may be nothing he could do about that but she wasn't going to take his house away from him. "Over my dead body," he added, in case his son hadn't taken the point.

"Stay here and it very well may come to that," Stuart said, getting to his feet. "Lock up tight tonight, Dad, because if anyone comes for you, I won't come running."

"Why are you on her side in this?" Graham asked. "I made one mistake, Stuart, one mistake."

"Yeah, but it was a bloody big one."

Graham watched in disbelief as his son unlocked the front door and walked through it, leaving his father to it.

***

Caroline had been to see a solicitor about a divorce. She was now sitting at a table in a small café, across from Jasmine who had gone with her but not gone in to see the solicitor, relaying the information she'd been given.

"Does your brother know where your father is staying?" she finished up. "The solicitor will need an address to be able to contact him in writing to let him know I've filed."

"I expect he does. He seems to have information on everything, and I expect Dad's told him," Jasmine said, taking a sip of her mocha coffee. "Are you sure you want to do this, Mum?"

Caroline nodded. "I could have forgiven a full-on affair easier, funnily enough. At least there would have been emotions involved and less likelihood of my catching something from him. And no," she added, catching Jasmin's look of horror, "there's no likelihood at all that I have—your father and I haven't, um, well…"

"I get it," Jasmine said. "Thank your lucky stars, eh?"

Caroline nodded and swallowed some of her own coffee. "Why did he do it?" she said unhappily. "I mean, really? Was he so miserable with me? With us?"

Jasmine shook her head, unable to answer without going on a huge rant. "I don't know," she eventually managed, "but you'll get by, Mum. There's someone out there who will be miles better than Dad ever was, just you wait and see."

Caroline smiled, although her eyes were brimming. She patted her daughter's hand. "I'm in my late fifties, Jazz. That's not going to happen now, is it? And, to be frank, I'm really not sure I would like to go through another relationship. Your father and I were together for so long; how could I adapt to someone different?"

"What if he was loving, kind, generous, hard-working? What if he absolutely adored you? I want that for you, Mum. You should want it for yourself, too."

Caroline looked at her daughter. "I thought I had that with your father."

Jasmine barked a laugh. "Dad? Kind, generous, hard-working? Seriously? He's always been a miserable old so-and-so; look at the way he talks about us all—he thinks Stu's a waste of space; he wanted me to have some high-flying job so he'd look good; he talked down to you all the time. You were just used to him and looked past it all. Come on, he semi-retired at fifty and spent all his time down in the basement in his 'office'. Was he working down there? Was he bringing money in? No, you've been living off savings and savings run out before you know it."

Caroline's head rocked backwards as she listened to what her daughter was saying, shocked at how little she apparently thought of her father. "Does Stu feel the same as you?"

Jasmine blinked. "Mum, Stu hasn't got along with Dad for a decade or more; he puts up with him for the same reason I do, because he's married to you. Every time he visits, Dad runs him down. Look at how he talked about Stu's business. He didn't think it would amount to a thing, did he? And look at him! SAS Investigations has been the making of my brother. He's involved, solving things, and—"

Caroline inclined her head. "And what?"

"Nothing," Jasmine muttered.

"—and if he hadn't started his business, he would never have known about what your father did. Is that what you were going to say?"

Jasmine pulled a face and nodded, not meeting her mother's eyes.

"Jazz, we also wouldn't have known that the burglary wasn't a burglary and that we weren't safe at home. He did us a huge favour, in all respects. I needed to know what happened because otherwise, I would have been living an enormous lie. Your father would never have admitted what he did, and, I have no doubt, he would have continued paying Madeleine for her services had he got away with it. Unfortunately, your father walked into something much larger than using a prostitute."

"What do you mean?"

Caroline shook her head. "I can't tell you – and it's best that you don't know."

Jasmine frowned. "What do you mean?"

"Just that," Caroline said, picking up her handbag and pushing her chair back signalling the end of the conversation. "Now, we've been out in the open too long already. Let's go home."

SAS Investigations Office

It was the end of what had been a long day and Stuart and Shakil had locked the office door, kicked off their shoes and were weighing up developments.

"You know one thing we haven't done?" Stu said, draining the last of the can of Bud he'd been drinking after relaying the details of his visit with his father and then the visit he'd made to the female client who wanted to know if her partner was cheating on her.

Shakil shook his head.

"We've accounted for two of Madeleine's clients, but we haven't identified Mr P, have we?"

"Do we need to?"

Stu nodded slowly. "I think we do, actually, yes. Look, Maddy knew Ted and Bobby by their actual names—and yes, I know Bobby was Robert Flanaghan, not Jones, so he pulled the wool over her eyes there, but she only knows Friday's client by an initial. Why is that—and what's the likelihood of her recognising anyone famous? She didn't know who Flanaghan was."

Shakil frowned. He pulled the laptop over towards him and opened the screen. "Let's find Flanaghan's address and see who he's friendly with, shall we? We can print out photographs of anyone with that initial either as a first name or a surname. Madeleine may be able to help us figure that out…"

A quick search brought up a list of current MPs and Shakil wrote down the names of any he thought could possibly be Mr P, then he searched each one independently until he found clear head and shoulder shots, switched on the printer, and began to print them out. By the time he'd finished, they had a file of around twenty men.

"Who'd have thought the initial P was so popular?" Stu said, flicking through it. "Now we just need to take these to Maddy and see if she recognises any of them. Do we tell her they are MPs?"

"I suppose we should," Shakil said.

Stuart picked up his phone and called Declan to bring him up to speed, his face changing as he listened to what Declan had to say. When the call had ended he turned to Shakil. "We can go through those photographs again. We're looking for someone called Patrick or Paddy. The conversation Declan recorded between Ted and Flanaghan mentioned both those names and we missed it in the excitement of finding Flanaghan. He thinks Patrick is our third man. Mr P."

The Clinic

Declan was sitting by Madeleine's bedside when his phone vibrated in his pocket. He tutted, unable to bring himself to move far from her side and not knowing whether it was because he simply felt sorry for her or if it was for some other reason that he hadn't attempted to work out yet. She ... *pulled* ... on him, somehow. When he saw that it was Sarah calling, he left the room and went into the corridor to update her on what was happening.

"Can we meet up later and talk about what to do next?"

"Yeah," Sarah said. She'd been staying at Declan's ever since they'd discovered her place was being watched and the pair had tag-teamed staying with Madeleine, barely meeting apart from once or twice a day when they updated each other on her progress. "Do you want to come here?"

"No. I think we need to go to SAS Investigation's office. Tomorrow at noon okay with you? I'll arrange it with Stu."

Jasmine

Jasmine was chewing the skin around her fingernails, wondering whether her mother would mind if she went out with the girls for the evening. "I'll have to let you know later," she told her best friend, Suki, who yelled, "Nooo! Just say yes for a change, Jazz! Nobody will die if you go out for a night!"

"Let who know what?" Caroline said, walking into the kitchen.

Jasmine blushed. "Hang on a mo'," she said into her phone, then turned to her mother. "It's Suki. She wants me to go out with the girls tonight. It's her birthday on Monday and she wants to celebrate it tonight."

"What are you waiting for?" Caroline said, puzzled as to why her daughter wasn't jumping at the chance. "You need a good night out. We all do, come to that."

Half expecting her mother to volunteer to accompany them, Jasmine spoke into the phone. "Okay, we're on. Where and what time?"

Details sorted out, Jasmine happily went off to shower and get ready leaving her mother grinning at her back, knowing that her daughter had thought she wanted to go too. As if, Caroline thought to herself, my days of partying are long gone, more's the pity. Plus, Jasmine wouldn't even leave the house much before ten pm and she'd be ready for bed by then. All this kerfuffle was leaving her drained.

Sure enough, Suki knocked at the door at ten thirty and Jasmine eagerly opened it. "You look lush!" she pronounced, looking her friend from top to tail. "I love that dress!"

"I do, too," Suki said, grinning from ear to ear. "I got it at Mudchurch, at that new place that opened up on the High Street."

"I'll have to go and have a look," Jasmine said. "I'm sick of this old thing." She tugged at the string straps of the tight-fitting, white mini dress she wore that fitted her to perfection. It was only the second time she'd worn it.

Suki laughed. "That dress is killer. You'll be fighting them off with spades!"

"God, I hope so. I haven't had sex in an age," Jasmine said, cringing when Suki's eyes widened as they moved past her and she realised her mother was in earshot.

"So long as you keep it on, that's all that matters," Caroline said without a hint of amusement in her voice as she came up the hall to say both hello and goodbye.

Jasmine sighed. "I'm twenty-two, Mother. If it comes off, it comes off—or up—"

Caroline swatted her daughter's behind. "Be off with you—you're making me jealous, the pair of you. You both look gorgeous! Don't do anything I wouldn't do, and remember to—"

"—keep my finger over the top of my drink, I know. They give out things to put over the tops nowadays, so don't worry."

"I was going to say don't forget to use a condom if you get lucky," Caroline said dryly, "but that's good to know, too."

Suki laughed at her friend's face. "Come on, Jazz," she said, linking her arm through Jazz's. "Mum's champing at the bit to drop us off; she's got a hot date with Liam Neeson apparently."

"What channel?" Caroline asked.

"I think she recorded it last night," Suki said regretfully as Jasmine began to drag her towards her mother's car.

"Have a wonderful time!" Caroline said, waving at Suki's mum as they got into the car. "Be good; and if you can't be good, be careful!"

Swearing under her breath, Jasmine slammed the car door shut. "Please just go," she begged Suki's mum, who obliged while she hid her own smile. Parents were the same the world over.

Four hours later, Jasmine, Suki and the rest of the gang, six in all, were on the dance floor thoroughly enjoying themselves, surrendering to the music in the way only people at nightclubs do. Like all of them, Jasmine had had too much to drink and their dance moves were more of a stagger than an actual dance but none of them cared a jot as they bobbed and weaved, slut dropping to the ground at sporadic intervals, ignoring everybody around them even while they were jostled by other dancing clubbers.

As she twirled around, Jasmine found herself meeting the eyes of a man who was dancing in front of her. He was drop-dead gorgeous with dark hair and equally dark eyes framed by long black lashes. Her heart skipped a beat. He grinned at her, an almost predatory, lop-sided grin. A thrill of excitement danced down her spine as she dared to smile back at him, encouraged by the lift of his eyebrow and the flicker of interest in his eyes. Pinning her with those eyes, he began to move with her, his hips dancing in rhythm with her own. He dared to put a hand on her waist and drew her closer to him and her excitement expanded at his touch. Together, they dipped and dived, one of his legs moving between hers so that his thigh moved against her groin as they dipped making her heart beat faster and her body fill with lust. She noted that she was having the same effect on him, his own enjoyment of their movements made obvious by the swelling she felt when she bumped up against the front of him. Jasmine smiled up at him in what she hoped was a sultry fashion and moved closer.

In answer, he tugged her completely into his arms and soon they were lost in each other.

"What's your name?" he whispered into her neck, his voice deep and lust-filled. The warmth of his breath sparked a thrill than ran from her neck directly to her groin.

"Jazz. What's yours?"

"I'm Jamie. Look, this isn't something I usually do, but do you want to get out of here?"

"Yes," she breathed, throwing caution to the wind. "I think I do. Let me just say goodbye to my friends."

He caught hold of her hand as she broke away from him and followed along behind her, smiling and introducing himself to Suki and the rest of the group.

"Do you mind?" Jasmine asked Suki, indicating Jamie.

"Go, have fun!" Suki flapped her hands at Jazz. "Ring me tomorrow so I know you're safe."

"I will." And then Jasmine was outside the club and Jamie's arm was wrapped around her shoulders. Half an hour after that, they were walking through his front door and he was pressing her against the wall, kicking the door shut behind them, his mouth joined to hers, his tongue exploring. His hands lifted her dress and grabbed her buttocks, and then he brought his right hand around to the front of her body, urged her legs apart and slid his fingers beneath her thong, making her legs buckle beneath her as they began to perform their magic. Moments later, she was naked on his kitchen table and he was buried deep inside her, driving her wild.

Chapter Thirteen
Saturday

The Clinic

At nine o'clock in the morning, Shakil knocked on Madeleine's door and then pushed it open slowly, not wanting to alarm the girl inside. She was sitting up in bed, propped up by a multitude of pillows, and turned her face towards the sound of the door, her eyes widening when she didn't recognise her visitor.

"Hi, I'm Shakil Barbosa," he hastened to explain, not wanting to frighten her any more than she already was. "Do you remember me? I've been in before, but you were sleeping. I'm here to discover who did this to you and I'd like you to look at some photographs, if that's okay?"

"I said no police," Madeleine said, her voice stronger than it had been but the quaver betraying her fear. Her hands clenched into fists around the plaster, her knuckles white. "I don't want any bother and this is all my own fault. I fell down the—"

"Madeleine, you're not in any trouble, I promise you, and I'm not from the police. I'm a private investigator. Your friends Declan and Sarah hired me and my partner, Stuart Dalgleish. We won't be doing anything that may put you in any danger."

Madeleine stared at him stolidly, her face betraying nothing of the turmoil that was going on inside her head.

Shakil continued, "We know about Ted Tennant and the person you know as Bobby Jones who did this to you."

"It wasn't Bobby," Madeleine said. "It was some random who barged his way in."

"We think Bobby arranged for it to happen," Shakil said as gently as he could.

Madeleine exhaled loudly and sank back into the pillows. Her mouth quivered. "How could he have wanted this?" she said, nodding towards each arm and then down the bed. "Why? It wasn't my fault Gra—"

When she abruptly stopped talking, Shakil continued her sentence for her, "—Graham came to see you and told you he'd seen something he shouldn't have seen on Monday, right?"

"How do you know?" Madeleine was now becoming visibly upset. Her face flushed and she tried to bring herself more upright in a bid to say what she needed to. "Did he tell Bobby? Is that why? Did that creepy snooper go to Bobby after he made me have sex with him?"

"Made you have sex with him?"

"He turned up again on the day this happened. He wouldn't leave. I stupidly asked him in and gave him a drink of water because I thought he was going to collapse on my doorstep and, ha, thought he might have been having a heart attack. I wish I'd bloody left him there! He told me he knew what I was and that he wanted to … to …"

"Become a client, too?" Shakil finished quietly.

Madeleine nodded. "He pulled out a tenner and said he wasn't going until he'd had sex with me. Said he'd tell everyone in the neighbourhood what I was if I refused. I didn't know what he'd do if I turned him down, so I …"

"So you let him. You did the right thing, Maddy. You had no way of knowing what he would do so you kept yourself safe."

"Kept myself safe? That's a laugh, isn't it? If he was the one who caused all of this, he should be in here, not me."

Shakil reached for her hand. "Madeleine, there's something you need to know about the man you call Bobby Jones. Are you ready to hear it?"

Madeleine swallowed. Then she nodded.

"Like I said, Bobby Jones is an alias. His real name is Robert Flanaghan. Maddy, he's the standing MP for Crickleby."

Madeleine stared at Shakil, open-mouthed. "He's military police?"

Shakil shook his head. "No, he's a Member of Parliament."

"What? Like Boris?" she named the ex-Prime Minister.

"Not as high up as he got, but yes, that's about the gist of it."

Madeleine's face paled. "I didn't know."

"We didn't think you did. Actually, we think that's why he came to you for so long. You weren't a threat to him until Graham turned up. Then you both became trouble with a capital T, unfortunately, which is why he hired a thug to keep you quiet."

He let her digest this for a few moments, then added, "Maddy, I need to talk to you about your third client, Mr P."

"Don't tell me, he's one of them, too," she said dully. "But I bet he's higher up the chain than Robert Flanaghan, is that right?"

Shakil reached into his pocket and pulled out two photographs. "Do you recognise either of these men?"

Madeleine peered at the pictures. Her first instinct was to deny any knowledge of either of them, but then self-preservation kicked in. "Yeah. The one on the right is Mr P. Who is he really?"

Shakil's lips thinned. "I'm not sure I should tell you—for your own safety."

Madeleine snorted. "If they come back it'll be to finish me off so you may as well tell me."

"That's Patrick Hackensach. He's the Secretary of State for Education. We need to beef up your security and as soon as it's safe to move you, that's what we're going to do."

"He works with *kids*?"

"Not directly, no. He decides what happens in schools but he doesn't actually go in to teach at any. He's not a teacher."

Madeleine flopped back against her pillows. "How can someone like him do a job like that?" she said, adding, "Don't bother answering, money talks, doesn't it." She changed the subject. "Where will you take me?"

"We have something planned. It's best you don't know and, as I said, we'll beef up your security in the meantime, and we only use people we really trust so you'll be safe. If anyone asks anything, any doctor or nurse, play dumb and then ring us to let us know, okay?" He reached into his pocket and pulled out a burner phone which he put on the bedside cabinet, beside the water container. "Our number is in there."

"Nice one," Madeleine said dryly. She nodded to each arm in turn. "How exactly am I supposed to do that then?"

Shakil grimaced. "You'll have to ask one of the staff members you do trust, I suppose," he said, mentally kicking himself. "Nurse Trudy, for example."

Madeleine fiddled with her bedsheets while she thought about it. After a short while, she nodded and said, "Can I tell Mum where I'll be going?"

Shakil swallowed the lump that appeared from nowhere in his throat, knowing she meant Caroline. "You mean the lady that came in to visit you?"

Not meeting his eyes, Madeleine nodded. "What's her name? I can't really keep calling her Mum, can I, even if she's been kinder to me than my own mum ever was?"

Shakil swallowed again. "She's one of us. Her name's Caroline and you're right, she's got a kind soul. She'll know and I'm certain she'll be in to see you. She's one of the good ones." He stopped talking, unsure if it would be a good idea to tell her that Caroline was married to the man who had brought all this trouble upon her.

"I know," Madeleine said quietly. "I know."

SAS Investigations Office

The office was almost uncomfortably full when Sarah and Declan arrived at noon. Stuart, Shakil and Caroline were already there waiting for them and Caroline had brought Chutzpah, the dog, with her to give him a change of scenery.

As the pair entered the office, Shakil tugged Stuart to one side. "I need to tell you something Madeleine told me, but Stu, your mum doesn't need to hear it."

Stuart closed his eyes and sighed. Pursing his lips into one thin line, he nodded. "I'll see what I can do."

Caroline rubbed behind Chutzpah's ears as Shakil told everyone Madeleine had identified both Robert Flanaghan and Patrick Hackensach as her Wednesday and Friday clients.

When he was done, Stuart said, "Obviously, she's still in danger. We've been warned off so we have to assume we're being watched, in which case, they may know about the

Clinic. Doc is going in to see her later today to see if she's fit to move. If she is, she's going to another location. I have a friend who has come up trumps for us. She doesn't know all the ins and outs, just enough that she wants to help. She's said Madeleine can stay there rent-free until she's well enough to work and the rent she'll charge when she can work will be the same as she was paying at her old place, although I'm not entirely sure that she'll be too happy with her continuing in her old line of business." He pulled a set of keys from his pocket, turned to Sarah and added, "The address is on the card attached to these. It's available now and she's happy for you to move in with Madeleine if you'd like to? We know you can't go back to your own place because it's being watched. However, there are two catches: one, it's not in Crickleby, it's in Mudchurch, the far side at the top of the cliffs, and two, it's unfurnished."

Sarah looked at Declan, who nodded at her and said, "That's a good idea. I know where we can get some furniture to tide you over."

She turned to Stuart who threw the keys towards her. She caught them with one hand, her eyes blurred by unshed tears. "I don't know how to thank you," she began. "If it helps, I own my house in Lakeland Road so I can put it up for sale. Would your friend," she looked at Stuart, "be interested in me buying the Mudchurch house from her? Assuming it's not too expensive, obviously."

"I'll ask," Stuart said, hiding his surprise as he jotted down a note to call Tammy and sound her out. If Sarah owned her own property, it would make sense for her to buy somewhere else once she'd sold her own and safer if she didn't have to go around viewing others. Although, "What if you don't like the Mudchurch house?"

"Then I'll think again. Either way, it's a safe space for us both at least for a few months. I'm truly grateful."

Stuart smiled at her. "Happy to help."

"So," Caroline interjected, "two questions: how are we going to get Madeleine safely out of the clinic; and how are we going to find out whether Patrick Hackensach was involved in what happened to her? We're rather assuming that it was Flanaghan who hired the thugs, both the one who beat Madeleine and those who came to our house, but Hackensach would come out of this worse if it became public knowledge because of his position. Madeleine is so young; it would be the end of his career, surely?"

"Yes, we need to figure out a way of getting to him," Stuart said, and the room fell quiet as they all considered this.

"We could always go to the middle-man," Declan said into the silence.

"What do you mean?" Shakil asked. "What middle-man?"

"Gregor."

"But we don't know where he operates from, do we?"

"No," Sarah said slowly. "But what if I was to call him and tell him I wanted to meet? That I'd been scared by what happened to Madeleine but was ready to go back to work?"

"You have a phone number for him? Why didn't you tell us?"

Sarah stared from face to face and shrugged. "Nobody asked and I didn't know it was important."

"That could be dangerous," Caroline said worriedly. "I mean, if he knows you know what happened, he'll want to safeguard himself."

"Exactly," Sarah said. "I'll be a honeypot."

"Honey trap," Shakil corrected, grinning at her. "But before we go down that route, can you let me have the number? I'll see if Terry can track where he is."

77 Lakeland Avenue

While Stuart, Shakil, Caroline, Declan and Sarah were in their meeting, Graham was peeling vegetables with the paring knife he'd sharpened the day before and staring blindly through the kitchen window, wondering what he could do to win his wife back. His texts hadn't worked, his daughter had warned him off and he had no other way of contacting Caroline unless she decided to respond to him. He was still feeling sorry for himself, still not allowing himself to admit that he'd done the wrong thing or that Caroline was well within her rights to be angry with him, and still longing for her to call him so he could try to sort things out. He could not get his wife out of his mind so when the doorbell rang, believing she'd come both to her senses and home, he put down the potato he was peeling and went down the hall eagerly, opening the door without looking to see who was there.

"Graham Dalgleish?" the dark-haired man who was standing on the doorstep asked in an amiable tone, putting his foot into the hallway so Graham was unable to close the door. He was conservatively dressed in a suit but low-key menace oozed from him, despite his air of apparent respectability.

"No, there's no Graham here," Graham said, blanching and unwittingly taking a step backwards.

The man on the doorstep put his hand on Graham's chest and pushed against it, moving forwards, an unstoppable force intent on gaining entry. When he was fully inside the house, he closed the door behind him, saying, "I need a quiet word with you."

"Why?" The word came out as a squeak. "Who are you? What do you want with m...Graham?"

"Who I am doesn't matter, and I think you know why, don't you?"

"N...no, not really," Graham managed, trying to paint an indignant picture with his face as he backed up the hall towards the kitchen.

He failed miserably. The man simply followed, smiling at him and shaking his head. As they reached the doorway into the kitchen, he caught hold of Graham's sleeve with a vice-like grip, stopping him in mid-track. Graham swallowed and turned to face him, knowing there was no way he could get free right at that instant.

"I see someone else was a bit upset with you." The intruder raised his hand and traced a finger against the remnants of Graham's healing bruises. "Why was that, I wonder?"

Graham jerked his head away. "The black eyes? I walked into an open door by mistake."

The man tutted. "Do you know how many times I've heard that little gem?" he asked conversationally. "Not always from women, you understand. No, it comes from the most cowardly of men, too. Are you a coward, Graham?"

"I told you; I'm not Graham," Graham said, trying to put as much emphasis into the words as he was able, his heart hammering up into his throat. "He's not here. He's split up with his wife and I'm housesitting while they try and get it back together. Graham's my brother."

"Let's pretend for an instant that I believe you; when will he be back?"

"Not for another month. He's ... *they've* ... gone away."

"Hmmn. That's too bad. You see, I've been having an interesting time with someone I think Graham may know. We met last night. Feisty little thing, she is—cracking rack and the peachiest of arses and, boy, did we have some fun! She's back at my place waiting for round two as we speak, although between you and me, her stamina is a bit on the short side, plus, I tend to bore easily. However, I have friends who, I'm sure, would love to play with her until her parents return."

"Let her go." Graham gave up the pretence as fear for his daughter flooded his entire body. He knew this man was talking about Jasmine. "I'm who you're looking for. I suppose this is to do with the girl down the road?"

"She's not a prisoner!" the man said in fake shock. "Look here." He took a phone from his back pocket and presented the screen to Graham where a recording was already playing on the screen. It showed a naked girl's body but her face was not in view. She was laying back on a table and someone was fucking her. The camera focus zoomed in between her legs as a penis slid in and out of her vagina and a man's thumb caressed around her clitoris. Graham could hear the girl's moans of apparent pleasure. Then the camera panned from between her legs and up to the man's face. It was the face of the man standing in front of him. He was smiling.

"That's not Jasmine," Graham said, praying he was right.

"Oh, Graham. Of course it is, look..."

The screen was back under Graham's nose. He watched as the man withdrew from the girl's body and urged her to turn over, saying he wanted to fuck her from behind. The girl's face came into view as she seemingly willingly complied and he heard her groan as the man gripped her hips and thrust himself deep inside her.

Graham had caught a glimpse of his daughter's face.

"You bastard!" he howled, rooted to the spot by the desperate fury that raged within him. "You must have drugged her! Let her go!"

"She can go anytime she wants, don't worry about that. At least, she can once she's learned to enjoy the things Madeleine liked to do before her little accident; she's a little vanilla at the moment, as you saw. It's a crying shame we lost Madeleine's services but I think Jasmine will come to appreciate the finer points of all that entails so she can take her place. She didn't complain when I slapped her arse while I was fucking her. Do you want to see? No? Okay, I understand. But you have to appreciate that it's your fault we lost Madeleine, so it's only fair you provide her replacement, and who better than your own daughter? I have no doubt Jasmine will come to love her new life, once she's learned her place in it and what she has to do to keep living it." As he spoke, the man pocketed his phone and brought out a set of knuckle-dusters. He slipped it over his right hand, clenching his fingers around it until it was properly in place. "And while we're talking about learning, you need a lesson, too. Haven't you heard it's rude to spy on people?"

Graham's vision tunnelled. As the fist slammed towards him, he realised he was still holding the paring knife and lurched forwards with his right hand outstretched in a vain attempt to ward the man off, ducking his head down as he did so. And then the world went black.

Jasmine

While Jamie was visiting her father, an unknowing Jasmine was languishing in a warm bubble bath, daydreaming about having just had the best sex of her life. She wouldn't have believed it possible before today that she could meet someone and want to hop straight into bed with them, but when she'd met Jamie the night before she couldn't wait to get out of her clothes. As she thought about him a warm throbbing began between her legs and her nipples hardened, despite the warmth of the water. She'd woken up content and replete in his arms having behaved like a complete slut for a change. Jamie had run her this bath and then popped out to get something in for lunch for them both and, more than anything, she wanted a repeat performance.

Unfortunately, just before she'd climbed into the bath, an incoming text from her boss told her someone was off sick from work and she'd been scheduled in, so she was going to have to leave before he got back. She towelled herself dry, dressed in last night's clothes – she was going to have to do the walk of shame – hunted for a pen and piece of paper and wrote him a note that explained what had happened. She left her phone number and then she reluctantly left his apartment and caught a bus to town to go to work.

SAS Investigations Office

Caroline, Declan and Sarah had left the office after their meeting not needing to hang around while they waited for Terry the Tech to do his business. Once they'd gone, Shakil updated Stuart with what Madeleine had told him about Graham's visit to her, hating every second of passing on the bad news.

"I didn't think my estimation of him could fall any lower," Stuart said when he'd finished. He went to the window and stared blankly out at the world beyond. "He blackmailed her and scared her into having sex with him. So she was pretty much raped twice that day. He's no better than any of her other clients, is he?"

"I think he just saw a chance and took it," Shakil suggested, trying to lessen the blow. "You can't call what your father did rape, Stu. Not really."

Stuart turned to face him, his eyes blazing. "She would never have had sex with him if he hadn't blackmailed her into it. It wasn't consensual; she had no choice. He planned what he was going to do, and he did it. That makes him no better than them—or any bloke who uses prostitutes."

Shakil winced at the rage that poured from Stuart and kept his mouth closed.

Stuart began to stomp around the room, unable to stay in one place. "Why did he do it? I mean, he had Mum, he had us – me and Jazz – why did he feel the need to blow it all away by shagging Maddy? She's younger than his own kids, for

Christ's sake! What kind of bloke gets his rocks off on girls younger than his own kids?"

Shakil shook his head, knowing his friend needed to get this out of his system before he'd be able to move on.

"I mean, I always thought blokes who use prostitutes are a step away from being incels. They can't get it naturally so they take their rage out on the girls who will for money. How wrong was I? Every single one of these blokes, Dad included, is married. They're all *respectable*," he spat the word out, "I don't think I'll ever be able to look at another middle-aged man and not wonder if he's up to the same thing."

Shakil nodded, he'd had similar thoughts.

"Poor Mum," Stu said, coming to a halt, his temper abating somewhat as he pictured his mother's face. "Thank you for not saying all of this in front of her."

Shakil shook his head, waving the words away. "I would never do anything to hurt her."

It was Stuart's turn to nod. "I know."

The phone rang.

"That'll be Terry," Shakil said. He waited a beat for Stuart to acknowledge what he'd said and then he took the call, scribbling down the information as it was passed to him. When it ended, he passed the note to Stuart. "We have a location for Gregor. His full name is Gregor Ivanov. Terry got a live hit on him coming from a house up in the Lakelands. The Lane, not the Road or Avenue. It's right at the very top so it's going to be enormous. Fancy a drive by it?"

"Let's go," Stuart replied.

"Hang on a minute," Shakil said, thinking fast. "We can't go empty-handed. This man's dangerous; he's got a lot to hide so we need to take protection."

"We're not going to be getting out of the car," Stuart said, tucking in his shirt tails and pulling on his jacket. "I don't think we'll have any trouble, do you?"

"We've been threatened already. Talking of which, when's the firm coming to fit the new door and windows?"

"Monday," Stuart said. "What do you want to take with us?"

"Harriet?" Shakil named the firearm he'd had since childhood. A doting uncle who was ex-force had given it to him for his tenth birthday, much to his parent's horror. It had once been a service weapon but his uncle had had it modified so that it could never fire. It looked impressive though and he and Stuart had spent many an hour playing cops and robbers during that year.

Stuart blinked his surprise. "You're really that worried?"

Shakil shrugged. "Better safe than sorry."

"Do you have it with you?"

"No, it's at home."

"Okay, you go and get that and I'll nip back to my parent's house and pick up Mack." Mack was the machete that Stuart had invested in the year his parent's lawn had become overgrown during the three-month Caribbean cruise they'd taken. He'd spent most of those three months high as a kite and it was only when his sister had yelled at him that he'd remembered he'd promised to run the mower over it once a fortnight. Mack had been an emergency purchase – hidden in the shed when he'd realised his parents owned a strimmer that would do the job much quicker.

"We may as well go together," Shakil said hurriedly, not wanting Stuart to bump into his father in the mood he was in. "Petrol prices and all that."

Stuart stared at him evenly. "I'm not going to hurt him, don't worry. With any luck, he'll have left anyway. I told him it wasn't safe for him to be there."

Shakil half-smiled. "Do you honestly think he listened to you?"

"Probably not. Okay, we'll take your car."

They locked up the office and went to Shakil's house first to pick up Harriet, then drove on to Lakeland Avenue. As they pulled up outside the house and Shakil made to open the car door, Stuart stayed him with a hand on his arm.

"Shaks, I've got a bad feeling."

Puzzled, Shakil leaned across Stuart to look at the house. "I can't see anything out of place."

"No, I know. I can just *feel* it. Something's happened."

Shakil nodded, accepting his friend's premonition. "Front or back?" he asked.

"I'll take the front; you go round the back. You can get in via Maud's." He nodded towards the neighbouring house. "If you walk confidently, nobody will think anything of it. Maud's almost blind and partially deaf, so she won't notice. She never locks her gate. Go through that way and jump the wall. You'll need to boot the door in—Dad had it locked when I was there last. I'll give you a minute and then I'll go to the front. We'll go in at the same time. Okay?"

"Okay. I'll have Harriet ready; we may be able to bluff our way through it if anyone's there that shouldn't be."

Stuart dry swallowed and nodded.

Shakil got out of the car and strode up Maud's path and on through her gate. Stuart counted to sixty slowly and then, his legs wobbling slightly, he too got out of the car and began to walk towards the front door. As adrenaline flooded his system, his pulse began to throb wildly in his temples and his senses heightened. Everything seemed too bright around him as he inched the key into the lock and turned it, praying his father hadn't put all the locks in place. He hadn't, the key turned easily and the door swung silently open. His eyes skimmed the hallway as he tried to listen for any noises inside the house but was unable to hear anything past the sudden premonitory roaring in his head. Nothing appeared to be moving but now his nostrils prickled as they picked up a familiar odour; one they'd smelled at Madeleine's house after her attack, the smell of iron. As sickening understanding bloomed in his brain, Stuart knew that he was smelling blood. He crept up the hallway wishing he had the machete, not understanding why he could see Shakil's ashen wide-eyed face, his open mouth, still at the window as he stared at something inside the kitchen.

Then Stuart was in the kitchen, taking in the surreal scene of pools of deep red that were congealing around two bodies that lay motionless on the floor, a blood-covered paring knife between them.

The rushing, pumping noise expanded and echoed in his ears. He went down to the tiles, lifting his father's head onto his lap and an unearthly, ululating howl filled the room. Now Shakil was able to move. He kicked the back door open and went to press his fingers against the neck of the stranger on the floor. He found no pulse.

"Stu," he said urgently. "Have you checked for a pulse? Is he still alive?"

Stuart wasn't listening. He was rocking his father in his arms in a world of private pain, recalling the anger he'd felt towards him not an hour before, remembering the fights he'd had with him. He was wishing he hadn't punched him, hadn't said the things he'd said, thought the things he'd thought, wishing he could tell him he loved him despite him being an old lech, and still the awful keening howl continued unabated from his throat.

Shakil picked his way around the dead body, avoiding the coagulating blood so his footprints wouldn't destroy any evidence and squatted by his friend. He gently reached his hand towards Graham's neck, being careful to explain exactly what he was doing in the vain hope that Stuart could hear him and would understand. Something must have got through because Stuart didn't try to fight him off and he allowed Shakil to gently move his hand away from Graham's head so he could feel for a pulse.

There was one there. It was thready and weak, but Graham was still alive. "Stu, he's not dead. Can you hear me? Your dad's alive. I'm going to get help, but you need to stop moving him around in case you hurt him more."

As the words began to sink in, Stuart stopped moving and the howl faded away. Now guttural sobs filled the air and tears began to course down his cheeks as he looked down at his father's lolling head. He moved his arm to cushion it.

"That's it, hold him still," Shakil said, patting his friend's shoulder awkwardly. "Don't move. I'll be back as soon as I've called for help, okay? Do you understand?" He waited until he saw the slight nod of Stuart's head and then he went down the hallway and out of the front door to ring for both the police and an ambulance. Then, almost on autopilot, he hid Harriet beneath the spare tyre in the boot of the car before going back into the house to sit with his friend.

Chapter Fourteen
Sunday

The Lakelands

After a police car and ambulance arrived simultaneously at 77 Lakeland Avenue, Graham was stabilised, hooked up to oxygen, put on a gurney and rushed to Crickleby Hospital. Stuart had been allowed to go with his father in the ambulance, leaving Shakil to give a statement to the police while they waited for the morgue van to arrive to take the dead body away for autopsy. He told them he had no idea who the dead man was but identified Graham as being the house owner and Stuart as his son and that they had popped in for a visit and found them like this.

The body had been removed and forensics were crawling over the house by the time Shakil was allowed to go. Praying no one would ask to search his car, he drove to the hospital in the early hours of Sunday morning and followed the police presence to the room where Stuart was waiting for his father to come out of surgery.

"How is he?" he asked, drawing Stuart into a bear hug and then pulling back to search his friend's ashen face.

"I don't know. They're not saying anything."

"No news is good news," Shakil said, aware of the platitude but unable to think of any other words of comfort.

"So they keep saying." Stuart took a step back and nodded toward the two officers in the room who shifted uneasily on their feet and directed their eyes away from the shared grief.

"Stu, does your mum know? Does Jasmine?"

"The police have gone to pick them up. I rang Mum when I got here, after they took him away."

"How did she take it?"

"She dropped the phone. Jazz said she'd collapsed."

Shakil's eyes slowly closed as he visualised the scene. When he opened them again, the door was opening and Caroline and Jasmine rushed into the room, straight into Stuart's outstretched arms.

***

The weather had turned by the time Stuart and Shakil left the hospital in the early hours of Sunday morning. The doctor who had finally come to speak to them all said that Graham had had an x-ray which showed he had a fractured cheekbone, and a brain scan that, thankfully, showed no sign of any bleeding inside his skull. He was stable and showing signs of coming around.

"He'll be taken to a ward soon so we can keep an eye on him, but unfortunately, only two people can stay," he finished.

"You stay with Mum, Jazz," Stuart said. "I'll go back to the house and pack a bag for him."

As they made their way down the three steps that led from the Accident and Emergency Unit, they walked into heavy rain. Within seconds, both men were drenched.

"Are you okay?" Shakil asked as they dashed towards the car park, slipping and sliding on the wet paving.

Stuart nodded. "He'll live. Christ, what a mess this is turning into."

"It really is. Stu, do you think we should have told the police what we know?"

"No," Stuart said immediately, saying the same thing as Shakil was thinking. "Once they know who's involved in this, it'll be covered up. I don't want the bastards getting away with it. The police can know when the time's right."

They'd reached the car by this point and got into it hurriedly, dripping rainwater all over the inside.

"Who'd have thought my old man would have the presence of mind to shank that bloke's groin?"

"I know, right?" Shakil said. Privately, he thought it had just been a lucky blow rather than a calculated move. Whichever, it had saved Graham's life. The knife had sheered through the femoral artery and the intruder had gone down and bled out within minutes.

"We need to get someone watching out at the hospital," Stuart continued. "Now we know for sure they know he was the one who saw Maddy and Ted together, he's in danger. Plus, Mum and Jazz are there. They could be followed."

"Already on it," Shakil said, having organised this straight after giving a statement to the police the previous day. "Didn't notice them, did you?"

"No," Stuart said, smiling for the first time. "Thanks."

"De nada. Do you still want to go take a look at this Ivanov's house?" Shakil asked, switching the engine on and then turning the heater dial up to full pelt in a vain bid to dry them out.

Stuart nodded grimly. "More than ever. Do you still have Harriet?"

Shakil grinned.

"Let's go see whether the police have finished at Mum and Dad's. We can collect some clothes for him and, if they've gone, I can nip out to the shed and pick Mack up."

***

Dawn was streaking the skies in pastel pinks, purples and blues as Shakil pulled his car to a halt at the very top of the Lakelands outside Ivanov's palatial house. The mansion, because that was what it could only rightfully be called, had pride of place directly at the top of the Lakelands, its outlook being the road ahead of it and the houses that were hidden from view on either side. It reeked of wealth and entitlement.

"Why is it the richest people get there by walking all over the poorest?" Shakil pondered as they both stared up at the high red brick walls surrounding the property, the locked double gates, the circular drive and the cream-painted house with an adjoining triple garage that was set way back from the road at the top of the hill. A pair of enormous Dobermans stood behind the gates, silently watching them, alert and ready for action.

"Beats me," Stuart said. "Crime pays."

"Sure does."

"So how are we going to play this? We can't exactly just ring the doorbell, can we? He's not going to open the gates and we can't scale that wall unless we want to be mauled to death."

"We'll wait until he leaves."

"Wait where?" Stuart said. "Look around you Shaks. I'm surprised the police haven't turned up to move us on already because I imagine he already knows we're here – look, there are two cameras up there and since we've been sitting here, they've been aimed at us. They must be motion activated."

"He'll be asleep. And even if he isn't, he's going to need to get out at some stage. It doesn't look like there's any other exit he can use," Shakil pointed out. "It may put him on edge, knowing we know who he is and where he lives. People on edge make mistakes."

Stuart thought about it. "Someone like him is going to have a hotline to either the police or a team of security. All he has to do is call them to have us moved on."

"So what do you suggest?"

"I think we move on now and park up further down the road; wait until he comes out."

"Yeah, but we don't know what he looks like or what car he drives, so we won't know if it's him."

Stuart laughed. "Shaks, his place is head on to the road. Wherever we park, we'll see those gates open. Plus, a guy like this? He'll have a Porsche or something similar."

"It's Sunday. He probably won't be going anywhere."

Stuart stared at him. "You think? I reckon someone will have told him what went down at my father's and he'll be having an emergency meeting with either Tennant, Flanaghan or Hackensach, if not all three." He narrowed his eyes, nodding thoughtfully, and then pulled out his phone. "In which case, we need to track them all. I'll ask Declan to go to Flanaghan's and stick a bug under his car while it's still early—he won't have a hope of getting near Hackensach's. We'll know when he or Tennant makes a move and we can follow them. Hopefully, we'll catch all of them together, Ivanov included."

***

Declan was in a deep sleep when Stuart called to ask him to place a tracker on Flanaghan's car. He'd spent most of Saturday figuring out a way to move Madeleine from the

Clinic to the safe house that he and Sarah had visited immediately after she'd been given the keys the previous morning. It was high up on Mudchurch cliffs, the best part of Mudchurch, with views over the ocean from the front, and rolling hills behind.

"This is gorgeous," Sarah had pronounced as she clapped eyes on it for the first time, and he had had to agree with her. It was.

The rest of Saturday had been spent ringing around ads on social media pages, tracking down beds for each of the girls to sleep in, a sofa for them to sit on, pots and pans, cutlery and food for the small, well-equipped kitchen that, luckily, was fitted with an integrated cooker, fridge-freezer and washing machine. When Tammy refurbished a house, she did so well. The inside, as the outside, was immaculate.

By the time Declan had collected his work van, fetched the beds and sofa, then got all of it installed in the house and taken Sarah food shopping, it was nine o'clock and they were both exhausted. They'd eaten fish and chips which they'd bought from a stand just above the beach, much further down the cliffs, and then Declan had waved goodbye to her and gone back to the Clinic to see how Madeleine was doing. He'd fallen into his own bed at just past midnight, so tired he was having trouble focussing.

"Sure I can," he mumbled sleepily when he heard Stuart's request, waking up fully when Stuart briefly told him what had happened to his father. "Is he going to be all right?"

"I don't know yet. He's stable but a head injury at his age isn't great."

Declan swore under his breath, then said aloud, "Are we anywhere near close to catching these bastards?"

"I imagine word will get around that the person they sent to kill Dad failed," Stuart said, putting him on speaker so Shakil could hear the conversation. "So once he's well enough to be moved he won't be going home again until this is all over with. I doubt they'll take kindly to one of their own being killed by an old guy."

"Where's he going to go?"

"I honestly don't know. I can't ask Tammy again, she's already let me have two houses, I don't think she'll happily let me have another even if she has one empty. I suppose he can come to stay with me, but whether he'll agree or not, considering I blacked his eyes and then had another stand-up row with him afterwards, I don't know."

"He won't have much choice, will he? Unless your mother takes him back—"

Stuart snorted. "There's no chance of that, I won't let her. I know he's suffering but he hasn't stopped lying about what happened with Madeleine."

Shakil, who was listening quietly to the conversation, wasn't so sure. He'd seen the panic on Caroline and Jasmine's faces as they arrived at the hospital. They weren't the faces of people who didn't love someone. He kept his mouth firmly closed.

Declan said, "Okay. Leave it with me. I'll put the tracker on and call you back. If we can get to these bastards before he's out of hospital, it may not be a problem."

Stuart and Shakil went to the office to wait.

***

When Declan arrived at Flanaghan's house he drove straight past it without slowing or stopping. Park Road was a dead-end road situated to the left of, and between, Lakeland Avenue and The Lakelands and was equally as leafy as either. Tall trees separated the road from the paving, offering shade to those who travelled on foot and to the front gardens of the properties depending on the time of day. The detached houses were as spectacular as any on the Avenue but not quite on a par with The Lakeland mansions.

Flanaghan's property was set in the middle of all the houses on the left-hand side of the road. Each property had its own short driveway, leading, in the main, to garages that were detached from the houses. It appeared that most of the property owners had second or third cars which were parked outside on the driveways so Declan was looking for one that had no vehicles outside and closed windows with drawn blinds or curtains, in the hope that the owners were not at home. He slowed his speed and found one such further up the road, approximately ten houses away from Flanaghan's. He pulled into the driveway, got out of his car and walked confidently around the side of the house, into the back garden. He was going to have to approach Flanaghan's house in the same way that he'd approached Sarah's.

Declan strode to the rear of the garden, a plot of around a quarter of an acre, and found a latched gate that led into a ginnel that ran parallel to the houses. He smiled grimly. This would be an enormous help. He opened the latch and stepped through, re-latching it behind him. He turned left and began to steal along the ginnel, counting houses until he reached the land at the rear of Flanaghan's house where his heart sank. Deep brambles edged the property and were a far more effective barrier than walls or fences. The properties to the left and right of Flanaghan's had high walls topped by spikes to deter burglars. He was going to have to rethink his plan.

He retraced his steps and got back into his car, backed out into the road and drove, more slowly this time, back towards the junction with The Lakelands and Lakeland Avenue. As he reached Flanaghan's property, he checked the driveway. A black top-of-the-range Mercedes A class with a personal plate reading 'FLAN 1' had been reversed in and parked close to the road. Declan smiled. He pulled up, engaged the handbrake, checked nobody was around to see his movements (or at least, that was nobody visible to him) and left the engine running while, keeping close to the perimeters of the property, he sneaked to the drive and planted the bug beneath the car. It took less than thirty seconds and Declan was off and away again.

He parked up again in Lakeland Road and checked to see that both bugs were working. Both Tennant and Flanaghan were stationary, both apparently at home and still sleeping. He rang Stuart to let him know.

***

At three pm, the trackers began to show the movement of both Tennant's and Flanaghan's vehicles.

"I'm still on Park Road," Declan rang to tell Stuart and Shakil, "so if Flanaghan comes this way, I'll follow him."

"Hang on," Shakil said. "We don't want to blow it, do we? I think we need to watch the trackers and see where they go; see if they're meeting somewhere. We can follow them from a distance and then scope them out."

Declan could see the sense in this but frustration swept through him as Flanaghan's vehicle passed him with Flanaghan at the wheel, heading towards town. His fingers itched.

Stuart's voice saying, "...do you think that's a good idea?" brought him back to earth.

"Sorry," he said. "I just watched FLAN 1 go past and had to sit on my hands. What were you saying, Stu?"

"I was saying we have a gadget that will let us hear what they say from a distance, and it records. Considering who we're dealing with, do we think it's a good idea to do that?"

"Absolutely!" Declan said. "Let's face it, we've not gone to the police with any of this and what are we going to do anyway? Beat them up? Kill them all? Are any of us killers? I know I'm not."

"Fair point," Shakil said.

Declan continued as if he hadn't spoken. "We need to put a stop to their shenanigans and the only way I can think of is to record what they have to say and put it, and the photos and possibly the recording of Flanaghan, out everywhere. Go to the papers, splash it over social media, let the world know what these bastards are like."

Shakil agreed. "So we follow at a distance. Keep your phone handy and we'll decide where we need to be to get the evidence we need once we know where they're headed."

"Will do. Now, can I tail the bastard? It looks like they're heading out of town." The trackers showed that both vehicles were taking the main A road out of Crickleby, a road that led towards the Broads.

The Broads

"Where are they going?" Shakil asked as he and Stuart followed the tracker with Declan hot on their heels. "It looks like they're making for the Broads but why would they want to go there, it's miles from Crickleby?"

"They probably want to go somewhere to talk without anyone recognising them. Plus, Ted's a loose cannon—he's not in the public eye like the others. I'm wondering if they're luring him here for another reason," Declan said on speakerphone.

"What, you think they might try to bump him off?"

"It's possible. There's a lot of marshland and water up here."

The three men continued following the cars, deep in thought. After a while, Stuart said, "So what the hell do we do if they *do* plan to kill him? Sit back and let them?"

Nobody answered. What could they do?

The tracker showed the vehicles turning onto the road known as the Treacle Straight, apparently heading towards Great Stodmouth, passing field after field of greenery. As they drove along behind them, the skies turned ominously dark, the pink sky of the morning warning holding true. The trackers showed the vehicles turning off before reaching the popular holiday resort and they began the winding route towards Racklesham.

Stuart, Shakil and Declan followed as it began to rain, spits and spots to begin with, but then lightning split the sky and thunder roared a few seconds later. The rainfall immediately became heavier and both drivers switched on their wiper blades.

"Why Racklesham?" Stuart said.

"Boats," Declan said as a clap of thunder roared and the heavens opened in earnest. Rain sheeted down the windscreen, travelling almost sideways in the wind that had whipped up from nowhere. He eased pressure on the accelerator and switched the wiper blade to its fastest speed so he was able to peer through the window. "Didn't you say Ivanov's place backs onto the Lakes? Those lakes feed into the river ways which feed into the Broads. I'd lay odds that Ivanov has a boat."

"We didn't think of that," Stuart said, as Shakil followed suit. "How do you know all of this?"

"I come out this way sometimes. If we turned off the Treacle Straight the other way, you'd be aiming for Rushem Marshes. It has an RSPB area down a cycle track. You can get a boat down if the tide's right or else you have to walk it. I, um, I know it quite well."

"Didn't have you down as a Twitcher," Stuart said, with some surprise in his voice.

"We're not all anoraks you know, Declan said defensively. "I do mostly physical work, I like the downtime. And we're not called Twitchers anymore. We're Birders. You get a lot of birds here that you can't see in other places. I like nature."

Stuart grinned at Shakil. "No judgement here. We all need downtime."

Declan sighed. "They're all up on the coast looking for Black Redstart this weekend."

"How do you all communicate; homing pigeon or Twitter?"

"No," Declan said after a beat. "And we don't all wear flat caps, britches and have whistles in our mouths, either."

"Lots of traffic ahead," Shakil said into the terse silence that had fallen.

"There is," Declan said. "Hopefully, if we do end up at Racklesham, we'll be able to find somewhere to park."

"They're caught in traffic, too," Shakil observed.

"Wonder if they're getting twitchy," Stuart said, unable to stop himself.

Declan inhaled sharply.

Shakil put his hand over the phone and turned to look at Stuart. "I think we'll get along better if you lay off the bird-watching jokes."

Stuart opened his mouth and closed it again after checking Shakil's face. "Okay."

After forty minutes of stop-start traffic, the trackers showed that their quarry had, indeed, been heading for Racklesham because they became stationary, a dozen or so yards apart.

"Looks like they've parked in Tays," Declan said. "That's a big shop, in case you didn't know. There's lots of parking there and it's right on the Broads. Lots of very expensive boats moor up there."

Ten minutes or so later, the three men reached Tays and, after queuing to access them, braved the attached car parks. Surprisingly, they found two empty spaces side by side at the far end and pulled into them with grins of relief. Deep puddles had gathered everywhere and fat raindrops bounced from their surfaces, splattering the heels of the few people scurrying to and fro their vehicles. Shrieks of laughter and loud complaints filled the air outside.

They braved the weather, Shakil lugging a bag with the equipment they'd need. All three were instantly drenched. Rain flattened their hair and streamed down their faces. It swept under their jacket collars and trailed down their backs. Their jeans became sodden weights around their legs.

"I doubt we'll get to hear much above this racket—if we can find them," Shakil said gloomily, as lightning streaked the sky followed by an immediate clap of thunder and the rain became torrential.

"It's right overhead," Declan said. "Hopefully, it'll pass as swiftly as it struck."

"We need to get to the dockside," Stuart said. "If you're right and they're meeting Ivanov's boat, we don't want them heading off before we find them."

Picking their way around the edges of the worst of the gathering puddles, they headed through the car parks, aiming for the waterfront to their right. Ducks huddled under bushes, quacking contentedly as ducklings, their yellow fluff flattened by the rain, scurried beneath their wings, peeking out and then retreating again.

Walking on a muddy path worn by thousands of feet, they passed between bushes and emerged on the dockside where a range of boats bobbed up and down in the water. People rushed past them in either direction, heads down against the rain.

"Odds on that one's his." Declan nodded towards a large white yacht with blue trimmings. A sign on the side bore the name *Greglorious*.

"Subtle, isn't he?" Shakil said, smirking.

"Doesn't look like anyone's on board," Stuart said, peering in the windows as they passed. "They could be below deck, I suppose."

"Or they could be in *there*." Declan nodded towards the pub on their left. Empty tables and chairs had been laid out across the dockside meaning people had to dodge around them if they were passing on through to the store. It was either that or enter the pub, which was probably, he conceded, the point of setting them out that way. "Shall we?"

"Don't mind if I do," Stuart said.

Inside, the pub stank of wet clothing, damp dogs and alcohol. Loud voices and laughter filled the air as the crowds avoiding the worst of the weather gathered and ordered drinks and food. Muffled conversations and dark glances were aimed by locals at the fair-weather holidaymakers as they sat comfortably at their small tables and booths, glowering at any who came too close.

"Far corner," Shakil said, turning his head to look at the chalkboard menu that was on the wall beside the bar to their left. "Your two o'clock, Stu. Don't look yet, Declan."

Being careful to move his eyes around the entire bar, Stuart looked where Shakil had indicated. Four men stood in a group, ignoring everyone around them, conducting a private conversation. Flanaghan was the only person whose face he could see, but Ted was recognisable as the man standing to his right.

"The gang's all here," Stuart muttered, turning back to the others.

"We won't get near them in here and we certainly can't record what they're saying," Shakil said glumly.

"No, but we do want to talk to Ivanov, don't we? I may know how to get to him."

Shakil and Declan looked at Stuart.

"We know that's his boat outside, don't we? Keep a look out; I'm going to hide on it."

"What will that do? You can't face him off on your own," Declan said. "Unless you have moves I don't know about?"

Stuart gave him a lopsided grin. "No moves. I'll stay hidden until he's well underway. What's he going to do? Push me overboard? Not if I take Harriet with me..."

"Harriet? Have you got a girl working with you that I don't know about? Is she the one with the moves?" Declan asked, wiggling his hips and making pretend karate chops with his arms. He accidentally elbowed the woman standing just behind him, making her spill her drink.

"Oi!" she protested. "Watch it. You're not Bruce Lee you know."

"Sorry, sorry, here, let me buy you a fresh one." Declan took her glass from her hand and sniffed it. "What is this? Vodka and orange?"

"Just orange," she said, grabbing it back again. "And I don't accept drinks from drunkards."

"I'm not—"

"Just leave it." Stuart nudged Declan. He smiled winningly at the woman. "It was my fault, he was demonstrating something to me—badly, I agree. Did you get any on your clothes?"

"What? No, no I don't think so," the woman said, momentarily disarmed by Stuart's dazzle. She looked down at her top. Stuart's eyes followed hers, a fact she noted as she looked back up at his face and his eyes weren't quick enough to follow. She crossed her arms in front of her ample chest, her eyes narrowing. "Not to worry, I was about to leave soon anyway."

"Are you all right, Kat?" The woman's male companion moved closer to the group, shoulders back and chest out.

"I'm fine, Max. And these gentlemen were just leaving, *weren't you*?"

"We were," Declan said hurriedly, pre-empting the scene that would draw attention to them. He reached into his pocket, pulled out a fiver and passed it across to Kat, who took it unthinkingly. "Please, buy yourself another. And I am truly sorry. Come on you guys." Grabbing an arm of each, he dragged Stuart and Shakil towards the door.

"We didn't even get a drink!" Stuart protested as they emerged into the rain.

"Good," Shakil said. "We don't want you drunk if you're going to pull this off. Let's go back to the car. I'll rig you up with a wire and we can collect Harriet. We'd better be quick though. We have no idea how long they'll be in there, do we?"

"I still don't know who Harriet is," Declan protested, running to keep up with the others who were streaking ahead of him and not even attempting to dodge the puddles.

A couple of minutes later he was leaning into the boot of Shakil's car, staring at the gun. "Is that *real*?"

"It is, or rather, it *was*, once. It's a Glock. I've had it since I was a kid. My uncle gave it to me. It's an old police gun that's been modified so it can't fire."

Declan shook his head. "That's no use. Stuart, do you even know how to hold it so it looks like you mean to use it?"

"Years of cops and robbers," Stuart said, grinning. He glanced around to see if anyone was nearby and seeing all was clear, took it from Shakil's hands, spun it expertly and aimed it at Declan's face.

"What are you going to do if he comes at you? Can you cock it? Does it sound like it's a working firearm?"

Stuart cocked the gun. Declan's lips pursed. "Don't get yourself killed. Remember the saying, if you pull out a weapon, you have to be prepared to use it. You can't use that. Don't you have anything else?"

"We have Mack," Shakil said.

"Let me guess, Mack the knife," Declan spluttered. "Do you guys have names for all your equipment?"

"Kinda," Stuart said. "He's right. Harriet will only work from a distance. If I'm close to him, I'll know she can't protect me, not properly, which means Ivanov might suss that fact out."

Shakil took Harriet back, uncocked it, and slid it into the waistband at the rear of his jeans. "I can handle myself in a fight. Stu, I think I should be the one to hide on board. I stand more chance of fending him off than you do and you know it." He passed the car keys to his friend. "Come on, wire me up and then keep an eye out while I go and hide on board the *Greglorious*."

The Greglorious

"Testing, testing, can you hear me?" Shakil whispered. He had hidden in the yacht's bathroom in the hope that Gregor wouldn't need to use it. If he came on board and went straight to the toilet, Shakil was in trouble.

"Ten-four." Stuart's voice sounded tinny in his ear. In the background, he could hear Declan laughing and saying, "You really did play cops and robbers, didn't you?" and it made him smile. Stuart's voice sounded again. "Radio silence; the targets are out of the pub. I repeat, the targets are out of the pub."

"Ten-four," Shakil whispered. "You'd better not talk to me once he's on board. We don't know if the sound leaks."

"Ten-four. Over and out."

Shakil silenced his earpiece and waited. Soon, male voices sounded on the dock and he heard the clatter of footsteps coming aboard. His heartbeat quickened. More than one person was boarding. He checked his wire was still in place and prayed that it would pick up any conversation. The footsteps came down the stairs and into the main living area of the yacht and soon the voices became clear.

"…don't understand how he managed to overcome Jamie," a male voice was saying. His speech was well modulated, his pronunciation crystal clear. "I let it pass whilst you explained it to the others, but I want to clear this up with you now we are alone."

"Sheer luck, I think. He'd been peeling spuds and still had the knife in his hand; he struck out as Jamie went for him and got an artery. Poor bastard went down and bled out in moments. Lucky for Dalgleish, eh? Next time, we'll have to be more creative."

"And you know all of this how?"

"When he didn't check in, I sent someone to see what was happening. He arrived at the same time as the ambulance finished loading Dalgleish and hung around. There were lots of onlookers so he was able to mingle and listen. The cops on scene were very talkative and not particularly quiet. It wasn't hard to put it together. Now, can I offer you a drink?"

"I see," the first speaker said, drawing the words out. "No. No drink, thank you, I'm not stopping." He fell silent for a few seconds and then spoke again. "Gregor, that's two failures. First Madeleine – and I was rather fond of her you understand – then the jackass who saw her with Ted."

"I know," the second speaker who Shakil now knew was Ivanov, said. "All I can do is apologise and explain. Firstly, I didn't put a hit on Madeleine—you know Ted suspected someone had been watching them together and you all wanted to know who it was. Carter was supposed to frighten her into giving Dalgleish's information up but she just wouldn't admit that he'd watched them at it and it wound him up. You know how volatile Carter is. He—went a bit Peaky Blinders on her."

"In my world, men never hit women," the first voice said evenly, seemingly unaware of the hypocrisy of his statement, "and I am not happy that this happened. There must have been a better way. Could you not have simply *asked* her about it?"

"They killed Polly," Ivanov said, evidently still on the Peaky Blinder's theme.

"I beg your pardon?"

"In Peaky Blinders. Polly. They killed her off. Look, Patrick, I agree it went too far and I agree none of this should have happened. But it has and we need to deal with it; tie up the loose ends."

Shakil inhaled sharply, then put his hand over his mouth in horror. The other person on the yacht was Patrick Hackensach. His heart hammered hard within the confines of his ribs as he wondered if his gasp had been heard by the others on board. He held his breath and let it out slowly when the conversation continued unabated.

"By that, Gregor, I take it you mean that you intend to locate Madeleine, who appears to have disappeared from the face of the earth, and silence both her and Dalgleish once and for all. Correct?"

Shakil heard the swallow. "Correct."

"Have you located her?"

"Not yet. We have people watching her house to see if she recovers and is stupid enough to go home. We're also watching the house of another girl who works for me. We think she's had something to do with Madeleine's disappearance because she hasn't worked since it happened."

They really don't know where Maddy is! Shakil thought happily.

"*Another* girl is involved? Explain, please," Patrick said, his voice betraying nothing of his feelings.

"She's one of my sex-cam workers. She lives in the same road as Maddy … but I wasn't aware they knew each other," Ivanov blustered.

"Let me get this straight. We now have a second girl who knows what happened to Madeleine and helped her to escape from under your nose. Does that sound about right? And now both of them are … somewhere … and you have no idea where? We have to assume she knows about us; about our arrangement with Madeleine. About me, Tennant and Flanaghan?"

Ivanov's silence spoke volumes, even to Shakil who was beginning to wonder whether Hackensach was the type of psychopath who would murder Ivanov on his own boat.

Patrick's voice broke the lengthy silence. "Tell me, are you intending to find and kill her, too? That smacks of shutting the stable door once the horse has bolted because we have no way of knowing who she has since spoken to. She obviously had other connections who have whisked them both off to safety without taking Madeleine to a hospital—I presume you *have* checked all the hospitals within, say, a fifty-mile radius? Where will this end?"

"They're in the wind," Ivanov said. "But we'll find them—and she can't have taken Maddy to a hospital or the police would be all over us."

"For your sake, Gregor, I hope you can find them swiftly. There is an awful lot at stake for me, as you are aware. If it comes out that I have … little peccadillos … my career is over. And if my career is over, so is your life. You have until midnight next Tuesday to tie up all the loose ends and I expect a text message at one minute past, telling me there is nothing to worry about or you won't live past twelve-thirty. In the meantime, as we were all discussing, you can send each of us a shortlist and video link of the girls so we can decide who will take Madeleine's place."

A stone of sickness plummeted into Shakil's stomach. They were planning on using another young girl – and she *would* be young, he was certain of that. They had to be stopped.

Now footsteps told Shakil the men were on the move, but this time they were receding from him. The last thing Shakil heard was Patrick saying, "Two things, Gregor: firstly, do not ever sully Madeleine's name again. She is not, and has never been, a Maddy. And secondly; it is considered bad form to name one's boat after oneself. Greglorious? Sounds cheap, dear chap."

And then they were gone. The footsteps moved across the boat and then one set returned to the engine room. Shakil was glad he'd stayed put as, before too long, the engine started up and the yacht began to move in reverse. He heaved a sigh of relief and switched on his earpiece. "Did you get all that?" he whispered.

"We did," Stuart's voice sounded triumphant in his ear. "We most certainly did. We're just watching Hackensach get into his Daimler. We missed it when we arrived; he'd parked it under a weeping willow so it was quite well concealed by the fronds. Now it's well concealed by bird shit."

Both men snorted quiet laughter.

"Murderous fucker, isn't he?"

"He is," Shakil agreed.

"Now, how are you going to get off that thing?"

"I'll wait until he stops, presumably he's heading home. I'll find a way off, don't worry about me."

The Hospital

While the three men were in Wroxham gathering evidence, Caroline remained sitting by her husband's bedside, holding his hand and chatting in the hope her voice would bring her husband around.

"I think it would be a good idea for us to put the house on the market," she said, expressing her private thoughts, hoping something would get through to him. "Not because I don't want you to have it if we divorce, but because I think we need a new place to create new memories if we don't.

Graham, I know you did a very bad thing. A very *stupid* thing, but I can get over it provided you promise not to do it again. Ever. So I need you to wake up and tell me everything will be all right because, at the moment, I don't know what to do." She squeezed the hand she was holding, hoping for an answering pressure against her fingers. None came.

Having bared her soul to him, Caroline found herself temporarily out of things to say. She glanced at the door for reassurance that the guards Stuart had hired were still outside but saw only an empty window. She frowned. Nobody had been in to see Graham since the last check an hour previously when the nurses had changed his fluid bag and emptied another, so where had the guards gone? It was getting late, perhaps they were changing shifts and others would appear momentarily. She released her hold on Graham's hand, went to the window and peered through it. Nobody was in the corridor. She eased the door open and peeked out. Not a soul was in sight. No nurses, no guards, nobody.

The hairs on the back of her neck raised. Something was wrong. Something was very wrong. Where were the guards? Why were there no nurses? She looked back at her husband, evaluating the hospital bed and the drip beside it that fed into the crook of Graham's elbow. She looked around the small room, noting the white coat that hung on the back of the door.

She came to a decision. She was moving her husband. She wasn't waiting for trouble to follow them, she wasn't going to allow him to become a sitting duck, she was going to be proactive. She took the white coat from the hook and slipped her arms into the sleeves, buttoned it up and prayed she looked like an official hospital worker. A badge on the left lapel proclaimed the owner to be Rajesh Singh.

Hopefully, nobody would look at that too closely if they were noticed. Next, she slid her handbag beneath the folded blanket at the foot of Graham's bed and looked at the wheels. She spotted the locks that were stopping the bed from moving and kicked them open. Now she opened the door fully, ensuring it caught the latch that would stop it swinging shut and wincing at the noise it made as it did so. She went to the head of Graham's bed, put one hand on the metal rail and another on the portable drip and began to push.

One of the wheels needed oiling. A piercing squeak assaulted her eardrums. Caroline's mouth dried and sweat began to form in her armpits and on her forehead. She ignored it all and kept pushing.

Manoeuvring through the door was tricky but she managed it with only minor scrapes. Once the bed was through, she carefully tugged the drip alongside and they were in the corridor. She stopped moving and listened. The only thing she could hear was the buzzing that was coming from an overhead light that was on its way out. It flickered on and off at odd intervals, sometimes catching fully, sometimes plunging that section of corridor into a twilight gloom. Apart from that small sound, nobody moved, not even to see why she was moving a patient from his ITU room.

Something was, indeed, very wrong.

Caroline went to the foot of the bed and shoved until it was facing in the direction of the lifts. She was going to have to traverse the length of the corridor to get to the internally locked doors that kept ITU patients separated from the rest of the hospital. The lifts were outside of these doors and to the right.

She pushed the squeaking bed and drip, walking swiftly and with as much confidence as she could muster. If anyone came from behind her, they may not realise who she was or who was in the bed. She reached the ITU entrance and left the head of the bed to press the button that opened the doors. A buzzing sound let her know the door was ready to open and she tugged on it. It opened and hit the foot of the bed. She was going to have to rethink this. She let the door close again and went back to the head of the bed. She grasped the rail and drip and tugged both, trying to turn the bed so that she would be able to get them both through, along with her, in one fell swoop. It took what felt like an age for her to swing the bed around to the opposite direction without banging it against the corridor walls and her hands were sweaty and slipped and slid on the rail, but she managed it without dislodging Graham or upending the drip. Her breath was now coming hard and fast, hitching in her chest. She wasn't sure whether this was from exertion or from the incalculable fear that was crawling up and down her spine and gathering intensity. She calculated the distance needed to be able to open the door so she could pull the bed through and re-hit the button to open it.

This time, she was able to pull it open to its fullest extremity. Keeping one foot pressed against the door to stop it swinging shut, she pulled the drip stand ahead of her and then tugged on the bed, easing Graham through. Now the bed banged against the door. Caroline held her breath at each tug and each bang and crash, the noise sounding immensely louder in her fever-pitched brain than it was in reality.

"Relax," she muttered to herself. "People hear this kind of noise every day. It's nothing new. Stop worrying." But her eyes darted from left to right and sweat dripped down her face and plopped to the floor in fat droplets. She kept tugging and finally, praise the Lord, *finally,* they were through.

The door to the ITU swung closed and sealed. Caroline turned the bed towards the lifts and went and pressed all the buttons available. As one arrived, she hopped from foot to foot, waiting to see if anyone was inside who may challenge her. Her luck was holding; the lift was empty. She pushed Graham and the drip inside and squeezed alongside the bed. Which way should she go? Up or down? Recalling every horror show she'd ever seen where people always pressed to go up and came unstuck, she pressed the lowest button marked B. Then, thinking cleverly, she also pressed the buttons marked 3, 2 and G, so that if anybody was trying to find them and thought to check the lifts, they'd have to try all four levels.

Of course, this meant that the lift stopped and the doors opened on all the floors. Pre-empting this, she angled the bed across the lift and waved away the waiting people saying, "Sorry, no room. I'll send it back," and pressing the 'close door' button several times in a bid to have it close before anyone ignored her words. After what felt like an age, the lift reached level B. Caroline had no idea what was down there but didn't actually care. As the doors opened onto an empty, undecorated corridor that had a rough cement floor, she exited and pulled Graham's bed through with her, remembering to grab the drip only when Graham's arm was moved by the stand's immobility.

Before the lift moved again, she pressed the buttons for every single floor and then she allowed it to depart.

The corridor they were in obviously wasn't part of the main building and it was cold down here. No voices floated towards them. No sounds of movement came from anywhere. The hairs on her arms prickled to attention in the chilly air. To her right, the corridor ended in a single room, the door to which had no window in it. To her left, the corridor turned. Leaving Graham where he was, she sped to her left and peered around the corner, seeing another room, the door to which had windows. Caroline ran back to Graham and pushed him to her right, towards the door that no one could look through. When they reached it, she pulled it open and found herself looking at a variety of discarded cleaning equipment that was stacked, higgledy-piggledy around the edges of a smallish cupboard. There was just about room for a bed. Caroline, Graham and the drip stand soon occupied that space.

Jasmine

After having sat with her mother at her father's bedside for some hours, Caroline had sent her daughter home. "There's no point both of us sitting here watching him sleep," she'd said, "so go and feed Chutzi and then catch some shut-eye yourself."

Jasmine hadn't argued. The doctors had said that her father was stable and she was exhausted, so, after kissing both her parents, she took herself off to the house they were currently living in. She eyed it balefully as she let herself in, missing their old house immensely. Chutzpah came running, his tail thumping on the floor, his rear end wiggling with excitement at seeing her.

Jasmine dropped to her knees and buried her face in the dog's fur, kissing his snout and the bit between his two piercingly blue eyes over and over again. "Was I gone forever?" she teased. "Do you need your din dins?"

Chutzpah chuffed his agreement, twirled around and led the way up the short hallway and into the kitchen. Jasmine followed him, laughing to herself as he turned to face her and then turned his face towards the cupboard where his kibble was. "It didn't take long for you to suss where that's kept, did it?" she said, opening the door and reaching into the bag to bring out a bowlful for him while the dog pranced around eagerly in anticipation.

She put him through his sit, down and high-five routine, then put the bowl down for him. Soon the room echoed with the sound of the dog happily chasing the bowl around with his snout as he attempted to get every last speck of food from it. Jasmine refilled his water bowl and placed that down for him too, then she put the kettle on and pulled out her phone. Jamie still hadn't called. She checked the signal – full bars – and huffed at the humiliation she felt crawling over her skin. What had she expected? She'd met a handsome guy at a club, gone back to his place where she'd willingly had sex with him and left, leaving only a note behind her. It was obviously the way he operated; he'd been the 'shag 'em and leave 'em to it' kind of guy she'd heard her friends talk about. More fool her.

Shrugging, she chalked it up to experience and made herself a cup of tea. While it cooled, she put the lead on Chutzpah and took him out for a quick walk around the block. When they got back, she downed the tepid drink and took herself off to bed where Chutzpah curled up beside her.

Chapter Fifteen
Monday

SAS Investigations Office

At one am, as Stuart and Declan were racing towards the hospital to check on Graham, Stuart's phone rang and showed Shakil was calling reverse charge. Stuart accepted the call and put it on speakerphone so Declan could hear, saying, "Shaks, are you all right?" as the call connected.

"Can you come and get me?" Shakil's voice was shaky.

"Where are you?" Stuart replied, his tone betraying his anxiety. "We've been waiting for you to call. After what we heard, we've been trying to raise the guards at the hospital, but they're not responding. We're on the way to see what's going on."

"I've only just found a phone box – they're rarer than hen's teeth nowadays. My phone died and so did the wire when I went into the water."

"You went into the water? What happened? Does Ivanov know you were on his boat? Did he push you overboard?"

"Stu, I'll tell you everything, just please come and get me before I end up with pneumonia."

"Where are you?"

"I'm in a village called, hang on, yeah, Thatcherton."

"Never heard of it," Stu said. He put his finger over the mouthpiece and hissed, "Declan, can you Google it?" He removed his finger and said, "Can you wait for us in the box? If you're wet, it'll be warmer in there than outside. Are you on the main road?"

Shakil laughed between shuddering shivers. "There *is* only one road here. It's the size of a postage stamp and there are only half a dozen houses. Ivanov's in one of them, I think. I was on the boat for about an hour before he moored up so I waited until I heard him getting off, left it for a bit and then went up on deck. If I stay here and he comes out, I'll be seen. I'm going to head out along the road and wait behind some bushes."

"How did you end up in the river?" Stuart asked.

"Got it," Declan said, interrupting. "It's about half an hour from here, about, oh, twenty-five or so miles if we put our foot down. It's a bit out of the way, but if we cut through from *here*," he held up the map he had pulled up on his phone to Stuart who glanced at it and nodded, "we'll pick up the main route to the hospital again without too much trouble. It'll add about … fifteen minutes or so. Take a left at the next roundabout and I'll direct you from there."

"I heard that," Shakil said. "Thanks, guys, I'll go and hide."

"Okay, so long as we can get there without too much delay," Stu said. "Shaks, how did you end up in the river?"

"Got to go, I see a door opening. See you in a while."

Stuart stared at his phone and then glanced at Declan, who shrugged and said, "Fell in?"

Stuart rolled his eyes. Of course, that was why Shakil had been so cagey about it. He grinned. "That's one to tell Tammy."

"Harsh," Declan said, also grinning. "Put your foot down."

They had a clear run and got there in twenty minutes, slowing as they reached the outskirts of Thatcherton to search for someone hiding behind a bush. There were no lampposts and it was pitch dark.

"There," Declan said, pointing as Shakil's face appeared from behind a large bush, just ahead of them.

Stuart pulled up alongside him, the rear door opened and Shakil threw himself onto the seat. "Turn the heater up a bit," he said, shivering all over.

Stuart reached for the heater knob and turned it to full blast, pulling away from the roadside smoothly as Shakil slotted his seatbelt into its rightful place. "There's a blanket on the parcel shelf, help yourself." He heard his friend shifting about and glanced into the rear-view mirror to see that Shakil had found it, shucked off his sodden jacket and pulled it around his shoulders. "So, Shaks, just how *did* you end up so wet?" he asked, glancing into the rear-view mirror again to catch his friend's expression and blinking in surprise at the mud that covered Shakil's face.

"He tied the boat to the end of a long wooden runway type thing," Shakil said, the words dragging from his lips. "It was dark and I didn't want to put the torch on so I just walked along it. There was a missing board or two and I didn't see the gap."

"So you fell in?" Declan said, making sure he was facing away from Shakil so he couldn't see his smile.

"I was bloody lucky to get out again!" Shakil said angrily. "I had to swim for the bank and there are weeds and *things* at the bottom of that river. *Living* things! Something caught at my foot and I had to shuck my shoe off to escape its grip. I lost one of my *shoes*! I paid a ton for these and now one's at the bottom of that, that, *stinking* quagmire! *And* the bank was high and slippery and I fell back in as often as I tried to climb out."

"Those bloody sharks will insist on leaving the sea to come into our rivers," Declan said, his voice bubbling with mirth.

"No, it was probably a piranha," Stuart said, straight-faced. "There's a family of ten, no, wait, you only have small feet, Shaks—a family of *six* living in it now. I bet their neighbours are all at the surface, clamouring for its pair…"

"Ha bloody ha," Shakil said. "Laugh it up."

"Oh, we will, fish boy," Declan said, turning to look at him, his face split by a huge smile. "Next right, Stu."

The jibes continued as the car sped towards the hospital and by the time they pulled up outside, all three of them were laughing at Shakil's expense.

"I'd better not come in."

"Have you dried out a bit?" Stuart asked, switching off the engine. "At least the rain's stopped now. How's about we go in and you keep a look out to see if you recognise anyone coming out."

"None of the four are going to be here, are they," Shakil said. It wasn't a question. "I'll wait here but can you leave me a phone? If you need backup, I can come at a run."

"You have no shoes," Stuart and Declan said simultaneously.

"I can still run in my socks if need be," Shakil said. "Now piss off before I lose my rag."

"Okay," Stuart said as both he and Declan opened their doors. He leaned back in just before he closed it. "We're hopping it now…"

Shakil shook his head as the door slammed and the two men hared towards the hospital steps and disappeared from view.

***

The cupboard was hot and stale. The room had no window or air conditioning and Caroline was now dripping with sweat and worrying about whether there was enough oxygen in the room. She'd long since stripped off the white coat and the jumper she'd been wearing beneath it. Now she was just dressed in her jeans and a vest top and that was becoming ominously transparent from sweat. She'd also been checking the drip and the bag was almost empty. She pulled out her phone to see if she was able to find a signal but still no bars showed. There was nothing for it; she was going to have to leave the cupboard. She needed to call her son.

Caroline pushed the door ajar gingerly, flinching at the blast of cool air that made her skin prickle and listening hard for any sounds coming from the corridor outside. When she heard nothing, she pushed it open wide enough to be able to slip out and left it that way so that the cool fresh air reached Graham. She checked her phone. No bars. She ran as quietly as she could up the corridor towards the corner that led to the lifts, searching for a signal that remained obstinately unobtainable. She rounded the corridor just as the lift door opened and a man wearing a white coat exited. His head jerked back in surprise when he saw her.

"My word, you gave me a start," he blurted, holding a hand to his heart as the lift doors slid shut behind him. "What on earth are you doing down here, sweet lady? If you're trying to find one of your relatives, I'm afraid the mortuary isn't open for visitors. Whoever you're looking for will be transferred to the funeral home once those arrangements have been made. You'll be able to visit whoever it is you want to see then."

"The, the *mortuary*?" Caroline managed, understanding why it had been so quiet and why it was so cold on level B.

"Yes, we keep the deceased in that room there." The man nodded reverently to the door that held windows, in the opposite direction to where Caroline had left Graham. "You went the wrong way anyway. There's nothing down there but our cleaning cupboard."

"I, I know," Caroline said, thinking on her feet. "I'm afraid I got a bit lost. I was trying to find the way out and must have hit the wrong button on the lift."

The man laughed. "Didn't you see all the floor levels? They're quite clearly marked. I'm so sorry I wasn't here to be able to help you earlier, there's been a bit of trouble up on ITU so it's been all hands on deck up there, and I was roped in, for my sins." He laughed again.

That meant Graham's departure from the unit hadn't gone unnoticed. "I was a bit upset when I got into the lift. I thought I'd hit the right button. I'm so sorry. Am I in any trouble?" Caroline allowed her lower lip to wobble.

"Oh no, dear lady. Not at all. Here, let me take you up." He turned and pressed the button to call the lift and when it arrived, escorted Caroline inside, his nose wrinkling in distaste when he found himself in close proximity with a woman who had been sweating profusely for the best part of several hours. When the door opened, he practically shoved her out. "Turn right and go straight ahead. You'll see the exit," he said as the lift doors closed once more with him inside it.

Caroline waited until she was certain he wasn't going to appear again and turned towards the exit. She checked her phone and found she now had a signal. As she walked towards the doors, she rang Stuart without looking where she was going, so it was somewhat of a shock when she heard his phone ringing directly in front of her, looked up and saw Stuart staring at her, looking equally as shocked to see her.

SAS Investigations Office

"Did you expect us to be working twenty-four-seven?" Shakil asked as Stuart walked into the office carrying two large Starbucks and yawning. He'd been listening to messages that had been left on the office answer phone.

"Nope," Stuart said, setting one of the cups in front of Shakil and plonking himself down onto the visitor seat opposite. "I feel like I should be knackered, especially after last night, but truth be told, sorting out what we're going to do with our recording has me buzzing."

"Me too. The thing is, we're neglecting our other clients and we've missed a load of calls. Some people have left us messages asking for help but we've also had a couple from people who are pretty pissed that we haven't called them back. We're going to need to take someone else on for the bread and butter stuff, and it would be a good idea to employ someone to work in the office. You know, someone to answer the calls and book appointments for us. I know Caroline wanted to help, but she's too busy with your father and I doubt she's going to want to come back."

"She needs some proper sleep, too. Who'd have thought she'd take it upon herself to keep Dad safe last night?" Stuart began to laugh. "I still can't get over her leaving him in the mortuary!"

Shakil began to chuckle too. "I wish I'd seen that."

"Declan's face was a picture," Stuart said, still laughing. "He got the proper heebie-jeebies down there. Still, she kept Dad safe because Ivanov's guys took out our guards far too easily. If she hadn't spotted them gone, they'd have been sitting ducks. It was perfect timing; the hitmen were busy locking the guards and nurses into one of the empty rooms when she got him out. A few seconds earlier or later and who knows what would have happened."

"I can't believe I missed all the action! Tell me what happened again."

"It was all on CCTV. I sat and watched it with one of the hospital security guards before the police showed up. They let me because it was me and Declan who found all the staff in the room they'd been locked in and let them out. A couple of porters went down to get Mum and Dad and they put him in another private room on a different floor – I kept the guards we used well away from them; they think he's been moved to another hospital for his safety so when you talk to them, play it that way because I'm not sure we can trust them. Anyway, after all the commotion, he began to come around, so they decided he didn't need to be in ITU anymore. It was odd," Stuart frowned as he recalled what he'd seen. "These blokes were professionals. They rounded everyone up using a firearm, locked them up and then went straight to Dad's room. They knew exactly where to go. But when they realised he wasn't in there they just kind of gave up and made a run for it. CCTV has them disappearing into the stairwell and then it catches them strolling out of the building. They didn't bother searching for him. If we'd got there any earlier, we'd have probably bumped into them." Now Stuart began to belly laugh. "Mum juggling Dad's bed and the drip stand was priceless; you should have seen her trying to turn him to go through the door. No wonder she was in such a state when we ran into her. I've never seen her so bedraggled."

Shakil's mouth twitched. Caroline was always super cool, in his opinion, and he adored her almost as much as Stuart did, so for her to be in that state, she must have gone to hell and back. "Poor Caroline," he muttered.

"I know. But she was much happier once we'd got Dad sorted out and another bag of fluids attached to his drip. I'll give her a ring in a bit, see if she got any sleep at all."

"That's a good idea. Now, what are we going to do about this place?"

"Oh, that!" Stuart waved a hand airily. "Yes, I agree with everything you said. We're going to be quids in once all this is sorted out so we'll be able to afford it."

"I still don't understand how we're going to make anything at all from this," Shakil said, frowning. "I mean; Declan's been working on this as much as we have so I doubt he's going to want to pay us what we quoted."

Stuart smiled triumphantly. "If things go to plan, we won't need him to."

"Explain."

After he'd finished telling Shakil that Declan had been right with what he thought they should do next, and how they were going to go about it, Stuart left him to return the most important calls and do one or two other things while Stuart headed for the Clinic, to help get Madeleine out.

The Clinic

"You'll be ready to leave later today," Doc cheerfully told Madeleine as she completed the last of her checks and slung her stethoscope around her neck. "Your nose is doing surprisingly well, it hardly shows that it was broken, and now that the swelling has gone down, your cheekbone appears to be knitting back into place nicely. The bites and burns on your breasts are healing but you need to accept that they may leave small scars. Are you still practising your deep breathing?" She waited to see Madeleine's slight nod and continued, "Is your ribcage still sore? I'm absolutely amazed you escaped pneumonia! Now, your arms will need to remain in plaster for some time, so are you certain Sarah will be able to look after you? She'll need to be able to take you to urinate and to keep that area clean, especially while the stitches heal and that means she'll be dealing with you when you menstruate, too. Would you like me to prescribe you with the pill? You can take it continuously for a few months to stop that indignity, at least."

Madeleine nodded again.

Doc scribbled something on her notepad and continued, "Your colostomy should be reversible with time, but she'll need to learn how to keep the stoma clean and how to replace the bags, too, until you have use of your arms. Do you think she's up for all of this? How's your sight? Are the creams and drops helping or is everything still blurry?"

Madeleine's head swam from the rapid-fire information. "Okay," she ventured, uncertain which question to answer first.

"So you can see me clearly?"

"My right eye has better vision than the left," she said. "There are strange black *swimmy* things, a bit like tadpoles, in that one."

"Floaters. Nothing to worry about there. You are a lucky girl. I didn't expect you to pull through and look at you now!"

Madeleine looked down at herself. She didn't feel particularly lucky. Aside from everything the doctor had just mentioned, her head itched, her bottom hurt and so did the soles of her feet. The itching was driving her mad. "When can I wash my hair?"

Doc smiled. "You *are* getting better. I'll have one of the nurses do it for you before you leave. Now, I have to get on. I'll have all the medicines you need ready for you to take away with you and a list of exactly how and when you need to take them. It is *vital* that you complete the course of everything I give you, especially the antibiotics, or you may yet come unstuck and I'll need to see you again in a week or so to check how things are going. I presume you won't want to come here if you're going into hiding. You *are* going into hiding, aren't you?"

"Stuart's found somewhere for us to live," Madeleine said.

"Well, tell him I need your new address so I can come and check up on you."

"I will."

The two women looked at each other for a few seconds.

"I'm glad you survived," Doc said eventually.

"I can never thank you enough," Madeleine said, smiling. The movement hurt and was slightly lopsided, but it was still a beautiful thing to see.

"No need," Doc said, beaming in return. "Besides, I'll be sending my bill out soon enough. You'll be crying then…" And then she was off without a backwards glance leaving Madeleine to wonder how the hell she was going to be able to pay for all the treatment she'd received and whether they would take cash—if she had enough saved up.

She was still fretting some hours later when Stuart and Sarah arrived to collect her, a fact that didn't escape either of them.

"What's up?" Stuart said, going straight to her bedside and stroking her freshly washed hair from her forehead.

"I can go home," Madeleine told him, and then she began to cry.

"Isn't that good news?" Sarah said, rushing to her other side. "Honestly Maddy, you're gonna love our new home. It's absolutely beautiful, right on the clifftop overlooking both the sea and rolling hills. It's so much nicer than either of our places in Lakeland Road."

"It's not that…" Madeleine choked the words out. "It's how I'm going to *pay* for all of *this*." She waggled her fingertips and nodded down the length of her body. "I have no way of earning now. I don't know how to do anything else! And I bet my money was stolen, wasn't it?"

Stuart bent over her and tipped her chin so she had to look at him. "You will not be paying a single penny for this," he said softly, staring deep into her enormous eyes as tears spilled down her cheeks. "Any bills and all your living expenses are going to be provided for many years to come. You won't *need* to work but you might find you want to study and that may lead to you doing something valuable later. Capiche?"

He could feel Sarah's eyes burning a hole in the top of his head as he watched Madeleine frown and then give a slight nod. She believed him but had no idea where this financial aid was going to magically appear from. She was well aware that the government wasn't known for its generosity, and suspected they wouldn't help her if they learned how she'd been earning a living up until now. Once a whore, always a whore seemed to be the opinion of the people she'd surrounded herself with for the entirety of her short adult life and, she suspected, also that of everyone else.

"Stop frowning," Stuart said, grinning. "Trust me. Now, what's this about your money? Isn't it in the bank?"

"The bank?" Madeleine sniffed. "No, I don't trust banks. I only have an account so I can pay bills and I put in exactly what I need to pay out every month. The rest of it is hidden."

"Hidden where? Would you like me to ask Declan to get it for you?"

Madeleine stared at him, her mouth working as it fleetingly crossed her mind as to whether she could trust Declan with her life savings.

"He won't do a runner with it, I promise." Stuart crossed his heart, licked his index finger and raised it to the air. "Cross my heart and hope to die," he pronounced soberly, keeping his eyes firmly on hers. "You wouldn't be here and alive today if it wasn't for him."

Madeleine couldn't help herself. She giggled.

"So, are you ready to get out of here?" Sarah asked, rather spoiling the moment that she sensed occurring, even if the pair in front of her didn't. She was a bit put out by the comment about Madeleine only surviving because of Declan when it had been she who had found her and called him. Plus, she knew Declan had feelings for Madeleine and didn't want Stuart cocking things up for him. She glared at Stuart when he glanced up at her.

"I need my meds," Madeleine said, turning towards Sarah. "And before you take me anywhere, you need to understand exactly what me getting out is going to mean for you." She explained what she remembered of Doc's instructions, watching Sarah's face closely, expecting to see her face fall, for the backtracking to begin.

Sarah didn't flinch once. "Maddy, Doc's been through this with me and it's not a problem. I nursed my father through cancer when I was ten years old," she said. "He died when I was fourteen. I can nurse you standing on my head— especially because this time, I know my patient will get better."

Madeleine's eyes filled with tears again. "What did I do to deserve you?" she sobbed.

Sarah watched in amusement as Stuart pulled himself to full height, put his hands behind his back and began to rock back and forth on his heels, obviously not having a clue how to deal with all the emotion in the room. She swiped a tissue from the box on Madeleine's bedside table, scrunched it up and held it to Madeleine's nose. "Blow," she said, wiping expertly when the girl did as she'd been told. She took out another tissue and wiped beneath Madeleine's eyes, removing the tears gently then she dropped both into the wastepaper basket beside the table.

"So," Stuart said, clearing his throat, glad the tears were over with. "Where did you hide your money?"

"Under my bed."

"Seriously?"

"Seriously. My rug goes partway under the bed. If you tell Declan to lift it up, he'll see one of the floorboards is slightly short of the other. If he hooks his nail in," she glanced at Stuart's hands, noted the shortness of his nails and realised Declan's would be similar, particularly as he worked with his hands, and amended her words, "or something thin like a wire coat hanger, it'll come up. There's an envelope in the gap below it."

"Okay. Let's get you installed in your new home and then Declan will go and get your cash for you."

"Really?"

"Really."

77 Lakeland Road

Having helped to install Madeleine in her new Mudchurch home, Declan reluctantly drove away to go and fetch her money, marvelling at the cloak and dagger stuff they'd had to pull to get her out of the Clinic without any prying eyes evidencing the move. He knew they couldn't be too careful, the men they were dealing with had money to burn, spies watching every move they made, and were prepared to use guns to make their point.

It had involved the use of a private ambulance, a Rastafarian friend and his non-Rastafarian wife, both of whom Stuart and Shakil knew from their old weed dealing days, and a couple of teenage ex-offenders who had served time for TWOCing who had come under the radar of SAS Investigations when a middle-aged housewife had called to ask for proof that the pair were casing local vehicles because she was worried they'd steal her old KA. The two lads were merely goofing around because they had nowhere else to go. Shakil had watched them from the woman's window for an hour or so one evening and then went out and struck them in conversation when he realised they meant no harm. He remembered being their age only too well, the looks he and Stuart had got when they'd hung out on street corners, the way people crossed the street when they saw them. He'd never known whether it was because people found them threatening – and that was kinda funny because they were hanging most days – or because of the colour of his skin and Stu's penchant for dancing on the spot—he'd never been able to stand entirely still.

This pair had reminded Shakil of those days. He'd advised them to hang around elsewhere knowing that the woman who had reported them would very probably also report what she was seeing to the police and that could be it for them as they were both on probation. The lads had been grateful and told him if he ever needed their help, to let them know, and then they'd taken themselves off to clown around in the park. When he had texted to ask if they'd be happy to help him out with something, they said yes, so Shakil passed them Declan's number and told them to call him to be told what they'd need to do. Declan had done so…

"You mean, you want one of us to stick a blonde wig on and pretend to be a chick? And the other one to dress like the gay boy in the photo?"

Declan, who had sent a picture of Stuart to them, bit back a laugh and said, "Yes."

"And then you want us to go to some private clinic place, find a blue Hyundai – can't you make it a Beemer?

No? Oh well – and then take it for a long drive wherever we want and drop it back at this other address about midnight?"

"Yes," Declan said. "And that's when you'll be paid. There'll be petrol in the car, you won't need to refill it, just don't go so far that you run out of juice and have to dump it, okay? And don't prang it!"

"That's lit, fam!"

Declan hesitated. "Does that mean you'll do it?"

"For a ton each? Hell, yeah, said so, din't I? Me mum's got a blonde wig, I'll nick it off her and take me clippers to it. She looks a right dog in it so I'll be doin' 'er a favour, innit, even if she gets salty."

"Oookay," Declan said slowly, having only understood about half of what the youngster had said but taking it on faith that they'd turn up and do what he'd asked. He gave them the details of where they had to be and when, and where the car keys would be left, and ended the call hoping Shakil was right and that they were trustworthy.

The Rastafarian, a friendly guy who went by the name Bobby M in deference to the infamous Mr Marley and who looked very much like him, from the lengthy dreads and thready beard to the colourful crocheted beret, had been extremely happy to play the part of an ambulance driver and his wife, Tansy, an overweight brunette with one side of her head shaved and the other cut into a long angular bob, the part of a paramedic, especially when they were told that it might be risky.

"Mon, me *thrive* on danger! An' me 'ave me protection 'ere," Bobby M sang, patting his crotch.

Tansy sighed and rolled her eyes. She thumped the top of her husband's arm. "Marcus, for God's sake, talk properly.

You're from Camden, not Jamaica, and you sound bloody stupid."

Bobby M sucked his teeth and gave his wife a dirty look, but he heeded her words. "Go over it again," he said.

So Declan did.

Bobby M and Tansy pulled the ambulance up at the rear of the Clinic at the appointed time, reversed towards the back door and waited with the engine running. Tansy hopped out and went to open the rear doors. The position of the ambulance left approximately a six-inch gap between the end of the slight incline that led from the building and the vehicle. Shortly afterwards, a hospital porter wheeled a hospital bed down the short ramp to the waiting vehicle attended by two nurses, one male and carrying a medical bag, the other female and holding aloft a drip, who both shielded the patient's face for the few seconds they were out in the open and were then swiftly hidden by the van doors. They fussed over the patient as the bed was carefully slotted inside then they got in with their patient, Tansy closed the door, signed a form that was presented to her by the porter and then got back into the driver's cab, beside her husband.

"Off we go Marcus," she said loudly as she hopped inside. "Let's get this poor old lady to the hospice before she pegs it."

In the back of the ambulance, Stuart, Sarah and Madeleine stared at each other and waited to see whether they'd got away with it. Inside, the Clinic had gone into lockdown mode.

Meanwhile, the two young ex-offenders who had gone into the Clinic in their usual garb of baggy, low-slung jeans that showed the backs of their underpants and garishly coloured, oversized t-shirts, came out of the front door slightly before the ambulance departed, dressed as Stuart and Sarah (who was giggling very much like he thought a girl would giggle; i.e., not at all convincingly if you were anywhere near them) keeping their heads down. As the doors to the Clinic were securely locked behind them, they loped around the building to the rear car park where they located the keys, got into Stu's Hyundai, and wheel spun the vehicle out onto the main road. They set off towards Brighton, a place both of them had fancied visiting during their TWOCing days but never managed to get as far as without being arrested. Behind them, a nondescript black Range Rover pulled out into the traffic and followed.

The ambulance, followed by a different black Range Rover, drove sedately along all the major roads where there were plenty of other vehicles to witness anything should the people in the Range Rover decide to do something stupid. It turned into the hospital grounds and drove straight to the A & E entrance. However, it did not stop there, it turned to the left and went through a guarded barrier that led towards a private area at the rear of the hospital where all ambulance transfers of patients from other medical establishments were taken to be admitted to the various wards. It was a strictly ambulance-only zone. Inside the ambulance, as they passed through the barrier admitting them to the area at the rear of the building, Marcus and Tansy grinned at the frustration on the faces of the two men in the Range Rover who were refused admission.

This had been where Declan had entered the fray. Shakil's new girlfriend, Trudy, had friends in the main hospital and had called to ask them to turn a blind eye to Declan's van accessing the staff car park just west of the ambulance-only area. This too was a private area that had strict staff-only access. As she had on previous occasions, she explained that the patient was being transferred home but the likelihood was that she wouldn't make it that far without help. Her friends, who knew the people she helped treat were those who wanted no attention drawn to themselves, were happy to help on the proviso that none of their names cropped up should things go awry. She'd given Shakil a staff pass card that, when presented at the barrier, unlocked the gates that led from the staff parking area to the private road at the rear of the hospital. It was considered one of the perks of the job, having their own staff car park, and one which very few other hospitals offered.

Declan had been ready and waiting. He'd put false plates on his van to throw anyone who might recognise it off the scent, applied a magnetic decal he'd borrowed from a friend who ran a flower shop, and the transfer of Madeleine, along with Stuart and Sarah, from the ambulance and into the rear of his van had gone seamlessly, as had the journey to the girls' new home in Mudchurch.

Now, as he approached Lakeland Road in the dead of night, his heart rate began to increase. He knew Madeleine's house was still being watched and wondered whether they would be watching the rear of the property. He was working on the surmise that, as nothing had happened here for over a week now, the watchers would have become sloppy from boredom. He drove past the house surreptitiously, looking into all the vehicles that lined this part of the road and smiled when he saw a couple of men whose heads rested against the side windows of a dark-coloured Suzuki jeep. Keeping an eye on it, he pulled the van still bearing the false plates and flower shop logo into a space a little further along the road and pulled on the handbrake. The men's heads did not move.

Brazenly, Declan strolled out of the van and up to the house belonging to the neighbours who had seen all the comings and goings at Madeleine's. Praying they were awake and would recognise him from the conversation he'd had with them in the garden, he walked up their short pathway and knocked quietly on the door, relieved to see a light glimmering from inside the house. He waited for a few seconds then saw the outline of someone shuffling towards the door.

"Yes," came the worried voice of an old woman from behind the door. "Who is it?"

"I'm the person you spoke to when your neighbour was attacked," Declan said, keeping his voice low.

"I can't quite hear you, dear," the voice said.

Declan sighed and was just about to say it again but louder when he heard a chain rattling on the other side of the door and it was opened. A blast of noise from a football match playing on a television inside the property hit his ears. The elderly lady looked at Declan and her face became pensive. "I know you from somewhere, don't I? No, don't tell me ... yes, you're the one who was in our neighbour's garden when she was attacked, aren't you?"

"Yes," Declan said, nodding. "And you're Mo and your husband is Reg, right? I'm Declan. Look, I'm sorry to bother you this time of night and I will explain, but can I please come in? I don't want the men who are watching her house to think I shouldn't be here."

The woman's face changed. She stuck her head outside, looking both angry and smug at the same time as she swivelled it from side to side, looking at the cars parked along the road. "Are those bastards *still* hanging ar—?"

"Please can I come in?" Declan interrupted before her voice raised any higher and attracted the attention of the men in the Jeep.

"What? Oh, yes, of course you can." She stepped aside and opened the door to admit him.

"Thank you," Declan said, passing her and stepping into her hallway.

She closed the door behind them. "Move ahead," she said, chivvying him with a flap of her hands. "Move ahead. Reg is in the sitting room. He's watching England play again and trying to figure out where they went wrong. I keep trying to delete the recording but he insists on watching it when we can't sleep. That's it, follow the racket, right to the end then turn right."

Smiling to himself, Declan allowed himself to be swept along by her. He went through the open door and Reg, the elderly husband, looked up from the match.

"Hello lad," he said with a smile. He pressed a button on the remote control that rested on the arm of the chair he was on and the sound level decreased. "Pull up a chair. How's the young lass from next door? It's good of you to come to let us know, we've been worried, haven't we Mo?"

"Yes, we have. Now turn that rubbish off," Mo said firmly.

"No need, no need," Declan said, bending his arms and holding his hands up in the traditional gesture of peace as he perched on the edge of a well-worn settee. "She's doing okay. It was a bit touch and go for a while, but she pulled through. Look, I'm sorry to disturb you so late but I need to get in next door. Madeleine left something behind and she's asked me to get it for her. I can't go in through her front door because of the people watching, so I need to go in round the back. Can I hop over your fence?"

"She's not coming back, is she?" Mo asked shrewdly.

"No. It's not safe for her here. She's moved somewhere else."

"Can we see her? I'd like to say goodbye."

Declan inclined his head. "I can pass your phone number on to her but I'm afraid I can't let you have her address for your own safety."

Mo and Reg shared a look. Declan waited.

"The thing is," Reg said. "Last time we spoke to you, we told you that one of the men who, let's not beat around the bush, *abused* that poor lass, was a friend of our son, Neil. We gave you a photo of him at Neil's fiftieth, didn't we? Well, um, we were wrong."

"I know," Declan said gently. "Do you know who it really was?"

Mo nodded angrily. "We do. Some woman knocked here last Friday pretending she wanted to find out how we're going to vote in the local elections. She gave me a leaflet with his picture all over it. I don't know how I kept my face straight! He's our local MP, Robert Flanaghan."

"Did you tell her you knew him?" Declan asked, his eyes wide with alarm.

"I'm not so green as I'm cabbage-looking," Mo said. Then, seeing the look of confusion on Declan's face, she added, "That means I'm not daft. No lad, of course I didn't tell her I knew him. She even asked me if I'd met him. Said he'd canvassed here a couple of years ago. I said no, he'd never knocked on my door—and I wasn't lying, was I!"

Declan gave her a wry grin. "Do you think she believed you?"

"Well, we're not dead yet," Mo said flatly. "And they're still watching her house, aren't they? We both pretend not to notice when we go down to town. They think we're a pair of daft old coots so we act the part. Who are we to tell them otherwise?"

"And," Reg volunteered, "I've taken quite a few photographs of the blokes who are hanging around, watching her house."

"Why did you do that?" Declan asked, astounded.

"Because we had the feeling you weren't going to let it drop and that you'd be back at some stage. Weren't wrong, were we? Do you want to take them with you? After you've nipped over our fence and gone next door, I mean?" Mo said, her eyes gleaming.

"I could kiss you both," Declan said, meaning it.

Ten minutes later, he had jemmied the lock on Madeleine's back door and was tip-toeing up the stairs in the dark, breathing through his mouth so he didn't gag at the stench within the small house. Luckily, it was a clear night and the moon shone brightly through her bedroom window meaning Declan was able to see the rug on the floor without having to use the torch on his phone. He tucked it back on itself and got to his knees to peer at the floorboard, spotting the short board and the gap between it and the neighbouring board immediately. He pulled out his penknife and eased it into the space then pressed down, raising the board enough to be able to slip his fingers beneath it and pull it up and out.

The space beneath the board was as black as Newgate's knocker. Hesitating only for a second, he plunged his hand into the gap and felt around, his fingers locating the envelope containing Madeleine's cash almost immediately. It was a large, fairly weighty envelope. He pulled it out and slid it inside the zipper of his jacket, then replaced the board and the rug and went back down the stairs.

When he got to the bottom, he hesitated again. When he'd been here before, after Madeleine had been attacked, he hadn't gone into the room where it had happened. Now he found his fingers edging towards the doorknob and turning it, seemingly of their own accord. Pushing the door open, he stuck his head through the gap and took in the scene of carnage; the dried blood on the walls, the table, the floor. The blooded cane and nipple clamps, the cigarette butts on the floor. He recalled how she had been systematically tortured and left for dead and his mouth worked and a muscle played along his jawline as he clamped his teeth together and white-hot rage spread through his body.

They were going to pay for this and then they were going to pay again.

A few minutes later, back in Reg and Mo's house, Declan asked them a question. The old couple shared a look and answered, "Yes."

On the doorstep, Declan leaned in and gave each of them a big hug. "Bye Nan, bye Grandad," he said loudly. Then, more quietly, he said, "We'll be in touch."

Chapter Sixteen
Tuesday

SAS Investigations Office

"The lads left the car for you I see," Shakil remarked as Stuart walked into the office early on Tuesday morning.

"They did. They added about five hundred miles onto the clock, though, so God knows where they went."

"Brighton," Shakil said. "Apparently they've never been before. They went down as far as Exeter, making sure the idiots followed them all the way and then shook them off and doubled back. They were quite chuffed with themselves."

Stuart barked a laugh of surprise. "How do you know all this?"

"I put a bug on the car and listened to them, on and off. Once they'd lost them, they went into a service station and took their disguises off, then they changed the plates like we wanted them to. By the way, it was good thinking to put their own clothes into the boot before you got Madeleine away."

"I texted to let them know," Stuart said.

"I know," Shakil said.

"Of course you do." Stuart rolled his eyes but smiled to let him know he didn't mean anything by it.

The door opened and Declan walked in with a grim smile on his face. "I got her cash," he said, pulling the envelope from the rucksack he had slung over his shoulder. "And I got a load of photographs of the cun ... sorry, *people*, ... who have been staking Maddy's house out since she was attacked. There are six of them and they've been working in pairs on eight-hour shifts."

He spent the next few minutes explaining what Reg and Mo had told him and how Reg had taken it upon himself to take up photography again, spreading the surprisingly clear photos out on the desktop as he talked. When he'd finished, he jabbed a finger at one person's face in particular. "That's the fucker who attacked her. They recognised him."

"Carter," Shakil said. "There'll be a special place in hell for him."

"He'll be making the devil's acquaintance sooner rather than later if I catch him," Declan said, cracking his knuckles. He cleared his throat. "How was she when you left her this morning?"

"Happy to be out," Stuart said. "Sarah's there, playing mother hen and clucking over her. Maddy loves the house—she couldn't stop remarking on how she could see the ocean from her bedroom window."

Declan's face relaxed. "Good," he said.

"She asked after you," Stuart said, watching Declan's face closely and seeing the flicker of interest.

"Yeah?"

"Yeah."

Declan's mouth twitched into a small, secret smile that disappeared as swiftly as it arrived. "What did you tell her?"

"That you were currently burgling her old house," Stuart said, unable to resist teasing him.

Declan's jaw dropped.

"Relax," Stuart said, "you know she knew you were going there. She was really happy when you got away without being followed."

"Reg and Mo are a pair of game old guys," Declan said, changing the subject. "They pretended to be my grandparents as I left but they didn't really need to; last night's watchmen were sound asleep in their Jeep when I arrived and they still hadn't moved by the time I left. Sadly, Carter wasn't one of them. All the cloak and dagger stuff wasn't really needed. Still, I'm glad I did it that way because I asked Reg and Mo if they'd be prepared to help us out, once we're ready and they said yes."

"What do you mean?" Shakil asked. "How else can they help us?"

"Well, I've been thinking. I'm presuming you've come up with some kind of plan to extort money from Flanaghan and Hackensach and I'm up for that—anything that'll help Maddy financially. There's no way I'm letting her go back to doing what she used to which means she'll need as much as she can get her hands on." Declan stopped talking and looked from Stuart to Shakil and back again. The two men nodded. "So what's your plan?" Declan asked.

Stuart swallowed. "Firstly, we're going to pay a visit to Ted Tennant's house where we'll play him the recording of Hackensach and Ivanov admitting to everything on the boat. That'll put the wind up him properly. We're going to tell him we will let him have the recording provided he pays us four million by midnight tomorrow."

"Four *million*!" Declan blinked. "Tennant won't have anything like that much. Why go to him and not Flanaghan?"

"The others will be expecting us to do *something*, but they'll consider Tennant so far beneath them they won't expect us to go to him. That's another thing I want to ask Tennant actually, what he has on the others—because you can bet your bottom dollar he has *something* on them for them to have allowed him into the threesome with Madeleine. He's not in government, he's nobody particularly special from what we have been able to find out, so why?

"And you're right," Stuart continued. "Obviously, he won't have four mill so he's going to panic. We'll suggest he call Flanaghan while we are there. Flanaghan will want to speak to us so we'll play the recording to him and let him knock us down to three mill. Then we'll tell him that he will be responsible for sorting out who pays what, but that we rather expect Hackensach to contribute one point five million, Ivanov a million, and Flanaghan half a million. It's a drop in the ocean for them, as bent as they are; they'll be able to lose it in the system somewhere but that's not our problem, obviously. He'll have until midnight tomorrow to transfer the entire amount into our offshore account and we'll leave Tennant with the details of where to send it."

"You have an offshore account?"

"One of the first things we did once we realised who was involved in this case," Stuart said wryly. "We had absolutely no idea if we'd ever use it but Mum stumped up the cash to pay for it when she came in to help us out. The account is in the name of a company that has been set up to help girls escape from sexual abusers. It's called Safe and Sound. SAS, get it? It's a legit company, run by us. She said it would be a good idea as if it all went, as she put it, tits up, it would be easy enough to close again."

Declan's jaw dropped.

"Maddy will get two million," Shakil continued. "Seven hundred thousand comes to the company, and you and Sarah will get three hundred thousand to split between you."

Declan's jaw dropped even further.

"You've done a lot of the work involved. It's only fair you be rewarded for it."

Declan shut his mouth so fast his teeth clacked. "I don't know what to say. We're supposed to be paying you. And you do know that Flanaghan will have his heavies on your trail as soon as he hears what Tennant has to say and realises you're actually with him."

"We'll be leaving as soon as we end the call. And you're right, we won't be home and dry yet," Stuart said. "We need to go to ground until the money's transferred and then the second part of the plan comes into play."

"What's that?" Declan said, fascinated by the machinations of Stuart's mind.

"We let Tennant have a copy of the recording, but once the money is in our account and we've safely removed it, we're going to release the lot. Hackensach and Flanaghan should not be in office. I mean, he's the Minister for *Education*! We keep hold of the originals—they're already in a safety deposit box, Shaks did that yesterday while we were moving Maddy. The copies will go to the Prime Minister's office email account, to the Home Office, to the Leader of the Opposition and out to the media and by that I mean the Mail, Mirror, Sun, Telegraph and Guardian. The email attaching the recording will be sent out to all of them at the same time. We'll tell them they have an hour to act on it and then we plaster it over social media, Facebook, Twitter, everywhere we can think of, and then, and only then, we send it to the police."

"You realise that's signing our death warrants," Declan said.

"Maybe," Shakil said. "But they'll have to get past the paparazzi and media hacks who will be camped on the doorsteps of all of them well within the hour, clamouring for interviews. They will deny everything, of course, but shit sticks."

A smile spread slowly across Declan's face. "Which is where Reg and Mo will come into play. They are willing to give statements to the police about having seen Flanaghan and Hackensach going into their very young, very pretty neighbour's house every week for the past couple of years and the noises of her being abused, plus the attack they heard taking place and how she was carted away the next day looking like she was dead. The only thing they won't tell them is Madeleine's real name. They're going to say she kept very much to herself but they'd heard both Flanaghan and Hackensach calling her Julie while they hit her during their loud sex sessions with her."

"Why Julie?"

"Apparently Mo used to go to a school with someone called Julie and didn't like her much. She said, and I quote, 'If we're going to have to paint that lovely Madeleine as some kind of paid trollop, even if she was one, we don't want her real name out in the public eye. She's been through enough; plus, I'd quite like to have Julie's face in my mind as I talk about her. She was such a bitch back then, she could have done with a good hiding. This is my way of giving it to her.'"

"Never mess around with an elderly lady bearing a grudge, eh?" Shakil said, laughing. "I'll have to get Terry the Tech to blank out Madeleine's name in the recordings that go out to everyone barring Tennant."

"What are they going to say when the police ask why they haven't reported any of this before?" Stuart asked.

"They know who Hackensach and Flanaghan are and were too scared until it appeared in the papers." Declan shrugged. "It's simple and easy to stick to and they'll be believed because they're old."

The three men looked at each other and grinned.

"Are we ready for this?" Stuart asked.

"Hell, yeah," said the others.

"Okay. Declan, do you still have your van?"

Declan nodded.

"Good. Bring it around the back and park in our slot. We need you to get all the gear out of here and if we're still being followed, you should be okay to use the back exit. Do you have somewhere you can keep it?"

"Yeah, I have a lock-up," Declan said, nodding. He cracked his knuckles. "Right, let's get going. Actually, no. Before you go off to Tennant's, I want you both wired in case anything goes wrong."

Edgar 'Ted' Tennant's House

It was Mrs Tennant who opened the front door leaning heavily on her cane when Stuart and Shakil, both dressed in their Men in Black sharp suits, called to see Ted.

"Mrs Tennant?" Stuart said, taking his sunglasses off as he stepped past her and into a vestibule that had been decorated tastefully with heavily embossed cream wallpaper that had dark green vine leaves climbing up it. Matching green and cream marbled tiles ran from the vestibule along the entire length of the hall and a cream-painted stairwell rose to the right of him.

"We have an appointment with your husband," Shakil told the woman as he stepped in behind Stuart. He turned and closed the front door leaving Mrs Tennant staring at them both in bewilderment.

"You do?" she said. "He didn't mention it."

"Yes. Point us in his direction and we'll go and tell him off for not letting you know." Shakil smiled down at her, trying to put her at her ease.

She smiled back at him. "Would you? He's rather away with the fairies these days, I'm afraid. He's in the conservatory. Go down the hall, turn right into the sitting room and you'll see him ahead of you. He's out there watering his cacti. If his back is to you, you may find you have to shout as he has his air pods in. He's listening to one of his audio books. He gets rather lost in them, you see. Would you like to take some tea?"

"That would be wonderful, thank you," Stuart said. He nodded at her once and then both he and Shakil followed her directions leaving her to shuffle off to the kitchen.

They turned into the sitting room, an equally tastefully decorated room, this time in the palest of pink with deep fuchsia accents.

"Nice," Shakil said, looking around him.

Ted Tennant was indeed in the conservatory which had, rather oddly, been constructed at a level three steps down from the sitting room. His back was towards them as his wife had expected and he was holding a watering can and allowing small amounts of liquid to fall from the spout. The two men crossed the room, slid back the door separating the two rooms and stepped inside, closing it behind them. Ted caught the movement and turned, his face dropping when he saw who was there. His hand slackened its grip on the watering can and water began to spill onto the tiling.

"What are you doing in my home?" he demanded angrily as the two men descended towards him. "Where's my wife?"

"Making us all a pot of tea, Mr Tennant," Stuart said smoothly. "Shall we take a seat?" He pointed to the set of conservatory chairs that had been set equidistant from each other around a square glass table and unbuttoned his jacket, opening it slightly to show Harriet resting in a holster around his middle.

Ted blanched. "What do you want?"

"If you do exactly as we say, Mr Tennant, there will be no need for anybody to be hurt," Shakil said, flicking his hand towards the chairs.

Ted went and sat down, putting the watering can to the side of his chair. He stared from one to the other as they each took a seat one to either side of him.

"We would like you to listen to something," Stuart said.

"Listen to something?" Ted frowned.

Shakil took out the recorder he had in his jacket pocket, laid it on the table and pressed play. Hackensach's voice filled the room.

"...don't understand how he managed to overcome Jamie. I let it pass whilst you explained it to the others, but I want to clear this up with you now we are alone."

Next came Ivanov's voice. "Sheer luck, I think. He'd been peeling spuds and still had the knife in his hand; he struck out as Jamie went for him and got his femoral artery. Poor bastard went down and bled out in moments. Lucky for Dalgleish, eh? Next time, we'll have to be more creative."

"And you know all of this how?"

"When he didn't check in, I sent someone to see what was happening. He arrived at the same time as the ambulance finished loading Dalgleish and hung around. There were lots of onlookers so he was able to mingle and listen. The cops on scene were very talkative and not particularly quiet. It wasn't hard to put it together. Now, can I offer you a drink?"

"I see. No. No drink, thank you, I'm not stopping. Gregor, that's two failures. First Madeleine – and I was rather fond of her you understand – then the jackass who saw her with Ted."

"I know. All I can do is apologise and explain. Firstly, I didn't put a hit on Madeleine—you know Ted suspected someone had been watching them together and you all wanted to know who it was. Carter was supposed to frighten her into giving Dalgleish's information up but she just wouldn't admit that he'd watched them at it and it wound him up. You know how volatile Carter is. He—went a bit Peaky Blinders on her."

"Interesting, isn't it?" Stuart said, pausing the recording and looking straight into Ted Tennant's eyes which were now so wide open it made him look owlish.

Tennant shook his head and pushed down on his seat as if to stand.

"No, no. Stay seated. Listen to what your friends Patrick Hackensach and Gregor Ivanov say next, Mr Tennant." He pressed play

"By that, Gregor, I take it you mean that you intend to locate Madeleine, who appears to have disappeared from the face of the earth, and silence both her and Dalgleish once and for all. Correct?"

"Correct."

Stuart let the recording play to the end, watching Ted's face, noting the way he closed his eyes and dry swallowed at the mention of people being killed. By the time it ended, his face was sickly green and he was pulling at his collar. He swallowed heavily. "What do you want from me?"

"Four million pounds," Shakil said.

Ted's face swivelled towards him, his jaw gaping. "I don't have that kind of money."

"Your friends do," Shakil said. "May I suggest that you call one of them? Between the four of you, that's you, Flanaghan, Hackensach and Ivanov by the way, I'm certain you can come up with it."

"You know about Robert, too?" Ted said.

Shakil raised an eyebrow. "Didn't you hear his name on the recording? We know everything. The money is mostly for Madeleine. I think you'll agree she deserves it. She was almost killed, after all."

As Ted considered this, his wife slid open the door to the conservatory. "Ted," she said, as three heads swivelled in her direction, "Can you please help me carry the tea tray through for us all?"

Shakil jumped to his feet. "Stay there, Ted, I'll help your delightful wife."

"No," Ted said, beginning to push himself off his seat. "We can't allow our guests to help out."

"Nonsense," Shakil said, pressing Ted back down. "Would you be so good as to show me the way, Mrs Tennant?"

Mrs Tennant smiled at Shakil gratefully. "Oh, you are kind," she cried happily. "That's utterly marvellous of you.

I've managed to bring it into the sitting room but can't manage the steps."

Shakil climbed the steps and followed Mrs Tennant into the sitting room. He noted the four cups and saucers and realised she intended to come into the conservatory with them all. "My dear," he said gently. "Let me pour your tea for you here. I'm quite sure you'd rather sit in comfort here than listen to our boring work talk."

Mrs Tennant's eyes lit up. "Would you mind so very much if I don't come in? Ted gets rather cross with me if I abandon him but I must say I would prefer to take my tea into my sewing room, just across the hall."

"How do you take it?" Shakil asked, pouring tea into one of the cups and adding the dash of milk she requested. "Lead on, dear lady. Allow me the honour of carrying it to the sewing room for you."

He returned to the conservatory with the tray now bearing three cups and set it down on the glass table. "She's a nice lady," he told Tennant. "Fragile boned. What is it that's slowly crippling her? Arthritis?"

Tennant nodded.

"I wonder what she would think of your visits to Madeleine... Shall we ask her?"

Tennant took his phone from his pocket. "Don't hurt her," he said as he keyed a number in. "I'll get you your four million."

Shakil, who had opened his mouth to tell Tennant he had no intention of hurting his wife, closed it again.

"Put it on speaker phone," Stuart said quietly as the call began to ring.

Ted complied.

"Ted? What are you doing calling me on my house phone?" Hackensach's voice said.

"Patrick, we have a problem," Ted said, staring at Stuart. "I have two ... gentlemen ... here in my home who want four million pounds from us."

"Four million pounds? Four mill ... what are you talking about?"

"They have a recording of you talking to Ivanov and it's rather condemnatory. We'll all be finished if we don't comply. They appear to know everything."

"Play the recording," Hackensach said tersely.

Stuart pressed play.

"Could be anyone," Hackensach said when it finished. "Tell them to fuck off."

Stuart took over. "Mr Hackensach, we can indeed do that. However, if we do *fuck off* as you suggest, the recording goes to the media, to the Prime Minister, the Home Office, the Leader of the Opposition and all over social media."

"As I said, those voices could belong to anyone. Try it and I'll sue."

"Okay," Stuart said. He grinned at Tennant. "However, we have something else that will go out along with the recording."

Shakil reached into his pocket and laid the photographs out in front of Tennant who blanched.

"You have nothing on me. Stop playing games and walk away now, while you still can."

"Is that a threat? Don't you want to know what we have?"

"I'm getting a little fed up with your sick games. You have nothing, I repeat, *nothing* on me."

Stuart grinned at Tennant again. "Mr Tennant, would you be so good as to tell Mr Hackensach what you are looking at?"

Tennant cleared his throat. "They have photographs, Patrick. I'm looking at them now."

"What photographs? More doctored crap?" Hackensach said, trying to sound bored. The slight quaver in his voice told a different story

"We have clear photographs of Mr Tennant accompanied by the MP Robert Flanaghan. If you remember, you mention both names in the recording we just played you. They're just about to go into the GC; I'm sure you've heard of the place."

"No," Hackensach said.

"No matter. We also have clear photographs of them both that were taken in the Den of Iniquity, an expensive, niche area that's part of the GC where lots of naked, underage girls perform sexual favours for cash. Oh, and after Tennant left, we made a video of Flanaghan. It very clearly shows him being rather creative with a bottle of beer on one of those naked girls. Rather a stupid move, abusing a young woman in a public place, don't you think? They're going live, too. Four million, Hackensach. You, Flanaghan and Ivanov can all afford it."

"Nothing to do with me," Hackensach said. "I wasn't there."

"No. But when you put it all together it makes a fascinating story for the public to hear about, doesn't it? Between the four of you, that's you, Flanaghan, Ivanov and Tennant here, we have the attempted murders of Madeleine Beaufort and Graham Dalgleish; one of whom sustained a violent and prolonged sexual assault and was left for dead—further incitement to murder both of them and another young sex worker—I think your words were something along the lines of, *'tie up all the loose ends'*. You're in it up to your neck."

"You cunts," Hackensach said venomously. "Think you're some kind of vigilantes, do you? SAS? You're a joke and yes, I know *exactly* who you are and let me tell you, you won't get away with this."

"I rather think we will. We'll leave Ted with the bank details. Make sure the money is in the account by midnight tomorrow, all four million, or everything I have just explained *will* happen. Oh, and if you should think of harming either of us, our families, or anyone else involved in this, remember that our solicitor has a copy and instructions to release the recording, the video and the photographs to the police and the Home Office. If he doesn't hear a certain phrase from us by a pre-arranged time, it all goes out. So call your dogs off. There's absolutely no point in you attempting to find the recordings; it won't get you anywhere. There are several copies, each dotted about the country with people we trust. We've uploaded everything to various forms of social media and the posts will go live at a particular time unless we cancel them. Emails with all the uploads are programmed to send from several different accounts, again, unless we cancel them. Game, set and match, you sick bastard."

"I can't raise that amount in such a short timeframe," Hackensach said, his voice dripping with hatred. "What am I going to tell the bank?"

"You're making a generous donation to a company which helps young girls whose lives have been ruined by abuse. You are the Minister for Education, after all. Hell, you'll probably be able to write it off as a tax break."

"I need a week."

"Or I could bring the time forward to midnight today. Your choice. It's easy enough to send everything out a day early."

"How do I know that you won't use the recordings to extort more from us at a later date?" Hackensach said heavily.

"You have our word."

"Your word? What's that worth?"

"More than yours," Stuart said, ending the call. He reached into his pocket and pulled out a sheet of paper "These are the bank details. Make sure the money goes in," he said to Ted. "You can keep the photographs but you might want to hide them from your good lady wife. Have a nice life Mr Tennant, and lay off kids young enough to be your granddaughter."

Hiding in Plain Sight

Stuart and Shakil left Tennant's house on foot. Walking swiftly and keeping their eyes open for anyone who could be following them, they used as many back roads and alleyways as possible as they made their way into the centre of Crickleby where they had to make a run for their pre-booked train that went into the centre of London. They entered a carriage that was rammed with people dressed in all the colours of the rainbow. It was National Pride Day which meant that, as the only people dressed in suits, they stood out like a pair of sore thumbs. They got on in the centre of the carriage and fought their way through the noisy crowd of happy, laughing people to go and stand one at either end; the best way they could think of to be able to survey the occupants and watch other passengers who embarked on this, or either of the adjoining, carriages. The doors closed with nobody who looked like they could cause trouble having appeared and the train groaned its way from the station and began its journey.

"They're going to the Pride carnival," Stuart muttered into his wire.

"You don't say," Shakil's voice came back in his ear. "Take your jacket off and lose the tie. We may get away with it."

Both men shucked off their jackets and ties, making sure not to dislodge the wires.

"Can you still hear us, Declan?" Shakil asked.

"Affirmative," came Declan's voice in both his and Stuart's ears. "Sounds like a party on there."

As he spoke, loud music began to blare and the majority of carnival goers began to sing and dance. Whistles began to blow in time with the beat.

"Ouch! That's deafening!" Declan groaned. "I got your equipment out safely, by the way. It's all in my lock-up and I wasn't followed."

"Are you sure?" Stuart asked.

"I'm still here, so pretty positive. No one's appeared yet."

The train lurched and Stuart found himself automatically putting out his hands to save himself. He found himself holding onto the shoulders of a teenage boy who was wearing a yellow tunic top that skimmed over pastel pink short shorts. A pair of red and blue platform shoes completed his ensemble. Stuart found himself wondering how he'd remained upright.

The boy looked up into his eyes, grinning. "Well, I was hoping to pull today but didn't expect it to happen quite so quickly," he said, eyeing Stuart from head to toe with interest. "Didn't you fancy getting dressed up? Oh, I get it—you've only just come out, haven't you?"

"I, er, I'm sorry. I didn't mean to—" Stuart said, taking in the pink and blue butterfly wings that had been beautifully and artistically painted on the boy's face.

The boy tossed his head. He had long dark hair which had been scraped back from his face by an Alice band and interwoven with rainbow-coloured ribbons. It briefly cascaded over his shoulders and then fell back into place as the movement ended. "It's fine, it's fine. Don't you worry your pretty little head about it. I'm not hurt and nor are you—you're not hurt, are you?"

"Me? No." Stuart removed his hands as the train stabilised and began to move ahead more steadily.

"I'm Xavier," the boy said, extending a hand that was clad in a lacy yellow fingerless glove that Stuart had somehow missed in his first evaluation of his outfit. The glove went up to his elbow and his nails had been artistically painted in consecutive colours of the rainbow.

"Stu," Stuart said. He took Xavier's hand and was surprised by the strength of the pump before it was released again.

"Do you mind?" Xavier asked.

Before Stuart could ask what he meant, Xavier reached out and undid the top two buttons of his shirt. Stuart froze. The wire was taped just above his left nipple and he didn't want it exposed. He glanced down and breathed a sigh of relief.

"That's better," Xavier said happily, misinterpreting the sigh. "Now, I'm not doing anything funny, so don't panic…" He reached lower and tugged Stu's shirt from where it was tucked into his trousers and began to unbutton it from the bottom upwards. When he'd undone what he considered to be enough buttons, he shucked the shirt upwards and tied the two flapping ends into a knot around Stuart's middle, exposing his midriff.

"That's *much* better!" Xavier proclaimed. "Now bend down a bit."

Stuart went with it, realising he'd blend in better with the crowd if he allowed this boy to have his way. He felt Xavier working on his hair, his hands ruffling it this way and that.

"What's going on?" he heard Declan say in his ear.

"The tousled look suits you," Xavier said, leaning back to look at his handiwork. "Roll those sleeves up; yes, that's it! Perfecto! Now, what's your favourite insect?"

"What?" Stuart said, his words falling on deaf ears because Xavier had turned away from him and towards the group of teenagers he was evidently travelling with, one of whom, a girl who was dressed as a fairy, complete with white tutu and wand, began to rummage in the backpack she had slung over her shoulder. When he turned back, he held a make-up palette in his hands.

Declan was openly laughing now.

"Your favourite insect? Quick! We'll be stopping soon and you will feel so much freer after this, I promise."

"Dragonfly," Stuart said, wondering where the word had come from.

"Oh, fab…u…lous! I can do them. Hold still!"

"I'm not sure—" Stuart began to say.

Xavier put a finger over Stuart's lips. "Hold still, no talking or it'll go wonky. You don't want a wonky dragonfly, do you?"

Stuart gave in.

The train was pulling into Mudchurch as Xavier finished his artwork. "Stu," he pronounced, almost tearfully, "you look adorable, doesn't he?" He grabbed hold of Stuart's hand and dragged him towards his group of friends, introducing him to all and sundry while they oohed and aahed at his transformation.

"Come on then," Xavier said, still holding his hand as the train came to a halt and the doors opened. "Let's go and paaartaaay!"

And Stuart found himself off the train and running up the platform, still hand in hand with Xavier. He caught a quick glimpse of Shakil who had also alighted the train and noted that he'd loosed his hair from its usual low pigtail and also removed his jacket and tie, unbuttoned his shirt and rolled up his sleeves. He'd also put on his dark glasses and looked way cooler than Stuart even if he *was* laughing his head off.

"I'll follow, don't worry," Shakil's voice said in his ear amidst spurts of laughter. "Cool dragonfly."

Chapter Seventeen
Wednesday

Mudchurch Pier

"Where are we?" Stuart mumbled. He squinted an eye open and immediately closed it again when brilliant white sunlight blazed straight in. His head throbbed and his throat felt like he'd swallowed a Brillo pad. He stretched his fingers and felt something cool and gritty flow between them. He opened both eyes. High above and to each side of him, enormous wooden beams appeared to be holding up a floating pathway that ran overhead.

"Beach," Shakil mumbled.

"Are we under the pier?" Stuart dug his elbows into the sand and raised himself to look around. Hundreds of people were either sprawled and asleep or sitting quietly chatting together all the way along the beach on either side of them.

"We are. You thought we'd be less obvious if we hid under here."

"Did I? And where are my clothes?" It was only now that Stuart noticed he was dressed only in his boxers and that a black-inked flowering vine that, he peeked to check, began just above his pubes, rose and spread across his pecs. Stuart stared at it in horror. "Did I get a tattoo?"

Shakil looked at him in amusement. "You did."

"Why didn't you stop me? I have flowers on my belly! Flowers! And where's oojamaflip? Zebedee, no, Zzzzz—"

"Xavier?"

"That's the one."

"He had to be home by two or he'd be grounded. He staggered off with his mates at about half past one. He's still at school, did you know? Final year, but still. Nice kid. He left his number for you and said to tell you if you call and his mother answers, to just hang up."

Stuart's skin drained of colour entirely. "Does he still think I'm gay? We didn't ... I didn't ... Tell me I didn't do anything stupid with a school kid. Please."

"Well, you had matching tattoos done."

"Nooo!"

"Oh yes." Shakil took pity on him as Stuart's face dropped even further. "Stu, he's a schoolkid, of course he didn't have a tattoo done. He did come and hold your hand while you had yours though. When you passed out – and that *was* amusing, let me tell you – he very solemnly told me that he thinks you're too scared of your own sexuality to let yourself go. His words, not mine. He said that anyone who drinks as much as you obviously has issues and he'd like to help you through them if you'll let him."

Stuart groaned. "What did we drink? I can taste liquorice."

"Most of us stuck to cider. But the liquorice will be the half bottle of absinthe you downed after it ran out."

"Absinthe? Absinthe! Where did I get that from?"

"A bloke was wandering along the beach, selling the stuff. You said you'd always wanted to try it. He warned you to add water to it and even tried to flog you a couple of bottles, but you decided you wanted it straight—another thing Xavier picked up on."

"Eh?"

"You were quite insistent on it being straight."

"Oh God," Stuart groaned again.

"Quite. I bought some anyway. Would you like a bottle?"

"Yes, please," Stuart said, dabbing at his new tattoo with a finger. "It stings. Is it supposed to have red all around it? And what happened to the wires we had on?"

"Oh, they're both in the sea somewhere. They came off when we all went for a swim around midnight. And yes, it's supposed to be red. It'll go down apparently, although you were supposed to keep it covered." Shakil passed a full bottle of water over to him and watched as Stuart drained it and began to look slightly less like death warmed up.

"So, Stookie. What's the plan for today?"

Stuart glared at his friend as a vague memory of him having happily responded to that name filtered into his brain. "Don't," he warned. He rubbed his eyes. "Do you have any more water?"

Grinning, Shakil passed another bottle to him. Stuart unscrewed the cap and tipped half the bottle over his head, then he downed the rest in great gulps. "That's better." Now feeling more alert, he thought for a moment and said, "Is everyone okay so far?"

Shakil rolled his eyes. "I wondered if you'd ever ask. Yes. Maddy and Sarah are safe at home, Declan's gone there too and he still has the flower shop decal on his van and the false plates so that should be okay. Your mum and dad are still safe at the hospital and they're hopeful that he'll come round today. His record has been temporarily hidden from their system and will be put back once it's all over, so nobody will be able to hack in and track what room they're in. It's a big hospital and someone would notice heavies wandering around searching for them. Trudi said she's got friends checking on them now and again, plus they've beefed up their security in general and he has a couple of coppers outside his door.

"Jazz is safely back at the house you rented from Tammy and I've told her to ring in sick at work today and checked she hasn't given them her new address so she can't be traced either."

"You've been busy," Stuart said. "Thanks. I don't know why I let myself get so drunk."

"We both needed to let off steam after yesterday, and going with the flow of the carnival mob and the after-party was the best way of hiding in plain sight. I'm not so sure the tattoos were a good idea though."

"Did you...?"

Shakil nodded sheepishly and pulled his trouser leg up to show Stuart the little red devil on his ankle. "I wasn't even that drunk." The two men looked at each other and suddenly burst into laughter that lasted for quite some time.

Eventually, once they'd pulled themselves together, Stuart said, "So where are my clothes?"

Shakil winced and pointed seaward. "The last I saw of them was when you and Xavier went for a paddle. You took them off and left them on the sand ... the tide's come in since then."

"Shit."

"Just jesting," Shakil said. "I already told you we all went swimming at midnight. I hid our clothes under that rock," he nodded to the large boulder behind them, "until we got back but then you refused to get dressed again. What do you think your head was resting on? Look, they're barbecuing sausages over there and I'm starving. Let's go and see if they'll let us buy a couple."

A Hospital Room, Somewhere in Crickleby General Hospital

Caroline had just fallen into a deep slumber when Graham woke up. He opened his eyes to the sound of machinery bleeping all around him and saw his wife slumped in a chair by his bedside and a lump came into his throat. He remembered a man charging at him and then … nothing. Somehow, he'd survived and ended up in hospital. How had that happened? Had Caroline found him?

His head hurt. He knew he needed to remember something. Something terribly urgent. Something that could mean life or death for someone. Who? Who was it? What wasn't he remembering? All of a sudden it came to him and he sat bolt upright in bed. Jasmine! Jasmine was in danger! The man who had attacked him had sexually assaulted his daughter and had her locked up!

"Jasmine!" he howled. "Jasmine! Jasmine!"

Caroline was awake in an instant. Befuddled by sleep, she was upright before she knew it, listening to Graham's calls for their daughter. "Graham, what is it? Jasmine's fine."

Graham stopped howling and clutched at Caroline's arm. "She's not fine. That man, the man who did this to me, he has her. He's … he's *done* things to her and he's got her locked up somewhere. We have to save her." He stared up at his wife unable to understand why she wasn't panicking, wasn't reacting as she should. "Caroline. He has her locked up! Call the police. He has to be found!"

A nurse came into the room having heard his cries. "Is everything all right in here?" she asked, moving towards the bed and checking Graham's fluids. "Are you in pain, Graham?"

"No! Yes! My daughter. He has my daughter!"

"Who has your daughter?" the nurse said, glancing across at Caroline, who shrugged in bewilderment.

"I don't know what he means," she said. "Graham, Jazz is at home. At our new place, I mean, not Lakeland Avenue."

"She isn't! She isn't! He has her. He showed me a video of her on his phone. He … he …" Unable to say the words, Graham stared, wild-eyed at his wife. "He …"

"He what?" Caroline said gently, taking his hand into her own.

"He *had sex with her and filmed it*!" Graham burst into tears. "He's going to sell her to his friends; we have to find him."

"Graham, are you talking about the man who attacked you?"

"Yes! He got away. He has her somewhere and we need to find her. She's not at home, I'm telling you. *She's not at home!*"

"Try and calm yourself," the nurse said, taking hold of his other hand and feeling his wrist to take his pulse. "Graham, your wife is telling you the truth. Your daughter is quite safe. She's been in to see you. I've seen her with my own eyes. About so high," she indicated with her free hand, "long blonde hair, pretty. She's Stuart's twin, isn't she?"

Graham stopped shouting and gawked at her.

A male head appeared around the door. "Knock knock. Everything all right in here?"

"Yes, officer. Graham's come around and he's a little confused," Caroline said. "Nothing to worry about."

"Mr Dalgleish, we will need to take a statement from you as soon as you feel up to it."

"Not now!" Caroline and the nurse snapped simultaneously.

The head disappeared.

"Did he say 'knock knock'?" the nurse asked, shaking her head.

"How …?" Graham asked, turning to Caroline who looked at the nurse, silently asking with her eyes whether Graham was well enough to know what he'd done. The nurse shrugged.

"Graham, listen to me," Caroline said. She pulled the chair closer to his bedside and sat on it, still holding onto his hand. "The man who attacked you is dead."

Graham stared at her. "What?"

"Do you remember what you were doing when he came into the house?"

Graham frowned. "I think I was peeling vegetables. Yes, that's right. I was expecting you to come home and wanted to cook a nice meal for us all."

Ignoring the fact that neither she nor Jasmine had had any intentions of going home at that point, Caroline said gently, "What were you using to peel the vegetables?"

"My little paring knife. You know I don't like using the peeler, the stupid swivelly bit gets stuck in the veg, and you'd taken it, anyway."

Caroline swallowed. "Do you recall whether you put it down? When the man came in, I mean."

"I don't know ... I think I did but," Graham's face was a picture of concentration and then his eyes widened. "I didn't, did I? I remember I had it in my hand when he came at me and I put my hands up to try to ward him off."

Caroline nodded. "That's right. And it's a good job you did because otherwise, you'd be the one who is dead."

"That little knife *killed* him?"

Caroline squeezed his hand, knowing how hard this news would hit her husband.

"That little knife killed a man? How? It isn't long enough to do any real damage. I got his tummy if I got anything."

"Actually, it went into his upper thigh just below his groin. There's a main artery in there and the knife hit it." Caroline chose her words carefully, framing them so it sounded like the knife had done the dirty work, not Graham. She watched to see how he was going to react but he simply stared at her, his gaze focusing on something that was going on inside his head.

"He went down and bled out in minutes. Less than minutes," Caroline said.

"It would have taken a bit long—" the nurse began, closing her mouth with a snap when she met Caroline's furious glare.

"*I* killed him? *Me*?"

Caroline squeezed his hand.

"And Jasmine is safe? You're not lying to me? How did she get away from wherever he had her?"

"He didn't have her," Caroline said, her brow knitting together as she wondered what he was talking about. "She was never taken."

"But ... but the video ..."

"It could have been doctored to look like her," the nurse said knowledgeably. "That happened to a friend of mine. A porn video went all over everywhere with her face on it. It wasn't her. At least, that's what she said."

A small noise sounded from the back of Graham's throat. "So I killed a man who hadn't hurt Jasmine at all?"

"Graham, it was you or him. What happened was the best thing that could have happened. You did nothing wrong, do you hear me? Nothing. He invaded our home and tried to kill you. You were just lucky to have still been holding the knife. It was self-defence, nothing more."

"I, I suppose it was," Graham said. He was silent for a moment and then ventured, "That was a policeman at the door, wasn't it? Am I under arrest?"

"No, not at all. They need to talk to you to hear what happened, that's all."

"Do you feel up to talking to them?" the nurse asked. "I'm not sure you're ready yet. You need to get your head around what happened before you talk to them, in my opinion. You know what coppers are like, they'll twist what you say and you'll be done for murder before you know it."

Graham's face fell.

"I'll tell them you've gone back to sleep, give you some time to process."

Caroline gave her a grateful smile as the nurse left the room and they both heard her loudly telling the waiting police officers exactly what she'd said she was going to.

Graham looked at his wife and his chin quivered. "I killed a man."

Caroline nodded and raised his hand to her cheek. "It was him or you," she said softly. "I'm glad it was him and not you."

Graham swallowed. "I'm so sorry," he said. "This whole mess is down to me, isn't it? If I hadn't tried to deliver that letter and looked through her window, and then acted like an utter fool, none of this would have happened."

Caroline remained silent, unsure of what she could say to any of that. He was right, it had all begun with him seeing something he shouldn't have, and had he not returned to Madeleine's none of this would have occurred. They would still be living in their house at Lakeland Avenue, Jasmine would be able to come and go without having to look over her shoulder, and not least, a young girl would never have been beaten to a pulp and Graham would not have been forced to kill somebody. Stuart and his partner, Shakil, would not be looking for the people responsible for it, dangerous people, people who would not hesitate to stop them by any means. She shuddered.

"I'm sorry," Graham said again. "Can you ever forgive me?"

"I forgave you when I heard you were in here," Caroline said, biting back tears.

"I don't deserve you."

"No, you're probably right. But still, here I am and here I'm staying for now, so get used to it."

"For now?"

Caroline nodded slowly. Her face full of regret, she turned to look him in his eyes. "Graham, I will always care for you; we were together for so many years. Yes, I can forgive, but I can't forget. There's no way back for us. I'm so sorry."

Jasmine

Chutzpah woke Jasmine a little after ten by licking her face and patting her chest with his great hairy paw. Grunting, she pulled herself up into a seated position and glared at him. "I was having a nice dream," she said crossly. "First Shakil woke me, then I had to lie to work, and now you. I suppose you want to go out while I sort out your breakfast?"

The dog's ears pricked at the word 'breakfast'. His tail thumped once and then he jumped off the bed and ran to the door where he stopped, looked back at her and whined.

"Okay." Jasmine slid her legs over the edge of the bed, stretched and got to her feet. "Let's go get you sorted, shall we?"

Chutzpah barked his agreement.

Downstairs, Jasmine opened the back door and let him into the garden. The dog raced to the far end and squatted, looking around to make sure nobody was going to jump on him while he performed his business. A black cat, which was sitting on top of the garden fence, hissed down at him and then delicately turned its face away, lifted a back paw, licked it and began to groom its ears. Chutzpah ignored it—he knew he was far superior to any hissing feline and his business was far more pressing than the primal urge he had to try and chase it away.

Job done, he turned his back on the cat and trotted back into the house where, he was happy to see, Jasmine was placing a bowl of food down for him to eat. He'd scoffed the lot within thirty seconds.

"Did you inhale that?" Jasmine asked as the kettle came to the boil and switched itself off. She made herself a cup of coffee and stuck two slices of bread into the toaster. When they popped, she buttered them and took both drink and food over to the table. As she ate, she began scrolling through the various sites she had permanently open and her eyes widened when a familiar face appeared on her news feed. She was looking at a picture of her lover, Jamie, the man she'd shared one night of passion with who had failed to call her afterwards. Now she knew why.

'Hit-man killed by homeowner', the headline declared. It was an updated post that had previously stated that one man was dead and another injured after an attempted house robbery had gone wrong. In the updated version, the police had released Jamie's image; one that had obviously been taken from a mug shot.

'James Woods, Contract Killer' was printed in italics beneath the photograph and beneath that, the words: 'James Woods, a prolific burglar and for-hire contract killer has been found dead after breaking into a property and attacking the homeowner who is currently in hospital in a critical condition. Woods, who has been on the police *10 most wanted criminals* list for several years, was found after having been stabbed in the groin after he launched a frenzied and savage attack against the homeowner whose name cannot be released due to an ongoing police investigation.'

Another picture, just below this information, showed a photograph of the kitchen in her family home. A huge pool of dried blood was on the tiled flooring along with a chalk outline of where Jamie's body had been found. Leadenly, Jasmine scrolled on:

'Woods came across the homeowner shortly after he gained access into the family home in a popular area of Crickleby, Pottershire. Woods immediately launched an attack on the homeowner, a man who is believed to be in his late fifties. It culminated when the homeowner, who had been peeling vegetables at the time of the attack, stabbed him, fatally piercing Woods' femoral artery. Woods was dead within minutes but not before he had critically injured the homeowner who was found by his son and a friend who raised the alarm.'

Beneath this was a 'Comments' section. Jasmine read on to see that the overwhelming majority of people were glad to see the back of James Woods and that he'd got what was coming to him. It was poetic justice. Many also called for the police to give the homeowner a medal for taking him out.

Jasmine's mouth dried out as she read and re-read the article. When she'd finished, she put her phone down, her head spinning. While she'd been moping over sexy Jamie, he'd been attacking her father. How could she have read him so wrong? What would have happened to her if she hadn't been called into work? Would he have murdered her father and come back for her? Would she have been next on his list? Her stomach churned and she made a mad dash for the kitchen sink, reaching it just in time to regurgitate the toast she'd just eaten while Chutzpah danced at her feet in worried attendance.

When she felt like there was nothing else to come up she picked up her phone and rang Shakil back.

"The guy dad killed," she said as soon as he answered her call. "It's all over Facebook and Twitter. Is it true? Did he go there to kill him? It wasn't just a burglary? Was he one of the guys who tried to break in when I was home alone at the start of all this? Would ... would he have killed me, too?" And then Jasmine broke down.

"Jazz, try to calm down," Shakil said, but it was no use, Jasmine couldn't hear him above the sound of the sea rolling in and her own tears. She continued to cry, great sucking sobs that tore at his heartstrings. He turned to Stuart. "We have to go to Jazz. She's just realised that the people who tried to break in weren't burglars and she's taking it pretty hard. Perhaps a bit too hard—I think there may be something she's not telling us."

Stuart was already on his feet, shucking sand from his shirt and trousers. "Tell her we're on the way," he said.

Shakil had thought of something else. "Jazz, listen. Sweetie, please stop crying for a moment .... Jasmine! Listen to me! Turn your phone off! We don't know if anyone's monitoring your socials and if they are, they might be able to track you. We're on our way. We'll knock three times, wait a bit, then knock twice more so you'll know it's us. Don't answer the door to anyone else. Do you understand?"

"Y ... y ... yes," Jasmine stuttered through her tears. "Thank you, Shaks." And then she killed her phone.

***

Shirtless, his hair still tousled and now engrained with sand, and still bearing the remnants of a dragonfly on his face, Stuart went into a shop sited at the base of the cliffs that sold garish t-shirts, shorts, baseball caps and flip flops. He bought a set for each of them plus four bottles of water, wincing at the astronomical prices being charged, then he and Shakil made their way to the public loos and had a quick wash and brush up and changed their clothes. Keeping a wary eye out for anyone who looked like they could be watching them, they climbed their way up the carved stone steps that led from the beach to the cliff top, stopping occasionally to catch their breath and take a drink. The bottles were empty by the time they reached the top.

"I am never drinking again," Stuart pronounced as they reached the top and he rested with his hands on his thighs, bending from the waist as he tried to catch his breath. Sweat oozed from every pore.

"Nor me," Shakil agreed, despite the fact he'd barely raised his pulse rate, much less any sweat.

Stuart side-eyed him enviously.

From there, keeping their heads down, they walked down the hill to Mudchurch High Street and purchased a couple of burner phones which they paid cash for and activated as soon as they left the shop. Then they trudged back up the hill and along the cliffside to the house where Jasmine and Caroline were presently living.

Shakil knocked on the front door three times, waited for a beat and then knocked twice more.

"Is that you, Shaks?" came Jasmine's voice from inside the house.

"Yes," Shakil said, rolling his eyes at Stuart. "We really need to give her some pointers on how to stay safe. Anyone could have said yes to that."

"Yes, but Chutzi would have barked if it hadn't been us. He knows how we walk and smell."

Shakil acknowledged this truth as Jasmine opened the door with the dog at her heels, her eyebrows raising at the state the pair were in. Despite the anguish she felt, a smile played around the corners of her lips as she opened the door wide and stood aside to let them in. Even the dog backed away, his tail wagging cautiously.

She closed the door behind them and, shaking her head, said, "You both stink."

"Cheers, Sis," Stuart said, going into the kitchen. "You don't look so hot yourself."

"Bastard," Jasmine retorted under her breath as she and Shakil followed in his footsteps.

"What's going on?" Stuart said, turning to face her once they were all in. "You worried Shaks."

Jasmine pointed towards the dining table. Taking a deep breath, she said, "Sit down and I'll tell you everything. And then you can go and take a shower."

By the time they'd heard her out and showered, it was getting on for one pm. Leaving Stuart to try to convince his sister that she'd been played by a pro and that she had nothing to feel guilty about, Shakil went into the lounge room and called Declan from his burner phone.

Declan answered without speaking.

"It's me," Shakil said, not identifying himself in case the person on the other end wasn't who he expected it to be.

He heard the answering release of breath and then Declan's voice sounded. "Where are you?"

"At Jasmine's. She had an unfortunate incident with the bloke Graham killed and Stu's consoling her at the moment."

"Was she hurt?" Declan asked immediately.

"Only emotionally." Shakil changed the subject. "Have you checked the account?"

"Nothing as of an hour ago. Want me to check again?"

"Yes, please." Shakil waited.

After what felt like an age, Declan returned. "Nothing."

"Shit." Shakil thought for a moment. "Okay, we'll have to scare him into it. Leave it with me." He ended the call and then rang Tennant's house phone. His wife answered the call.

"Hello Mrs Tennant, this is Mr Barbosa, we visited you and your husband recently, do you remember? You were kind enough to make us tea?"

"Yes," said Mrs Tennant. "How are you dear?"

"Fine, thank you. Would you please tell Ted that Madeleine needs him to help solve a problem?"

"Madeleine? I don't know a Madeleine," she said, sounding confused.

Hating what he was doing, Shakil said, "No, but Ted knows her. Would you mind passing the message on?"

"Certainly, wait one moment and I'll go and fetch him."

Shakil waited. Soon enough Tennant was on the other end of the line, almost apoplectic with anger. "You told her about Madeleine!"

"Ted, Ted, Ted. That's just the beginning. It's all going out. Be prepared."

"Why?" Ted appeared to be utterly confused.

"The money hasn't gone into the account?"

"What?" Tennant said, alarmed. "I've just been talking to Flanaghan and he said it was being transferred as we spoke."

"Looks like he lied to you. Okay, Hackensach has until midnight and then, well, hold on to your hat—everything is going live." Shakil ended the call and yelled, "Stu, we have a problem."

Chapter Eighteen
Thursday

Caroline and Jasmine's Rented House

By the time the whole clan had gathered together at Madeleine and Sarah's house, it was in the early hours of Thursday. The deadline had passed and no money had been put into the account. Six of them had squeezed themselves into a lounge room that was really only big enough for three, maybe four people at a push, and Caroline and Graham were attending via Zoom, much to the nursing staff's disgust.

Madeleine was at that particular stage in her recovery where everything was irritating, something Graham could relate to but which also included him. She kept side-eyeing the laptop and glaring at him whenever he caught her eye. She was in pride of place in the room, propped up in a recliner armchair, the extendable base of which raised her feet taking the pressure off her back and bottom and she was only in that because she had had a full-on tantrum when a worried Declan had mooted the idea of her staying in bed and them coming to her room.

"The perv who caused all this will be at the meeting, won't he?" she'd shouted, interspersing a variety of curse words that Declan had been contrarily awed by. "He's seen enough of me already! I'm not comfortable with him seeing me in bed, too!"

"Fair point," Declan agreed. He'd carried her downstairs, installed her on the recliner and grabbed every cushion available to prop her up until she was both comfortable and happy. At least, she had been until the Zoom call began and she saw who was sitting beside Graham.

"You!" she said, the hurt she was feeling evident in her voice. "You and *him*?"

Everyone fell silent at the pain in her voice.

Caroline nodded. "He's my husband."

"And you're still with him? What, are you soft in the head?"

"No, I'm not still with him. We're not together like that anymore. I'm here because Graham was seriously hurt, like you were," Caroline said, ignoring Graham's hurt look, "and we were married for an awful lot of years. I'll also say that yes, he's been a prat but he knows he has and he's dreadfully sorry—and he's paid a high price for it."

"I haven't heard him say sorry once," Madeleine hissed. When Graham opened his mouth, she got in first, cutting him off from whatever he'd been about to say by raising a hand and aiming it at the laptop. "No. Don't even bother. It's too late now." She put her hand down and turned her attention to Caroline. "Why did you visit me? I *liked* you! Did you just come to gloat at what happened to me? Did you think I *deserved* it?"

"What? You went to see her?" Graham said, aghast.

"Shut up." Caroline elbowed Graham aside so that only her face appeared on the screen. "Yes, I'll admit I came to see you originally because I wanted to see who had turned my husband's head so easily." She swallowed down the original emotions she'd had that threatened to surface again so surprisingly quickly. "I thought I'd see a hard-faced tart if I'm honest. But instead, I saw you; a beautiful young girl who had been so badly damaged because of my husband, even if he didn't intend for it to happen, that I couldn't turn away. You had no one, from what the nurses told me and nobody should ever have to go through what you went through alone.

"I looked at you and kept thinking; what if you were my daughter? And then you called me Mum, do you remember? As soon as you said it I wanted to protect you from the world you'd been living in, I wanted you to feel loved and I wanted to take care of you. That had nothing to do with Graham and everything to do with you. He was just the means of bringing me to you."

Madeleine's lower lip quivered. "Did you? Did you really?"

"Yes. Really. I still do."

"Even when this is all over?" Madeleine found herself saying.

"Of course!" Caroline said, keeping the thoughts that told her that was when Madeleine was going to need the most support to herself.

Nobody knew quite what to say after that and the meeting fell awkwardly silent.

Jasmine broke it. "I've always wanted a sister."

"So have I," Stuart said, grinning and nudging her side.

"Oi!" Jasmine squealed. She thumped his arm. "You already have one!"

"Could have fooled me! Do you know, when we were growing up, Jazz took great pleasure in blaming everything that went wrong on me. Do you remember Dad's watch, Jazz? The wind-up one?"

"Ye...es," Jasmine said slowly. "The one you broke?"

"I broke? *I* broke! You got hold of it and said Dad hadn't wound it up, so you turned the little wheel on the side of it so far and so fast, it fell off. Remember?"

"That wasn't you?" Graham said, looking at Stuart. "But you took the blame."

"That's what brothers do," Stuart said, shrugging. "It was easier for you to blame me. Jazz was upset enough that she'd done it. Remember?"

"Oops, that's right, it was me who broke it. I'd forgotten about that." She glanced at the laptop. "Sorry, Dad."

"But Stuart was punished for something he didn't do!" Graham said. "That wasn't fair."

"Life isn't always," Madeleine said dryly.

"No," Graham said, grateful for the chance to speak to her. "Madeleine, I am so sorry for what happened to you just because I…" he swallowed, "…because I was a Peeping Tom."

Madeleine glared at the laptop while the others held their breath. Eventually, she huffed, her face softened slightly, and finally she nodded. "Look, I know you didn't mean for all this to happen but I can't forgive you. I mean, look at me." She flapped her hands up and down. "I'll never be the same again. Peering through people's windows is an ugly thing to do. I just hope you won't do it ever again."

Graham shook his head, his face red and expression sombre. "No," he said. "That I can promise you."

"And you need to promise that if you do see something you shouldn't, you won't blackmail them into sleeping with you like you did me."

"I won't," Graham said, studiously avoiding looking anyone in the eye.

"We'll talk about that later," Caroline muttered, her voice low.

"Okay," Stuart cut in. "Anyway, the reason we're all here is because the money's fallen through and we need to discuss when will be the best time to release all the information we have. Tonight," he glanced at his watch, "actually, this morning, obviously isn't the right time because people are in bed. We want maximum impact."

"They called our bluff," Shakil said gloomily. "I'm so sorry Maddy, and both of you." He nodded towards Declan and Sarah in turn. "We shouldn't have got your hopes up."

"What are you talking about? Were you expecting them to shell out money to *you* for what they did to *me*?" Madeleine asked, astonished at the thought. "I mean, what the hell?"

"We have enough on them that we thought they'd pay to stop it being released," Shakil said guiltily. "We asked for four million pounds." Seeing the women's shocked faces, he added, "We wanted to give you enough money to not have to worry for the rest of your life."

"Four *million*?" Jasmine squeaked.

"A couple of thousand would have helped," Madeleine said, "and they may have given me that. Did you seriously think they'd just hand over *four million pounds*? What were you thinking?"

"We were going to let them knock us down to three," Stuart said defensively. "We didn't expect to get four."

"But these are men who'll stop at nothing!" Sarah said. "I mean, I get that you wanted compensation for Maddy, but four million pounds? That's insane! Did you know about this?" She turned to Declan, who squirmed uncomfortably, unable to meet her eye. He nodded. "So all you *men* decided to keep us *little women* in the dark? No wonder! You knew we'd have put a stop to it. There's a huge difference between gathering information that can bring them down and extortion, because, not to put too fine a point on it, that's what it was—you tried to extort money from them!"

"Why didn't you talk to me about it?" It was Caroline's turn to add her thoughts. "It'll all come out, you know. Even if you go to the police with whatever evidence you have, those men will drop you in it. I presume you told them you'd get rid of whatever it is you have if they paid up? That's blackmail."

The room fell silent as the men contemplated the truth of the women's words. Eventually, Stuart muttered, "Well, it's a bit late now. It's done. They can't prove anything. We'll just deny it."

"Do they have your bank account details? I mean, I presume you weren't expecting them to hand that amount over in cash," Caroline asked.

"The offshore account," Stuart mumbled.

"Did you handwrite the details?"

Stuart nodded.

"You bloody idiot!"

Stuart nodded again.

"This wasn't about money," Caroline said furiously. "You should have gathered the evidence you needed to prove they intended to kill Maddy and then gone to the police."

"But I didn't want the police involved!" Madeleine interjected. "I never wanted the police involved. I know what they're like. They'll just see a sex worker who got caught out when things went too far. They wouldn't care. People like me are ten a penny!"

"We've changed your name in the recording, don't worry about that," Shakil said, speaking up for the first time since the issue was raised.

"What recording?"

"What's going out first?" Declan asked, unwittingly speaking over her. "Are we doing it as we discussed?"

"Yes, I think so," Stuart said, relieved that the conversation was moving on. "Shaks has programmed everything up, all we need to do is add a time and press send."

"Hang on one cotton-picking minute!" Caroline used an expression that only her family were familiar with. It meant she wasn't happy. "What *are* you three talking about? Programmed what? What recording?"

Shakil brought out the recorder. "This one."

He played the entire group the recording he'd made of Ivanov and Hackensach. When it was over he said, "We have photographs and a video too, but I don't think you women will want to see those..." And then he ducked as a variety of cushions and other items rained towards his head.

When the commotion had died away and the photographs and video had been passed around and tutted over, he spoke again. "Right. Who do we send the recording to first?"

It seemed that everyone had their own ideas about this and the conversation went on for some time. The majority of the group weren't convinced that the current Prime Minister would do anything at all if the story wasn't leaked to media sources.

"We already know he's a spineless git who'll try to sweep it under the carpet," Declan said. "He has form."

Stuart agreed with him. "So we need to release it elsewhere at the same time. The papers?"

Shakil had been thinking. "We could broach them first, tell them we have a story about two government officials that will be huge and see which paper bites." He shrugged. "We may get some money from this yet."

Madeleine interrupted. "I don't want to make money from this. Don't you get it yet? It was never about money, not for me. I want them stopped from ever doing this to anyone else, and that recording ends with Hackensach telling Gregor to line someone else up. *That's* what I want stopped. I want to see them go down for a very long time."

"I'm with Madeleine," Caroline's voice piped up. "It shouldn't be about money. She's right, they need to be outed and put away. Asking for money from journalists makes it all feel … I can't explain it properly … it makes it feel somehow as though what those men did to Madeleine was acceptable and she could be bought off … it wasn't, and she can't.

"Stu," Caroline looked to her son, "I know you mean well by trying to get money for her as compensation but it won't make anything right, not really. Just let them have the recording. See what happens from there, provided Madeleine is okay with that?"

Madeleine nodded. "I want them put away. Send it everywhere, all at once. The Prime Minister, the police, the papers and social media. Let everyone see what they are."

"Okay," Stuart said. "Shaks, can you do that?"

"Yeah. What time should it go out?"

Everyone looked at their watches. It was now five am.

"About eight?" Caroline suggested.

Shakil looked at Stuart who shrugged. "It's as good a time as any."

Shakil nodded. He fired up the laptop, cued up all the draft messages, attached the recording to each and, at exactly eight o'clock, he pressed 'send'.

Chapter Nineteen
Friday

Crickleby Police Station

"Why didn't you come to us?" Detective Inspector Schnell shouted. He leaned over the desk until his nose was practically touching Stuart's.

"Our client didn't want us to."

"Yet you've released a recording with her name clear enough for anyone to hear!"

Stuart leaned forwards, too, and their noses grazed. "It's a common enough name. Look, you have my father's information, you know what happened to him, now you know who ordered the hit and why."

"Proud of him, are you?" Schnell said bitterly, leaning away from Stuart who was now glaring at him. "Sorry, sorry. But we could have got them sooner had you told us! You pre-warned them and now both Hackensach and Flanaghan are on the run!"

"I doubt they'll get far. Their faces have been plastered all over everything. It's gone viral."

"I know!" Schnell shouted, leaning back. "I bloody know! You've made us look right fools. I could do you all for obstructing police business."

"But it wasn't your business," Stuart said. "Our client was assaulted and she didn't want to report it because she didn't want a ton of coppers looking at her like she was dirt because of her job. She had the right to make that decision, didn't she?"

"We wouldn't have done that! Things have changed nowadays."

Stuart laughed. "You can't honestly stand there and tell me that you'd have worked to find her assailants as hard as you'd have worked if she'd been an office worker, can you?"

"You didn't give us the chance!" Schnell yelled. "And do you know who this other girl is that they're talking about?"

Stuart ignored the question. "We found who did it, we've provided addresses and we've given you all the evidence you need. You got Ivanov and Tennant didn't you? I'd lay odds both of them are talking. Plus, I believe you've had eye-witness testimony from Julie's neighbours by now. They recognised both Hackensach and Flanaghan and they heard what they did to her when they visited her every week for years."

Schnell's eyes narrowed. "One last question: who is the other girl?"

"No comment," Stuart said blithely.

"Interview terminated," Schnell snapped, switching off the recorder. "Get out of my sight. But don't leave the country, we're not done with you yet."

***

"They're a bit pissed off with us, aren't they?" Shakil said, as he and Stuart walked down the steps from the police station.

Stuart grinned. "That they are. Did you get told not to leave the country?"

"Yeah."

"Did they ask you for Maddy's real name"

"Yeah. I told them Julie was who she identified as."

Stuart laughed. "Did they ask about Sarah?"

"Yeah. I said no comment, as we agreed. You?"

"Yeah."

Both men nodded in satisfaction and continued walking companionably towards the car where Caroline sat, waiting for them. She, along with Graham, had been interviewed at the hospital but both of them had pleaded ignorance of what their son and his partner had been doing and the police had no evidence to say otherwise.

"I've been thinking," Shakil said while they were still a fair distance from the car.

Stuart looked at him.

"I have the feeling we're going to get a lot busier after all of this, so we'll need to take more people onto the books. I mean, it's been all well and good hiring security, but we need our own people. People we can trust."

Stuart nodded. He'd had similar thoughts.

"And we need a secretary, and not your mother. No offence."

Stuart's mouth twitched. "I agree."

"What about Sarah?"

"Can she type?"

Shakil shrugged. "We could put her onto a training course, if she's interested."

"We could," Stuart agreed.

"Plus I think Declan is going to be looking for a new job now, so why don't we take him on to work with us?"

"So long as he doesn't think SAS stands for Stuart and Shakil and want to add his initial too. We don't want to be known as SADS do we?"

Shakil snorted laughter. "And we could ask Madeleine to work front of house, greeting clients and answering the phones."

Stuart stopped walking. "Do you really think we're going to be that busy?"

"Mate, our answering machine has run out of room."

The two kept walking.

"We need to sort out Gordon King, the security chief at the clinic, and we still need to catch this Carter, the guy who actually attacked Madeleine," Stuart said.

"We do," Shakil said. "But can we bask in the limelight today and worry about them tomorrow?"

Stuart grinned. "I think we can do that, yeah. Pint?"

"Is the Pope a Catholic?"

"I do believe he may be."

The two men nodded at each other with satisfaction and made their way to the car where Caroline still waited.

"To the pub, Mum, and don't spare the horses!" Stuart said, sliding into the seat beside her as Shakil got into the back.

"For sure," Caroline replied, grinning. "To the pub it is."

The end (for now)

© JM Turner
17th August, 2022

Printed in Great Britain
by Amazon